WILL JORDAN
BETRAYAL

arrow books

Published by Arrow Books 2014

2 4 6 8 10 9 7 5 3 1

Copyright © 2014 by Will Jordan

First published in Great Britain in 2013 by
Arrow Books
Random House, 20 Vauxhall Bridge Road,
London SW1V 2SA

A Penguin Random House Company

Penguin
Random House
UK

www.randomhouse.co.uk

Addresses for companies within The Random House Group Limited can be
found at: www.randomhouse.co.uk

The Random House Group Limited Reg. No. 954009

A CIP catalogue record for this book
is available from the British Library

ISBN 9780099574484

Penguin Random House supports the Forest Stewardship
Council® (FSC®), the leading international forest-certification organisation.
Our books carrying the FSC label are printed on FSC®-certified paper.
FSC is the only forest-certification scheme supported by the leading
environmental organisations, including Greenpeace.
Our paper procurement policy can be found at:
www.randomhouse.co.uk/environment

MIX
Paper from
responsible sources
FSC
www.fsc.org   FSC® C016897

Typeset in Palatino (10.5/14pt) by SX Composing DTP Ltd, Rayleigh, Essex
Printed and bound by CPI Group (UK) Ltd, Croydon, CR0 4YY

For Susan; who showed me what matters

Acknowledgements

For me, *Betrayal* was an important story to tell. More than that, it was a story I wanted to tell right. But dealing as it does with sensitive subject matter, I knew it was never going to be an easy book to finish. The fact that it appears before you now is due in no small part of the dedicated and talented people I've been lucky enough to work with.

As always, my thanks go to my editor Georgina Hawtrey-Woore for her help and advice in shaping this book, and to my agent Diane Banks for being my guide in the weird and wonderful world of publishing. I'd also like to acknowledge the tireless work of my copy editor Mary Chamberlain, who somehow managed to keep the complex events of this series in some kind of order!

Lastly my thanks go to my friend Irene Houle, who I was finally able to meet in person last summer. Her thoughtful advice and kind words of encouragement on my early writing forays helped me realise how much I wanted to be an author, and for that I'll always be grateful.

Betrayal

Prologue

Numbed by fear and exhaustion, Natasha glanced up from the old scarred wooden floorboards that had been her sole point of focus for the past several hours.

Her captor was standing about 10 yards away, puffing absently on a cigarette, the bulky frame of an assault rifle cradled in his arms as he took another deep draw. His features were crude and blunt, characteristic of the men in this part of the country; all pockmarked skin and stubbly beard. His eyes, grey and soulless, were fixed dead ahead, seeing nothing.

What was going on behind those expressionless eyes?

A muted cough nearby drew her attention back to her immediate surroundings. More than 500 men, women and children of all ages were packed into the school exercise hall, crowded in so close that there was scarcely enough space even to sit down. The heat was stifling. The smell of sweat, fear and stale urine was pervasive.

They had been held for two days and nights without rest or relief, forbidden to move, forbidden even to talk. When they had first been herded in here, their passage marked by shouting and gunshots, many of the children had been near hysteria with panic. Some had pleaded in vain to be allowed to leave, as if this were a sports day that they could somehow be excused from. Others, too young to understand

1

what was going on, had sought the only reassurance they knew and clustered around their teachers like sheep.

But two days and nights of constant fear, lack of sleep and threats of violence had worn the jagged edges of their nerves down until all Natasha could hear was the occasional cough, groan and strangled sob. These were a group of people defeated in body and spirit, grimly waiting for what was to come.

Most of them had their eyes turned downwards, trying not to be noticed, trying not to do anything that would single them out. They had all learned the value of anonymity. On the first day their captors had executed one man simply for failing to kneel quickly enough, and another for speaking in the local Ossetian language instead of Russian.

On the second day they had rounded up twenty of the fittest, most capable-looking men and taken them upstairs to the second floor. Moments later, a thundering boom had rolled through the corridors, followed by the chatter of automatic gunfire. None of the men had come back.

Natasha's empty stomach growled, the muscles in her abdomen cramping painfully. She hadn't eaten a thing since this had all begun; a fact that her body was reminding her of with increasing urgency. A slender girl of twelve years, she had had little enough meat on her bones to begin with, but now she was starting to feel weak and light-headed as malnutrition took hold.

She licked her dry lips, trying to silence thoughts of cool, refreshing water. How many times had she pushed her glass of water aside at the dinner table, pestering her father for fruit juice or a sugary soft drink? She would have killed for that glass now.

Her thoughts were interrupted as shouts echoed from the corridor outside the gym hall, making her and the rest of the captives jump in fright. But despite the sudden pounding of her heart, Natasha strained to listen, trying to discern the cause of the commotion. Despite the obvious anger, they didn't seem to be arguing amongst themselves. It was more as though they were yelling for the sake of it, venting their frustration and trying to rally their flagging resolve.

They were speaking in Chechen. She couldn't understand what was being said, but it didn't matter. Even she could sense the change in them.

Some, like the smoking man nearby, were older, calmer and in control of their emotions. But most were young, filled with fire and bravado. As the uneasy stand-off dragged on without any end in sight, they were growing more frustrated and aggressive. Things were not playing out as they had expected. Something was wrong.

'It's going to happen soon,' Natasha whispered.

'What are you talking about?' It was Yelena, the friend she'd known for so long she couldn't remember a time without her. She was a plump sort of girl – not fat as such, but rounded and soft in body, the kind who would blossom into a voluptuous beauty in her teenage years before growing big and matronly as her youth faded.

The girl, her dark hair hanging limp and damp around her face, didn't look up from the floor, but Natasha could see her eyes were red from crying.

Natasha leaned in closer and nodded towards the gunman who had discarded his cigarette and was now pacing back and forth in front of the door, his broad shoulders hunched with tension. 'They're getting more worked up all the time. They're going to do something soon.'

'Like what?'

'I don't know.' She swallowed even though her throat was dry and sore. 'Maybe kill us all.'

'They can't! The soldiers outside will stop them.' It was a weak protest, delivered without conviction.

Cut off and isolated as they were, neither could tell what was happening outside. Certainly they had heard the rumble of big vehicle engines, the beating of helicopter blades and the occasional shouted exchange with the gunmen, but nothing more. The entire Russian army could be outside, but it didn't make the slightest difference to them.

'They didn't stop all those men being killed yesterday,' Natasha reasoned. 'Why would it be any different today?'

'Maybe they'll surrender? They can't want to die here.'

Even Natasha sensed the flawed logic in her argument. 'Or maybe they're like the men who flew planes into those buildings in America. Maybe they don't care about dying.'

Yelena sniffed and shrugged, as if it made no difference to her. 'So what? What can we do about it?'

That was the question. Natasha wasn't a soldier. But like all living things, the overwhelming, primal instinct in her young mind was to survive.

'Be ready to move,' she said, because wasn't that what people said at times like this? She hoped she sounded more confident than she felt. 'When it happens, stay by me.'

Seeing the growing defiance and desperation in her friend, Yelena's eyes opened wider. 'You're going to get us killed!' she hissed.

The girl raised her chin, a tiny flame of anger kindling within her.

'Better than letting these bastards kill us,' she said through gritted teeth. She turned her eyes on her friend again. 'Yelena, look at me. *Look at me.*' With great reluctance, her friend's eyes crept up from the floor to meet her own. 'I can get us out of here, but only if you trust me. Do you trust me?'

4

Yelena's eyes shone with tears, but she nodded all the same. 'Yes.'

Natasha reached out and clasped her hand. 'We'll get out of this. I promise.'

No sooner had they spoken than a fresh round of shouting began in the corridor outside. But this was different from before. The men weren't just yelling to fire themselves up; they were arguing amongst themselves, their aggression growing in intensity.

And then all of a sudden there were two more gunmen in the gym, both of them young, gaunt and wild-eyed like horses caught in a stampede. They were brandishing their assault rifles like they intended to use them, and sensing this, the hostages tried in vain to shrink away. It was useless. They were hemmed in by the sheer mass of bodies.

The smoking man was weighing in to the argument now as well, standing in their path to stop them getting any closer, trying to make them back down. He was a formidable figure, as tall and wide as a doorway to Natasha's young eyes, but his younger comrades were apparently beyond such intimidation now.

They had come here to act, and nothing was going to stop them.

It happened fast. The older man reached out to grab the nearest one by the arm, but the young man reacted by shoving him away with enough force to put him off balance. Growling with anger, he waded back into the fray, drawing his rifle to swing it like a club. But the second young gunman was ready for him. Raising his assault rifle, he aimed it dead centre in the older man's chest and fired.

The resulting cacophony of noise echoed around the gym like the pealing of thunder, mixing with the frightened screams of the hostages as the weapon discharged. The older man crumpled to the ground like a sack of potatoes, his blood staining the floor.

People were scrambling away in terror now as the two gunmen moved further into the room, yelling and screaming as if they had lost whatever self-control they possessed. One of them raised his assault rifle and fired a burst into the ceiling, sending chunks of plaster and broken wood raining down on them.

Natasha gripped her friend's hand tight. This was it. This was the moment. They had to act now. Her heart was pounding hard in her chest, blood rushing through tired muscles, investing them with new strength.

It started as a faint whooshing sound from outside, barely heard against the screams and shouts of 500 men, women and children. But it soon grew in power and intensity until everyone in the hall could hear it. Natasha turned towards the source of the sound, perplexed despite her fear, wondering what it could mean.

The flash lasted only a fraction of a second, but it was bright enough to burn its way on to her retinas to leave a blurry after-image flashing across her vision. An instant later, the flash was replaced by a ball of fire that tore through brick walls, reinforcing struts, beams, wooden floorboards and fragile human bodies without mercy.

Natasha was thrown off her feet by the blast, her head slamming on to the hard floor with bruising force. For a moment she saw and felt nothing but blackness, sheer and absolute. She was in her own world now, a world without pain or fatigue or fear, a world of nothingness.

Then, as if heard from a great distance, she became aware of sounds around her. Panicked voices, screams of pain and fear, the rhythmic thud of automatic gunfire, the pounding of her own heart, and a distant roar that she couldn't identify.

With great effort she forced her eyes open. The world around her was a nightmare.

Something had demolished the far wall of the gym, blasting through the bricks and mortar, and turning them into a deadly hail of shrapnel that had torn apart anyone unlucky enough to be caught in their path. There was blood everywhere, and the screams of the wounded and dying mingled horribly with the cries of those now seeking a means of escape.

The explosion had also set the roof ablaze, and fire was already clawing at the wooden rafters, filling the air with thick dark smoke. She could feel the heat even from the other side of the room.

More gunfire erupted around them, both inside and outside the school. A full-scale battle had apparently flared up between the gunmen and the Russian police and army outside. The building shook to its foundations as another massive explosion rocked it.

Natasha stared again at the hole in the wall. It was a ragged, smoking gap about 8 feet wide, partially blocked by fallen rubble and dead bodies. But beyond the haze of smoke, she could see daylight.

That was it! That was their way out! Hope surged through her. This was their chance.

Turning away for a moment, she reached down for Yelena, who was lying on the ground beside her. 'Yelena! Get up. We're getting out now!' she yelled, coughing as the smoke seared her lungs. The fire was raging above them, pieces of burning wood and insulation falling everywhere.

The young girl didn't move. She lay curled in a foetal position, knees drawn up to her chest, eyes staring straight ahead without seeing anything.

'Yelena! Wake up!' In desperation, Natasha drew back

her hand and slapped her friend across the face with all the strength she could muster. The shock of the blow seemed to snap her out of her reverie, and she looked up at Natasha, eyes wide with fear.

'Come on!' Natasha yelled, pulling her friend up. 'We have to go.'

People were running everywhere in blind panic, some trying to help injured friends, some just searching for a way out. Still clutching Yelena's hand, Natasha pushed her way forwards, getting jostled left and right as people crowded in, all making for the gap in the wall.

Her foot caught on something, and she glanced down in time to see the body of one of her friends splayed out on the floor like a rag doll. His torso had been shredded by shrapnel, exposing ribs and charred muscle, and one of his legs had been blasted away. For a moment she found herself transfixed by the shattered bone and torn flesh where his leg should have been. His lifeless eyes stared upwards, reflecting the flames in the roof overhead.

She knew she should have felt horror, should have felt revulsion and grief at the sight, but there was no time to feel such emotions. Her mind was in survival mode, dealing only with the things it needed to deal with to keep her alive. Instead she stepped over the body, pushing the horrific image from her mind, concentrating only on getting out.

The shooting was growing more intense now. She could hear the whoosh of what sounded like rocket launchers, accompanied by heavy thuds as missiles impacted on the school building. Everywhere there was smoke and fire and confusion and yelling, people clambering over the bodies of the dead and wounded in their terror.

She was almost there now. She could see daylight outside.

'Yelena! Keep moving!' she screamed, yanking her friend's

hand with a fierce strength that defied her malnourished body. 'We have to—'

She never got a chance to finish. A mother of one of the children, running in blind panic, tripped and fell into her from the side. The impact of the larger and heavier adult knocked her off balance so that she landed hard on the ground. She tried to keep hold of Yelena's hand, but they were being pulled in opposite directions and before she knew what was happening, her friend was gone.

'Yelena!' she cried, trying to get up. But every time she did, someone would run into her or trip over her, knocking her down once more. 'Yelena, wait!'

She gasped in pain as a boot slammed into her chest, bruising her breasts and forcing the air from her lungs. She coughed, trying in vain to breathe the hot, smoke-filled air. She felt as if her ribcage had been caved in.

Then, above the roar of the fire, the chatter of machine-gun fire, the pounding of her heart and the screams of terrified people, she heard her friend's high, thin voice. 'Tasha! I can't! I can't!'

She caught a momentary glimpse of the young woman's frightened face as she was carried away by the press of people, and just like that her friend was gone.

She tried to follow, but instead found herself jerked backwards as strong hands clamped around her neck, dragging her away from the hole in the wall. One of the gunmen had seized her, she realised. In desperation she kicked and struggled against his hold, summoning up the last reserves of her failing strength in a vain effort to break free.

It was no use. He was twice her size and many times her match in strength. With one arm locked around her neck, he used his free hand to cuff her across the side of her head. White light and pain exploded through her mind as she went limp in his arms.

With a hard yank, she was pulled right off her feet and hauled back through the burning gym. Vaguely, through clouded vision, she realised she was now in the corridor running between the gym and the school cafeteria. The corridor was streaked with bloody footprints, and on her left she saw a body lying curled against the wall, clothes and flesh shredded by bullet holes.

Rounding a corner, her captor dragged her into the food hall. The place was in chaos, windows smashed out, chairs scattered everywhere and tables upended to serve as temporary barricades for the dozen or so gunmen who had decided to make a stand there.

'They've betrayed us!' one of them shouted in Russian as he fumbled to insert a magazine into his weapon with trembling hands. 'They're going to kill us all!'

His companions were firing indiscriminately at the row of apartment buildings beyond the school gates, the roar of their weapons deafening in the confined space. The floor was covered with broken glass, empty bullet casings, discarded magazines and blood.

'Move!' her captor yelled in her ear as he pushed her towards the windows. 'Move!'

She tried to comply, but her legs wouldn't work. She was still groggy from the blow to her head, but a hard kick to her back was enough to move her. She fell forwards, gashing her knees on the broken glass. She barely felt the pain now.

Staring out into the open space beyond the windows, she froze in horror at the scene unfolding before her eyes. The school yard was littered with the bodies of children, teachers and parents unlucky enough to have been caught in the crossfire between the two sides. Amongst them, curled into a ball as if to hide, she saw the body of a plump girl with dark hair. Yelena.

Whatever grief she should have felt at the sight, there was no time for it to sink in.

A deep rumble off to her left caught her attention, and she stared open-mouthed as the massive bulk of a battle tank rumbled through the brick wall that marked the boundary of the school yard, crashing through the solid barrier as if it wasn't even there. Its domed turret swung around in a measured, unhurried fashion, the long barrel of its main gun eagerly searching for a target. Then it stopped, a brief moment of inaction passed, and with a roar that shook the very ground, it fired. The shell hit one of the classrooms on the first floor of the main building, sending glass and burning debris raining down on the playground.

She was not alone by the windows, she realised now. Several men and women of various ages had been lined up next to her, and all stood unmoving, some crying in fear, others strangely silent as if resigned to what was happening. Gunmen were crouched behind them, using them as human shields.

Before Natasha could recover enough to get up, she was once more grabbed by the arm and forced to her feet. She could feel the bulk of his body armour pressed against her back, and the rough bristle of his beard brushing her cheek. Thunder erupted beside her as he opened fire, spraying bullets into the school yard almost without bothering to aim.

To her left, one of the hostages cried out in pain and fell to the ground, blood flowing from his chest and legs. He was followed a moment later by the woman beside him, who took a round to the head that shattered her skull like an eggshell. She crumpled without as much as a sound.

With dawning horror, Natasha realised that it wasn't the gunmen who had killed them, it was the Russian soldiers fighting their way into the school. She bucked and lashed out with her feet, screaming, arching her back in a last desperate attempt to get away.

This wasn't real, her mind screamed at her. This couldn't be happening. Her life had been one of safety and security, each day like the one before. Things like this couldn't happen to her. This wasn't—

All such thoughts were silenced when a 7.62mm projectile penetrated her chest, shattering ribs, tearing through internal organs and blasting out through her back before doing the same to her captor. Her legs gave way beneath her and she fell to the floor, eyes staring blankly up at the ceiling as the last few seconds of her short life played out.

She felt no pain now. She felt nothing except a vague sense of sadness and regret that she would never see her family again, never hear her mother's laugh or listen to her father chastise her for not drinking her water at dinner.

Her last thought was a simple one. Why us?

Then her vision faded and she saw and thought no more.

Part One

Intrusion

In what became known as the Beslan Massacre 334 people were killed and 728 injured. The majority of those casualties were women and children.

Chapter 1

CIA Headquarters, Langley, 19 December 2008

Ryan Drake watched as the man before him shifted his weight from one foot to the other, trying and failing to find a comfortable firing stance. The M4 assault rifle at his shoulder was held at an awkward angle that he was sure would cause problems when the shooting started, but he made no move to intervene.

He was here as an observer, nothing more. His role was to evaluate the candidate's performance and ultimately decide whether or not he was suitable to join the Shepherd programme. It was a task he didn't relish. Drake wasn't accustomed to sitting back and watching good men fail.

'Candidate ready?' he asked when it seemed the shooter had settled down. He couldn't blame the man for being nervous. They both knew what rested on this.

There were no second chances when it came to the Shepherd teams. Either you made the grade first time, or you went home.

'Been a while since I heard that.' Cole Mason glanced at him and managed a strained smile, before turning his attention back to the rifle range stretching out in front of him. The tension in his body was obvious, even to Drake. 'I'm ready.'

'Go hot,' Drake instructed, watching as he thumbed off the safety on his weapon. It was loaded with live ammunition

for this exercise, and even amongst experienced profession-
als there was no room for complacency.

Giving Mason a few seconds to prepare, Drake checked
his ear protectors were firmly in place, then pressed the little
remote trigger in his hand to start the live-fire exercise.

Straight away the light levels on the rifle range decreased,
and the strained silence of moments earlier was replaced with
the loud boom of explosions, the chatter of heavy machine-
gun fire and the screams of panicked civilians, all of it blasting
through speakers strategically placed around the room. The
explosions were accompanied by strobe light flashes and
vicious orange glows, designed to simulate the confusion and
disorientation of a real combat situation.

To his credit, Mason stood his ground, unfazed by the dis-
turbing visual and aural stimulus. He'd experienced this stuff
for real plenty of times and certainly wasn't going to panic at
a simulation. Anyway, he knew what he was looking for.

And a few moments later, it came.

The cardboard representation of a gun-toting militant
sprang up from behind a wall, accompanied by another burst
of simulated gunfire.

Mason reacted immediately. Swinging the barrel of his
assault rifle left, he paused a heartbeat to take aim, leaned
into it and fired a burst. His shots impacted a couple of inches
off-centre, but still within the kill zone. The target toppled
backwards, effectively 'dead'.

'Come on, Cole,' Drake whispered, willing the man to
succeed.

His next grouping was better, landing more or less dead centre in a target that popped up just 10 yards away. Maybe he'd
been wrong, Drake thought. Maybe Mason's years of experience and training would overcome his physical limitations.

His hopes were soon dashed when the next target popped up

in the window of a building at the far end of the range, meant to represent a sniper taking potshots at them. Mason's first burst missed entirely, and though his second found its mark, the rounds were scattered all across the cardboard figure. Drake saw Mason flinch at the weapon's recoil, rolling his shoulder as if to loosen it up. Already the air reeked of burned cordite.

Hastily ejecting the spent magazine, he reached for a new one on the table in front of him and slapped it into place just as three more figures popped up. Two of them were innocent civilians, meant to represent hostages, while the third was their captor.

Knowing he had only moments to react, Mason brought his rifle to bear and, driven by the pressure of the moment, opened fire.

His hastily aimed burst slammed into the cardboard hostage next to his intended target, undoubtedly dealing a fatal injury had it been a real person.

Drake looked down, unwilling to watch as the exercise continued. Already he knew the result, but delivering it was one task that the machines here couldn't help him with.

That unpleasant duty fell to him alone.

It was a cold, damp Friday evening in the capital, with icy flurries of sleet carried on the fitful breeze as commuters fought their way through rush-hour traffic. This close to Christmas, many were heading home via the nearest shopping mall, hoping to grab a few last-minute bargains before the weekend.

A woman paused at a busy intersection, waiting for a gap in the traffic so she could cross. She was dressed in a heavy winter overcoat, the collar drawn up to offer some protection from the chill wind. Her short blonde hair was hidden beneath a black stocking cap.

A leather gym bag was slung across one shoulder. Just another DC office worker squeezing in a workout before the excesses of the festive season. An older woman, plump and tired, offered her a sympathetic smile as she passed by. She didn't acknowledge it.

Spotting a let-up in the traffic, she moved with fast, measured steps across the road, heading down a quieter residential street towards an apartment building overlooking the nearby freeway. The rumble of traffic and the occasional blast of car horns filtered through the air towards her as she turned left and strode towards the main entrance, unlocking the security door.

The public stairwell beyond was clean and well maintained, just as it had been the last time she came here two days ago. There had been a bike chained to the stair banister then, but it was gone now. The place wasn't heated, but warmth from the various apartments had bled out into it, raising the temperature a few degrees higher than outside.

Wasting no time, she made for the stairs and started up them. The contents of the sports bag were both heavy and bulky, and by the time she'd reached the third floor she could feel beads of sweat on her forehead. The stocking cap clung uncomfortably to her head, but she ignored it.

'Hey, you okay?' a male voice asked from the third-floor landing. 'Need a hand?'

She looked over at the tall, slightly overweight man with glasses and a goatee, who had just emerged from his apartment. He was dressed for the winter weather and had likely been on his way out when he'd spotted her.

'Nah. I'm good, thanks,' she replied, flashing a grateful smile. 'It's a better workout than I get in the damn gym.'

He smiled in response, warming to her immediately. 'I hear ya. Should do a little more myself,' he added. She noticed he had drawn his stomach in, as men often did when talking to women about exercise.

Turning away, she resumed her difficult climb to the top floor. She was grateful when she heard his footsteps receding below, followed by a heavy clang as the front door opened and shut. He might remember her later, but it wouldn't matter. She'd be gone by then.

The building's roof was accessed via a short flight of steps, with a fire door at the top which, naturally, was alarmed. She had already disabled it during her visit two days before, bypassing the door sensor to fool the system into thinking it was locked.

Glancing back down the steps for a moment to check she wasn't being watched, she pushed firmly down on the bar to open the door and stepped out. Straight away she was greeted by a gust of cold wind that tugged at her coat and made her eyes water. After the relative warmth of the stairwell, the sudden change in temperature was almost a shock to the system.

Still, it provided a welcome moment of refreshment. Her body was by now well adapted to cold climates, and compared to some of the places she had visited, winter in DC was of little concern.

Letting out a breath that steamed in the chill air, she surveyed the area that would act as her vantage point. It was perfect for her needs. Like most buildings in America, the roof was crowded with heating vents, satellite dishes and air-conditioning outlets. The general clutter would provide excellent cover as she went about her work.

Stretching out before her like a river of concrete was the 395 freeway, clogged with slow-moving evening traffic. That was good. The slower her targets were moving, the easier her job would be.

Chapter 2

Seated in his small, cramped and cluttered office on the second floor of Langley's Old Headquarters Building, Drake looked up from his computer at the knock on the door. He had a fair idea who was there.

'Come in,' he called.

Sure enough, the door opened to reveal Cole Mason. A tall, good-looking man in his late thirties, Mason possessed the dark eyes, olive skin and jet-black hair characteristic of his Italian ancestry. Only his name seemed to let him down on that front – the result of his grandmother moving to America to escape Mussolini's Italy in the 1930s. Smart move on her part.

He had showered and changed out of the T-shirt and combat trousers he'd worn during the live-fire exercise, donning a grey business suit that did little to hide his broad-shouldered and muscular physique. He had been hitting the gym hard over the past few months, determined to regain his former strength and fitness.

But despite this outward display of robust physical health, the look in his eyes betrayed his lack of confidence as he stepped over the threshold. Nonetheless, he managed a wry smile as he glanced around Drake's disorganised work space.

'Some things never change, I see.'

Drake avoided his gaze. Some things unfortunately did change.

Mason wasn't some eager young recruit fresh off the Agency's basic training programme, but a seasoned veteran who had served alongside Drake on a dozen occasions in the small but elite group known as the Shepherd teams. Their job was to travel to some of the most hostile and dangerous places on earth and recover lost, missing, captured or, in rare cases, rogue Agency operatives. As such, only the best of the best made the cut.

Experienced, quick-thinking and cool under pressure, Mason had been a natural choice as second in command during their ill-fated mission into Russia the previous year. Drake had been handed the daunting task of breaking into a Siberian prison and rescuing an operative known only by her code name, Maras. Against the odds they had achieved their objective, but a stray round had shattered Mason's shoulder during their escape, putting him out of action and very nearly ending his life.

It was a shitty thing to happen to a good man, and more than once Drake had agonised over his responsibility for it. Now, after eighteen months, several surgeries and a gruelling period of rehabilitation, Mason had applied to rejoin the Shepherd teams as an active field agent. Whether or not he was capable of fulfilling this role had been left to Drake to decide. Talk about a poisoned chalice.

'Have a seat, mate,' Drake said, gesturing to the chair opposite.

Mason eased himself down and crossed his legs, fidgeting uncomfortably in the awkward silence that followed. Drake hated this shit, hated having to give bad news to good people, hated deciding men's futures from behind a desk. It wasn't him. It wasn't who he was.

Still, he was here, and he had a job to do.

'First of all, I want you to know that you've done an

21

incredible job to get back here,' he began. 'The work you've put in over the past year—'

'Ryan, we've known each other a long time,' Mason interrupted. 'You don't need to bullshit me. Let's just get down to it, okay?'

He was smiling as if this was just good-natured banter between friends, perhaps hoping to ease the tension, but Drake could sense the nervous anticipation beneath that disarming smile. He supposed he would have felt the same way in Mason's shoes.

If Mason wanted the truth, Drake would give it to him.

'All right, here's the deal.' He leaned forward, his elbows on the desk as he eyed his friend. 'There's no easy way of saying this, so I'll just say it. I'm afraid you haven't made the grade. I'm sorry, mate, but I can't certify you fit to return to duty.'

For a long moment, Mason said nothing. He didn't react at all. He just looked at Drake across the desk, as if waiting for him to say something more, to add in something that would turn it all around.

It didn't happen. Drake had nothing to give him.

The Shepherd teams had no time for guys who made the cut on their third attempt, when they knew what to expect and how to deal with it. Just as there were no second chances out in the field, so it was with training and selection. They were ruthless because they had to be.

'You know the standards they set for Shepherd operatives,' Drake went on, more to fill the silence than because he thought his words would offer much comfort. 'The bar is pretty fucking high, and I can't lower it for anyone, no matter how much I might want to.'

'So that's it, huh?' Mason finally said, an undertone of bitterness and simmering frustration creeping into his voice. 'I'm done. You pack me off and send me home?'

'Of course not. There are other jobs in the Agency—'

'Doing what? Flipping burgers in the fucking canteen?' Mason snapped, rising to his feet as his temper got the better of him. 'That what you think I'm fit for now?'

'That's not what I meant,' Drake said, knowing he had to handle this delicately. 'You've got years of experience in the field. You could get into training, mission planning . . . whatever you wanted. There are plenty of opportunities—'

'No, Ryan,' the older man said, shaking his head vehemently. 'I'm no more cut out for that shit than you are. We're both field ops – always have been, always will be.'

Except one of us doesn't have the tools for the job any more, Drake couldn't help thinking. It was a harsh thought to entertain about a man he considered a friend, but theirs was a harsh profession that didn't make allowances for weakness or injury.

Calming himself a little, Mason continued. 'Look, we worked together for years, right? You know me, you know what I can do. So I didn't ace every test they threw at me today – so what? I can still do my job *out there*, where it matters.' He paused a moment, as if sensing the line he was about to cross, then went for it anyway. 'It . . . wouldn't be hard to change my scores a little. We both know it's been done before, so why not now? You know I'd have your back if the situation was reversed.'

This was a very different man from the one he'd parted company with after the prison raid, Drake realised now. The Cole Mason he'd known then never would have contemplated what he'd just suggested. Then again, that had been before the painful surgeries, the punishing months of rehab, the financial trouble that came with existing on half pay while his future hung in the balance.

Drake understood why he was doing this, why he felt the

23

need to regain everything he'd lost, to prove to himself that he wasn't a useless cripple who couldn't even fire a gun properly. He might well have felt the same way in that position, but this was one line of thought that needed to be stopped right now.

'Cole, listen to me,' he said, rising from his chair. 'I'm going to tell you something you don't want to hear, but for both our sakes you need to hear it. I know you'd never let me down if you could help it. You were one of the best operatives I ever worked with, but the fact is you're a liability now. That's a shitty deal, but it's the truth. If I clear you for field ops, I'd be risking the lives of any team you ever served with. You saw what happened on the rifle range earlier. That could have been me, or Keira, or some innocent civilian caught in the crossfire. You want to live with that for the rest of your life?' He sighed and looked down at his desk for a moment. 'You said you'd have my back if the situation was reversed. Well, if it was, I'd expect you to give me the same lecture I just gave you. I'd be pissed off with you, and I'd probably resent you for a long time, but eventually I'd realise you were right. I'm asking you to let this one go, mate. Don't make it any worse for yourself.'

That was enough to blunt the edge of Mason's anger. Drake saw him hesitate, realising that his shortcomings today weren't just bad luck or pedantic adherence to some arbitrary standards, but a simple and unavoidable fact. Despite all the operations and the rehab and the training, he simply wasn't the man he'd once been.

'I'm sorry, but this was my decision.'

'Must have been a tough call, huh, Ryan?' he said bitterly.

Drake said nothing.

Sensing he would get nothing more from his friend, Mason raised his chin a little in a flash of defiance.

24

'Well then, I guess we've got nothing more to say,' he decided, his tone now cold and businesslike. 'Thanks for the opportunity. Maybe I'll see you around some time.'

He shook hands with Drake, his grip crushingly strong as if to demonstrate the strength he still possessed.

'Funny old world, huh?' he said at length, releasing his hand and leaving the office.

Letting out a breath, Drake eased himself back into his chair. He'd just destroyed a man's career from the comfort of an office desk. The computer on which he was writing up his final assessment of Mason's performance was his weapon now, and it was just as cruel as any rifle.

This wasn't him. This wasn't who he wanted to be.

He rubbed his eyes and pushed himself away from the desk, swinging his chair around to stare through his small office window at the dimly lit world beyond. Past the trees that surrounded CIA headquarters lay the distant lights of DC, shrouded in sombre grey clouds. It was early evening in December and getting dark fast, with flurries of sleet pattering against the window.

Again he replayed the events of that night last year: the dangerous raid on the remote Russian prison, the decisions he'd made, the things he could have done differently. He'd been through it more times than he could count, but Mason's appearance today had triggered the memories once again.

In retrospect, nothing good had come out of that mission. The rescue of that enigmatic prisoner had started a chain of events that had very nearly ended Drake's life, not to mention that of his sister and her family back in the UK, ruined his career and left him trapped in an uneasy stand-off with powerful men who wanted him dead. And yet again today, he'd been confronted with another reminder of the consequences of his actions.

'Fuck this,' he growled, rising from his chair.

The report could wait until tomorrow. It was nothing more than an autopsy anyway. Whatever he noted in it, it wouldn't change the fact that the patient was dead. Explaining how and why it had happened was a task he didn't feel up to completing tonight.

Grabbing his coat off the back of the door, he jammed his hands in the pockets, feeling for his car keys.

Laying aside the heavy sports bag, Anya knelt down and unzipped it, exposing the carefully wrapped package within. A KSVK sniper rifle, stripped and dismantled for easy transport.

With the efficient, unhurried ease born from long practice, she set to work reassembling the weapon, clipping together the breech mechanism before attaching the enormous metre-long barrel. A quick test pull of the trigger confirmed that the firing mechanism was in good order, after which she attached the scope to the rail mounted on top of the weapon.

The last task was to insert the magazine. She didn't slam it into place the way they did in the movies, but simply applied firm pressure to push it home until she felt the click as the locking pins engaged. A slight downward pull was enough to assure her the magazine was secure.

Reaching into her pocket, she fished out a Bluetooth earpiece and fitted it to her left ear, then powered up her cellphone and dialled a number from memory. It was answered immediately.

There was no greeting; the ringing simply stopped.

'I'm green,' she reported. 'When do we start?'

'Our friends are on their way. Fifteen minutes.'

'Understood.'

There was no need for further conversation. Both she and

her contact knew what had to be done; it was simply a case of doing the most difficult part of any sniper's job – waiting.

Drake emerged from the liquor store clutching a carefully wrapped bottle of wine, his head down and his coat turned up against the driving sleet and hail that pelted him with each gust of wind. It was a miserable evening, and not likely to get much better by his estimation.

He'd gone for a five-year-old bottle of Sauvignon Blanc, thinking it was fairly forgiving stuff that most people could drink easily, but now he was starting to wonder if he should have bought a Chablis Chardonnay instead.

'Jesus Christ, Ryan, it's a bottle of wine,' he said under his breath, giving himself a mental slapping.

In this case, however, it was more than a bottle of wine – it was a peace offering. It wasn't much in the way of recompense considering how he'd treated the intended recipient over the past couple of months, but it was the best he could come up with.

He was just approaching his car when he felt his phone go off in his pocket, signalling an incoming text message.

For a moment Drake was tempted to leave it. He suspected it was work-related, and was in no mood for dealing with some boring administrative issue at 6 p.m. on a Friday.

Still, he wasn't the sort to leave a message unread; curiosity and a frustratingly innate sense of duty compelled him to take a look. Laying the bottle down on the passenger seat, he opened the text. His curiosity soon intensified when the sender came up as Anonymous.

But more intriguing still was the message itself.

Ryan – We need to talk. 1st Street and Delaware Avenue. 10 mins.

Drake felt a chill of anticipation run through him as he scanned the message again. It was impossible to tell from

27

such an impersonal form of communication, but the style matched that of a woman who was accustomed to arranging such clandestine meetings at short notice.

A woman he hadn't seen since his return from a mission in Afghanistan four months ago that had seen one of his team dead.

A woman he couldn't afford to ignore now. If she had taken the risk of making contact in the heart of DC, she must have something important to tell him.

Either way, he knew he had to get to her.

Pocketing the phone, he jumped in the driver's seat, glancing for a moment at the bottle of wine lying on the other side. He felt a fleeting moment of regret, knowing what it represented.

Peace offerings would have to wait for now, he thought, as he fired up the engine and pulled out into the busy road, gunning the accelerator hard to avoid hitting an oncoming bus.

Chapter 3

Central DC was in a state of organised chaos as Drake tried to fight his way through the rush-hour traffic, manoeuvring his car through spaces it had no business trying to fit into, taking side streets and any possible short cuts he could think of.

Despite his best efforts, he was forced to abandon his car in a residential area several blocks south of the meeting place and make his way there on foot, doing his best to ignore the stinging hail and sleet that had been getting dumped on the capital all day. It was a miserable evening, but in truth his mind wasn't on the weather.

If he was right, then the person waiting for him a few blocks away was someone he'd spent much of the past eighteen months searching for.

Anya, the woman he'd been charged with liberating from a Russian prison last year. Once known by her code name Maras, she'd been one of the Agency's best field operatives in her time. She had also been an infrequent but profound influence on his life ever since that night, her presence often heralding great upheaval and danger.

But as much as it galled him to admit it, she was also his lifeline; the one person on this earth who could unravel the web of deceit and betrayal that reached to the top echelons of the Agency. Only time would tell whether she held the key to setting things right.

However, there was always a chance that his enigmatic contact wasn't Anya at all. If so, he intended to be ready. Reaching into his pocket, he felt the solid frame of the 9mm Sig Sauer automatic, taken from the glove compartment of his car just before he'd dumped it. He always kept a weapon there these days.

The corner of 1st Street and Delaware was, on the whole, a pretty unremarkable area for such a meeting. Looking around, he saw little of interest on the unassuming tree-lined roads except an apartment complex to the north-east, with rows of two-storey residential houses opposite. The cars parked beside them confirmed his suspicion that this was a less-than-affluent neighbourhood.

A Baptist church stood on the south-east corner. Judging by the sounds drifting out on the cold air, it was the kind of place where they did a lot of gospel singing and tambourine banging. At least someone was having a good evening.

Traffic chugged past on both main roads, less congested here than on the big freeway a short distance to the north, but enough to make crossing a dicey affair. There were almost no pedestrians, save for an overweight old man out walking his dog on the grassy area near the low-rise apartments. Drake couldn't hide a flicker of amusement as the man pretended not to notice his charge hunker down and leave a big steaming turd on the grass, walking on as if nothing had happened. He'd used the same tactic himself when forced to take the family dog for morning walks as a kid.

The only thing missing in this picture of urban blandness was Anya. That wasn't surprising in itself. She always controlled the time and place of their meetings, and saw to it that he didn't find her until she wanted to be found, but it wasn't in her nature to be tardy.

Pulling his jacket collar up, Drake looked down at his

watch. It had been well over ten minutes since her text message. Where was she?

The light levels were falling rapidly up on the roof. It was winter, the sun had set about half an hour earlier and darkness was descending on the capital. For Anya, it was perfect. The brightly lit highway in front of her made picking targets easy, while the gathering dark kept her position safely obscured.

Not that she had to worry – there were few buildings in the vicinity that overlooked this rooftop. That was one of the reasons she'd chosen it in the first place.

'One minute.'

Gritting her teeth, she heaved the bulky weapon up on to the metal air-vent cover beside her, allowing it to rest on its integral bipod as she worked the bolt action, drawing the first round into the breech.

The KSVK held five rounds of 12.7 x 108mm armour-piercing ammunition; powerful enough to punch through the metal skin of the average APC and kill anything on the other side. Two targets, five rounds, no time to change magazines.

'Thirty seconds.'

Anya reckoned the wind speed at about 6 or 7 knots, blowing more or less straight towards her from the east. It wouldn't divert the rounds off target, but it would contribute to a slight drop in shot as each projectile had more air to travel through. She adjusted the scope's lateral compensation a couple of notches and settled in behind it, finding a comfortable position for the butt against her shoulder.

'Twenty seconds.'

Closing her eyes, she allowed her breathing to come slower and deeper, her heart rate to calm, her muscles to relax. Sniping was one of the most difficult skills for any operative to master; years of training and preparation all coming down to a single moment of truth. One shot, one chance, one kill.

'Ten seconds.'

Opening her eyes once more, she leaned into the scope, surveying the traffic on the freeway until she found what she was looking for. A pair of silver Mercedes-Benz sedans travelling in loose convoy in the centre lane. Distance, 700 metres. Speed, approximately 40mph.

'Five seconds.'

She needed no prompting now. Sighting the second car in the convoy, she focused in on the left side of the windshield. The glass was tinted as it often was on official vehicles, making it difficult to see the driver, but it didn't matter. She was familiar with the make and model of the car and knew exactly where he would be seated.

Her gloved finger tightened on the trigger.

'Now.'

Exhaling slowly, she fired.

The recoil of a single 12.7mm round slammed the weapon back into her shoulder with bruising force. The blast from the muzzle caused a shockwave to spread across the metal vent cover in front of her, raising tiny showers of water, while the boom of the discharging round left her ears ringing.

Half a second later she watched as the toughened windshield exploded inwards, accompanied by a sudden cloud of red that coated the broken glass.

Straight away her right hand was moving, working the bolt to eject the spent cartridge and draw a fresh one into the breech. There was a loud click as the moving parts worked, followed by a dull ping as the spent casing clattered on to the rooftop, smoking and sizzling where it rested on the damp surface.

She was no longer looking at the second car in the convoy. That was done now. It would only be a matter of moments before the driver of the lead vehicle looked behind and realised something was wrong.

There was a brief blur of movement as she shifted her aim, focusing on the lead vehicle. Her shoulder was aching now from the impact, but she ignored the pain as she worked the bolt action, lining up her second shot. Vaguely she was aware of the growing panic on the highway as her first target slewed sideways, crashing into a people carrier and pinning the lighter vehicle against the freeway's concrete wall. Horn blasts and the screech of brakes filled the air as motorists tried to work out what was happening.

The driver of the lead Mercedes had picked up on it too, but unlike the bored commuters around him, he knew exactly what to do and jammed his foot down on the accelerator. His training would have kicked in now, telling him to speed up, put in evasive manoeuvres, get clear of the kill zone as fast as possible.

Anya could tell he was heading for an off-ramp about 100 yards further down the freeway, part of a big interchange between two other main drags. Unfortunately, to get there he had no choice but to come straight at her.

With the second round now chambered, she swung the long eager barrel left, tracking her target as it tried to weave through the dense traffic. The driver's efforts were in vain as she sent a round straight for him, punching through the windshield and killing him instantly.

Caught in the midst of a sharp left turn, the Mercedes yawed hard left and slammed into the central reservation before flipping and rolling over.

Two shots, two kills. She had done her part. The rest was out of her hands.

Drake started at the muted boom of the first shot, wondering for a moment if he had heard the crack of thunder in the darkened skies overhead. However, the second shot a few seconds later, followed by a crash and the blare of car horns on the nearby freeway, quickly shattered that illusion. Someone was firing on the slow-moving traffic.

He knew the sound of a high-powered sniper rifle well enough, and his experiences of urban combat told him it had come from nearby. Straight away his mind switched gears, his training as a field operative taking over without conscious thought, quickly assessing what he knew so far and combining it with experience and intuition to decide on a course of action.

It was no coincidence that such an attack should have happened at the same time and location he'd agreed to meet with Anya. For all he knew, the sniper might have been sent specifically to take her out. In which case, she could be injured or even dead already. He had no idea how they had learned of the meeting, and now wasn't the time to ponder such questions. What mattered was what he did in the next few seconds.

He himself was standing at an open crossroads, totally exposed and easy prey for a skilled sniper. He certainly couldn't stay here, and fleeing would be an exercise in futility. Modern sniper rifles were accurate at up to 1,000 yards or more, and he had no desire to put that to the test. No, his best chance was to get to them and take them out.

The only question was where they had located themselves.

Urban environments with lots of high walls and sharp angles can do strange things to the acoustics of gunshots, deflecting the sound waves and making it difficult to pinpoint the origin of individual shots. In part, this is why snipers flourish in city fighting. The only way to find the shooter in this case was to consider his or her possible firing positions, pick one and hope it was right.

In the space of a second or two, Drake quickly took in his surroundings, noting nearby buildings that would make good vantage points.

The 395 was an elevated freeway, meaning most of the low-rise residential buildings and shops in the vicinity were beneath road level. To the north, an office building that he vaguely recognised as belonging to Michigan State University rose up into the night sky. Certainly it was tall enough to provide a good field of fire over the freeway, but buildings like that had cameras, armed security guards, alarms – all of which would have to be meticulously bypassed and neutralised. Not a good place for a sniper to set up.

There was the church across the way. Its bell tower was certainly tall enough to overlook the freeway, but there was no way anyone could get a sniper rifle past a full congregation and make entry to it, no matter how hard they were banging their tambourines.

Then at last he saw what he was looking for. The residential apartment block, easily five storeys high and overlooking the big interchange between the 395 and two other main drags heading north and south. Its flat roof offered a perfect field of fire for a skilled sniper, and security was likely to be light there.

He was moving before he even had a chance to finish that thought, reaching for his cellphone and quickly dialling 911 as he sprinted across the road, ignoring the angry horn blasts that followed him.

'911 emergency,' came the crisp voice of a female operator a few moments later.

'Shots fired on the corner of 1st Street and Delaware, the apartment building at the crossroads,' Drake said, making a beeline for the nearest door. 'Sniper, probably targeting the freeway. Send everything you've got in the area right now.'

With that, he closed down the call. He had no time to give a detailed description of what he'd seen and heard. He had more important matters to attend to.

Drawing the Sig, he shoved his way through the main doors and into the bland, clinical-looking communal stairwell beyond. To his left stood an elevator, with an *Out of Order* sign affixed to it.

Good. One way in, one way out.

Gripping the weapon tight, he sprinted up the stairs, taking them two at a time as he made for the roof. His breath was soon coming in deep gasps, his heart pounding, but his pace showed no signs of slowing. Adrenaline was doing a good job of maintaining his energy.

On the top floor he spotted a teenage girl in a black hoodie emerging from one of the apartments, earphones on and head down as she flicked through songs on her iPod. Taking one look at Drake and the weapon he was clutching, she let out a startled cry. 'Oh fuck!'

With that, she retreated into her home and slammed the door shut.

She wasn't what he was looking for. Drake paid her no heed as he focused on the stairway leading to the roof. Glancing at the weapon to check the safety was disengaged, he advanced up the stairs, keeping his eye on the sliver of light around the edge of the door.

Halting at the top, he took a deep breath to get his breathing under control. His wait lasted only a second or two. Never delay longer than you have to, he'd been taught long before. The anticipation only works against you.

Go now!

A single hard kick to the release bar was enough to send

the door flying outwards, allowing cold air and hard pellets of frozen rain to rush in. Ignoring it, Drake advanced on to the roof, his eyes and weapon sweeping the area, eager for a target.

The sniper's weapon lay on the gravel-covered roof next to a big box-like air vent. He didn't recognise the model, but it definitely wasn't British or American in origin. However, it was a beast of a gun, easily 6 feet long and probably weighing at least 25 pounds. The kind of heavy-duty sniper rifle designed to punch through light vehicle armour.

The weapon was less of a concern to him at that moment than its owner, who had abandoned the gun and was standing on the low parapet at the edge of the roof as if he or she intended to jump. The face was hidden, but the general build and height suggested that the sniper was a woman.

The moment he emerged on to the roof, she started to turn. He saw a sudden movement, the distinctive action of someone reaching for a concealed weapon, and instinctively brought the Sig to bear.

'Freeze!' Drake ordered. At this range he could hardly miss.

Drake watched as the lone figure on the edge of the roof turned to face him, revealing attractive, finely chiselled features, a straight nose, a firm jaw and strong, intense blue eyes that were locked with his.

In an instant, everything around him faded away into darkness. The weapon in his hands seemed to lower of its own volition as he stared in disbelief at the woman he knew all too well.

'Anya,' he gasped, the rush of his pursuit giving way to shocked disbelief.

She looked at him for a long moment, saying nothing. As always, it was impossible to know what was going on behind those icy blue eyes of hers. Then without warning she took a single step back over the edge of the parapet, and disappeared.

Drake let out a breath. The image that had appeared before him and then vanished so abruptly felt like a dream. It didn't seem real.

Only when he saw the rope affixed to one of the rooftop heating outlets did reality snap back into place. He rushed over to the parapet in time to see the woman disengage herself from the abseiling gear 50 feet below.

Casting a brief glance up at him, she turned and sprinted off, vanishing into the shadows beneath some trees on the edge of a park area below.

Just as suddenly as she had reappeared in his life, Anya was gone.

Chapter 4

For the next few seconds Drake just stood there, trying to make sense of what he'd seen and heard. As inconceivable as it sounded, it appeared Anya was responsible for a sniper attack on a crowded freeway in central DC. And judging by the chaos on the multi-lane highway below, she had caused casualties.

But who or what had been her target?

Peering through the gloom and rain, he did his best to survey the scene. At least six or seven cars, vans and trucks had been involved in the smash, probably as collateral damage rather than because they were specifically targeted. The two vehicles that seemed to have borne the brunt of the attack were a pair of luxury Mercedes-Benz S-Class sedans; both silver coloured and both likely to have been travelling in convoy.

Drake had seen enough foreign diplomats arriving for high-level conferences to recognise the kind of vehicles they liked to cruise around in. Powerful, manoeuvrable and sturdy enough to bear the weight of concealed armour plating and toughened glass, these two Mercs were prime candidates for such duty.

But whatever countermeasures they'd been fitted with, it hadn't been enough to protect them from Anya's attack. One had crashed into the central reservation, rolling several times before coming to a halt as a mangled, deformed mess, while a second had swerved to the right and broadsided a Ford people carrier, forcing it into the opposite wall.

Already he could see the distinctive flashing lights of an ambulance approaching the crash site, the backed-up traffic moving aside as best it could to make way for the emergency vehicle. It screeched to a halt beside the second of the two Mercs, the rear door flew open and a pair of paramedics leapt out.

The glow of headlights on the freeway made it hard for Drake to discern what was going on, but he frowned in surprise when the doors slammed shut and the ambulance accelerated away after just a few moments, leaving the other crashed vehicles unchecked. Either they had been advised that other medical units were inbound, or they had a patient on board with critical injuries.

But if so, how had they managed to get them out of the wreckage so quickly? And for that matter, how had they arrived on the scene mere seconds after the attack? Even if other drivers on the freeway had called in the crash immediately, it would take at least thirty seconds for their calls to be answered and processed, and emergency services vectored in.

Everything about this was setting off alarm bells in his head.

Holstering the Sig, he reached for his cellphone.

'Sir, put your hands up where I can see them!' a voice called out from behind. Deep, powerful, authoritative. The voice of a cop with his gun trained on a suspected terrorist.

Drake closed his eyes for a moment, realising that his warning to the Metro PD might have worked rather better than he'd expected. Never had he imagined they would arrive so quickly, and at such an inconvenient moment. Being caught in the sniper's nest with the weapon itself mere yards away was going to take some explaining.

'I'm not the man you're looking for,' Drake said, raising his hands slowly. Cops only used their weapons as a last resort, but he didn't want to give the man any excuse to open fire. 'I called this one in. I'm on your side.'

'So we'll take your word for that, huh?' A different voice this time: high, young, female. Cops usually travelled in pairs.

'We'll get to that later, sir,' the first cop decided. 'Right now I want you to get down on your knees with your hands behind your head.'

Shit. Explaining himself from the back of a police cruiser could waste hours. Meanwhile Anya and the mysterious ambulance on the freeway below were getting further away by the second. Not to mention the inevitable questions that would arise over why he was here in the first place, and the text message on his cellphone. He'd deleted it of course, but even he knew that a skilled technician could recover it with ease.

Drake's heart was beating faster as he considered his options. The sudden arrival of these two cops less than two minutes after his 911 call, much like the ambulance on the freeway, bore all the hallmarks of a set-up. Had someone called this in before he'd even arrived? If so, who?

'Sir, I'm not gonna ask you again,' the cop went on, sensing his hesitation. 'Get down on your knees. Come on, pal. This isn't worth it.'

Resisting arrest wasn't going to do him any favours. There were two of them and only one of him, and he had his back to them. They had the drop on him.

Slowly he lowered himself to his knees, the rough gravel of the rooftop biting into his skin as he did so, and placed his hands behind his head. He'd put enough targets in this position to know they were about to handcuff him.

He heard the squelch of a radio. 'This is Unit Seven. Possible suspect apprehended on the roof at previous address,' he heard the female cop say. 'Requesting backup to secure the scene.'

The crunch of boots on gravel as the first cop approached. He would have holstered his weapon and reached for the cuffs at his belt while his partner covered him. Securing the suspect was the most dangerous part of any arrest, because you had to come into contact with them in order to snap the cuffs on. In that short time before you had them subdued, you were vulnerable.

And just like that, Drake had settled on a course of action.

It happened fast. Just as Drake felt a strong grip clamp around his left wrist to snap the cuffs on, he clenched his right hand, twisted around and drove it into the cop's groin with all the force he could summon. Normally he would have aimed for the abdomen to knock the wind out of him, but like any street cop he was almost certain to be wearing a ballistic vest. They were more effective at stopping bullets than fists, but the last thing he needed was to break his hand on an inconveniently placed piece of armour.

In any case, his aim was true and the cop let out a grunt of pain as Drake's fist connected. Before he could double over, Drake had wrenched his other hand free of the man's grip and jumped to his feet, instinctively reaching for the holster at the cop's right hip. Really he had no idea if the weapon was on the left or right side, but since most people were right-handed he was prepared to take a chance.

Sure enough, he felt his fingers close around the butt of an automatic. Yanking it free from the holster, he brought it up and jammed it against the cop's neck, forcing the man to turn so that he was positioned between Drake and his partner. The entire action had taken just over three seconds.

Fortunately for Drake, the man he was now using as a human shield was more than up to the task. Standing a couple of inches above 6 feet, his heavy frame suggested a passion for weightlifting, though poor diet or lack of cardio training had left him bulked up and barrel-chested rather than lean and trim. Still, he was a serious-looking man who could easily overpower Drake in terms of brute strength. Only the gun now pressed against his flesh was keeping him under control.

His female comrade had been unable to intervene. She was too far away to get involved physically, while a bit of careful positioning on Drake's part had prevented her getting a clear shot.

Now she was trying to decide what to do; whether it was worth the risk of opening fire. Drake surveyed her, quickly sizing her up. She was young, probably mid-twenties, with a full figure that was tending towards plump, and short black hair tied back tight. Her dark eyes and olive skin suggested Hispanic origin, and the name *Cortez* printed on the tag on her jacket confirmed it. If he had to guess, he'd say she was a rookie, probably partnered up with an older and more experienced officer until she learned the ropes.

Today, however, she was about to learn a different kind of lesson.

'Forget it,' Drake said, crouching low to hide himself behind the cop's considerable frame. Neither of them had seen his face, and he wanted to keep it that way. 'Lower the gun and step back, and you both get to live.'

She shook her head vehemently. 'Bullshit. I lower it, you kill both of us.'

She wasn't about to give up her only leverage. Credit

where it was due, she was tougher than she looked. But being tough was a poor substitute for being smart, and he needed her to see that her position was untenable.

'I've got no interest in either of you, Cortez,' he promised her. 'I'm not responsible for this attack, but I can't let you take me in. You can either walk away from this, or you can get yourself and your partner killed trying to stop me. It's up to you.'

Even as he said this, he was edging closer to the stairwell door, keeping his human shield in front. Instinctively Cortez took a step backwards, keeping her distance. She couldn't get a decent shot at Drake, so aside from shooting through her partner, there was little she could do to stop him.

'You're wasting your time, man,' the first cop warned him, his deep baritone voice seeming to resonate through his entire body as he spoke. 'We've got backup inbound. You won't make it two blocks.'

'Then there's no reason not to let me go,' Drake countered, still moving towards the door. 'Better than getting killed.'

He saw Cortez's eyes waver for a moment, saw the barrel of her automatic lower just a little. She wasn't giving up her weapon, but the meaning was clear all the same. She was letting him go, just as he'd known she would.

Movies often depict the heroic cop finding an ingenious way out of such situations, whether it be shooting the hostage-taker in the leg to disable him or using some trick to distract him, but the reality was often far more pragmatic. Cortez didn't want to die here, and she didn't want her partner to die either.

Neither death was worth the life of some anonymous nut job, and they all knew it.

He was close enough. Releasing his grip on his hostage, Drake planted a firm kick in the small of his back that sent him staggering towards Cortez, blocking her shot for a few precious moments.

Without waiting to see the results, he turned and sprinted through the door, slamming it shut behind him. The security bar would only allow it to open from inside, and short of blasting the entire door apart, there was little chance of Cortez and her partner giving chase.

Still, Drake wasn't hanging around to find out. Rushing down the stairwell and back outside, he passed the police cruiser parked outside the apartment block and headed west, away from the freeway and the heavy traffic that was already starting to back up around it.

Once he was sure he was out of sight of the apartment building, he turned south and picked up the pace. His car was two blocks away, and he needed to get to it fast.

Keeping his head down, he turned off the main drag and took a footpath running through a grassy area between two residential buildings, then fished out his cellphone and hurriedly scrolled through the list of apps until he found one with the innocuous title *DateCalculator*.

At first glance it appeared to be nothing more interesting than a personal organiser, but in reality it was a sophisticated piece of encryption software developed by the Agency to allow their operatives to make calls without fear of interception. In Drake's case, it allowed him to speak freely with other people on the same encryption scheme – even the Agency itself couldn't listen in.

Inputting his personal access code, he waited a few seconds while DateCalculator enabled secure mode, then finally dialled the number he wanted. Technically it was after hours, but Drake knew the man he was calling didn't keep to office hours any more than he did. It was one of the perks – or otherwise – of being the director of the CIA's Special Activities Division.

As he expected, it rang several times before it was answered. The recipient of the call would have to input his own access code to allow DateCalculator to link the two phones and create a secure line.

'Yeah, Ryan?' Dan Franklin answered at last, sounding more harassed than usual.

Drake and the director of Special Activities had served in the same composite unit in Afghanistan years earlier, and had forged a strong friendship during their tour together. Their lives and careers had taken different paths since then, and the burden of leadership had strained their relationship more than once, but Drake still considered Franklin a friend. And he had few enough of those nowadays.

In this case, however, he wasted no time on greetings. 'Dan, we've got a problem.'

'What kind of problem?'

'The kind when someone caps off shots from a high-powered sniper rifle into a busy freeway.'

That was enough to get his friend's attention. 'And you know this how?'

'Take a guess.' Drake paused a moment, waiting until he'd passed by a runner out for some evening exercise before carrying on. 'I was opposite the building when the shooting started. It was overlooking the 395 just west of Garfield Park.'

'Jesus. Are Metro PD aware?'

'You could say that. Two of their guys just tried to arrest me.'

His words weren't lost on Franklin. 'What do you mean, "tried"?'

Drake winced inwardly. 'Had to give them the slip.'

'Christ, Ryan. You're supposed to be a case officer, not Jason fucking Bourne. You aiming for a spot on *America's Most Wanted*?'

'You don't understand – they turned up right after I did,' Drake hurriedly explained. 'Unless they happened to be passing by when the shooting started, there's no way they could have got there so fast. Which means they were tipped off in advance. Someone was trying to set me up, Dan.'

'Possible, but who?'

He paused for a moment, wondering whether he was doing the right thing by dumping this on his friend. But he knew he couldn't sit on it and do nothing. Franklin had to know. 'Anya.'

At that moment, any lingering doubts Franklin might have had about the severity of this call vanished. 'You're sure?'

'Pretty sure,' Drake said, recalling that moment up on the roof. 'She was standing right in front of me. Looks like she was the shooter.'

'Any idea what the target was?'

'I saw a pair of luxury Mercs on the freeway that looked like they'd been fucked over. Couldn't make out the plates, but I think they were part of a diplomatic convoy. Join the dots and it looks a lot like an assassination.'

His friend exhaled, digesting everything he'd just heard. 'Talk about stirring up a hornet's nest. What the hell is she up to?'

'Your guess is as good as mine right now,' Drake admitted. 'Listen, I need you to do me a favour.'

'What's that?'

'The police weren't the only ones to arrive in a hurry. An ambulance pulled up at the crash site within seconds, then left in a big hurry. I couldn't see what they were up to, but it didn't look right to me. Can you check around the local hospitals and see if they brought in any crash victims? The closest one from here is George Washington University.'

'I'll see what I can do. What about you?'

47

'I'm getting the fuck out of here,' he replied, fully intending to put as much distance between himself and those two cops as possible.

'Good. Try to stay out of trouble.'

'You know me,' Drake assured him.

'That's what I'm talking about.'

There wasn't much Drake could add to that. Closing down the call, he pocketed the phone and pressed on, keeping his head down to shield himself both from bad weather and from curious onlookers.

His car, a black Audi S5, was still sitting where he'd left it. A quick flash of the key fob disabled the alarm. Drake couldn't get inside fast enough, eager both to escape the biting wind and to get away from the crime scene.

Within seconds he was off and moving. And once again he fired up his cellphone.

Chapter 5

With a strained, breathless cry, Keira Frost closed her eyes, arched her back and dug in her nails, the taut muscles of her body held rigid as the sensations within her built to an unbearable crescendo, and then finally exploded with glorious release.

Breathing hard and still quivering with aftershocks of pleasure, she opened her eyes and collapsed on top of her partner, for the moment absolutely spent.

'Fuck yeah,' she said, her voice low and husky. She could feel the fast and powerful beat of his heart as she rested her head on his chest.

Rick Berkeley, a mechanic at her local bike shop. Mid-twenties, tall and well built, with scruffy blond hair and a jawline permanently roughened by several days' growth, he'd caught her eye the very first time she'd met him. She'd known he felt the same way about her, though it had taken him a couple of months to work up the courage to ask her on a date.

Normally she had no time for men who were indecisive or timid, but in his case she'd sensed another motive for his hesitation. He'd been trying to play the gentleman by not making his interest too obvious. Fortunately for him, Frost wasn't looking for a gentleman.

She'd told him as much about an hour ago.

'Worth waiting for,' he said breathlessly, the words rumbling against her ear.

Grinning, Frost sat up, leaned over him and picked up a half-empty bottle of Corona from the bedside table, downing it in one gulp. Still flushed with the post-orgasmic glow, she was feeling pretty good about herself at that moment.

All things considered, she liked Rick. He was smart without being a smartass, confident without being a domineering jerk, and as she'd just discovered, he wasn't entirely clueless between the sheets either.

Might be worth keeping around for a while, she mused. And maybe putting his skills to the test again later.

She turned towards him, curious as to whether he was ready for Round Two, only to find him staring at her. But his look wasn't the glassy-eyed stare of a satisfied partner. Rather, she saw curiosity, surprise and even a hint of suspicion in them. And she knew why.

Sitting upright and naked as she was, it was inevitable that his eyes would stray across her exposed body. The demands of her difficult and dangerous job as a Shepherd specialist had endowed her with the firm musculature and toned physique of a professional athlete, but they had also left another legacy that she was less enthusiastic about.

'What did you say you did again?' Rick asked, eyeing the jagged knife scar on the left side of her ribcage; a little memento of an operation in Somalia where she'd discovered that stab vests weren't all they were cracked up to be.

Frost felt a brief flash of annoyance and, much to her chagrin, self-consciousness. She'd never had any hang-ups about her body, had never fretted and agonised in front of the mirror wishing her breasts were bigger or her ass smaller. But in situations like this the physical toll her work was taking was becoming harder and harder to hide, and it wasn't something she liked.

In any case, what was she supposed to say? She certainly couldn't tell him that she was a highly trained CIA operative who took part in clandestine operations in foreign countries. For one thing it would put Rick's job selling engine parts at the bike shop into serious perspective, and for another she simply wasn't allowed to talk about it.

'I didn't,' she replied, leaning forward and kissing his neck as she allowed her hand to stray down to his crotch. 'Isn't it more interesting that way?'

His mind might still have been filled with questions, but it was obvious enough what his body wanted. And as her movements became more forceful, the body began to gain control over the mind.

She was just beginning to feel her own desire rise when her phone started ringing, abruptly shattering the moment.

'You're fucking kidding me,' she said under her breath.

'Leave it,' Rick grunted, kissing the sensitive skin on her neck and working his way down to her breasts.

Frost hesitated, looking over at the phone on her bedside table. There weren't many people who knew her private cell number, and she had worked hard to keep it that way over the years. She had no time for idle chit-chat, and even less for telemarketers.

If someone was calling, it was likely a family member or . . .

'Hold that thought,' she said, pulling away from him and snatching up the phone.

It was Drake.

'What is it, Ryan?' she began, unable to keep from sounding a little flustered. And typical of Drake, he picked up on it right away.

'Caught you at a bad time?' She could have sworn the son of a bitch was smirking.

'I'm allowed a life outside work,' she pointed out irritably. 'Even if you're not.'

51

'Fair one.' He was wise enough not to rise to her rebuke. 'I need your help.'

She heard movement on the bed behind her and felt Rick's hands encircle her waist, moving upwards to cup her breasts, gently squeezing and caressing. Normally she wouldn't object to such a move, but right now she needed to concentrate.

'With what?' she asked, trying to shrug out of his embrace.

'There's been a sniper attack on a freeway in central DC. Looks like a possible assassination.'

Rick wasn't getting the message. It was time for a less subtle approach. Reaching behind her, she got a good grip of his genitals and twisted; not quite hard enough to cause damage, but enough to show she could if he didn't back off. Straight away he let go.

'And you're involved?' she asked as if nothing had happened.

'I am now,' Drake remarked. 'An ambulance was on the scene right after the attack. I want to know where it went.'

'Maybe a hospital?' she suggested with unveiled sarcasm.

'Thanks for the insight, but I doubt this one was on the books. It happened too fast.'

'You think it was a lift?'

'Maybe. Either way, someone went to a lot of trouble to set this up, and I want to know why. I need someone who can backtrack surveillance footage of the attack, and you're the best I can think of.'

Frost rolled her eyes. 'Fuck off, Ryan. Flattery doesn't suit you.'

'I'm working on that. The attack happened ten minutes ago, on the 395 just west of Garfield Park. Can you access traffic-cam footage and figure out what happened?'

She reached for her beer and downed the dregs. With her

Agency security clearance, she could access virtually any police or civilian system. And like any technical specialist, her home set-up was easily on a par with anything she could put together at Langley.

'Okay, fine. I'll save the day for you – again. Just remember this shit the next time we're discussing my annual bonus.'

'No promises,' he said. 'Call me when you have something.'

'What a novel idea.'

He didn't bother replying to that, and instead hung up.

Tossing the phone on the bed for now, Frost stood up and scanned the discarded pile of clothes on the floor, finally finding her vest top and underwear. She tried to ignore Rick's look of disappointment as she hurriedly dressed.

'My boss. Duty calls,' she said by way of apology. 'Get your clothes on.'

The younger man looked at her in disbelief. 'Seriously?'

'Yeah, seriously.' Reaching down, she grabbed his jeans and tossed them to him. 'Sixty seconds from now you're leaving, with or without your clothes.'

Rick glared at her in annoyance, but nonetheless started to pull the jeans on.

'Your boss is a real asshole, you know that?'

Frost flashed a crooked smile. 'Yeah. Yeah, he is.'

Chapter 6

Anya was cruising north on the interstate highway in a rented Chevy Aveo, keeping her speed at a steady 70mph to avoid police attention. Just as well really, because she doubted the underpowered saloon was capable of much more.

Still, she had made good progress in the past hour. After making her escape from the rooftop, it had been a brisk walk three blocks north to her car. She could have run such a distance easily, but running attracted attention. That was one thing she didn't need today.

Instead she chose a steady ground-covering pace that saw her in her car within five minutes. Nobody challenged her, nobody suspected her, nobody even paid attention to her in fact. She was a Caucasian woman, dressed in respectable clothes and displaying completely unthreatening behaviour. Why would they?

She hadn't even broken stride as a Metro PD cruiser roared past, sirens wailing and blue lights flashing. She had known the cops inside hadn't seen her, just as the people she walked past on the street didn't really see her. Living in a large city like DC, they were used to not seeing people.

Less than seven minutes after the attack, and with emergency services only just starting to vector police units to the scene, she was in her car and on her way out of DC.

Now, an hour later, she was approaching Wilmington; just

one of thousands of other motorists rumbling down the big interstate highway.

She exhaled, allowing herself to relax just a little. The first phase of the operation had been a success. She had done her part and escaped more or less without incident, leaving her free to move on to her next objective.

But her relief was tempered by unease at the unexpected arrival of Drake in the very midst of the attack. Such interference had brought her to the edge of disaster. Had he interrupted at the crucial moment, she might have missed her shots entirely. Demochev would still be free, and her plan would have been in tatters.

Her grip tightened on the wheel. Such an encounter simply couldn't have been random chance – Anya had long ago stopped believing in coincidences. Her sniper position had been nowhere near his home or place of work, or any logical commuting route between the two. He'd been there because he'd intended to be, but why? And why had he drawn a weapon on her?

She was reluctant to consider him a threat after everything they had been through together, but Drake's interference was an unwelcome and dangerous variable in a plan that depended on many elements working together in perfect harmony, each event creating the conditions for the ones to follow. A man like him could unbalance everything, whether he intended to or not.

She could not allow that to happen.

She reached for the bottle of water in the cup holder to her right and took a drink. It wasn't exactly champagne, but then she didn't exactly feel like celebrating. A lot still had to happen for her to reach her goal, and as she had learned already tonight, a lot could still go wrong.

She was just replacing the bottle when her cellphone

buzzed with an incoming text message. Glancing down at it unobtrusively in case an unmarked police car happened to pull her over for the minor violation, she opened the message.

Have dropped Brett off. He was very grateful. See you for drinks on Sunday.

Anya wasn't sure whether to feel good about that or not. 'Brett' was their code word for Demochev, which in this case meant he had given up the information they needed. She doubted he would have given it up willingly, though she preferred not to think about what had been done to him to force him to talk.

In either case, he was certainly dead by now. If what she'd heard about him was true, his death wasn't undeserved. Still, such things were out of her hands.

She had other tasks to accomplish, chief amongst which was getting herself out of the United States as soon as possible. According to her dash-mounted GPS it was over 450 miles to the Canadian border, and another 50 or so more to Montreal International Airport.

She had a long night ahead of her if she wanted to make her morning flight, and was beginning to wish she'd brought a Thermos of coffee for the ride. Settling back into the driver's seat, she flicked on the radio and waited while it tuned to a local station.

As she'd expected, it was dominated by coverage of the attack.

Chapter 7

By now well clear of the crime scene, Drake was ensconced in a small coffee shop near Union Station on the north-east side of central DC. His mood was as dark as the steaming liquid in his cup, not helped by the constant coverage of the sniper attack playing on a TV mounted above the service counter.

Anya's handiwork laid out for the world to see. But why?

Police follow-up from his escapade on the rooftop was unlikely now. Neither officer had seen his face, and he'd made good his escape from the immediate area before backup could arrive. He'd been obliged to buy a new jacket and jeans from the nearest department store to eliminate the chance of a clothing match, but he could live with that. The only thing they could use against him was his English accent, and even that was unlikely to help much in a city that saw a regular influx of foreign tourists.

For now at least, he was in the clear.

His unhappy contemplation was interrupted when his phone started ringing. It was Franklin. Snatching it up, he inputted his DateCalculator access code and hit the green button to take the call.

'What have you got, Dan?'

'News, and none of it good,' his friend began. 'You were right about those Mercs. They were part of a Russian diplomatic convoy fresh in from Andrews AFB.'

It didn't take much effort to spot the link to Anya. She had been incarcerated in a Russian jail when Drake had found her. The exact reasons for her imprisonment were unknown, but clearly she was important to them. And it seemed she was now returning the favour.

'We're still getting police reports in, but we know both drivers were killed by high-velocity sniper rounds. The damn things punched right through the bulletproof windshields like they weren't even there.'

'Yeah, I saw the gun,' Drake confirmed. 'Looked like it could take out a tank.'

'It gets better. The survivors were executed at close range by small-arms fire. Double taps to the head – real professional.'

Drake wasn't surprised. He would expect nothing less from any operation that Anya was part of. 'So the "paramedics" I saw were there to finish the job.'

'This wasn't just an assassination,' Franklin went on. 'According to the convoy manifest, we've got an MIA. Anton Demochev, director of the FSB's counter-terrorism branch.'

Drake felt as though he was immersed in a bad dream, and it was getting worse by the minute. The convoy that had been hit belonged to Russia's Federal Security Bureau, better known as the FSB.

When the Soviet Union dissolved in 1991, the old KGB broke up into a number of successor agencies, all vying for power and influence. The FSB had eventually emerged as the dominant entity and was now the main intelligence service of the Russian Federation, responsible for both foreign and domestic security.

Essentially they were the CIA and the FBI rolled into one. As such, their power and resources were considerable. And as many in Russia and elsewhere had learned to their cost, they weren't shy about flexing their political and military muscles.

'So this was an abduction,' he said, stating the obvious.

'Looks that way. The Russians are going apeshit over this. If they hold him to ransom, it will be a PR disaster.' Franklin was silent for a moment, and Drake could almost feel his growing anger. 'Anya might have caused a goddamned international incident.'

Drake looked down at his coffee. He could think of nothing to say to that, because his friend might well be right. Her actions this evening had already resulted in several deaths, not to mention incurring the wrath of one of the world's most dangerous intelligence services.

'What are we doing about it?' he asked instead. With an incident of this magnitude, an Agency response was inevitable.

'We're coordinating with FBI and Homeland Security, trying to figure out where they took him. But it's slow going.'

Drake could guess why. Cooperation between America's security services was less than impressive at the best of times, and with a sudden attack like this, just piecing together what had happened could take hours. They were a sledgehammer, when what was needed was a scalpel.

Fortunately Drake had just the instrument in mind.

'I have to go, Dan,' he said, as his phone buzzed to let him know another caller was trying to reach him. 'I'll call you back if I have anything new.'

'Likewise.'

Ending his call with Franklin, Drake immediately hit the accept button to take one from Frost. He could only hope she had good news.

'Yeah, Keira?'

'I think we've got them,' the young woman announced without preamble. 'Our friends from the freeway dumped the ambulance at an underground parking lot on the east

59

side of DC. Then they switched vehicles. They must have handled the transfer in a blind spot because I couldn't see it on any of the security cameras, but thirty seconds later they left in a blue Chevrolet Express.'

Drake's heartbeat had stepped up a gear now. 'Did you get a look at the plates?'

'No need,' she explained. 'I tracked them to a self-storage facility in Capitol Heights, and I doubt they're there to offload old furniture.'

Drake was already up and moving, heading for his car, which was parked outside. 'Good work. Text me the address.'

Capitol Heights was on the east side of the city, no more than a couple of miles away. Assuming he managed to avoid the worst of the traffic, he could be there in five minutes or less.

'I hope you're not planning on going in there alone?'

'You know me,' he evaded. He needed to know what the hell Anya was involved in, and one way or another he intended to get some answers.

'That's what I'm afraid of, Ryan. If . . . *she's* there, I'd go in wearing fashionable Kevlar. And a tank.'

'Duly noted,' he promised, closing the phone down.

As he approached his car, Drake instinctively reached into his jacket and felt the reassuring shape of the Sig automatic. He might be going in for Anya, but he was under no illusions about what he might find when he got there. If the welcome was less than friendly, he would do what he had to do to defend himself.

Chapter 8

She couldn't move, couldn't see, couldn't breathe. All around her was darkness, cloying and suffocating. The gag in her mouth pressed tight into her flesh, making it difficult to swallow and impossible to cry out. There was no way to summon help, no chance of escape.

With her hands and feet bound behind her back and a thick burlap sack drawn over her face, she lay helpless on the hard, cold, metal floor of the van. Her body, bruised and battered after the crash that had almost killed her, ached with the pain of countless small injuries, while her head throbbed as blood pulsed through it.

All she could do was lie there with the coarse material of the hood pressed suffocatingly against her face, listening to the sounds of the brutal torture session going on outside.

Even through the thick fabric and the metal walls of the van she was being held inside, she could hear Demochev's agonised screams as his captors went about their grim work.

Anton Demochev, the man whose safety had been entrusted to her, was being tortured to death mere yards away. And she could do nothing to help him.

All she could do was lie there, fighting back the growing feeling of nausea as she listened to Demochev's screams echoing around the interior of the van.

*

Ten minutes after leaving the coffee shop, Drake, along with five members of an Agency tactical team, were crammed into the rear compartment of a Ford Econoline Transit van as it hurtled through the eastern suburbs of DC.

With the Agency on alert after the freeway attack, they had several such units on standby throughout the city. A call to Franklin was all it had taken to place the nearest one at Drake's disposal for a limited duration.

Drake's role as a Shepherd team leader afforded him certain powers that most other government officials could only dream of. He could pass through US airports without being searched, enter most government buildings without difficulty, and even commandeer police and military resources in the pursuit of his objective. It wasn't something he was expected to make use of on a regular basis, and such authority was always strictly monitored, but it did allow him to cut through a lot of red tape in a hurry.

Police and FBI units were converging from all over town to establish a perimeter around the site and support them, but so far they had the lead. If they moved fast, there was a chance they could end this thing quickly, capture the instigators of a major terrorist attack and perhaps even recover Demochev alive. How Anya would fit into this equation remained to be seen.

Their target was, according to Frost's online forays, Xcell Self-Storage, a commercial storage facility in the Capitol Heights district of the city. Secure, and used only by the occasional delivery truck, it was the kind of place where one could hold a man hostage for a long time without fear of discovery.

Drake gripped one of the wall-mounted handles as the van rounded a corner at high speed. It was raining hard outside. He could hear the heavy drumming of it on the vehicle's thin metal roof, and the rhythmic whine of the wipers up front as they fought to keep the windshield clear.

'According to the facility manager, the only lock-up to have been accessed in the past hour is Unit D7,' the lead operative said, studying the blueprints of the facility that had been transmitted to his PDA direct from Langley. The name tag on his body armour read *O'Rourke*. 'It's about the size of a double garage, but according to the plans it's one big open space so we shouldn't have trouble locating our target.'

Assuming he's still there, Drake didn't add. Despite their rapid response there was a chance their opponents had switched vehicles again after reaching the facility. It certainly wasn't the kind of place one would dig in and defend.

Still, they wouldn't know for sure until they got there.

'We've got a friendly in there so watch your fire,' O'Rourke added. 'But be advised, tangos are armed and should be considered extremely dangerous. Try to take them alive if possible, but don't take any chances. Clear?'

He was met by a chorus of affirmative remarks. Each of the tactical operatives was geared up for the assault, both mentally and physically. Drake had seen that look enough times on soldiers about to go into battle to recognise it.

Curious how far they still had to go, he craned his neck to see up front, trying to make out the world beyond the rain-streaked windshield.

Capitol Heights was a run-down area, with dirty litter-strewn streets and dreary low-rise apartment buildings crowded close to the main drag. Many of the street lights were out, either because they'd been vandalised or because the bulbs had blown and never been replaced. The few shops that he'd seen all had heavy security shutters down, while most apartments had their curtains closed as if the occupants were trying to shut the world out. Drake couldn't blame them.

The cars were mostly old Buicks and Chevys; all battered and poorly maintained like everything else around here. There weren't many people out on the streets given the weather conditions, but a few brave souls trudged doggedly onwards, heads down and shoulders hunched against the rain. They looked as miserable as the buildings around them.

Christmas hadn't yet come to Capitol Heights, it seemed.

Turning his attention back to the tactical team leader, he leaned forward and tapped O'Rourke on the shoulder. 'So what's the plan?'

'Simple breach, sir. We go in hard through the front door, use flashbangs to cover our entry, and secure Demochev as fast as possible. With luck we can take them by surprise.'

'What if they make a run for it?'

O'Rourke shrugged. 'There's nowhere for them to go. The entire facility's surrounded by chain-link fence and security cameras. Only way in or out is through the main gate, and we'll have that covered.'

He paused, bracing his large frame, bulked out by body armour, against the wall as the van swerved. As their course stabilised, he reached into a bag by his feet and handed Drake one of the little portable radio units the assault team wore.

'Take this. It's already tied into our radio net.'

The unit was familiar enough to Drake, similar to the ones he'd used as a Shepherd operative during similar assaults. The microphone was attached to a Velcro strap that wrapped around the throat, so that it picked up the actual vibrations in the user's voice box and allowed them to be heard clearly even when surrounded by loud ambient noise.

After strapping the unit in place and checking it was switched on, he hit the transmit button. 'Radio check.'

O'Rourke nodded. 'Good, copy.'

'This is it,' the driver called as they began to slow down. 'Ten seconds!'

Sure enough, the drab grey housing of Capitol Hill had given way to drab grey commercial storage units; essentially long brick sheds of varying size, with corrugated-iron roofs and rolling steel-shuttered doors. Access to each locker was controlled by a key-card entry system similar to that used in modern hotels, which cut down the chance of theft and also allowed the storage company to monitor usage, since each card swipe was electronically logged.

Alerted in advance of their arrival, the lone security guard manning the main gate had made sure the barrier was open, allowing them to drive right through and into the network of storage lock-ups unhindered. Their van was disguised as a regular commercial goods vehicle, hopefully allowing them to park near the lock-up without raising suspicion.

They would find out soon enough, Drake thought as the van skidded to a halt, the tyres slipping on the slick tarmac.

O'Rourke turned to the rest of the team. 'Ready up.'

Most of the team were armed with the venerable Heckler & Koch MP5; a compact and reliable sub-machine gun that had been in use with SWAT and Special Forces units for more than forty years. It lacked the punch and range of heavier assault rifles, but it was ideal for use in tight spaces.

Drake also spotted a couple of big Mossberg 590 breaching shotguns, designed to blast open locks and reinforced doors. He'd seen them in action himself on a few occasions and knew the devastating damage they could deal at close range.

Taking up position at the rear of the compartment, O'Rourke gave a single nod to show that he was ready, unlatched the cargo door and shoved it outwards. Two operatives armed with MP5s went first, taking up position on either side of the van to cover their flanks while the rest of the team deployed.

O'Rourke was next, with Drake right behind him. Leaping down on to the wet tarmac, he immediately found himself in the midst of the heavy downpour. Doing his best to ignore the freezing rain that was quickly soaking into his clothes, he turned his attention to the storage lockers around them.

A long row of breeze-block structures stretched out before him, with letters and numbers printed on their doors. As far as he could tell, the storage yard was laid out in a basic grid pattern, with a letter assigned to each section. The number indicated the location within that section.

With that in mind, lock-up D7 should be just around the corner.

Turning to O'Rourke, he nodded off to the right. 'Send two of your men around the other way. I want to box them in.'

The operative nodded understanding. 'Telford, Cartwright. Circle around this section. Radio when you're in position.'

'Copy that.'

As the two men hurried off to encircle the lock-up, Drake advanced to the next intersection with the Sig gripped tight in numb fingers. The splash of boots in the puddles behind told him the rest of the team were close.

Backing up against a rough breeze-block wall, he took a breath and waited for a signal from their flanking force.

'I see it,' a voice reported over the radio a few moments later. 'Doors are shut. No vehicles, no sign of activity.'

'Copy that,' Drake replied. 'Watch the rooftops. We're moving in now.'

Drake had been in this situation countless times before, preparing to make entry to a building with no idea what was on the other side of the door, wondering if they were going to be fired upon at any moment, anxiously watching every corner, every shadowy recess.

Taking another breath and wiping the rainwater out of

his eyes, Drake rounded the corner and advanced towards lock-up D7. At the same moment he spotted the two operatives moving in from the opposite intersection, weapons up and ready.

As they had said, there was no sign of any activity in the lock-up. The rolling steel doors were down and locked. Drake couldn't tell if there were any lights on inside.

'Telford, get that breaching gun ready,' O'Rourke ordered, motioning forward one of the operatives armed with a heavy-gauge shotgun. 'Flashbangs on standby. Everyone ready?'

Before anyone could reply, they froze as an engine suddenly rumbled into life inside the lock-up. Someone had just started up a vehicle in there.

'They're getting ready to move!' Drake hissed, realising the priceless opportunity that now presented itself. In order to leave, they would have to open the lock-up doors. 'Flashbangs on my order. Everyone else get ready to move in. Understand?'

He was met by a round of affirmatives. Backing up beside the lock-up, Drake checked his weapon and waited, his heart pounding. Adrenalin was keeping his body temperature up, allowing him to ignore the freezing rain that had by now soaked him to the skin.

All his attention was now focused on the steel doors beside him.

He heard an electronic buzz from inside, and suddenly the doors began to roll upwards, their metal links folding around the mechanism at the top as the winch inside clanked and groaned under the strain. Harsh light spilled out from the gap now opened – headlights from the vehicle or internal lighting, he couldn't tell.

Either way, he'd seen enough.

'Breach!' he called out. 'Flash out!'

Stepping out from cover, two of O'Rourke's operatives pulled the pins on their stun grenades and tossed the little metal cylinders in through the gap. There was a pause, perhaps a second or so, followed by twin explosions that echoed around the confined space of the storage lock-up like the crack of thunder.

The flashbang grenades, producing a blinding flash of light and a concussive boom designed to temporarily blind and deafen potential enemies, would hopefully buy the assault team a few precious seconds to move in.

They didn't waste a heartbeat.

'Go! Go!' Drake yelled, ducking beneath the doors that were still rising, his weapon immediately sweeping the interior of the storage lock-up. The reek of burned chemicals from the grenades stung his eyes and nostrils, but he ignored it, concentrating instead on taking in his surroundings.

The big storage lock-up, bare brick walls and a corrugated-metal roof, was dominated by the blue Chevrolet Express van that sat to one side, its bodywork still dripping from the recent rain. The engine was idling, the headlights almost blinding in their intensity, yet even as he advanced he saw a figure stagger out from behind the vehicle.

Dressed in a set of plain blue overalls that reminded Drake of a courier or delivery company, he was holding one hand against his ear and blinking furiously. Clearly the blast from the flashbang had deafened him and probably overloaded the photoreceptors in his eyes. His unsteady gait suggested the grenade had also disturbed his equilibrium.

'Don't move!' Drake yelled, levelling his weapon at the man's centre mass. 'Get down on the ground!'

But his target had no intention of surrendering. Drake saw him reach for something in his overalls, saw the glint of a weapon as he brought it up to fire.

There was no choice. Without hesitation Drake put two rounds in his chest, the Sig kicking back in his hands as the rounds discharged. He saw an explosion of red mist exit from the man's back, heard an almost surprised grunt, and just like that he went down.

'Tango down!' Drake shouted, advancing towards him and kicking the weapon clear of his grasp. He didn't have time to examine it in detail, but it looked like an automatic of some kind. 'Secure the van!'

'Roger that,' O'Rourke replied. 'No other Tangos in sight!'

Drake's eyes swept the darkened room, looking for more targets. As O'Rourke had suggested on the way here, the storage lock-up was one big open space about 8 yards square. Big enough to hold a couple of delivery trucks parked side by side, but in this case more or less empty. Nowhere to hide.

The internal lights were switched off. The only illumination was provided by the dim red glow of the van's rear lights.

'Clear left!' another operative called out.

He heard a click and a faint groan as the van's cargo doors were hauled open. 'Vehicle's clear. Nothing inside!'

But that didn't interest Drake now. His attention was focused on the lone figure strapped to a cheap plastic office chair in the far corner of the room. The prisoner wasn't moving, and from what he could see in the crimson glow of the vehicle tail lights, he doubted he or she ever would.

'I've got something over here,' he called out. 'Far corner. Bring some light.'

Flashlight beams pierced the gloom around him, illuminating the chair's inhabitant, though Drake quickly caught himself wishing they hadn't.

They had found Demochev all right, or what was left of him.

Stripped to the waist, his expensive suit thrown idly to one side, the FSB's director of counter-terrorism bore the grim hallmarks of the torture he'd endured. His head lolled back, no longer supported by conscious effort, his eyes staring blankly at the roof as raindrops continued to patter off the thin sheet metal.

His face was battered, bruised and swollen, rendered almost unrecognisable by the terrible beating he had taken, while three fingers of his right hand were missing, sliced off by a pair of wire cutters that was now lying on the concrete floor, covered in blood. Looking down, Drake could see that the man's left foot had been given similar treatment. All five digits had been crudely snipped off.

His throat too had been cut; likely to finish the job. The angle of his head had pulled open the gaping wound, exposing the torn flesh and severed windpipe. Drake opted not to devote too much attention to that.

Instead he tried to take in the scene as the sum of its parts, concentrating on each detail and gleaning what information he could from it. Out of all the injuries inflicted on him, the one which drew Drake's attention was the series of deep lacerations across Demochev's chest. Carved into his flesh with a sharp blade was a single word written in Cyrillic:

ПОВИННЫЙ

Drake was familiar with a few words in that language, but this wasn't one of them.

He inhaled, tasting the pungent odour of human excrement. He guessed Demochev had soiled himself, probably at the point of death. It was an unpleasant reality of executions like this, and far from rare.

'Poor bastard,' he heard one of the operatives remark. 'Carved up like a fucking roast.'

'It's in Russian. Any idea what it says?' O'Rourke asked.

'You got me, sir.'

Drake was no longer listening. Instead his attention had been drawn back to the floor at Demochev's feet, where the wire cutters and the body parts they had been used to remove were lying scattered around. Amongst the gruesome remains he saw something else. Small and black, gleaming in the glow of the operatives' flashlights.

Something that had no rightful place there.

'Give me your torch, would you?' he said, motioning to O'Rourke.

The man glanced up, disturbed from his inspection of the body. 'Huh?'

'Your flashlight,' Drake repeated irritably. 'Hurry.'

Catching the portable light that O'Rourke tossed to him, Drake knelt down to examine what appeared to be a black wooden chess piece sitting alone on the floor. It was a rook, intricately carved and quite old, judging by the wear around the top where countless hands had picked it up and moved it over the years.

O'Rourke knelt down beside him to examine it. 'Whoever did this is one seriously messed-up individual,' he decided. 'This a Russian thing, leaving chess pieces at murder scenes?'

'Russian Mafia,' Cartwright said, nodding sagely as if he was an authority on such matters.

Drake said nothing as he considered everything he'd seen. Like the word carved into Demochev's chest, the chess piece clearly meant something to whoever had planted it. What he needed was to understand the message this person was trying to convey, and why.

'There was more to this than a simple murder,' he said at length. 'This man was tortured systematically. They wanted information from him.'

O'Rourke had heard enough. His job had been to secure the scene, not to ponder the motivation of the men who had created it. Leaving Drake, he rose up and hit the transmitter on his radio. 'Charlie, you copy this?'

'Roger that,' came the reply.

'Call it in. We've found the hostage, he's confirmed KIA. One Tango down. Get forensics down here to start a sweep.' He released the transmit button on his radio. 'And will someone kill that goddamn engine before we all suffocate.'

The van's exhaust fumes were slowly building up inside the lock-up, creating a choking haze that was making it difficult both to see and to breathe.

As one of the team leaned into the cab to switch off the idling engine, Drake made his way over to the man he'd just taken down. He was lying sprawled on the ground where he had fallen; his blue overalls were stained crimson with blood from the twin chest wounds, and his eyes were blank and staring, seeing nothing.

Drake felt no remorse at having killed him. The moment he'd gone for his weapon, he'd sealed his fate. Instead Drake concentrated on examining him.

As far as he could tell, the man was in his mid-forties, neither tall nor short, though with a noticeably stocky build. His receding hair was close cropped, his face wide and strangely flattened. His ruddy complexion was already starting to pale from blood loss.

Drake was about to unzip his overalls to look for some form of ID when the engine at last fell silent.

Drake, however, made no move to continue his examination. He had stopped, head cocked slightly as he listened for something. A muted thumping sound; the hammer of fists against metal. It was coming from inside the van.

His eyes opened wider as he looked up at O'Rourke. 'You said the van was clear?'

'It is,' he confirmed. 'There's nobody in there.'

Frowning, Drake rose to his feet and strode over to the vehicle, pulling the doors open once more to survey the interior. As O'Rourke had said, there was nobody inside. The only thing in there was a loose piece of plastic sheeting laid across the floor, perhaps to protect delicate cargo from damage during transit.

The banging was more noticeable now, accompanied by a muffled groan. A hostage, gagged and bound, desperately trying to be heard. O'Rourke and the rest of the team had gathered around, all of them having heard the same thing.

'Shit, we've got a live one,' Cartwright said, raising his weapon.

Grabbing the edge of the sheeting, Drake pulled it aside, revealing a metal hatch welded into the centre of the floor. A simple deadbolt held it shut, though the hatch reverberated from time to time as something struck it from within.

Gripping the Sig tight, Drake clambered up into the cargo area, reached out and grasped the bolt. He took a breath, readying himself, then slid the bolt back and hauled the hatch open in one quick movement.

'Oh shit.'

Chapter 9

The compartment hidden beneath the steel floor was dark and cramped, much of its space taken up by a bound figure that was now writhing and kicking against the sides of the claustrophobic prison.

He or she was dressed in what had once been a smart business suit, though the fabric was ripped, torn and stained with blood in places. Muffled cries echoed from the burlap sack pulled over the head, but the pitch and timbre of the voice confirmed that it belonged to a woman.

'Jesus Christ,' O'Rourke gasped.

Leaning in, Drake reached down and pulled the bag away, revealing a tangled mass of shoulder-length black hair, matted in places with congealed blood. A pair of dark eyes glared back at him; a mixture of anger, fear and pain.

'It's all right,' Drake said, still startled by his discovery. 'We're here to help you.'

Glancing at O'Rourke, he held out a hand.

'Give me a knife, mate. Now.'

He felt the haft of a knife pressed into his hand, and immediately went to work on the bonds securing her wrists and ankles. The blade was as keen as it looked, and a few quick thrusts were all it took to saw through the ropes.

The instant her limbs were free, her arm shot out, pushing him back. Her other hand reached up and tore away the gag.

'Who are you?' she demanded, blinking in the harsh glare of several flashlights now pointed right at her. 'What do you want with me?'

She was on the verge of losing it. Drake had no idea what she'd just been through, but having men with guns crowding in close wasn't helping matters.

'O'Rourke, back these guys off, okay?' he instructed, waving the team back. 'Give her some space.'

'Who are you?' the woman repeated, teeth bared like an animal.

'My name's Ryan Drake. I'm with the CIA. We're here to help you,' he explained, holstering his weapon. 'Are you hurt?'

She frowned, as if failing to understand.

'Are you injured?' he repeated. He saw lots of cuts and bruises, but it was hard to tell if there were more serious injuries to contend with.

'No . . . No,' she said, shaking her head.

'You're FSB, right?'

She nodded slowly. 'Part of Director Demochev's security detail.' Suddenly her eyes lit up as awareness returned. 'Anton! Where is Anton?'

Drake winced, regretting the news he was about to deliver. 'I'm afraid he didn't make it. We got here too late.'

The woman let out a breath as if she'd just been punched in the gut, though she seemed to recover her composure quickly. 'I want to see him.'

'Probably better that you don't.'

Anger flared in her eyes as she began to pull herself out of her makeshift prison. Drake moved forward to assist her, but she angrily shoved him away.

'Get off me!'

With difficulty she managed to clamber out and rose unsteadily to her feet. For a moment she seemed to falter, clutching the side of the van for support, but somehow remained on her feet as she stepped down on to the concrete floor of the lock-up. The rest of the tactical team, obeying Drake's instructions, backed up to give her plenty of room.

Straight away her gaze fastened on the body strapped to a chair in the corner of the room. Walking with faltering steps, she approached her former commanding officer and let out a strangled breath that might have been called a sob.

'I'm sorry,' Drake said quietly, wishing there was more he could offer her.

She swallowed hard. Even in the poor light, he noticed how pale she looked. 'I heard gunfire,' she said, her eyes fixed on the body.

'We arrived just as your captor was leaving. We took him out, but I'm afraid we were too late to help Demochev.'

She said nothing to that.

'Do you know what this word means?' O'Rourke asked, pointing to the gory symbols carved into Demochev's chest.

'"Guilty",' she said after a moment. 'It says "guilty".'

The tactical team leader frowned. 'Guilty of what?'

The woman was breathing harder now, her balance growing unsteady. She staggered sideways a step, and Drake quickly moved in to support her.

'It's all right,' he said, gently but firmly steering her away from the scene of her boss's gruesome death. She didn't need to see this any longer.

'I just need some air,' she said, backing away and heading towards the doors. It was cold, dark and wet outside, but anything was better than the stench of blood and shit in that lock-up.

A short while later, the woman was sitting in the rear of the van that Drake and the tactical team had arrived in. After paying a quick visit to the security hut at the entrance to the storage facility, Drake returned with a steaming Styrofoam cup of instant coffee. She was shivering from a combination of cold and thinning adrenalin in her bloodstream. Survival was less of a priority now; shock was taking hold.

'Here,' he said, gently handing her the cup. 'You look like you could use it.'

She glanced up at him, her dark eyes reflecting a moment of surprise, but she accepted the drink all the same. 'Thank you.'

'Don't thank me till you've tried it,' he warned, then held out his jacket to her. 'I'm afraid the CIA haven't got their own clothing line, but this'll keep you warm at least.'

He saw a glimmer of a smile but nothing more. He couldn't blame her, given what she'd been through today.

'Sorry, bad humour,' he amended.

'I appreciate the gesture anyway, Agent Drake.' She held up the cheap cup he'd given her. 'My first American coffee.'

'Yeah? How does it taste?' he asked as she took a sip.

She paused for a long moment, considering the question. 'Like shit.'

Despite everything, he couldn't help but smile at that. At least her sense of humour was intact. 'Do you feel up to answering a few questions?'

She took another sip of coffee, grimacing at the taste. 'Yes.'

'What's your name?'

'Miranova,' she answered. 'Anika Miranova.'

'What happened on that freeway, Anika?'

Sighing, the woman looked down for a moment, trying to piece together the hazy memories of the crash. 'We were hit by sniper fire. Our driver was killed. We crashed . . . I think I was knocked unconscious for a few moments. When I came round, that was when I saw the ambulance.'

Drake's brows rose. 'What happened then?'

'When they pried open the door and I saw the paramedics' uniforms, I thought we were safe. Then I saw the guns in their hands.' He could see the pain and grief in her eyes as she replayed the encounter. 'They executed Andre Lagonov, Demochev's aide. One round, right between the eyes. Then they turned the weapon on me.'

He looked at her, intrigued by how the attack had played out. 'But you survived.'

'I made a grab for the weapon, tried to break his arm. The gun went off.' Reaching down, she pulled her shirt up to reveal the slate-grey material of a Kevlar vest. 'The vest stopped it, but I was thrown to the other side of the car and winded. By the time I recovered, they had bound my hands and thrown me into the back of the ambulance along with Demochev. We changed vehicles at some point, because the two of us were forced down into that . . . compartment beneath the floor. I could hear him breathing beside me, though I suppose he had been gagged just as I had. Then when we arrived here, they took him.' She clenched her teeth, impotent anger flaring up inside her. 'It was my job to protect him, and I did nothing.'

Drake sympathised, but self-pity would have to wait for now. He needed information. 'How many were there?'

'Three that I saw before they put the hood over me. There may have been others.'

'And were they speaking English or Russian?'

She shook her head slowly. 'I don't know. I heard none of them talking. They knew what they were there for – they did not waste time communicating.'

'Do you think you could describe them to one of our artists?'

Again she shook her head. 'They were wearing surgical masks. I did not see their faces.'

Drake thought it over for a moment. Clearly this had been a well-planned and well-executed hit. With Anya involved, he would have expected nothing else.

'Look, I know this doesn't mean much, but I'm sorry about your boss,' Drake said. 'That can't have been an easy thing to see.'

'I have seen worse,' she assured him, a flash of defiance showing in her dark eyes. 'Russian Mafia do similar things to informants, though they usually don't stop with fingers.'

Drake decided not to dwell too much on that one.

'Can you think of anyone who might have wanted Demochev dead?' Drake asked quietly.

She shrugged. 'We have many enemies at home and overseas. Just like the CIA, I imagine,' she added. 'We will find them.'

The look of absolute, cold-blooded hatred in her eyes was enough to give even Drake pause for thought. He didn't doubt for a moment that she meant what she said. And with the resources of the FSB to call upon, she was more than capable of making it happen.

'Speaking of which, how did you find this place?' she went on.

'We backtracked traffic-camera footage of the freeway attack,' he said, deciding to leave out the part about his meeting with Anya. 'Lucky for you, we've got some good people working for us.'

She took another sip of her coffee, surveying him in thoughtful silence for a long moment. 'And you, Agent Drake? How is it that a British CIA man finds himself rescuing hostages on American soil?'

Drake sighed. 'Long story,' he said truthfully. 'The short version is, my job is to find people who go missing. I didn't expect to be doing it on my way home from work tonight, but that's life.'

explosion that knocked them both flat on the rain-slick concrete.

Stunned and half-deafened by the blast, Drake shook his head and looked over at what remained of the lock-up. Smoke and flames from the Chevy's fuel tank were billowing from the shattered roof, impervious to the rain that was still falling steadily all around them. The heat was causing his skin to prickle at such close range.

The lock-up must have been rigged with explosives linked into the mains lighting circuit. The moment they'd flicked the switch, it had set them off. Only sheer luck had found Drake and the others outside when the bomb went off.

Beside him, O'Rourke and his two teammates were rising unsteadily to their feet, staring in disbelief at the raging inferno that was all that remained of the storage lock-up, the van, Demochev and their unlucky comrade.

Drake turned away, preferring not to look at it. Only now was he starting to realise what they were up against, the war they had become embroiled in. This evening was rapidly going from bad to worse, and he had no idea where it was going to end.

Samantha McKnight was lying curled up on her living-room couch, a half-empty glass of white wine and a weighty leather-bound copy of Dostoyevsky's *Demons* resting side by side on the coffee table before her. Outside, wind-driven rain and sleet lashed against the window of her apartment, the cold winter night making her all the more glad of the warm, snug apartment she now called home.

The book was a gift from her grandfather; part of the complete set that lurked menacingly on the top shelf of her bookcase. An avid reader, he had given her the daunting stack of books on her sixteenth birthday, making her promise to read them all . He hadn't lived to see it, but she was slowly making good on her promise.

Every holiday season she took another crack at them, slogging through the heavy tomes with the dogged persistence of a marathon runner. It was one of the few times of year when she actually had the time and the motivation for such things.

Today, however, neither the wine nor the book held her attention. She was focused instead on the TV on the other side of her living room, and the ongoing news coverage of the sniper attack on the DC freeway. Apparently an explosion had been heard at a storage facility on the east side of the city, believed to be linked to the sniper attack.

She was just reaching for her glass when her cellphone started ringing. Abandoning the wine, she raised her head to glance at the caller ID and decide if it was a call worth taking.

It was.

She stretched out and picked up the phone, hitting the receive-call button. 'Ryan,' she began. 'What can I do for you?'

Her greeting wasn't entirely effusive, and they both knew why. McKnight had left behind her dangerous but very worthy role defusing unexploded ordinance in Afghanistan to come and work for the Shepherd programme. She had relocated to DC, bought an apartment here, moved her entire life halfway around the world, and she had done much of it because of him. And yet she had barely seen him in the three months she'd been working here.

One or both of them had often been out on active operations, making it difficult to meet up, but she'd sensed there was more to it than that. She felt as if Drake had been actively avoiding her these past few months, always finding an excuse not to see her.

Much as she hated to admit it, she was beginning to wonder if she'd made a mistake coming here, and that doubt had soon manifested itself as frustration towards Drake. If he hadn't wanted her here in the first place, why let her go through all the upheaval of switching jobs and moving home?

'Sam, I'm sorry to call so late,' he began, his voice urgent. 'I need your help.'

'Funny how that works, huh?' she said before she could stop herself. Immediately she regretted both the tone and the words, not that they weren't deserved.

Drake hesitated, stung by the recrimination in her voice. 'I'm sorry,' he said at length, his tone suggesting he was apologising for more than just the inconvenient hour of his phone call. 'But I wouldn't call if it wasn't important.'

That got her attention. This was no social call – he was very much in work mode. But wherever he was calling from, there was a lot of ambient noise in the background.

She frowned. 'Why can I hear police sirens?'

'You been watching the news?'

'Yeah.'

'There you go,' he said, seeing little need to elaborate. 'I'm at a storage facility in Capitol Heights. Or what's left of one.'

She glanced at the TV, and the ongoing coverage of the sniper attack, and immediately made the connection with the reported explosion on the east side of the city. She felt a knot of apprehension tighten in her stomach.

'You okay?' she asked, regretting her earlier censure even more now.

'Not a scratch,' he assured her, much to her relief. 'But other people haven't been so lucky. I could use your help down here.'

It didn't take a genius to see why. Samantha's area of expertise was explosive-based weaponry; everything from field artillery to surface-to-air missiles to improvised bombs.

If a device had just detonated down there, it was a safe bet that Drake wanted to know more about it – where it had come from, who might have manufactured it and where they could be found.

'I need a full forensic sweep of the scene. Explosive residue, fragments of the detonator . . . anything that might tell us—'

'You want to carry on telling me my job?' she asked impatiently.

A moment or two of uncomfortable silence greeted her.

She managed to force calm into her voice as she continued. 'Before we go any further, you mind telling me what the hell you've gotten yourself mixed up in now?'

'Long story. The short version is that I want to know who was behind this attack, and why. And I need those answers discreetly.'

She frowned. 'This is off the shelf?'

Calling her up on a Friday evening to summon her to the scene of an explosion was one thing, but doing it without any kind of sanction from the Agency was quite another.

'For now,' he admitted. 'Look, I'm asking for your help, Sam. I need someone I can trust to work on this, and believe me that list is pretty short these days.'

McKnight hesitated. That was enough to cut through any interpersonal issues she might have had. If he was asking for her professional assistance, she wouldn't refuse.

'Fine,' she conceded. 'What kind of device are we talking about?'

She was starting to wish she hadn't drunk that glass of wine earlier. It wasn't enough to intoxicate her, but the alcohol had slowed her normally sharp analytical mind at a time when she needed to be on the ball.

'Your guess is as good as mine right now. All I know is

that it went boom, and it was powerful enough to destroy a storage lock-up and everything inside.'

Which told her nothing at all, she thought with the faint exasperation of an expert dealing with a layman. The only way she'd find anything of value was to get down there herself and survey the site.

Rising from the couch, she looked out the rain-lashed window at the distant lights of central DC glimmering in the darkness of the winter night.

'Okay, give me the address,' she said at last.

She heard a faint exhalation on the other end. 'Thanks. I mean that.'

'Don't thank me yet,' she advised. 'I might find nothing at all. Either way, I expect to be told exactly what this is all about before the day's over.'

'You will be. I promise.'

McKnight glanced down at the heavy leather-bound book on her coffee table. It seemed *Demons* might have to wait until next Christmas.

She could live with that.

Chapter 10

CIA Headquarters, Langley

Even if Drake hadn't been personally involved in the events in central DC, a quick stroll down the corridors at Langley would have told him something serious was going down. Analysts hurried back and forth, some clutching sheets of paper hot off the printer, others speaking into their cellphones with hushed, urgent voices. All wore the same look of quiet panic that takes hold as a big organisation wakes up to a crisis unfolding around it.

Drake now found himself in Franklin's office on the third floor of the New Headquarters Building, having been summoned there shortly after arriving back at CIA headquarters to give his summary of events in central DC.

He had little in the way of good news for his friend.

'In short, they knew we'd track him down to that lock-up,' Drake said, taking a deep pull of his coffee. 'They left Demochev with that message carved into his chest because they wanted someone to find it, but they also didn't want any useful evidence falling into our hands.'

And in that respect, they had apparently succeeded. Several pounds of high explosive combined with an almost-full tank of fuel had done their work well, incinerating the contents of the storage lock-up and any evidence they might have yielded. There was little left for the FBI forensics teams to examine.

'So it seems,' Franklin agreed. Rather than sitting behind the polished mahogany expanse of his desk, he was standing by the window that overlooked the darkened woodland beyond the Agency perimeter. Drake knew why – back injuries sustained in the line of duty years earlier now left him with painful muscle cramps if he stayed seated too long. 'And now we've got a major international incident to deal with. You can imagine our counterparts in Moscow aren't too pleased with how tonight panned out.'

Which brought them neatly on to something that had been bothering Drake ever since he'd seen those diplomatic licence plates.

'What was that FSB delegation doing in Washington in the first place?'

His friend glanced at him over his shoulder. 'Believe it or not, they were on their way here, to Langley. They were supposed to attend a conference on strengthening cooperation between our two agencies. Joining forces in the War on Terror, all that good stuff.' He snorted with grim amusement. 'You can imagine how this looks – they spend five minutes on American soil and it turns into a bad day in Baghdad. And less than three miles from the White House to boot. The FBI, the Secret Service . . . they're going apeshit over this.'

Drake couldn't blame them. An attack of this scale in the nation's capital was enough to ruin anyone's day, particularly if foreign diplomats were involved.

'And all because of one woman,' Franklin added with a pointed look.

'Anya's a soldier, not a terrorist,' Drake said, refusing to countenance such thoughts. 'She would never kill innocent people.'

Franklin leaned forward. 'You sure about that, Ryan? She's a rogue Agency operative who spent four years in solitary confinement in a Russian jail. She could very well be psychologically unbalanced. At the very least she has a clear grudge against the Russian government, and the training and experience needed to act on it. And you said yourself she was at the sniping point. Think how this would look to anyone else.'

It was difficult to argue with that reasoning. Anya was certainly a ruthless and highly trained operative who wasn't afraid to use both of those attributes when they were needed, but even he had difficulty believing she would stage an attack on a freeway packed with innocent civilians for no reason.

'I know how it must look,' he conceded. 'But Anya's no murderer – I'd bet my life on that. Whatever her part in this, she must have her reasons.'

'And she hasn't contacted you before today?' Franklin asked. 'She hasn't made any attempt to send you a message or communicate in any way?' Seeing Drake's look, he added, 'You know I have to ask.'

Drake shook his head. He'd heard nothing from Anya since his return from Afghanistan four months ago. There had been no sightings of her, no activity, nothing. She had dropped off the face of the earth.

'Does anyone else know she was there?' he couldn't help asking.

Franklin raised an eyebrow. 'You mean, has Cain found out?'

Marcus Cain, the newly appointed deputy director, had once been Anya's mentor, her handler and her sponsor within the Agency. But their relationship had long since turned sour, and the two former comrades were now bitter enemies. Cain's restless attention was always on finding the enigmatic woman, and he had formidable resources to call upon.

'Not yet,' Franklin continued. 'But don't expect it to stay that way for long. Anya crossed a line tonight – the kind of line you don't come back from. She killed innocent people, she took part in the abduction and execution of a major player in the Russian intelligence service, and she damn near caused a major international incident. Whatever she was before today, she's now a liability. To the Agency, and to us.'

'So what are you saying? We just hang her out to dry and be done with it?' Drake challenged him. 'Is that what she deserves?'

'What she *deserves*?' Franklin repeated. 'Ryan, you're lucky to still be breathing after what she's put you through, never mind walking around as a free man. But sooner or later your luck's going to run out. What Anya deserves doesn't come into it. When are you going to realise that?'

Drake hesitated, stung by his friend's cold detachment. Somehow he was reminded of how Mason must have felt standing in Drake's office as his hopes of resuming his career were crushed.

'We need her. She's the only one who can end this.'

For the past eighteen months Drake and his companions had lived with a sword hanging above their heads; a sword wielded by none other than Marcus Cain. It was clear the CIA deputy director would like nothing better than to bring it down on Drake's neck, and sooner or later he'd find a way to do it.

Only Anya possessed the knowledge and the resources to stop him. She was the key, the thread by which their fate hung. If they lost her, they lost everything.

Franklin shook his head, chuckling with grim amusement. 'You still don't get it, do you? There'll never be an end to this. Anya's doing exactly what she was trained to do – build trust and dependency, manipulate her targets, expose their vulnerability, get them to take risks and sacrifice themselves for her. You go after someone like that, and you'll wind up dead or in prison just like she was. That's the only end waiting for you, and I'll be damned if you're taking me down with you.'

At that moment, Drake knew he'd heard enough. It was as if something had snapped inside him, as if some dam had been breached and all the pent-up frustration and longing and guilt it had been holding back was unleashed.

'You wouldn't even have your precious career if it wasn't for her, Dan. Let's not bullshit each other – we both know how you landed this promotion, and it wasn't through hard work and patience. What would happen if Anya exposed Cain for the lying piece of shit he is? Would he drag you down with him?' he asked, his eyes narrowing. 'Don't give me that crap about trying to look out for me. This is about one thing: saving your own arse.'

He'd gone too far, and he knew it right away. Slamming his fist down on the desk, Franklin rose up from his chair, ignoring the pain in his back as he glared at Drake. He was visibly struggling to contain his fury, but there was more than just that. There was pain and sadness in his eyes at his friend's accusation.

'As your boss, I should have you relieved of duty for that,' he said at length, his voice now dangerously cold and clinical. 'As your friend, I should beat the shit out of you. So you tell me now, which one will it be?'

The undertone of quiet, restrained menace was enough to cut through the fog of Drake's frustration. He exhaled slowly and unclenched his fists, his anger dissipating.

He was ashamed of himself for lashing out like that, and equally taken aback by his friend's change in demeanour, no matter how justified it might have been. Normally composed and self-possessed, Franklin had just shown a side of himself that Drake had never seen before. A side that had only started to emerge since he took over as director of the Special Activities Division.

'Dan, look . . . I'm sorry for that,' he said after a few moments, having calmed himself a little. 'It was wrong, and I apologise.'

'You're goddamn right it was,' Franklin hit back, though his tone had lost some of its vehemence. 'If you were any other agent, *any other*, I'd have you fired right now. I mean that.'

He sighed wearily, his anger apparently expended. Leaving the window, he lowered himself into his expensive leather chair, the strain of his job seeming to weigh more heavily on him at that moment. He looked tired and worn, though he was barely into his forties.

He leaned forward, staring intently at Drake as if trying to reach out to him. 'As your friend, I'm asking you to give this up, before you cross the same line as Anya. You're so caught up in following her, little by little you're becoming her. Let this one go, Ryan. Please. *Let it go.*'

Drake was silent for a moment, surprised by the conviction, the raw emotion in his friend's voice. In his own way Franklin was trying to help him, trying to guide him, trying to save him from himself. And in part of Drake's mind, he knew the man was right. Few people could have listened to his words and not been moved by them.

But he also knew what his answer would be, just as Franklin did. Anya had saved him, in more ways than one. The bond between them was stronger than either was prepared to admit, but both acknowledged it all the same.

He couldn't give up on her. He *wouldn't* give up on her.

'You know I can't do that.'

The director of Special Activities slumped back in his chair, defeated.

'Then whatever you're going to do, you'll have to do it without me,' he said. 'I can't support you on this. I'm sorry.'

And that was it, Drake realised. Franklin had just pulled the plug on him. Drake was on his own now, with no resources to call upon, no backup, nothing.

'Yeah,' Drake said, rising from his chair. 'So am I.'

Chapter 11

Montreal International Airport, Canada,
20 December 2008

Three o'clock in the morning was a graveyard shift by anyone's standards, but like any major airport, Montreal International's food outlets never shut down completely. No matter how ungodly the hour, there was always someone around who needed to eat or drink.

'One black coffee, no sugar,' the barkeeper said, laying down the steaming brew on the wood-veneer counter in front of Anya. A gangly young man barely out of his teens, his jet-black hair was worn long and brushed forwards so that it almost obscured one eye, in what she assumed was the fashion these days.

'Can I get you anything else?' he asked in a tone that suggested he really hoped the answer was no.

'Just the coffee, thanks.' Anya flashed a weary smile as she handed over a ten-dollar bill, playing the part of the strung-out traveller. And in this case, it wasn't entirely fictitious.

After an uneventful and thoroughly boring eight-hour drive from Washington, DC, she had crossed the loosely policed Canadian border without incident, her fake ID barely checked by the officers on duty. From there it had been a short hop to Montreal airport where she had returned her rental car and made for the check-in desk.

Security had been a mere formality, consisting of a glance

at her passport and a quick swipe through the biometric reader. Unlike America, Canada was still somewhat relaxed about international travellers, hence the reason she'd chosen to escape via Montreal instead of Dulles or Newark.

Ahead of her lay another nine hours of transatlantic inactivity; a prospect she greeted with a mixture of relief and trepidation. On the one hand it would mean a chance to grab some much-needed rest, but on the other it would mean being stuck on an aircraft over which she had no control.

She'd always disliked flying, and that sentiment had only increased in recent years. She hated the cramped seating, the dry stale air, the press of humanity all around her, and most of all the feeling of imprisonment that descended on her every time the outer hatch sealed shut.

Anya had spent a good part of her life incarcerated in one form or another. And as loath as she was to admit it, those experiences had left their mark on her, both physically and emotionally.

She pushed those thoughts aside as she took her first sip. She wasn't particularly thirsty, but like most travellers with time to kill before their flight, grabbing a coffee just seemed like the thing to do. Most of the retail outlets were closed anyway.

A TV was mounted overhead, tuned to a news channel that was replaying coverage of the sniper attack in Washington. Anya was careful to keep her attention elsewhere, lest the barkeeper see something in her eyes that stuck with him. She had no desire to dwell on the gory results of her handiwork.

'Ma'am?'

She looked up from her coffee, instantly on edge. Perhaps she hadn't guarded her expression as well as she'd thought. Or perhaps the CIA had just released a picture of her to the world's media, and her friend behind the bar was about to pick her up on it.

She turned her eyes on the young barkeeper, her mind already switching gears into survival mode. If it came to it, she knew she could take down a man like him with ease, but getting out of the airport would be another matter entirely.

He nodded towards the TV overhead, looking nervous. 'I couldn't help noticing you weren't watching the news.'

Anya tensed, readying herself to act.

'You . . . mind if I turn the volume down?' he asked sheepishly, then held up a couple of dog-eared textbooks he'd been keeping beneath the bar. 'I was kinda hoping to do some revision, and the noise breaks my concentration.'

Anya might have laughed had she been less on edge. She understood now why he'd been so unenthusiastic at her arrival – he was a college student, probably working the graveyard shift for some easy money while he was studying.

'Of course,' she said, hoping her relief wasn't too obvious. 'Feel free.'

At this, his previously sombre face broke into a smile. 'You're a lifesaver,' he said, using a remote to mute the TV. Within moments he had the books open and spread out on the bar.

'What are you studying?' Anya asked out of idle curiosity as she took another sip.

'History,' he replied without looking up. 'Cold War history. I've got to write a paper on the Soviet defeat in Afghanistan bringing about the collapse of the USSR. And it has to be handed in by Monday or *I'm* history.'

Anya couldn't hide a faint smile of amusement. He could scarcely have found a better person to interview than the woman sitting right in front of him, and he'd never know it. She was also struck by the realisation that he probably hadn't even been born when she was fighting for survival out there.

She felt her cellphone buzzing in her pocket. Excusing herself from the bar, she retreated a short distance to take the call, adopting a conversational tone when she spoke.

'Good to hear from you again,' she began.

'I assume there were no problems?' Her contact felt little need to reciprocate the upbeat tone, speaking instead in the clipped, efficient, almost mechanical voice she'd come to recognise as emblematic of his personality.

'Nothing I couldn't handle,' she assured him, unwilling to talk about Drake. Aside from startling her and prompting a hasty withdrawal from the rooftop, he had caused no real damage. Yet.

With luck, he'd have enough sense to stay out of something that was none of his concern. If not, she'd have no option but to deal with him. She hoped for his sake that it didn't come to that.

'Good. Our party has drawn a lot of attention. We're popular these days, it seems.'

She knew that both the CIA and the FSB would now be working furiously to track them down after the attack in DC, and that they would leave no stone unturned in their pursuit. But then, that was exactly what their plan called for. The only question was one of timing.

Timing was everything.

'So you're free to meet on Sunday?'

'Just as we planned,' he confirmed. 'I'm looking forward to seeing you again.'

'And you,' she replied, closing the phone down.

Returning to the bar, she downed the remainder of her coffee and set the cup down. The young man didn't even glance up from his books.

'Good luck with your paper,' she said, content to leave him to it.

Chapter 12

Drake was in a foul mood as he threw open the front door to the disorganised, neglected space that he called home, with Franklin's earlier words of admonishment still ringing in his ears. A chill early-morning wind followed him in as he slammed the door shut.

For a few seconds he just stood there, soaking up the quiet darkness around him and allowing his restless mind to relax a little. After a long day and night of ringing phones, whirring computers and tense meetings, the silent and empty house was a welcome relief to his senses.

His house in Bethesda on the north-west side of DC was much like his office: cluttered and untidy, with coffee cups, magazines, books, dirty plates and various other bits and pieces scattered about. The curtains were drawn, blotting out the murky grey morning that was slowly taking shape outside.

Discarding his coat, he turned his attention to the sideboard, seeking the bottle of Talisker whisky that resided there. Drake couldn't stomach the American brands. His drink of choice was a good Scottish single malt, preferably from the Western Isles for the smoky taste they imparted.

Pouring himself a generous measure, he eased himself down on the couch with a sigh and took a pull on the Scotch. The drink was warm, rich and powerful, lighting a fire inside him. He wasn't prone to drinking to excess these days, but right now he needed something to take the edge off.

Things weren't looking good, and there was no sense in ducking that fact. Franklin had effectively withdrawn his support, leaving Drake few resources with which to pursue a woman who had eluded the world's premier intelligence agency for the past eighteen months. But more than that, Drake felt the loss of support even more on a personal level.

Dan Franklin, his friend and one of his few remaining allies within the Agency, had effectively cut him loose.

'Fuck,' he said at length as he took another drink, feeling that one word rather aptly summed up his situation.

With nothing more to be done at Langley for the time being, he had returned home to consider his next move, and to brood on everything that had happened.

Maybe Franklin had been right, he reflected in a moment of brutal honesty. Anya had neither the need, nor apparently the desire, for his help. Maybe it would be best for everyone if he stood down from this one.

He closed his eyes, and for a moment found himself back in that small border village in Saudi Arabia where he'd spent his last night with Anya. He was talking with an old man, grey-haired and overweight; one of the few people on this earth who could rightly call Anya a friend.

'She will not listen to reason, will not back down. I see her standing alone, surrounded by enemies. And when that happens, she will fall . . . I think there will come a time when you have to choose, either to stand with her or against her.'

Drake sighed and took another drink. The events of those tumultuous few days, and the heartache and danger that had come with them, felt like a lifetime ago now. So much had happened since then, it was almost possible to forget it had ever been. It was almost possible to forget the feelings she had stirred up in him; the brief moment of peace, of belonging, of connection he'd felt with her.

Almost, but not quite.

He was reaching for his cellphone almost before he knew it, quickly dialling McKnight's number from memory. It rang a half-dozen times before a weary voice answered.

'Ryan?'

Drake felt a stab of guilt at calling her so early. She'd pulled an all-nighter just as he had, but she had no personal stake in this. She was doing it because he'd asked her to, even though he had no right.

'Sam, where are you?'

'In the forensics lab at Langley. Running that analysis we talked about. Why, where are you?'

'At home. There's been some . . . changes, but I'd rather talk face to face. You think you and Keira could meet me here?'

She paused for a moment, considering his request. 'I don't know about Keira, but I'll be finished here in about half an hour. With luck, I should have some results for you.'

'Bring everything you've got. I'll have some coffee waiting for you.'

'Thought you Brits drank tea?' she asked, a faint trace of her old humour returning.

'Only on TV,' he assured her. 'See you soon.'

As it turned out, it was just over an hour before Drake heard a loud knock at the door. He'd had enough time to shower and change clothes, and although this had done nothing to remedy his lack of sleep, it had at least made him feel a little more on the ball.

The knock was repeated, louder this time.

'I'm coming!' he called, pulling a T-shirt on as he made for the front door.

His brief explanation seemed to satisfy her, for now at least.

'There is one more thing,' Miranova said, her voice softening a little now. 'I did not get a chance to say this to you before, but . . . thank you. All of you. If you had not found me . . .'

She trailed off, seeing no need to finish that line of thought. Drake wasn't too inclined to ponder it either. Instead he simply nodded acknowledgement, glad that something good had at least come out of today.

Beyond the open van doors, O'Rourke and two of his teammates emerged from the lock-up, wary of contaminating the crime scene before forensics could analyse it. In reality they just wanted to get away from the gory spectacle within. O'Rourke reached into his trouser pocket for a pack of cigarettes, likely needing something to take the edge off.

Miranova was apparently of like mind, and stared at him until she made eye contact. 'Can I have one?'

Without saying a word, he tossed her the pack, then fished a lighter from his pocket.

'My first cigarette in eight years,' she said as he lit it for her. She took a long, slow draw and breathed deeply, managing to hold it a few seconds before coughing a little.

Drake couldn't blame her. She'd earned it today.

'Yeah, well, you never really quit,' O'Rourke acknowledged as he lit up his own. 'You just go a while between smokes.'

Further off, they heard Cartwright call out to one of his comrades. 'Hey, Charlie, I can't see shit in here. Switch those overhead lights on, will you?'

Drake was just turning back towards Miranova when a blinding flash suddenly illuminated the drab storage yard around them, followed a moment later by a thunderous

'Then move your ass!' an angry female voice retorted. Definitely not McKnight. 'Before I freeze mine off.'

Unlocking the door, Drake was practically barged aside as Frost pushed her way in, closely followed by a gust of cold wind. Her bike leathers were glistening with rainwater that was already dripping on the carpet, her dark hair a dishevelled mess. A laptop carry-case was slung over one shoulder. She spared him little more than a passing glance as she made straight for the living room.

'Good to see you too, Keira,' he remarked.

'She hasn't had breakfast yet,' McKnight warned as she stepped in out of the early-morning drizzle. Unlike her leather-clad companion, she was dressed in casual jeans and a black winter coat, the collar turned up against the chill breeze.

Drake made a face as he motioned towards the living room. 'Bad news for all of us.'

Frost had already made herself at home, tossing her jacket aside and flopping down on the couch where she unpacked her laptop. She also removed a curious-looking device from her carry-case, set it down on the coffee table and switched it on. Resembling a walkie-talkie with four separate plastic aerials protruding from its top, it was a portable signal jammer designed to disrupt any electronic surveillance equipment within 50 yards.

A single green light on the side confirmed the jammer was on and functioning. The house, and everything in it, was now immune to any form of electronic eavesdropping. It wasn't the first time they had resorted to such measures, particularly when it came to Anya. This was one conversation that they certainly didn't want Marcus Cain to find out about.

'I love coming here, Ryan,' Frost said as she glanced around at the disorganised living space. 'Makes my place seem like a palace.'

'Yeah? Well, I suppose everything seems big from your point of view,' he remarked to the diminutive specialist, moving behind the breakfast bar to fire up the coffee machine. He guessed they could all do with some.

'So how did things go with Dan?' McKnight asked, guessing that was part of the reason he was at home and not at Langley.

Drake glanced up as the machine started to dribble black liquid into the first cup. 'Put it this way, I wouldn't count on any more support from his end. He doesn't think it's worth the risk trying to find Anya.'

'Can you blame him?' Frost asked. 'She's connected to a major terrorist attack. She's about as burned as they come.'

'She's not a terrorist,' he said firmly. 'She must have had a reason for this.'

'Okay, so maybe she's trying to spread love and peace through the medium of bullets. Either way, we know she was the sniper.'

'Let me worry about the motive,' he said, handing her a steaming cup. He knew she'd have kicked off if he didn't offer her a coffee. 'All I need from you is the method. Did you get anything from the cameras at the lock-up?'

She shook her head. 'The lock-up itself wasn't covered by any cameras, so I missed the vehicle changeover. But the main gate logs all vehicles coming in. I managed to catch our friends as they arrived with Demochev.'

Turning her attention to her laptop, she called up an image file and maximised it so that it filled the screen. Sure enough, the Chevy cargo van was plainly visible as it pulled up to the main gate, the driver leaning out to swipe his access card through the reader.

'Can you zoom in?' Drake asked.

Manipulating the black-and-white image, Frost focused in

on the driver. He was wearing a baseball cap and was careful to keep his head tilted away from the camera, denying them a good look at him. The only thing Drake could tell for sure was that he was of lean build, and apparently fond of tattoos, judging by the symbols and images etched into his exposed forearm. There was scarcely a square inch of skin left untouched, and he had a feeling he knew why.

'The local tattoo parlour did well out of that guy,' McKnight remarked.

'Those aren't professional,' Drake said as he surveyed the crude hand-inked images. 'Those are prison tattoos. Russian.'

Tattoos were a big thing in Russian prison culture, the arcane and seemingly random pictures and symbols forming a complex and richly diverse language that could reveal a great deal about their owner. Drake had seen more than a few in his time. After all, many of the warlords and organised crime leaders the Agency operated against had spent time in Russian jails.

Seeing one he recognised, he looked at Frost again. 'Can you zoom in any tighter on his hand?'

Increasing the resolution to maximum, Frost focused the screen on the driver's outstretched hand, the image now rendered grainy and pixillated by her efforts. But sure enough, a single word had been etched into his skin in simple, bold letters.

СЕВЕР

'What's that?' the young woman asked.

'It's the Russian word for "north",' Drake explained. 'Our friend there did time in a Siberian prison.'

She said nothing, though for once she actually looked impressed with his insight.

'And the devil?' McKnight prompted, nodding to the image of a demon near his wrist.

'That's for someone who holds anger and hatred towards the government.'

'Figured as much,' Frost said. 'Shame he didn't get his name and address on there too. Would've made our job a lot easier.'

Drake folded his arms. The tattoos might have given an insight into the man's background, but not his identity. Or more importantly, his intentions.

'What about the vehicle they left in? Did we get any images of that?'

The young specialist shook her head. 'This place wasn't exactly Fort Knox. They only log vehicles as they enter.'

'They must have brought it in at some point to have it standing by.'

'No shit. But it could have happened weeks or even months ago. You want to cross-reference every vehicle that's passed through those gates in the past six months, be my guest.'

He didn't. 'So who was the lock-up registered with?'

'Some outfit called Marcell Removals. They took out a short-term lease about a month ago.' She shook her head. 'It's a bullshit company – there's nothing on them.'

He wasn't surprised. 'What about Anya?'

Frost made a face, suggesting the news wasn't good. 'There were no cameras in the apartment building she fired from. I was trying to backtrack her movements using traffic cams, but it was slow going. Knowing her, I wouldn't be surprised if she disappeared like a fart in the wind.'

Neither would he. Anya had made a career out of evading detection, and had survived on the run for the past eighteen months despite Cain's best efforts to capture her. He doubted she would allow herself to be caught now.

With no progress on the security-camera front, Drake turned his attention to McKnight. 'Sam, anything from you?'

He held a second cup of coffee out to her, but she shook her head. Unlike Frost, she didn't live off the stuff.

'Well, the sniper rifle's a dead end. No pun intended,' she added. 'Serial numbers and ID marks were removed. No hairs, fibres or prints were found on it. It's a serious piece of hardware, though – a KSVK 12.7 Russian, designed by the Degtyarev plant for taking out armoured vehicles and concealed snipers. It packs more punch than a Barrett Fifty Cal, and it's lighter. According to the intel I was able to dig up, they were only ever issued in small numbers to special forces teams in Chechnya. The Russians really know how to build guns.'

They've had plenty of practice, Drake thought.

'And the explosives?'

She nodded, consulting the chemical analysis results she had printed out. 'According to this, it's a compound called Danubit. Some company in Slovakia manufactures it. Normally it's used for industrial applications like mining and rock blasting. Packs a hell of a punch, though – I'd guess it took less than a pound of the stuff to vaporise that lock-up.'

'So who would have access to it?'

'Virtually anyone,' she admitted. 'It's exported to mining and construction companies all over the world. Anyone with a licence to drill or build could get their hands on it.'

He sighed, disappointed she hadn't found anything more specific. They needed something to narrow down their search, and this, like the rifle, seemed to be a dead end.

'There was one other thing,' she added, turning her attention back to the printout. 'The chemical analysis turned up some unusual trace elements in the explosive. Nickel, cobalt, cadmium, selenium . . . lots of heavy metals that aren't part of the explosive reaction.'

He frowned. 'Sounds like the stuff you'd find in your

average car battery. Wouldn't it have come from the van when it blew up?'

She shook her head. 'No, this stuff was everywhere, in equal quantities. The van's battery was still more or less intact even after the explosion. Whatever it was, it was part of the bomb itself. The blast must have rendered it aerosol.'

Drake raised an eyebrow, intrigued but not sure how it could be used to their advantage. 'Any theories?'

She shrugged. 'If I had to make a guess, I'd say the explosives were contaminated somehow, either during manufacture or storage.'

'So where would you find nickel, lead and all that other crap?' Frost wondered.

'A chemical plant,' Drake suggested.

The young woman made a face. 'Plenty of those to choose from.'

McKnight shook her head, still mulling it over.

Then, just like that, her eyes lit up as an idea came to her. 'Blacksmith.'

'Huh?'

'If this contamination came from some kind of airborne pollution, all we need to do is find a site that matches it,' she explained, growing more excited as the idea took shape. 'The Blacksmith Institute is an environmental agency that monitors industrial pollution all over the world. I used a bunch of their papers to write my thesis back in college. If anyone can tell us where this contamination came from, they can.'

She turned her attention to Frost, and the laptop she was still holding.

'Keira, if I give you the list of trace elements, can you tie in with their servers and do a search for possible sites that match?'

Frost made a face. 'Could be a hell of a long list without any search parameters.'

'Then narrow it down to construction and mining complexes,' Drake suggested.

'And focus on Russia and Eastern European countries,' McKnight added, the ideas seeming to flow easily when she had Drake to bounce them off. 'Everything we've seen so far is of Russian origin. It seems logical that the explosives were as well.'

'On it,' the young woman said, already bringing up Google to search for the site.

Chapter 13

Deputy CIA director Marcus Cain looked up from his computer at the knock on his office door. Normally his private secretary would be there to screen anyone seeking an audience with him, but this early in the morning he was alone.

'Come in,' he called out, knowing already who was on the other side.

The door opened. Sure enough, Dan Franklin strode into the room, his posture tense and his expression hard, as it often was when Cain called him into his office. He hated the deputy director almost as much as Drake did; the difference, however, was that Cain now owned Dan Franklin. He had made a deal with the devil last year, and if anything happened to his unlikely benefactor, he would be ruined as well.

'Dan, good to see you again,' Cain said with false equanimity.

The younger man wasn't impressed. 'You asked to see me?'

Cain nodded and gestured to a chair opposite. 'Take a seat.'

He knew Franklin preferred to stand, just as he knew he hated it when people made allowances for his injury. Saying nothing, Franklin eased himself into a chair, doing his best to hide the pain as he did so. Cain sat easily in his own chair, regarding his subordinate for a few seconds before speaking.

'Been a busy night, huh?'

Franklin nodded. 'It has.'

'Especially for some of your staff,' Cain added, eyeing him hard. 'Maybe you could tell me what your friend Drake was doing at the scene of that sniper attack? Because from what I've heard he made quite an impression. Ruffled a few feathers, if you catch my drift. I was hoping you could tell me why.'

'Ryan's a loose cannon, always has been,' Franklin said, allowing a hint of irritation to creep into his voice, as if Drake was just as much a problem for him as he was for Cain. 'He sees something happening and he feels he has to get involved. Mostly against my better judgement. I've already brought him in and reprimanded him for his actions.'

To his credit, Franklin remained surprisingly composed under this scrutiny. There weren't many men who could sit opposite Marcus Cain and blatantly lie to his face without sweating.

Still, Cain allowed it to pass. 'So tell me, what is Drake doing now?'

Franklin shrugged. 'Going home with his tail between his legs, I'd assume. There's nothing more for him to do.'

'Of course,' Cain agreed. Despite his genial tone, his gaze was cold and penetrating as he stared at the younger man across his desk. 'And there's nothing else you'd like to share with me, Dan? No other issues that you want to bring to my attention?'

For a moment, a tension hung in the air between them, heavy and brooding. The very air in the office seemed to press down on them.

This was the crucial moment; the tipping point where Cain decided whether Dan Franklin was a man he could control and ultimately mould into something useful, or whether his loyalty to Drake represented a threat that would have to be eliminated. For a heartbeat, he caught himself wondering whether his subordinate understood just how much rested on what he said next.

And just like that, Franklin shook his head, meeting Cain's gaze without fear. 'I've got Drake under control.'

Cain smiled and nodded, the tension evaporating. 'Good. I'm glad to hear it. We have to be careful about the people working under us, don't you think?' His smile faded a little as he held the other man's gaze. 'You never know when they might do something . . . unwise.'

'Couldn't agree more,' Franklin said, rising from his chair. 'Now, if it's all the same to you, I wouldn't mind heading home for a few hours' sleep. There's nothing else, is there, Marcus?'

'No.' The smile was back. 'No. Nothing else.'

Hesitating a moment, Franklin nodded, turned away and walked slowly from the room, making a point of not retreating too quickly. But Cain could tell from his body language that he couldn't wait to get out of there.

The door closed and Cain leaned back in his chair, his eyes pensive as he stared at the image on his computer screen. It was an artist's impression of the woman seen entering the apartment building in central DC shortly before the sniper attack.

Blonde hair, blue eyes, mid-thirties to mid-forties, tall and athletically built, attractive features with a slightly foreign look about them. Even if it was based on one civilian's chance encounter in a dimly lit hallway, the picture bore enough of a resemblance to Anya that Cain was willing to bet his life it was her.

The entire attack bore all the hallmarks of the snatch-and-grab operations she used to run in Afghanistan two decades earlier. Anya; audacious as always, launching an attack of this scale just a few short miles from Langley itself. Perhaps she was trying to send him a message, letting him know that no one was safe from her, no matter how well protected they felt.

He didn't fully understand the depth of her participation yet, but he had a suspicion he knew what, or rather who, her ultimate goal was. What he did know for certain was that Drake, predictable as always, was already working to track her down.

For now at least, Cain was content to let Drake do his work for him. Keeping the man alive just might prove to be the best decision he'd ever made. Cain was adept at manipulating people into doing what he wanted, but as he had learned from long experience, the best spies were the ones who didn't even realise they were working for you.

'I think I've got something,' Frost said, now hunched over her computer, her eyes glued to the screen. 'I've accessed the Blacksmith Institute's soil- and air-sample database. It's one of the most boring things I've ever looked at, but if the comparison tool finds something it should return a result within minutes.'

Drake could do nothing but wait as Frost went about her task, her eyes flicking constantly back and forth across the screen while her fingers danced over the keyboard, inputting information, navigating from page to page, scrolling through lists of results. The only time she interrupted her work was to reach for her coffee cup and take a gulp.

'Got it,' she announced at last, leaning back on the couch with a triumphant smile. 'It's a perfect match for soil samples taken around the nickel-smelting plant at Norilsk in Siberia. They even have their own mining operation right next door. Twenty bucks says that's where your explosives came from.'

'Can you access the local police department, bring up a list of recently reported crimes in Norilsk?' McKnight asked.

The technician frowned. 'I think so. Why, what are you looking for?'

She raised an eyebrow. 'Thefts.'

Frost got the idea. Accessing the Norilsk central police database and running its contents through an online translator program, she began to scan the list of recently reported crimes. Such occurrences were often kept available online in case some helpful citizen happened to browse through and spot something that jogged their memory.

'Epic win for us,' she announced. 'Norilsk Nickel reported a theft of explosives from one of their warehouses about two weeks ago.'

McKnight leaned in closer, her expression serious. 'How much?'

'Erm . . .' She scanned the badly translated report. 'About three hundred pounds.'

The older woman took a step back. 'Jesus,' she said quietly. 'That's enough to level a building.'

For Drake, the revelation presented an altogether more sinister conclusion – there were going to be more attacks. Still, they had a lead. A tenuous lead, perhaps, but a lead all the same. The next course of action was obvious.

'If the trail leads to Norilsk, that's where I'm going.'

Why the group responsible for this would have travelled all the way to Siberia for explosives, he had no idea. But like the chess piece and the cryptic message on Demochev, it was somehow part of some larger plan.

'It's not going to be easy,' Frost warned, having called up detailed information on the city. 'Norilsk is a closed city – kind of a hangover from the Cold War. I guess the mining operation is considered highly sensitive. Even people who live there need a special permit to enter or leave. It could take months to get one, which puts you shit out of luck, Ryan.'

Drake let out a breath, for the time being daunted by her revelation. Franklin wouldn't support any kind of covert insertion, and there was no way for him to make his way there legitimately. Without the resources and backing of the Agency, he was little better than a tourist.

'There has to be a way in,' he persisted, unwilling to concede defeat.

Frost spread her hands. 'Unless you're real cosy with someone in the Russian government, I don't see how.'

That notion stirred an idea in him. It was a risky and decidedly unwise idea, but if it paid off then it just might give them what they needed.

He knew of someone in the Russian government well placed to get him access to restricted areas. Someone with a vested interest in catching the people responsible for the attack. Someone with whom he had already established a tentative element of trust.

'There's one person we could try.'

It didn't take McKnight long to see where he was going. 'Ryan, tell me you're not suggesting Miranova.'

'Fine, I won't tell you.'

'She's FSB, for Christ's sake,' she reminded him. 'In case you hadn't noticed, we're hardly top of their friends list right now. Not to mention the fact that you're talking about launching an unauthorised operation into a foreign country, and cosying up to one of our biggest rivals at the same time. How do you think this would look if it got out?'

'I don't care how it looks,' he bit back. 'I care about answers.'

McKnight folded her arms. 'Then here's an answer for you. If you do this, forget about your career; you're putting your life on the line. These people don't play games, even if you do.'

Drake remained for a moment in brooding silence. To go any further, to go against Franklin's wishes and join forces with the FSB, might mean opening a permanent rift between them. It might mean the end of his career entirely.

Yet doing nothing could mean sitting back and watching Anya destroy herself in a war she could never hope to win. She was without doubt one of the most capable and resourceful people he'd ever met, but she was still only one woman. She couldn't take on the whole of the FSB by herself.

And if he lost Anya, he lost his only chance of taking down Marcus Cain and getting his life back. The man might have been held in check by Franklin's threats of exposing some of his past misdeeds, but that would only serve to delay the inevitable. Drake, and those around him, was a thorn in his side that Cain would find a way to remove sooner or later.

Drake's only chance was to get there first, and the only person who could make that happen was Anya. She alone possessed the knowledge to bring down one of the most powerful and dangerous men in the Agency.

'I can't afford to lose her, Sam,' he said at last. 'I have to find her.'

And that was it. Just like that, the decision was made. The line was crossed.

Whether he would come back from it was another matter.

'Then I'm coming with you,' McKnight decided.

Drake shook his head. 'No, you're not.'

He was prepared to stick his neck out on this one, but he wasn't prepared to put the rest of his team at risk – not over something like this. He'd done that too many times already.

For a moment, anger flared in her eyes. 'I'm an explosives

expert, and you're hunting for missing explosives. You need me.'

'I don't need you dead.'

He'd known she would insist on going, and he'd known she would offer a perfectly logical argument to back it up, but that still didn't mean he wanted Samantha there. He especially didn't want her there if his connection to Anya was discovered and the FSB decided to throw him in the same hellhole prison he'd once rescued her from.

'Well, that's handy because I've got no intention of dying.'

'Neither did Keegan,' Drake remarked sadly, thinking of the teammate they'd lost during their mission in Afghanistan several months earlier. His death had left a raw wound on the team, particularly on Drake and Frost.

'That's low, Ryan. Bringing him up like that.' McKnight folded her arms and stared at him, her eyes filled with simmering anger. 'Anyway, you sure there's not another reason?'

'What's that supposed to mean?'

'You want me to draw you a diagram?' she said accusingly. 'It means you've been ducking me ever since I got to DC. If you've got a problem, I want to know about it. Now.'

Drake looked up at her then. 'My problem is that I made it personal in Afghanistan, and I got a good man killed.' He shook his head, willing those memories to subside. 'Never again. This is my risk to take, not yours.'

McKnight stood her ground, undaunted by his refusal. 'Last time I checked, this was an unsanctioned operation. Which means Keira and I aren't specialists, and you're not our team leader. So you can't stop either of us from coming.'

'She's got a point, Ryan,' Frost conceded, looking infuriatingly pleased with herself.

'You stay out of this,' he said, his attention focused on McKnight. Other people might have been unnerved by his

114

penetrating glare, but she didn't flinch for a moment. No way was she going to back down now.

For a moment, the tension in the air between them grew until it became almost palpable, each of them pitted against the other, refusing to give an inch. This was more than just an argument about inclusion in one operation and they both knew it. It was the culmination of months of building frustration and mutual distrust, of disappointment and recrimination.

'We're all involved now, Ryan,' McKnight said at last, her voice calmer and softer now. She knew him well enough to know she couldn't force the issue – she had to persuade him. 'Whether we stay or go, it makes no difference. We've all got swords hanging over our heads, but I think we stand a better chance together. Let us help you. And for Christ's sake, stop punishing yourself for something that wasn't your fault.'

Drake glanced from one to the other, still reluctant to involve them and yet aware that he was both outmanoeuvred and outnumbered. She was right and they both knew it. He did need her help. He needed both of them.

'Fine,' he said at last, practically having to force the word out.

'Fine,' she repeated, satisfied at having won this victory but still looking far from pleased. He had conceded the argument, but nothing had truly been resolved. 'I'll stop off at Langley to pick up my gear.' Heading for the door, she stopped and turned to look at Drake. 'One thing I'll say about you, Ryan. You don't make things easy. For anyone.'

With that, she turned and left, closing the front door a little harder than necessary.

For several seconds, an uncomfortable silence descended on the living room, broken only when Frost rose from the couch. 'That was awesome,' she said with a knowing smirk. 'Let me know when you guys are ready for Round Two.'

'Piss off. If I want advice I'll watch Jeremy Kyle.' Seeing her blank look, he added, 'It's a Brit thing.'

She shrugged. 'So is soccer. Doesn't mean I give a shit.'

Drake didn't have the energy to follow that one up. Anyway, he had more important things to focus on. 'Listen, can you access security-camera footage from here?'

She thought about it a moment. 'I've got remote access to the Agency's network. The download speed will probably be shit, but yeah, I can probably make it work.' She interlocked her fingers and bent them backwards to crack the knuckles. 'What do you want this time?'

'I need to know where Anya went after the sniper attack, but I need you to find out without anyone knowing about it. If this Norilsk lead doesn't pan out, we need a Plan B.'

'Is there a Plan C?' she asked with a dubious look.

'Not unless you want to knock on Cain's door and ask for help.'

'I'll pass.' Frost looked at him, her usual cocky arrogance fading. 'Look, you know I have to ask this. Are you sure this is what you want, Ryan? Even if you find Anya, you really think you can stop her?'

'Nobody can stop her,' Drake admitted. 'But she trusts me, and she might listen to me. Maybe that'll be enough.'

'Yeah, good luck with that.' She sighed and ran a hand through her short black hair, leaving thick strands of it sticking up. 'Okay, fine. I'll see what I can dig up.'

'Thanks.' Rising from the chair, he grabbed his coat, which was still draped over the edge of the couch. 'Help yourself to whatever's in the fridge.'

'You know I will. What are *you* going to do while I'm working my ass off?'

Drake needed people he could rely on, and enough of them to make a viable investigative team, but he knew he couldn't approach any of the other Shepherd specialists through the regular channels. Franklin would shut him down before he'd even made his first phone call.

'We need more manpower,' he decided. 'I'm going recruiting.'

'Anyone I know?' Frost asked.

'Yeah. Agent Off.'

'First name Fuck, by any chance?'

'Got it. By the way, sorry for . . . interrupting you earlier,' he added.

For a moment or two, she actually had the good grace to look embarrassed. He didn't think it was possible to embarrass Keira Frost.

'It's cool,' she said, quickly recovering. 'Anyway, he's still chained to the bed—'

'I didn't hear that,' he called over his shoulder as he made for the door.

Chapter 14

Cole Mason grunted, startled out of sleep by the harsh buzz of his cellphone. He blinked a few times, his eyes slowly adjusting to the darkness around him as his mind snapped awake. In his profession, one learned to sleep light and wake quickly.

The phone carried on ringing and vibrating, moving an inch or so across the hard table surface with each surge. With his head starting to pound as a hangover kicked in, he reached over and snatched it up.

'Yeah?' he mumbled, rubbing the sleep out of his eyes. His throat was dry as sandpaper, and it was reflected in his voice.

'Cole, it's Ryan.'

If the fact that Drake had called at such an early hour wasn't enough to rouse him, the urgency in his friend's voice was more than enough to convince him something was up.

Mason frowned, torn between curiosity and lingering resentment towards the man who had only yesterday killed any hopes he had of resuming his career. 'So what's on your mind?'

'How's the shoulder?'

'It works,' Mason replied, managing to keep from groaning in pain as he sat up and pain blazed outwards from the old injury. 'Why?'

He reached for the plastic bottle of painkillers on his bedside table and emptied a couple into his hand. These weren't the kind you could buy over the counter at the local super-market, but they did the trick. For a long moment he stared at them in the half-light filtering in through the window blinds. Then, with a resigned sigh, he popped them in his mouth and swallowed.

'I might have work for you, if you're up for it.'

'What do you mean, work? You refused to reinstate me. Or have you forgotten? Because I remember it pretty clearly, Ryan.'

Even after half a bottle of Scotch.

He could almost hear Drake wincing at his stinging rebuke. 'It's complicated,' Drake said tersely. 'I'd rather talk about it in person.'

Mason hesitated, unsure what to do. The fact that Drake wasn't willing to discuss the matter over the phone suggested this was some kind of unofficial job, which immediately started alarm bells ringing. He wanted to return to active duty the right way, not taking on shitty unsanctioned work that might land him in jail, or a coffin.

And yet, surveying the cheap, cramped, low-rent apart-ment that was all he could afford on the half pay he'd been forced to subsist on since his injury, he knew one thing for sure – he couldn't carry on living like this.

'Okay, let's talk,' he allowed at last. 'Where are you?'

His response came a moment later with a knock at the front door.

'You've got to be shitting me,' Mason said, killing the phone and swinging his legs over the edge of the bed. He quickly pulled on a pair of jeans and a T-shirt before heading out to greet the unexpected visitor.

Drake was waiting for him in the hallway as he unlatched the door, his coat glistening with rainwater and his hair damp.

119

'A little presumptuous, don't you think?' Mason asked, irked by his arrival.

Drake shrugged. 'What I have to say isn't a conversation for an open line. Anyway, I assumed you'd at least hear me out. You're not *that* much of an arsehole.'

'You'd be surprised,' Mason remarked, though reluctantly he moved aside to let Drake pass. 'Lucky for you I'm in a forgiving mood.'

He'd showered and shaved since the last time they'd met, but there was a drawn and haggard look about Drake that spoke of a long and sleepless night. It gave Mason a faint sense of satisfaction to know that all was not well in the other man's life either.

Drake surveyed the dingy apartment, his expression making it obvious how little he thought of it. And for a moment his eyes rested on the bottle of Scotch on the cheap coffee table in the centre of the room. The top was still undone, and the pungent smell permeated the whole apartment. Then again, it was probably leaking from Mason's pores as well.

'You came all this way to talk to me,' Mason said, easing himself on to the threadbare couch. He made no move to offer Drake a seat. 'Well, let's talk.'

Drake exhaled slowly, marshalling his thoughts for what was clearly going to be a long and difficult explanation. 'It's about Anya,' he began at last.

For the next ten minutes, Mason listened in silence as Drake did his best to outline everything that had happened since they'd parted company yesterday. The anonymous text message requesting to meet, the shots fired from the apartment block, the encounter with Anya and the desperate race to recover Demochev before finding him brutally tortured, and finally the trail that seemed to be leading them deep into Russia.

'That's what we've got so far,' Drake concluded. 'The next step is to approach Miranova and see if she'll cooperate.'

Mason was stunned by everything he'd heard. Never had he imagined the depth of the conflict Drake had become caught up in, or the lengths to which he was willing to go for the woman who had started it.

'So let me see if I've got this straight,' he said, rising from the couch. 'Your plan is to rock up to the front door of the Russian embassy, ring the bell and say, "Hey, remember me?" Then, assuming they even let you speak to this . . . Miranova, and assuming she's dumb enough to agree to help you, you're going to hightail it to some shitty town in the middle of Siberia on the remote chance that you can find the guys who supplied the explosives to blow up that storage locker. Then, assuming you find them, and assuming they know anything that's worth a damn, you're going to use them to track down Anya, make contact with her and get her to stop what she's doing, all under the very noses of the FSB?'

Drake shrugged. 'Like I said, I don't expect it to be easy.'

'It's a clusterfuck just waiting to happen,' Mason cut in. 'If the FSB find out you knew who was behind the sniper attack the whole time, they will *kill you*, Ryan. There won't be any trial or prison sentence for you – you'll disappear for good. That's assuming Anya doesn't kill you first, of course.'

'She won't,' Drake said, with a confidence that seemed entirely unwarranted. 'I'm about the closest thing she has left to a friend.'

'That's beautiful, Ryan,' Mason said with unveiled sarcasm. 'You're going to die for your friend.'

Drake looked at him, his eyes hardened with resolve. 'I've made it this far without getting killed – I've got no intention of starting now. And as for the rest, finding people is what I do. I know I can get her.'

Mason folded his arms, leaning back in his seat as he eyed Drake critically. 'And say you do somehow manage to track her down. What then? What's your endgame?'

'I get her to stop what she's doing before she makes things even worse. At the very least, I can find out why she's doing this.'

Mason wasn't convinced. 'And it never crossed your mind that she doesn't need or want your help?'

At this, he saw the stern resolve waver just a little, saw the long-buried pain that his words had drawn to the surface. 'Anya's a fighter,' Drake said at last. 'She's been betrayed all her life, broken down, forced into a corner . . . and she'll fight back any way she can. It's all she knows. It's the only thing that's kept her alive all this time. But now . . . it's the thing that's going to get her killed. I can't explain it, but I know it. I have to find her, Cole. And I'm asking for your help. I can't make you do it, but I came here because you're one of the few people I still trust.'

Mason sighed, torn between admiration and pity. If Drake was hoping to appeal to his sense of duty and loyalty, it was misplaced. 'If I agree to this – and Christ knows there are plenty of reasons why I shouldn't – what exactly do I get out of it?'

'I can offer you the daily rate for a specialist,' Drake said, clearly unhappy at the tone of Mason's demand. 'Best I can do, I'm afraid.'

Since this operation was off the books, any payments and expenses would have to come out of Drake's own pocket. He was hardly rolling in money, but he had savings that he could if necessary use to finance Mason's services.

Mason smiled, though it was a cynical, ironic smile. 'You're asking me to break the law, disobey orders, take part in an unsanctioned operation and risk my life to help a woman who destroyed my career? If you want all that, you'll have to do better than standard pay, buddy. I don't want your money. I want my life back.'

'How, exactly?' Drake asked, though he had a feeling he knew what was coming.

Rising from the couch, Mason took a step towards Drake. Even injured and diminished as he was, he remained a large and formidable figure. 'When this is over, you're going to bring me in for retesting. You'll make sure I pass the exam, and recommend that I be reinstated to full active status.'

Drake felt his heart sink. He'd suspected Mason wouldn't let this go, but to hear it laid out in such stark, calculating terms was nonetheless far from easy to stomach. What his friend was asking of him was the very thing he'd refused to do yesterday, for very good reasons.

'Consider this job a field trial,' Mason went on, sensing his doubts. 'I screw up, we call it a day. But if I do right by you, in the field where it matters, then I want a second chance. I *deserve* a second chance.'

'If you screw up, there won't be any second chances – for either of us,' Drake said.

Mason eyed him hard. 'Those are my terms. You either accept them, or we have nothing more to say to each other. Your call, Ryan.'

He was trying to play the part of the cold, detached negotiator, but Drake sensed an underlying current of desperation in his friend. This was his chance, perhaps his last chance, to get back in. If he failed, his future would hold little beyond unemployment, incapacity benefits, isolation and bitter reminiscing over what once had been.

For that reason if nothing else, he knew Mason would give everything he had to this operation. And even injured and out of practice, he was still a formidable operative with years of experience to back him up.

And he was the only man Drake could rely on.

'All right,' he finally conceded. 'If you get through this, we'll talk. Deal?'

The older man reached out and shook hands with him.

'Deal.'

Chapter 15

Keira Frost sat back on Drake's couch and rubbed her eyes. They were dry and gritty and unfocused after staring at a screen all morning, yet still she persisted, determined to fulfil the task set out for her.

Her makeshift workstation had gradually expanded to take over much of the living room in the past couple of hours, now encompassing Drake's own laptop whose password encryption she had broken with ease, and even the TV in the corner that was now wired into her own unit to provide a bigger screen area. In the absence of Langley's formidable computer labs, she needed all the resources at her disposal.

It wasn't a desire to impress Drake with her technical prowess that drove her on, but rather a stubborn refusal to admit defeat, particularly to someone like Anya.

In a way, she almost felt relief at the knowledge that she'd been right about Anya since the beginning. From the first time they'd met, Frost's instincts had told her the woman was bad news; a suspicion apparently confirmed when Anya attacked her and tried to take her hostage mere minutes after her escape from the Russian jail. Only prompt intervention on Drake's part had persuaded her to back down.

True to her word, Frost had resumed her painstaking trawl through CCTV camera footage in the area of the sniper attack, trying to discern where Anya had gone after firing those two fatal shots.

Such a task was daunting at the best of times. There were no viable cameras within two blocks of the apartment building – she knew because she'd wasted an hour trying to find one – and nobody knew which direction Anya had gone after the attack. Thus Frost had been forced to randomly search through traffic and security footage in the general vicinity, hoping to get lucky.

Truly it was like looking for a needle in a haystack, only there were thousands of other needles mixed in with it, and the limited technology at her disposal only allowed her to view one at a time.

'I know you're out there somewhere,' she said, reaching for the takeaway pizza box next to her workstation. Two empty cans of Red Bull sat crumpled next to it, pilfered from Drake's fridge. 'There's no fucking way you're getting the better of me.'

She was about to crack open her third when at last she spotted something.

A figure in a dark overcoat striding down a busy street north of the freeway, head down and partially covered by a black hat. A woman. Tall, athletically built. A woman who walked with the confident, ground-covering stride of a soldier, who didn't even look up as a police car sped past on the main road with its lights flashing and sirens wailing.

Frost leaned closer, staring intently at the image as the woman raised her head, finally exposing her face to the camera. Straight away her hand shot out and hit the pause button, capturing a perfect shot of Anya getting into a car.

'Goddamn, I'm good,' she said, slumping back on the couch, flushed with success and relief. Technology, intuition and sheer hard work had triumphed over age and experience.

Now all she had to do was figure out where Anya was heading.

Chapter 16

It was an hour or so before Drake returned to his house with Mason in tow, having delayed to give his friend time to pack some of his gear. He was feeling a mixture of relief and unease at the deal he'd just brokered with Mason. On the one hand he was a step closer to realising his plan of finding Anya, putting a stop to whatever scheme she was involved in, and perhaps saving her life to boot.

On the other hand, he was now all too aware of the consequences of failure.

Frost and McKnight were waiting for him when he entered; the latter having returned from her work at Langley. It was still a little strange to think of them taking over his home while he was away, but he had to admit it was preferable to returning to an empty house. He just hoped they had good news for him.

The younger of the two women recognised Drake's companion immediately, having known her fellow specialist almost as long as Drake had.

'Well, fuck me,' she said, rising from her chair and throwing her arms around him. 'If it isn't the ghost of Christmas past.'

Mason looked almost nostalgic as he returned the gesture with equal enthusiasm. 'It's good to see you again, Keira. I heard you were still working with Ryan.' He flashed a playful grin. 'Can't believe he kept you around this long.'

'We've come close a few times,' Drake said, glancing at her with the long-suffering patience of a schoolteacher eyeing up a troublesome student.

'Ignore Mr Negativity over there,' Frost advised. 'So what the hell are you doing back here? You on the clock again?'

'For now,' Mason said, giving Drake a meaningful look. 'Ryan needed my help. After this, we'll see.'

'How's your shoulder these days?'

Mason's relaxed confidence faltered for a moment, though he quickly recovered. 'A few months of rehab was all I needed. Never felt better in my life.'

The young woman paused. She had seen the fleeting look of anger in his eyes, and seemed poised to question him further when Drake jumped in.

'Cole, this is Samantha McKnight,' he said, gesturing to the other woman who had hung back to let Frost greet her old friend. 'She's an explosives specialist who joined the team a few months ago. Sam, this is Cole Mason.'

Mason shook her hand, adopting a more formal approach for the new addition. 'Looking forward to working with you, Specialist McKnight.'

'Likewise. And do me a favour – call me Sam,' she added, flashing one of her disarming smiles. She too had seen the friction between him and Frost when she mentioned his injury. 'Never was one for formalities.'

Mason relaxed immediately, the brief moment of tension forgotten as his easier manner reasserted itself. 'That makes two of us.'

Drake almost let out a sigh of relief. The last thing he needed was for his hastily assembled team to fall apart during their first meeting.

'I'm afraid that'll have to do as far as introductions go,' he began. 'Now that we have a team of sorts, our next priority is to contact Miranova and get her to cooperate with us.'

After being cleaned up by paramedics and given a short debriefing at Langley, the FSB agent had been returned to her own people, who were no doubt also anxious to hear her account of the attack. With luck, she would still be at the Russian embassy just a few miles away.

'Before you do that, you might want to hear what I've found,' Frost interrupted.

'Hit me.'

'Tempting,' she acknowledged. 'I've got a lead on Anya.'

Drake paused, stopping in his tracks. 'Go on.'

She smiled, knowing she had him. 'It's a long and tedious story, believe me, but the short version is that I was able to find the rental car she escaped from DC in. I traced the licence plate, and found the fake ID she was travelling under. She crossed the border into Canada in the early hours of the morning, then ditched the car at Montreal International. I had to hack their security system—'

'I didn't hear that,' Drake said.

She grinned. 'And I didn't say it. The point is, I had to do a little snooping to find out which flight she'd boarded.'

'And?'

Her grin broadened. 'She's on a transatlantic flight to Moscow.'

Drake was stunned by how much she'd been able to uncover in just a few hours.

'It gets better,' she went on. 'After Moscow, Ms Vorontsova is booked on a connecting flight to Grozny in Chechnya.'

Drake's excitement evaporated.

Chechnya was a country well known to the Agency. A Russian republic that had tried to break away after the dissolution of the Soviet Union, it had twice fought wars of independence against its far larger parent nation, achieving little except widespread destruction and suffering. These days it was a hotbed of racial tension, ethnic nationalism, sporadic fighting and terrorism.

There were an awful lot of Chechens who harboured deep hatred towards the Russian government, many of whom were capable of planning an attack like the one mounted last night.

'Ryan, do you understand what I've just told you?' Frost said. 'I've got reliable intel that Anya is heading for Chechnya, and I'm pretty sure she's not there for a fucking vacation. This could be the build-up to another attack.'

'I hear you,' Drake confirmed, his mind racing. 'Does anyone else know about this?'

'Nobody yet. I was careful to cover my tracks.'

McKnight was quick enough to see the implications. 'Ryan, we know which flight Anya's on, we know what she looks like and what ID she's travelling under – we could have a team standing by in Georgia to intercept her. We could end this thing today.'

And get Anya killed in the process, he thought. He was quite certain she wouldn't surrender willingly, and an armed confrontation in a busy airport wouldn't end well for anyone. And even if they did somehow manage to take her in alive, it would be impossible to do so without Cain finding out.

There it was right in front of him – a simple choice. Give up Anya and perhaps prevent another attack like the one in DC, or do nothing, protect her anonymity and watch as more people died.

Drake could feel his heart beating faster as various possibilities whirled through his mind, none of them good. He knew the right thing, the logical thing, to do was to confess what they'd uncovered and give the FSB everything they had on

Anya. Such a course of action might well save innocent lives.

He knew this was what he was supposed to do. Any case officer worth his salt would have considered Anya compromised by now, and would have burned her long before.

'Ryan, I know this is a shitty position to put you in, but it's your call,' Frost said quietly, sensing his difficulty. 'I'll go with you either way, but if it comes out that we had intel that could have prevented a major terrorist attack, you don't need me to tell you that we're all fucked.'

'Keira, I . . .' He closed his eyes, trying to master the conflicting emotions now vying for dominance within him.

One word from him could put an end to this. Just one word.

It happened almost before he was aware of it.

'No,' he said, shaking his head as if to reaffirm the decision. 'No. I won't do it.'

'Ryan, are you sure this is what you want?' McKnight pressed. 'You make this choice, there's no coming back from it. For any of us.'

Drake swallowed and raised his chin, facing up to the truth of what he was doing. 'I understand. Keira, erase everything you've uncovered so far. No matter what happens, this doesn't come back to you.'

'Fuck off,' she said, making a dismissive gesture. 'If Sam's going all the way with you, you really think I'm going to walk away now?'

Drake sighed, partly through vexation and partly through relief. He knew she wouldn't bend on this one. Trying to change Keira Frost's mind once it was made up was an exercise in futility. And if he was honest, part of him was glad to have her with him.

'Thanks, Keira. For all of this,' he said quietly. 'We wouldn't even have made it this far without you.'

'Stop it, you're embarrassing me,' she said sarcastically, flashing a crooked smile. However, it soon faded as she returned to the more serious matter at hand. 'So what are you going to do now?'

That was a good question. It seemed to him they now had two avenues of investigation: the explosives in Norilsk, and Anya's as-yet-unexplained journey towards Chechnya. The explosives might well yield clues to the group behind this and prevent further attacks, while the Chechen connection would offer a chance of intercepting Anya before she got herself into even more trouble.

Given the scale of the attack, it was clear to him now that Anya was merely one piece of a larger puzzle, and taking down her alone was unlikely to derail whatever plan she was part of. Even he wasn't prepared to sit back and watch innocent people get killed.

Likewise, putting all their resources into finding the man who had supplied explosives to the group might ultimately help them track down those responsible for the attack, but would fail to achieve their main goal of finding Anya before things got even worse.

Two trails, neither of which they could afford to neglect, but which they didn't have the resources to pursue equally.

'I'll follow up the Norilsk lead,' McKnight said, sensing his dilemma. 'I know what I'm looking for, and I think I know how to find it.'

Drake nodded. By her own admission McKnight was the logical choice to investigate the contaminated explosives, but he was relieved that she'd made the decision of her own free will. Norilsk was unlikely to be a picnic for her, but it was infinitely safer than the war-torn country he was planning to venture into. And the woman he was planning to take on.

'Better pack your thermals,' Frost cautioned her. 'I checked the weather report for Norilsk earlier. Right now it's a balmy twenty below zero.'

'Then you'd better do the same,' Drake added. 'You're going too.'

The young woman rounded on him. 'Wait a second. I didn't agree to that shit.'

'We work as a team, remember? Sam needs someone to back her up, and you're the logical choice.'

She eyed him suspiciously. 'Is this a woman thing?'

'It's a common-sense thing. If these people were able to steal explosives from a secure warehouse, they might have falsified records to try to hide the theft, doctored computer inventories, whatever. That sort of thing is your speciality. Either way, I want you around to help out.'

He hadn't said it out loud, but he was very aware of the fact that his own mission to intercept Anya was going to be more dangerous, and require a lot more muscle, than either of the two specialists could provide. Frost and McKnight, despite their obvious skills and expertise, were basically technicians. Drake needed a soldier to back him up.

'So I guess you and I are going to sunny Chechnya,' Mason remarked with a touch of grim humour. 'Better pack the fashionable Kevlar. I hear tourism isn't what it used to be.'

Drake was less concerned about the dangers on the ground. If things worked out as he hoped, they wouldn't have to venture beyond the airport. How exactly he would intercept Anya without Miranova and the rest of the FSB finding out, he wasn't sure. But as with many operations he'd taken part in, he would work out the details once he was there.

'Our goal is to find Anya and put a stop to whatever she's part of,' Drake reminded his friend. 'The rest of it can wait.

What we need is to give Miranova a compelling reason to let us into Chechnya in the first place.'

'It would kinda defeat the purpose if you told her about Anya,' Mason remarked, echoing his thoughts.

Drake chewed his lip. Much as he disliked what he was contemplating, he could think of no other option than to add 'falsifying evidence' to the list of crimes he'd committed over the past twenty-four hours.

'Keira, can you fake an image of our tattooed friend from the lock-up showing him boarding Anya's flight?'

Frost's brows rose at this, and she spent several moments weighing up what he was suggesting. 'Possibly. Might not hold up to detailed scrutiny, but it should be enough to get us in.'

Drake rubbed a hand along his jaw. It was a gamble, but he couldn't think of anything better at that moment. And in the cynical part of his mind, he figured they had already broken enough laws to land them in jail – one more transgression was unlikely to make much difference.

'Do it,' he said at last.

Frost sighed and nodded. 'Normally I'd ask if you're sure you know what you're doing, but I think we both know the answer already.'

Drake said nothing to that. Instead he surveyed the small room, taking in each of the teammates that had agreed to help him, had agreed to put themselves at risk for him. They might each have done it for different reasons, but they were all here, all willing to follow him.

Never had he felt that responsibility more keenly.

'Thank you,' he said, not knowing how else to sum up his thoughts. 'All of you. I know this one isn't exactly on the books, but we work by the same rules as any other job. We go into this as a team, we work as a team and we come home as a team. And nobody puts the rest of the team at risk by trying to be a hero,' he added, giving Mason a brief glance. 'Everyone clear?'

He was met by a round of affirmative nods.

'All right. Then let's have a talk with our Russian friends.'

Chapter 17

Located on Wisconsin Avenue in north-west DC, the embassy of the Russian Federation was only a few miles from Drake's house, and therefore an easy drive on the quiet Saturday-morning roads. The embassy compound itself was dominated by a massive white cube-shaped building that served as the administrative centre of the diplomatic mission here. With luck, Miranova was somewhere inside.

Security was tightened, as was to be expected in the wake of the freeway attack yesterday, with armed guards in Russian army overcoats patrolling the extensive grounds and high perimeter fences.

Pulling to a halt at the main checkpoint, Drake rolled down his window as the duty officer approached. He was a serious-looking customer; mid-forties and heavily built, with the kind of eyes that suggested his career hadn't always consisted of standing guard at diplomatic missions. A quick glance at the licence plates confirmed that Drake was not a Russian official.

'What is your business here?' the officer asked without exchanging pleasantries.

'I'm here to see Anika Miranova. She's an FSB agent involved in the attack yesterday,' Drake explained. 'My name is Ryan Drake. I work for the CIA.'

This prompted a frown. 'You have identification?'

'Of course.' Drake handed over his card, and waited while the officer retreated to the armoured booth that controlled the security gates. He watched as the man radioed the situation in and requested instructions, his facial expression giving nothing away.

Finally he nodded, returned to the car and handed Drake's ID back.

'Bring your car inside and park by the main building,' he instructed. 'An officer will search you and escort you inside.'

'Thank you.'

Following the instructions, Drake found himself in a world of immaculate green lawns, carefully maintained trees and shrubs, and even an elaborate fountain in the courtyard in front of the embassy building. The place was very much emblematic of the new Russia – modern, efficient and above all, conspicuously friendly to Western eyes.

Parking, he killed the engine and stepped out. He'd barely closed his door before he was approached by a younger man in a dark suit. From his crew-cut hair and thick muscular neck, it was clear he was some kind of security officer.

'Please hold your arms outstretched,' he said, speaking perfect English, though his tone made it clear this wasn't a request.

Drake did as commanded, seeing no need to provoke him. A quick and efficient search was soon conducted, during which his wallet, cellphone and car keys were removed, with the promise they would be returned to him when he left the embassy grounds. He wasn't pleased by this, and was glad he'd brought only a prepaid phone with no sensitive information on it, but nonetheless he complied.

Satisfied at last that Drake posed no obvious threat, the agent handed him a blue security badge to pin to his jacket. It was written in both Cyrillic and English: *Visitor – Escorted At All Times*.

'Do not lose this,' he instructed Drake, then gestured towards the main building. 'Follow me, please. I will take you upstairs.'

Drake did as he asked, eager both to find Miranova and to escape the miserable winter weather. She was waiting for him in one of the embassy's conference rooms on the upper floor, his escort explained as he was conducted through the main lobby and up several flights of stairs, the younger man taking the steps with the ease born from strenuous daily exercise.

Even Drake was a little out of breath by the time they halted outside a room on the top floor. The security agent glanced at him, a flicker of amusement in his eyes as he swiped his card through the electronic reader. The doors clicked once as the locks disengaged, and swung inwards to reveal an expansive conference suite.

With thick carpeted floors, a polished wooden conference table surrounded by expensive leather chairs and floor-to-ceiling windows offering a fine view of the city, it was clearly the kind of room reserved for high-level briefings and important visitors. Drake should have felt honoured, but his mind was on other matters at that moment.

The room's only occupant was standing by the reinforced windows, staring pensively out at the buildings of central DC beyond. Hearing the buzz of the door's electronic locks disengaging, she turned to face him. For the first time since he'd met her, Drake took a moment to really look at Miranova.

She was in her mid-to-late thirties, he guessed. No longer young and inexperienced, either as an operative or as a woman, but still with a certain vitality and energy about her that only youth could impart. She was of pale complexion, in stark contrast to the dark, almost black hair that he suspected was dyed. He could see the slightly artificial glint of it in the electric lights overhead.

Her features stopped short of beautiful, at least by classic standards. Her nose was a little too long, her mouth a little too wide, her cheekbones a little too prominent. A thin scar, long since healed and faded to silvery grey, traced its way along her jawline on the left side, suggesting she'd been glassed or knifed at some point. She could have used make-up to conceal it, but hadn't.

And yet despite this, there was something undeniably attractive about her. Perhaps it was that same lack of perfection that made her more human, that somehow made the whole greater than the sum of its parts. Or perhaps it was the unselfconscious manner in which she bore the facial scar, knowing it was nothing to be ashamed of.

In either case, he sensed in Miranova a tough, resourceful and confident personality. The kind of traits Drake normally found appealing.

Like himself, she'd showered and changed into fresh clothes since last night. All in all, her appearance was much improved from the bruised, bloodied and bedraggled figure Drake had first encountered in that dimly lit storage lock-up the previous evening. Still, he was surprised to see her back on duty so soon after an ordeal like that. Clearly she hadn't been exaggerating when she'd said FSB agents were expected to keep going no matter what the circumstances.

'Agent Drake,' she said, looking both surprised and relieved to see him. 'I did not expect to see you again.'

'I didn't expect to be seen,' he said as the door was closed behind him. 'But things have taken a different turn since last night. I came here because I wanted to speak to you face to face.'

She folded her arms, regarding him warily from the other side of the room. 'About what, exactly?'

Drake helped himself to a seat at the conference table,

taking his time about it. He had to play this one cool, had to make Miranova believe he was holding all the cards.

Once he was comfortable, he looked up at her. 'Over the past few hours we've been running our own investigation into the attack,' he said, beginning his gambit. 'I can't go into details yet for obvious reasons, but we've found evidence linking the explosives at the storage lock-up to a mining operation in Norilsk.'

At this, her eyes opened wider. 'In Siberia?'

'That's right. Our working theory is that they were stolen or smuggled from a storage warehouse out there. Finding the person who supplied those explosives might just give us a lead on the group behind the attack. We also have reason to believe at least one of the men behind the attack may have boarded a flight to Chechnya a short time ago. You don't need me to tell you that both of these places are inside Russian sovereign territory. The CIA can't send people in without the permission of your government.'

'Of course you can't.' Apparently her command of English was sufficient to convey her sarcasm.

'All right, let's be honest with each other. Things are . . . delicate between Russia and America after this attack. The last thing the Agency needs right now is to be caught sending covert teams into Russian territory.' He sighed and drummed his fingers on the table, feigning frustration with the politicians who were holding him back from doing what he knew to be right. 'The upshot is, we're stuck. They won't go near this thing, even though we've got credible intelligence to act on.'

Miranova was neither stupid nor naive. It was obvious enough to her where this conversation was leading. 'Correct me if I'm wrong, but you are suggesting a joint investigation, Agent Drake.'

Drake made eye contact with her. 'You're not wrong.'

Miranova said nothing to that, though he could sense her pondering the implications, the difficulties, the dangers and the possible rewards of what he was proposing.

'Look, we have a team standing by and ready to go,' he said. 'They're good people, and I've worked with all of them before. If there's anything at all to be found, they'll find it. All we need is your cooperation. Get us permission to enter Russia, let us do what we do best, and we'll find these men for you.'

'And what would you do with them, if you found them?'

He shrugged. 'Our goal is to see them punished. Who does the punishing doesn't make much difference to us.'

Watching him for a long moment in silence, Miranova walked away from the window, took a chair and sat down opposite him. 'Tell me, Agent Drake, do you speak for the whole of the CIA on this?'

She was testing him, trying to make him sweat. This was where he had to concede something, had to make her think she'd rumbled him. If he tried to present her with a deal that sounded too good to be true, she'd never buy it.

'Like I said, the Agency's not prepared to make a move on this. Not officially, at least. The truth is they'd prefer to distance themselves entirely from this whole mess.'

She cocked an eyebrow. 'And you?'

'It seems to me that stepping back isn't helping anyone. I prefer to act, and I told my bosses as much. They'll support me in the sense that they won't actively stop me, but they also won't officially acknowledge what I'm doing.'

'Unless you succeed.'

He smiled a little. 'Exactly. Then they'll take the credit, so it's win-win for them.' He leaned back in his chair. 'That's the deal I'm offering. Let me and my team in. We'll share

141

our intelligence with you, work to follow up leads, and if we happen to take these men down at the end of it all, they're all yours.'

It seemed like a good deal on the surface, but clearly Miranova was no stranger to such games. 'And what do you get out of this, Agent Drake?' she asked. 'It seems you are offering us much, and asking nothing in return.'

He smiled, playing the part of the ruthlessly ambitious opportunist. 'The Agency might take the credit on the surface, but behind closed doors it'll be a different story. Especially if you make sure they understand how invaluable my help was.'

He saw a knowing look in her eye. Taking risks to advance one's career was apparently not a concept unique to the CIA. Now they were talking the same language.

'I'm offering you my help, Agent Miranova. If I fail, you lose nothing. If I succeed, it'll cost you nothing. You're not likely to get a better deal, but it's your choice.'

For the next few seconds she was silent, her natural caution and pragmatism vying with her desire for vengeance. Then gradually he saw her expression change as one emotion began to gain control. He saw her jaw tighten, saw her chin raised a little, and in that moment he knew that he had her.

'I will make some calls,' she finally said.

Chapter 18

Like all of the secure conference rooms at the Russian embassy, the one now occupied by Drake and Miranova featured a sophisticated communications suite, allowing them to create high-speed encrypted data links to any computer or satellite comms array that was willing to receive them. In this case, that meant setting up a teleconference with the FSB's central office in Moscow. Miranova's job was to convince them that Drake's offer was legitimate and had a reasonable chance of success.

Drake was no expert on the Russian language, but it was obvious from the tone of her voice and the expression on her face that she was dealing with a situation of both gravity and sensitivity.

Still, after several minutes she finally relaxed a little. Cupping a hand over her cellphone, she turned to Drake. 'We are being transferred to the office of Viktor Surovsky, the FSB's director. He wants to speak with us personally,' she explained, seemingly in some doubt as to whether or not that was a good thing. 'They are setting up the satellite link now.'

Sure enough, the big flat-screen television mounted on the wall at the far end of the room flickered into life, displaying a test screen for several seconds while a secure link was established. And then, just like that, Drake found himself staring at the grim, unsmiling face of the FSB's Director of Operations.

Drake knew little of Viktor Surovsky's history beyond the fact that he'd served in the KGB during the Cold War, but he'd seen file photographs of the man and had even watched a couple of videos of him at public events. However, the reality confronting him on the TV screen was quite different from the carefully managed public image.

The first thing that stood out was his age. He couldn't tell if Surovsky's public appearances had been recorded under more forgiving lighting conditions or if he'd been wearing stage make-up, but the face on the video link clearly belonged to a man whose life had been neither short nor easy.

His skin was lined and weathered, pockmarked and sagging visibly under his jaw. His cheeks and eyes were hollow as if he'd lost a lot of weight in a short time, his hair grey and thinning. His lips were compressed into a thin line as he stared back at them, his dark eyes surveying the almost-empty conference room.

'Director Surovsky,' Drake began, feeling as though he had to say something to break the uneasy silence. 'It's an honour to speak with you, sir. I'd like to say how sorry I am for the loss—'

'Spare me your apologies,' Surovsky replied impatiently. 'Apologies will not bring dead men back to life.'

Not one for small talk then, Drake concluded, though he couldn't exactly blame him for being abrupt. With the death of several agents and one of his senior executive officers, Viktor Surovsky's day had hardly got off to a good start.

The old man's piercing gaze switched to Miranova. At least, Drake assumed he was looking at Miranova on his own video feed. The different positions of camera and screen meant that he was staring at a point somewhere over her left shoulder.

What followed was a minute or two of dialogue in Russian,

with Surovsky doing most of the talking and Miranova somehow managing to squeeze in the odd sentence here and there. He couldn't be sure, but Drake got the impression she was slowly starting to win the director round to whatever she was proposing. Her face remained a mask of stoic self-control throughout the discussion. Somehow Drake doubted that emotional outpourings would cut much ice with a man like Surovsky.

Still, with some agreement apparently reached, the old man turned his attention back to Drake, as if he were a tiresome task that had been put off as long as possible. 'Who are you?'

'My name's Ryan Drake, sir. I'm a search-and-rescue specialist with the CIA.' He certainly wasn't going to go into details about the highly classified Shepherd programme with this man. The term 'search-and-rescue' seemed a lot less threatening.

'Agent Miranova tells me you were useful in tracking down Deputy Director Demochev,' he said, with the faintest nod of acknowledgement. 'You have my thanks for this.'

If expression and body language were anything to go by, that was a complete lie. Surovsky's words had no more meaning than if he'd been reading from a teleprompter. Still, it was a gesture of recognition, even if it was a fake one.

'I'm only sorry we couldn't recover him alive,' Drake replied.

'As am I,' the director confirmed, his voice heavy with implied threat. 'Mr Drake, you can assume I was not pleased to learn that one of my best men, along with his protective detail that I sent to *your country* on a peaceful mission, was attacked and killed just minutes after touching down. You can also assume that I want the cowards responsible for this to answer for what they did.'

If Drake had been wearing a tie at that moment, he'd have been sorely tempted to reach up and loosen it. 'We're already pursuing a number of leads, sir.'

'Of course you are.' His contempt was thinly veiled at best. 'But you will pardon me if I don't entrust the entire investigation to the CIA. I have already dispatched an investigative team of my own. Once they land at Andrews Air Force Base I will expect you to turn over to them all information relating to this attack.'

Drake knew right away that such a proposal wasn't going to wash. The idea of allowing a Russian intelligence group free rein to operate in central DC was absurd. The idea of turning the entire investigation over to them was even worse. Surovsky was pushing, seeing how far he would go before he drew the line. He had to bring this man around to his way of thinking, and he had to do it fast.

'You've spoken very candidly, sir. So I'll do the same,' he said, going on the assumption that Surovsky wasn't one for diplomatic bullshit. 'It's no coincidence that this attack was launched on American soil, while your people were on their way to broker a deal between our two agencies. It seems logical to assume at least part of the goal was to split us apart and make us waste time throwing blame around. If we start fighting over who has jurisdiction here, we're giving them exactly what they want.'

'I assume you have an alternative?' the FSB director prompted.

'We've both lost people. We both know the CIA has to conduct its own investigation, regardless of what the FSB does. The question you have to ask yourself is what you want to do now. You want to sit on your hands for the next ten hours while your own team flies here? Fine. You want our two agencies to be working against each other and duplicating

146

each other's efforts? I can't stop you. But it seems to me it would make a lot more sense for us to work together.'

Surovsky said nothing. He just sat there waiting for Drake to go on. At least he hadn't shouted him down, or even worse, killed the video link right away. The older man's lack of objection encouraged him to go on.

'Our evidence trail seems to be leading us back to Russia, and if we follow it quickly then we might have a chance of stopping the group behind this, but we can't do it without you. My proposal is a joint operation, using my investigative team and overseen by Agent Miranova. You'll be kept in the loop on everything we're doing, and you'll have equal access to any intel we recover.' He kept his eyes locked with Surovsky's, trying not to let his nerves show. 'We both want to find the men who did this, so let's go after them together.'

Surovsky leaned back in his chair, surveying Drake for a long moment in thoughtful silence. Drake said nothing further. He'd made his case as best he could; now it was up to the FSB director to decide whether he was prepared to buy what Drake was selling.

'Assuming I agreed to this, I would want your guarantee that if we catch these criminals, they will be remanded to FSB custody,' he said after a long moment.

As far as Drake was concerned, Surovsky could do whatever the hell he wanted with Demochev's killers – he had no sympathy for them. Anya, however, was another matter. No way was he letting this man get his hands on her.

Somehow he had to get to her before the FSB did, had to find a way to reach out to her, to work out why she was involved in this and what she was trying to achieve. And more important than that, he had to stop her before she made the situation even worse.

He had no idea how he was going to accomplish any of

those things at that moment, but he would cross those bridges when he came to them. Right now the priority was getting the FSB on his side, and convincing them he was on theirs.

'You have it,' he said without hesitation.

The FSB director nodded slowly, his expression one of grudging agreement. 'Then I accept your proposal. For now.'

Whatever rush of relief Drake felt was soon dispelled as the FSB director's expression darkened and he leaned forward, staring right into the camera.

'But consider yourself warned. If you withhold information from us, if you try to manipulate this arrangement for your own benefit, or if I or Agent Miranova suspect you are serving another agenda, there will be serious repercussions between our two countries. And for you, Mr Drake. Do I make myself clear?'

It didn't take a genius to see what he was hinting at. If Drake tried to play games with them, they had a game of their own – *How many years must you spend in a gulag before you learn not to play games?*

'You do,' Drake assured him.

Surovsky nodded. 'Agent Miranova, I will expect daily reports from you on this investigation. I also expect to see some tangible progress within forty-eight hours. Good luck.'

Reaching out, he pressed a button to kill the link. The screen went blank, and for several seconds the conference room was silent. It felt like the aftermath of a hurricane; stunned survivors crawling out of their basements to survey the damage.

'Must be a great guy to work for,' Drake remarked.

Miranova gave him a disapproving look. 'Director Surovsky has had much to deal with since yesterday. You should be grateful he even agreed to speak with you.'

Drake didn't feel particularly grateful at that moment.

An awful lot of things had to go right for him to achieve the result he desired. And all it took to ruin everything was for a single thing to go wrong.

Still, they were on their way. They had taken the first step. The next step would lead them to Russia, to Demochev's killers, and hopefully to Anya.

'I'll be grateful when this is over,' he said, meaning every word. 'Now if you'll excuse me, I need to make a few phone calls myself.'

Drake waited until he was outside in the embassy courtyard before firing up his cellphone. It had been returned to him, along with his other possessions, by the security staff at the gate. He wouldn't put it past the FSB to fit a listening device within the phone's casing, though in this case he'd left a 'tell' – a tiny piece of red plastic inside that would fall out the moment anyone opened it.

Satisfied that all was well, he dialled Frost's number. Miranova might have shown a little faith in him, but he doubted the same could be said of her FSB masters.

As he'd expected, Frost picked up right away. 'How's it going?'

'We're in business,' he replied simply.

'Great. Not sure if I should be celebrating or shitting bricks.'

'A little of both, I suspect,' Drake advised. 'Listen, I need something else from you. I need you to do some digging on two people – Viktor Surovsky and Anika Miranova.'

'Ryan, I'm shocked. You telling me you don't trust our Russian comrades?'

Drake glanced over his shoulder. The security agent who had escorted him into the building was watching him through the plate-glass windows of the reception area, his face impassive. 'I don't trust anyone, least of all the FSB.

But if someone's got you by the balls, you want to know if they're going to squeeze.'

'What a lovely image. Okay, I'll see what I can dig up on them.'

'Thanks. Tell the others to meet me at the Russian embassy when you're done. We've got a flight to catch.'

'Can't wait,' she said, her sarcasm obvious.

Part Two

Incursion

Of the thirty-two hostage-takers at Beslan, the majority had been remanded to FSB custody for suspected terrorist activity in the months leading up to the massacre. All were subsequently released without explanation.

Chapter 19

One thing Drake had to commend the FSB on – when it came to getting from place to place, they did it in style. No expense had been spared in the Ilyushin IL-96M executive airliner that had ferried Demochev and his team to DC only the previous day, from the luxury leather seating to the cutting-edge workstations to the fully equipped communications centre just aft of the cockpit. There was even a small drinks bar at the rear of the plane, though Drake had opted to steer clear of it so far. He had enough problems without adding alcohol to the mix.

So far at least, things seemed to be going to plan. Frost had duly produced her doctored image of the tattooed man, choosing one of the passengers on Anya's flight to become their fake suspect. On the face of it they seemed to have a pretty solid case, and Drake's photographic evidence combined with the revelation that another attack could be imminent had been enough to convince Miranova to split the investigation into two subgroups.

Frost and McKnight had duly been dispatched to Norilsk to follow up on the stolen explosives, while Drake and Mason, accompanied by Miranova and several other FSB agents, were en route to Grozny. All things being equal, they expected to land there about an hour ahead of Anya's flight, giving them plenty of time to set their trap.

Drake felt a twinge of sympathy for the innocent man they

had chosen, knowing he was likely to be in for a rough time when the FSB caught up with him. Still, they would hopefully realise their mistake sooner or later and send him on his way. Drake himself would be left with some serious explaining to do; he only hoped he'd accomplished his real mission by the time that happened.

He was disturbed from this dark contemplation when Miranova, seated at a small workstation near the front of the aircraft, beckoned him over. Gripping the headrests to steady himself as they hit some light turbulence, he made his way forwards and sat down opposite her, easing himself into one of the padded leather chairs. Mason joined them a moment or two later.

'I have been going over the deployment plan at Grozny airport. You should familiarise yourselves with it,' she began. 'In addition to myself and the operatives on this flight, we have six agents from our regional bureau situated at various points throughout the arrivals area, ready to move in on my signal. Our best chance to find our target will be in the disembarkation area, where the terminal creates a natural choke point. Once we have a confirmed sighting, we will move in, surround the target and subdue him.'

'And where are we supposed to be in all this?' Drake couldn't help asking.

'The two of you will keep your distance,' she said. 'I do not want either of you directly involved in the takedown. This is to be an FSB-only operation.'

Mason frowned. 'You realise you might learn more by tailing this guy instead of arresting him?'

'My superiors feel it is too dangerous. If we try to follow him then we risk being compromised,' she explained. 'This way we guarantee a prisoner that we can question. Believe me, we will find out everything he knows.'

'And if he doesn't feel like talking?' Mason asked.

Her dark eyes held a dangerous glint. 'We can be very persuasive.'

Drake didn't doubt it. The FSB didn't exactly have a good track record when it came to human-rights abuses. Then again, neither did the CIA. Both sides tacitly recognised that 'coercive interrogation', better known as torture, was a vital weapon in the arsenal. They just preferred not to talk about it.

'I bet you can,' Mason added in a faintly derogatory tone.

Miranova was quick to pick up on it, and cocked her head. 'Do you have a problem with this, Agent Mason?'

'Let's just call it what it is. We're talking about torture here, based on circumstantial evidence at best.' Mason folded his arms and met Miranova's gaze without flinching. 'You know this guy might actually be innocent?'

'Five of my fellow agents are dead, plus a senior director of the FSB. Men with families, children, people who will never see them again. The group responsible didn't have any reservations about what they did, and our evidence suggests they are planning another attack. If one man has to suffer some discomfort to put a stop to this, I can live with it.'

'Is that the official FSB line?'

Miranova snorted with amusement. 'If you are here to lecture me about the evils of our repressive country, maybe you should look to yourself first,' she suggested. 'What exactly do you think happens at Guantanamo Bay, or Abu Ghraib prison, or Parwan in Afghanistan? The CIA's hands are just as bloody as ours, Agent Mason. They are simply better at washing it off.'

This conversation was going nowhere fast, and Drake knew it. Squabbling amongst themselves was exactly what he'd sought to avoid, and he had to fight to hold in check his mounting anger towards Mason. What the fuck was the man doing provoking Miranova?

'Cole, why don't you stretch your legs and grab me a coffee?' he suggested, without looking at the man. He didn't want Mason to see the look in his eyes.

'You want me to help you drink it too?' Mason asked irritably.

'Go now, Cole.'

Mason hesitated a moment, his hostile gaze still on Miranova, then finally seemed to relent. 'Of course,' he said, slowly rising from his chair. 'Not like I've got anything better to do.'

Miranova watched him go, waiting until he was well out of earshot before leaning back in her seat. She had remained thoroughly unruffled throughout the confrontation, as if Mason were no more than a passing irritation to be patiently endured, but Drake could see her relax a little as the man departed.

'Interesting company you keep,' she observed dryly.

'I'm sorry about that,' Drake said, irritated at Mason for causing such needless friction before they were even on the ground. 'He was out of order. It won't happen again.'

'You are not responsible for his thoughts,' she said, dismissing the apology as unnecessary. 'But tell me, is everyone at Langley so prejudiced against us?'

'Can't say I've noticed.'

In truth, the FSB were seen by most as nothing but a different incarnation of the KGB; the enemy from behind the Iron Curtain that had been the Agency's nemesis for decades. Old habits died hard in a place like Langley.

Miranova didn't seem convinced by his words. For a moment, he caught a look of sadness, of disappointment in her dark eyes.

'I don't blame you, you know,' she said.

'For what?'

'For hating us.' She said it so simply, so matter-of-factly, as if it were something that both of them already knew and accepted. 'I understand why you would feel that way. We are different to you, born from different circumstances and serving different needs. Because of that you see us as oppressors, as criminals, as torturers. But the truth is, we are what we need to be. And we do what we need to do to survive, to keep our country safe. The men we face are ruthless and focused on nothing but their final objective. If we expect to defeat them, we must be as they are. We must think as they think.'

'Didn't Friedrich Nietzsche say something about the dangers of fighting monsters?' Drake said, referencing the famous quote describing the dangers of ruthlessly pursuing a goal regardless of the cost. He knew that better than anyone.

He saw a flicker of amusement in her eyes. 'I believe he also said that fear is the mother of morality.'

'I'll take your word for that.' He had pretty much reached the limits of his philosophical knowledge.

'My point is that we can leave no room for fear. Not in ourselves, or those we work with,' she added, with a meaningful glance in Mason's direction.

'He'll see this through,' Drake promised, not sure how confident he felt. Mason certainly wasn't afraid to face danger, but his behaviour so far had been inconsistent at best, and downright insubordinate at worst. Eighteen months of inactivity hadn't just eroded his skills as an operative, but apparently changed his outlook on dealing with others.

'As you say,' Miranova conceded, though she didn't look convinced. 'And you? Do you have the stomach for this, Agent Drake?'

If she had met him five or six years ago, she wouldn't have

asked that question. He had been a very different man back then, fighting a very different kind of war. He wasn't proud of some of the things he'd done as a black operative, but he knew one thing for certain – they had left their mark on him for ever. The lessons he'd learned back then would never leave him.

He noticed a faint smile on Miranova's face as her eyes met his. 'I think I know the answer already,' she said, suddenly intrigued by the man sitting before her. 'Tell me, what is it you said you did for the CIA?'

Drake could feel himself tensing up. 'I find people.'

'But it was not always this way.' It was delivered as a simple statement of fact.

She'd know from his body language that she was right. There was little point in pretending otherwise.

'We've all done things we'd rather leave behind.' His tone was carefully neutral. He was still on edge, and couldn't help wondering how much she really knew about him. 'I imagine it's the same for you.'

Miranova settled back in her seat, satisfied to have her theory validated. She said nothing further, though he was uncomfortably aware that her gaze remained on him, cool and assessing.

'Forgive me,' she said a few moments later. 'Perhaps we could start again, Agent Drake? If we are going to be working together, I would prefer we did it amicably.'

'It's not "Agent".'

She frowned. 'Excuse me?'

'You called me Agent Drake. I'm not an agent – that's not how it works in the CIA,' he explained. 'I'm a case officer.'

'So what should I call you? Case Officer Drake?'

'You could start with Ryan. I never could be arsed with formalities.'

That seemed to suit her. 'Anika,' she said in return.

'Good to meet you, Anika.' He reached over the table and shook her hand; a gesture which she apparently found quite amusing.

'And you, Ryan.'

Deciding to leave while the conversation was on a high, Drake gestured to the galley at the rear of the plane. 'I'd better see how that coffee's doing,' he said, excusing himself.

In truth, he was eager to have a word with Mason. Drake might have managed to salvage something from the earlier disagreement, but that didn't change the fact that Mason had very nearly dropped them both in the shit.

'Hey, buddy,' Mason said nonchalantly as he approached, holding out the coffee he'd just finished making. His earlier anger and belligerence had inexplicably vanished. 'Milk and no sugar, right?'

'What the fuck was that, Cole?' Drake demanded, keeping his voice low to avoid being overheard. Only his eyes betrayed the depth of his anger. 'Do you actually *want* us to fail?'

'It's called running interference,' his friend said, laying the cup down. 'You just scored a touchdown because of me.'

'Do I look like a football fan?'

'Look, I gave you what you both needed – a common enemy. I took a pop at her, you stood up for her, now she trusts you a little more than she did before. She'll be willing to listen to you, and take you at your word. You're welcome, by the way.'

Drake hesitated, briefly daunted by Mason's casual rationale. It was the clichéd good-cop, bad-cop routine employed in movie interrogation scenes.

'You could have warned me,' he said, still angry that Mason had taken such a gamble without bothering to discuss it. 'That could have gone a lot worse.'

Mason shrugged, apparently unconcerned. 'Wouldn't have been authentic then. Anyway, I know you better than that. You're good with people. Especially the ladies, though Christ knows what they see in you. I knew you'd win her round.'

Drake was in no mood for flattery. 'I'm not in the mood for games, Cole.'

'Neither am I. I'm helping you win their trust, and it's working. So relax, would you? You should know me by now.'

He wasn't so sure about that.

'Look, things have changed since we last worked together,' Drake said, forcing calm into his voice. 'You have no idea the kind of danger we live in every day. If you did, then believe me you wouldn't be so eager to get back into the Agency. Either way, next time you have an idea like this, do me a favour – don't do it.'

Just for a moment, Drake saw the same rippling under-current of anger and resentment he'd seen when Frost questioned his injury. It was a mere glimpse, but it was there all the same.

'Fair enough, Ryan. We'll do it your way,' he said, his voice oddly calm. He glanced down at the cup still resting on the shelf beside him. 'Your coffee's getting cold.'

He moved past Drake, heading for his seat.

Drake watched him in brooding silence, wishing he knew what was going on in the man's head. The situation was delicate enough without him rocking the boat.

He was about to rejoin Miranova when his phone went off. It was Frost.

'Yeah, Keira?'

'Can you talk freely?' the young woman began.

Drake glanced over at Miranova, seated on the other side of the conference table. She had been watching the interplay between himself and Mason with some interest, but had now returned to her work.

'Yeah.'

'Good. I've done some digging on your buddy Surovsky. The Agency keeps a detailed dossier on him, so most of my work was done for me.'

'Can you give me the short version?'

'He's not a man to fuck with,' she said simply. 'He's old-school KGB, did a lot of counter-insurgency work back in the eighties, especially in Afghanistan. Apparently he had a reputation for brutality, especially when it came to interrogation. The Agency even gave him the code name Sickle. Anyway, he transitioned into the FSB after the Cold War and went quiet for a few years, mostly moving through different admin positions. It wasn't until 2003 that he popped up again.'

'So what happened?' Drake asked.

'Russia got hit by a bunch of terrorist attacks from Chechen separatists. They blew up an apartment complex in Moscow, downed a couple of airliners and shot up a school in Beslan. Needless to say, the boys in the Kremlin weren't pleased with the FSB. The hardliners in Moscow were demanding action, so Surovsky was shoehorned in as interim leader. He must have done something right, because domestic terrorism was all but wiped out after that. Even organised crime's taken a big hit. And most important, Surovsky's still in power five years later. Not bad for an interim leader, huh?'

Drake could guess that Surovsky's crackdown had been orchestrated with the same brutal efficiency he'd learned in places like Afghanistan. No wonder he'd been so angered by the attack in DC – his reputation had just taken a serious hit.

'He doesn't seem like the sort to step down voluntarily,' Drake agreed. 'What about the other search?'

'Miranova? Not much. She's been with the FSB since the

late nineties, started out working undercover against organised crime – stakeouts, drugs busts, that kind of thing. In 2005 she moved into anti-terrorism. She was a senior advisor to Anton Demochev.'

Drake rubbed his jaw. Russian organised crime had flourished in the wake of the USSR's collapse. Now it was a world unto itself, the brutality and ruthlessness of its rank and file members making the Mafia look like children's entertainers by comparison. Working undercover against such people must have taken nerves of steel.

Miranova had just gone up a little in his estimation.

'Good work, Keira. Thanks.'

'No problem. I've got nothing else to do on this flight,' she admitted. 'Just answer me one thing, Ryan. What's our situation?'

'SNAFU.'

He heard a faint chuckle on the other end. SNAFU – Situation Normal: All Fucked Up. 'Figured as much.'

Chapter 20

Making her way up the shaky and draughty jet bridge towards the main terminal, Samantha McKnight was thoroughly glad to be on solid ground again after the hair-raising descent into Alykel airport. Crosswinds had hammered them all the way, the big aircraft lurching from side to side as the pilots fought for control. Normally a comfortable flyer, she had found herself gripping the armrests tight as they landed with a heavy, shuddering thump, the undercarriage groaning under the strain.

This was turbulence, Siberian style.

They had left Andrews Air Force Base a good hour after Drake and the others had departed for Chechnya, and though Norilsk was much further east, their journey was actually rendered considerably shorter by flying north of the Arctic Circle. Thus they had a head start on the other group, and she intended to use it.

'Christ, I hate flying,' Frost mumbled beside her.

McKnight glanced at her travelling companion. Frost's diminutive frame was bulked out by a thick padded jacket over which she had slung her laptop bag and electronics kit, while her feet were encased in heavy boots that would have made professional mountain climbers jealous. She had woken up only ten minutes earlier. With her eyes still bleary from sleep and her dark hair sticking up at all angles, she looked thoroughly unimpressed with their new surroundings.

'I thought nothing fazed you, Keira.'

Frost gave her a sour look. 'There are only three things in life that I hate. Warm beer, cold weather and bad flying. So far we're two-and-oh.'

McKnight was spared further grumbling when their FSB minder strode back down the jet bridge to join them, having gone on ahead to clear the way for their arrival.

A powerfully built man with a shaved head and a black goatee beard, Stanislav (or Stav as he referred to himself) was there to serve as their official liaison, translator and guide. In reality his job was to keep an eye on both CIA operatives and ensure they didn't do anything they weren't supposed to.

He spoke passable English, and contrary to their expectations of stoic, brooding silence, he'd been happy to use his language skills incessantly on the flight out here. In the past eight hours McKnight had heard his views on everything from the war in Afghanistan to the relative merits of McDonald's versus Burger King. He and Frost had even got into a heated debate on which was the best gun to use in *Modern Warfare*.

'We go this way, my friends,' he said, jerking a thick finger up the jet ramp. 'Stav has taken care of things. No passports, no problems.'

Another thing McKnight had learned about him over the past eight hours – he liked to refer to himself in the third person.

Still, in this case he was telling the truth about there being no problems. His status as an FSB agent allowed the entire group to breeze straight past whatever security checks were in place here, and into the public terminal beyond.

The building was a wonder of 1960s Soviet architecture – a big, square, uncompromising concrete structure that looked as if it hadn't changed since the day it was built. The walls were bare whitewashed stone, with big concrete pillars rising up from the cracked tile floor.

Hot air vents blasted heat from all directions, and there were angry red signs everywhere telling people to have their travel documents ready for inspection. The air was thick with the smell of tobacco and greasy food.

The few people milling around were a sombre-looking bunch, mostly men in their forties and fifties standing in silence, with the grim resignation of condemned prisoners walking the green mile. Everyone looked depressed and pissed off. Not that she could blame them – she was far from pleased to be here herself.

'We have car outside,' Stav said. 'Follow me.'

Without waiting for a reply he turned on his heel and strode towards the main doors on the other side of the concourse, moving with the confidence of a man used to owning any situation he's in.

The cold air struck McKnight's exposed face as soon as the automatic doors shuddered open. A frigid wind was blowing in from the north, picking up scraps of old newspaper, empty crisp packets and other small bits of trash scattered around, and carrying with it occasional wisps of dry frozen snow. The sky overhead was completely black, the few working street lights rendering the muddy, oil-stained car park even more grim and depressing.

'Jesus, what a shithole,' Frost whispered, echoing her thoughts.

As if to emphasise her point, another frozen blast of air whipped against them, seeming to penetrate right through the heavy layers they both wore. Suddenly the blustery wind and sleet in DC didn't seem nearly so bad.

She glanced at their chaperone. 'What time is it, Stav?'

He glanced at his watch and did some quick calculations

in his head, no doubt trying to account for the time zones they'd crossed. 'Three-twenty in morning.'

'What time's sunrise?' Frost asked.

He grinned at her. 'February.'

McKnight couldn't hide a faint smile of amusement. This far north of the Arctic Circle, the darkness of the polar night was constant and absolute. It would be several weeks before Norilsk even saw the sun again.

'You said there was a car for us,' she reminded him, eager to get down to business.

As if on cue, a big silver Mercedes M-Class cruised in from the other side of the terminal building and slid to a stop in front of them, chained tyres rumbling on the potholed road. Its paintwork was caked with frozen mud and ice, the twin exhausts billowing steam.

Never had a vehicle looked so out of keeping with its surroundings.

The driver's door flew open and a giant of a man emerged. He was a serious-looking guy, easily 6 foot 4 and built like two brick shithouses stacked on top of each other. His neck was as thick as the average man's thigh, his dark hair shaved into a brutal flat-top.

He'd been squeezed into a grey business suit for the occasion, but it was obvious he was more of a jeans-and-jacket man. Saying nothing, he thrust out one huge hand, obviously waiting for the new arrivals to hand over their bags.

Frost merely shook her head, clutching her laptop bag a little tighter. As much as a good soldier never allowed his weapon to be more than an arm's length away, so she refused to be parted from the tools of her trade. She might have been half his size, but the hostility in her eyes was unmistakable.

Stav said something in Russian to the giant, perhaps sensing her mood and thinking it best to avoid confrontation. The giant shrugged, not caring one way or the other, and returned to the driver's seat, the suspension sagging noticeably under his weight.

'Okay, no problem,' Stav said, clapping his gloved hands together. 'We go.'

With the matter apparently decided, the small group piled in – Frost and McKnight in the back, Stav up front with the driver. As the doors slammed shut, the relief was instantaneous. The frozen, litter-strewn car park seemed a distant memory – now they were in a world of crisp leather, gleaming consoles and walnut dashboards. Without saying a word, the driver gunned the engine and off they went in a spray of snow and exhaust fumes.

The airport was about 30 kilometres west of Norilsk itself, forcing them to take the scenic route to reach the town. Though perhaps 'scenic' was the wrong word. The landscape they were passing through made the Somme battlefield look lush and verdant by comparison.

The winds that whipped across the open steppes must have been absolutely brutal, scouring and flattening anything that dared to grow more than a few feet tall. This was Arctic tundra, some of the coldest and most inhospitable territory on earth.

Trees grew in the more sheltered spots, or *had* grown once upon a time. Today they were little more than tortured, leafless skeletons, acid rain from the smelting complexes having long since killed them off. Even the snow on the lifeless fields was dirty grey.

At one point they passed the remains of a massive factory or warehouse about 100 yards from the road. McKnight had no idea as to its original purpose, but all that remained now was the metal framework, standing like the mighty skeleton of some long-extinct animal.

Everything here looked faded, grey and decayed. Despite the warmth and comfort of the vehicle they were travelling in, she couldn't quite suppress a shiver as another blast of icy, filthy rain slammed into the windscreen.

'Mind if I ask you something?' Frost said, stirring her out of her thoughts.

There was something strangely comical about the way the fiery and temperamental specialist was sitting in the big leather expanse of the rear seat, with her jacket puffed up and her equipment bags piled all around. She looked like a reluctant child on a boring family day out.

Without waiting for a response, she immediately launched into her question. 'What was all that shit between you and Ryan earlier?'

McKnight felt herself tense up. She shrugged, trying to appear nonchalant. 'I had a few things I've wanted to say to him for a while now. I guess that seemed like the right time.'

'You mean you were pissed at him for shutting you out?'

McKnight gave her a sidelong glance, saying nothing.

At this, the young woman chuckled and shook her head. 'Jesus, it's like being in high school again. Fucking hormones flying around all over the place.'

'I'm glad you find all this so amusing,' McKnight said, torn between irritation and curiosity at her reaction. 'I gave up a lot to be part of this team. Now I'm starting to wonder if it was worth it.'

Sighing, Frost looked at her frankly, a twinkle of amusement still in her eye. 'You think he's giving you the cold shoulder, huh?'

'I'm just calling it like I see it. I've barely seen him since I moved to DC. He's done everything in his power to avoid taking me into the field. Hell, I had to practically twist his arm just to be part of this job.'

'Sam, for a smart woman you can be frighteningly dumb at times.' Frost's annoyingly smug smile was still there. 'Let me tell you something about Ryan. He's an asshole.'

The blunt, matter-of-fact way she said it caught McKnight off guard, and she actually laughed for a moment. 'Thanks for that insight.'

'I'm serious,' Frost persisted. 'He's overbearing, socially dysfunctional, a workaholic and a control freak. And most important, he's overprotective of people he cares about.'

What she was saying made little sense to McKnight. 'So he pushes me away, shuts me out and generally treats me like a piece of shit, all because he cares about me?'

The younger woman shrugged. 'I said he was dysfunctional, didn't I? And he's a guy, which means he can't deal with all that emotional-attachment shit. Instead he just runs away from it. Which in this case means running away from you.'

McKnight hesitated. On the face of it, Frost's assessment seemed ridiculous. And yet even she had to admit it did fit with Drake's behaviour, however bizarre it seemed.

'But he cares about you too,' she protested. 'And he never hesitates to take you into the field. What's the difference?'

Again she saw that crooked grin. 'Because he knows I'd break his arms if he tried that shit with me. Maybe you should do the same thing.'

McKnight made a face. 'Not that I haven't been tempted . . .'

'I'm serious,' Frost persisted. 'Ryan's got no time for people who won't stand up for themselves. Keep that in mind.'

The next twenty minutes or so passed mostly in silence as the Merc bumped and skidded along the slush-covered, potholed highway, trying to avoid the spray from rust-encrusted haulage trucks as they roared past. Even Stav was quiet, perhaps sensing the atmosphere in the back seat.

Then, at last, they caught a glimpse of their destination.

The first signs were the great plumes of steam rising up into the darkened sky, accompanied by a fiery orange glow reflecting off the low-lying clouds as if from some immense volcano smouldering away beneath.

McKnight was finally confronted with the full might of the Russian industrial centre cresting a low hill, almost a city in itself. The glow of furnaces was visible within the monstrous square buildings, conveyor belts and machinery running without pause, chimneys belching smoke and steam. The whole smelting complex was surrounded by immense slag heaps, almost mountains in themselves.

If she'd been asked to describe a vision of hell on earth, she doubted she could have come up with a better example than this place.

Just west of this industrial nightmare was the dingy grey town of Norilsk. Even from this distance she could see the towering apartment blocks glowing like beacons in the gloom, though the light appeared hazy and indistinct. Smog from the factories and smelting works, still running at full capacity despite the early hour, lingered over the city like a blanket.

'Wow,' Frost breathed, awed by the sight.

'I've seen pictures of Norilsk online,' McKnight said as she watched the vast pillars of glowing smoke. 'Don't do the place justice.'

Up front, Stav twisted around in his seat. He'd seen the same things they had seen, but through different eyes. 'It is cool, yes? The factories provide many jobs here. People come to work for a while, then move on.'

She got the picture. Norilsk's population was one of transient workers. They would stay for a few years, enduring the appalling conditions while slowly amassing a small fortune in the refineries, then leave for more pleasant climes.

Which was just about anywhere.

'How far to the smelting works?' she asked.

Stav exchanged a few words with the driver. 'Five, ten minutes. But we have office at Norilsk police station. We set up there first, yes?'

She shook her head. Setting up a base of operations could wait. Getting answers was her goal right now.

'Just get us to that refinery.'

The sooner they completed their mission and got the hell out of here, the better.

Chapter 21

Grozny, Chechnya

Drake recalled reading once that Grozny was the city most heavily bombed and shelled since the Second World War, and if the view from his window was anything to go by as they descended towards Grozny airport, he believed it. Even from 5,000 feet it was a mess of bombed-out buildings, big areas of waste ground where damaged structures had been bulldozed and never replaced, and shell craters that nobody had bothered to fill in.

The weather was lousy as the big aircraft lumbered in to land, with heavy rain showers and blustery squalls buffeting them all the way. Drake could hear the creak and groan of the airframe as the pilots fought to keep their heading, the engines occasionally whining with increased power.

After what seemed like an age the wheels finally made contact with the ground. They landed hard, bumping and rumbling on the rough concrete runway.

'Give me a flight to LAX any day,' Mason remarked beside him.

Drake wasn't inclined to argue as they taxied towards the main terminal.

Reconstructed by the Russian army after being shelled into submission a decade earlier, Grozny airport served as a transport hub for both military and civilian aircraft in the region. It hadn't yet opened to international routes, but it did

172

handle domestic traffic from several Russian cities, which was probably why Anya had first flown to Moscow before taking a connecting flight.

In their case, however, the FSB jet was heading for a separate terminal reserved for military usage. In short order they had taxied to a halt, a set of stairs were connected and the outer hatch was hauled open. Eager to be off the aircraft that had been his home for the past eight hours, Drake virtually sprang from his seat, with Mason close behind.

Outside, a storm of heavy rain greeted them, lashing the tarmac and drumming against the aircraft's fuselage like the pounding of hammers. Dark grey rain clouds hung low over the airport, promising that there was plenty more to come.

'They ever have sunshine in this fucking country?' Mason asked, surveying the rain-soaked runways with distaste. The last time the two of them had ventured into Russia together, they had had to contend with sub-zero temperatures and snowstorms.

'Let's go,' Miranova said, leading the team down the stairs.

The tarmac beneath their feet was rough and uneven, and patched with newer material in places. Judging by the pattern of repair work, Drake was willing to bet a cluster bomb had been dropped in this area during the Chechen War. It reminded him of the buildings in Berlin: old shell and bullet holes covered over with cement, the battle damage repaired but never quite erased.

Miranova led them straight towards the terminal building, which was a new three-storey structure with concrete blast barriers and armoured glass everywhere. A group of big satellite uplink dishes on the roof loomed over them.

Clearly this was more than just an airport terminal, Drake realised as he approached. He suspected it was some kind of regional headquarters building, either for military intelligence or for the FSB themselves. Having their headquarters at an airport made sense if they wanted to quickly and unobtrusively move personnel or other assets into the country.

The appearance of a smartly dressed man flanked by a pair of armed agents behind a set of glass doors up ahead only furthered his theory, and Drake kept his eyes on the man as they approached.

He was of average height, neither tall nor short, and just starting to develop middle-aged spread, judging by the tighter buttoning around his waist. Drake guessed him to be in his fifties, his features rugged and characteristically Slavic: wide and rounded face, high cheekbones and a long downturned nose that seemed to push his lips into a disapproving pout.

One of the agents beside him held the door open for Miranova and the others as they hurried inside, all eager to escape the wind and driving rain.

The reception area beyond was very much representative of the building's exterior – modern, refined and expensive. The floor was polished marble, mirror smooth and clean, making Drake feel oddly uncomfortable as he clicked and squeaked his way across the open space, leaving muddy footprints in his wake.

Drake's mind wasn't on the decor at that moment, however. His attention was focused on the sharp-suited man as he strode forwards and perfunctorily shook hands with Miranova. There were no cordial smiles from this guy – he was all business.

A few words were exchanged in Russian, with Miranova doing most of the talking. Judging by her deferential body language, she was very much subordinate to this man.

Having apparently been briefed to his satisfaction, his attention turned to Drake, his pale grey eyes shrewd and assessing as he surveyed the younger man.

Miranova handled the introductions. 'Ryan, this is Ivan Masalsky, regional director of FSB activities in Chechnya.'

His suspicions had been proven right. Masalsky was the FSB's top man in Chechnya, responsible for keeping a lid on the simmering melting pot of racial tension, infighting and attempted terrorism that much of the country had become. Drake certainly didn't envy his job.

'Director Masalsky, this is—'

'You are the CIA agent leading the investigation into Anton Demochev's murder,' Masalsky interrupted, forgoing any actual greeting. His English was about on par with Miranova's, which was to say it was excellent. 'Ryan Drake.'

Drake nodded, hoping he looked less apprehensive than he felt. 'That's right.'

'I understand you have been tracking one of the suspects.' It was phrased less as a question and more as a challenge.

'We think so, sir. We'll know more when his flight lands.'

There was no point in guaranteeing something that wasn't going to happen. By being non-committal at this stage, Drake was hoping to let him down gently when the time came.

'You think so?' Clearly he was neither impressed nor shy about letting Drake know it. 'We are about to shut down a major airport based solely on your evidence, Mr Drake. I would hate to think it was all a false alarm.'

'So would I, sir,' Drake said, deciding to play the wounded-pride card. 'I flew five and a half thousand miles to get here in time for this.'

Sensing the tension between the two men, Miranova jumped in. 'The flight will be landing shortly, sir. We need to be in position when it does.'

Masalsky grunted something that might have been grudging acceptance or disgust – Drake couldn't tell which.

'Then you had better come with me,' he said. Without waiting for a reply, he turned and strode off down a corridor leading deeper into the building.

'I see you're working your usual magic,' Mason remarked with a wry smile. Thus far he had managed to stay out of the discussion, and therefore Masalsky's line of fire.

'Fuck it,' Drake decided in lieu of a more rational course of action. 'We're here now. Let's just get it done.'

'Great plan. You worked out what you're going to do if you see her?'

He'd thought about almost nothing else on the flight out here. Indeed, it was during the flight that a possible solution had first come to mind. It certainly wasn't a foolproof plan, and it would involve Mason sticking his neck out more than he would have liked, but it was the only one that had come to mind.

'I'll need you to run interference for me again,' Drake said quietly as they hurried to catch up with Masalsky. 'If you catch my drift.'

The look on Mason's face told him that he did.

Chapter 22

If McKnight had thought the smelting complex daunting when viewed from a distance, it was even more so now that she was inside one of the main buildings. The place was truly immense, reminding her of old WW2 pictures of town-sized Soviet factories churning out munitions night and day.

Situated in an overseer's office three floors up, she was able to look out on the vast operation as if it were a huge model laid out before her. Smelting furnaces glowed with intense heat, conveyor belts moved constantly, bringing in unrefined ore to be melted down, while machines worked to crush and compact and sort it all. Loaders and forklifts rumbled back and forth, their exhausts venting diesel fumes. Steam and smoke shrouded the entire area, rising to the vaulted ceiling high overhead to form ominously glowing clouds.

The men whose job it was to keep the vast operation running seemed tiny by comparison. Small, dirty, forlorn figures moved amongst the endlessly toiling machines, virtually hidden by the smoke and exhaust gases.

Dragging her eyes away from the industrial nightmare beyond the windows of the small office, she turned her attention back to the man sitting opposite. An overseer of the mining and smelting operation, he was one of the more senior managers on hand when she had arrived with her FSB escort. He was also the one who had filed the police report on the missing explosives, which made him an ideal point of contact.

He was a small, thin man with greasy dark hair and a thick moustache that made him look a lot older than he was. His face was lean and angular, his complexion darkened as if the airborne dirt had somehow become part of him. Most workers spent three or four years here before moving on, but this man must have been around a lot longer to have risen to his current position.

'You said the explosives went missing from your storage warehouse here,' she began, going over his official statement. 'I assume there's no other way they could have stolen it.'

'We always have some in the mine itself for blasting, but most of it is kept under lock and key,' Stav said, acting as interpreter for both parties.

He might have been jovial and garrulous on the flight out here, but it was a different story now they were on site. Stav had his game face on as he stood blocking the door to the small office, dark eyes watching the shift manager like a hawk, his broad rugged face immobile as if carved from granite. He'd explained to her in advance that he'd act only as an interpreter, saying nothing in between for maximum intimidation. Judging by the way the manager's eyes kept flicking towards him, it was working.

'And the warehouse has security guards?' she continued.

He nodded, throwing an anxious glance at Stav. 'Of course. We questioned all of them, and so did the police. None of them saw or heard anything suspicious.'

McKnight frowned. They could question the guards again, and with Stav on board they might well learn more, but she wanted to consider other possibilities first. 'Who's responsible for moving explosives from the warehouse to the mine?'

'Whichever foreman is on duty for that shift. They have to sign for everything they take. There are three of them in total, plus their assistants.'

'Could one of the foremen have requested the explosives and then offloaded them on the way to the mine?'

His thick brows drew together. 'He would have to falsify the log afterwards to cover his tracks.'

'But it's possible?' she pressed.

Swallowing, he looked at Stav again, then nodded.

She was getting somewhere. Now she had to narrow down her list of suspects. 'Do you know if any of the foremen are from Chechnya?'

The flash of recognition in his eyes told her he did. 'I am not comfortable with these questions.'

McKnight glanced at Stav for a moment before going on. 'Maybe not, but I need you to answer. Lives could depend on it.'

She suspected Stav had added 'including yours' or something similar to the end of her translation, because the colour seemed to drain from the overseer's face.

A hard, unblinking look from Stav was enough to demolish whatever remaining reticence or loyalty he might have felt. Coughing uncomfortably, the overseer turned to his computer and set to work, calling up several personnel files. It took a minute or two to compare their records, not helped by his apprehension as Stav moved in close to watch what he was doing, but soon enough McKnight had her answer.

'I am not responsible for hiring the foremen,' he hastened to remind them. 'But one of them has family in Chechnya. His name is Borz Umarov.'

McKnight folded her arms, giving Stav a look of gratitude before resuming her interrogation. 'We need to speak to him.'

'He is on shift today,' the manager said. 'I can summon him here . . .'

'No need,' McKnight cut in. 'We'll go to him.'

Chapter 23

Grozny, Chechnya

The civilian terminal at Grozny airport was about as far removed from the sleek, modern and efficient FSB building as it was possible to be. With walls stripped down to the bare concrete beneath, cracked tiled floors and cheap lighting overhead, it reminded Drake more of an underground car park than an airport.

Still, it was obviously a work in progress. Scaffolding had been erected here and there, on which electricians and carpenters clambered like very slow worker ants. Some had removed whole sections of the false ceiling to fit new cabling and heating ducts, while others were repainting walls and patching over damaged sections of concrete.

For what felt like the hundredth time, Drake glanced up at the arrivals board overhead to confirm the ETA of Anya's flight from Moscow. Ten minutes out.

Right now it would be on final approach.

'Would you stop looking up at that thing,' Mason said, taking a sip of his beer.

Drake looked over at his companion. Normally drinking on the job was a big no-no in their line of work, but considering what Drake might need him to do in the next few minutes, he supposed a little Dutch courage wasn't unwarranted.

'It's an airport,' Drake replied quietly, not wishing to draw too much attention to the fact that he was speaking English.

There weren't many non-Russians in this neck of the woods. 'People look at arrivals boards.'

The two of them were seated at the edge of the arrivals area in a small bar, café and restaurant all rolled into one. It was a lively place that sold everything from Shashlik kebabs to cheeseburgers, with some kind of bizarre Russian folk-pop combination blaring from speakers overhead.

'I know. It's just irritating, that's all,' Mason explained, taking another drink. 'Oh, and for the record I think your plan sucks.'

Drake couldn't blame him. All eyes were on them at that moment, Masalsky having seen to it that every surveillance camera in the airport was now under FSB control. Nearly a dozen agents were spread out across the arrivals lounge, all waiting for the same thing as Drake and Mason.

Well, almost the same thing. The difference was that the target they had been given didn't exist. On the other hand, the woman Drake had come all this way to find was very real. The difficult part was going to be getting to her without every man and his dog realising what he was up to.

If he spotted Anya amongst the disembarking passengers, he was going to need Mason to draw attention away from him while he made contact. And the only way to do that was to fake a sighting of their target.

It certainly wasn't going to win them any friends amongst the FSB, but with luck it would buy Drake enough time to get close to Anya. He'd pretend to bump into her as he pushed his way towards the ruckus created by Mason, and with luck he'd be able to slip her a little piece of paper advising her in no uncertain terms to call his cellphone if she wanted to be alive tomorrow. She would be unarmed in the airport, and perhaps more inclined to listen to him if she thought he might call in the big guns of the FSB.

As for what he would say to her when the call came, he didn't know.

'Answer me one thing, Ryan,' Mason went on. 'You ever ask yourself if this is all worth it? If she'd do the same thing for you?'

'She's already risked her life for me, more than once,' Drake said, keeping his eyes on the board. In Afghanistan just a few months earlier, at great risk to herself, she had infiltrated a heavily guarded compound to stop the man intent on killing Drake and his team.

'Very noble. But you know, somehow I can't imagine her taking a bullet for *me*.' A pause, probing, demanding. 'What do you think about that, Ryan?'

Drake could feel the tension growing within him, just as he felt Mason's eyes boring into the side of his head. Mason's injury had happened during the mission to rescue Anya from a Russian jail, so it was perhaps inevitable that some of his resentment and bitterness was directed towards her.

'I think you need to get your game face on, mate,' he replied tersely. 'Remember why we're here.'

'I know why I'm here, Ryan.'

Mercifully, Drake was spared further barbed remarks when his concealed radio earpiece crackled with an incoming transmission.

'Ryan, it is Anika.' Miranova's voice sounded tinny and hollow through the little speaker. 'Acknowledge.'

She was posted in the building's security centre alongside Masalsky and several other FSB staff, their eyes no doubt glued to the feeds from countless security cameras located throughout the airport; all searching for anything out of the ordinary.

The transmit button was hidden inside the cuff of his jacket. Reaching over, Drake gently pressed it. 'Go.'

'We just had confirmation from air traffic control. The plane is on approach now. Five minutes.'

He felt his heart start to beat faster, though he managed to keep his voice calm as he spoke his reply. 'Copy that.'

Five minutes.

In five minutes he would risk his career, his freedom, even his life, for a woman who might or might not be willing to listen to him. Who might or might not try to kill him if he got in her way.

Mason had asked him if this was all worth it. Soon enough he would know.

Anya was uncharacteristically tense and agitated as the aircraft ploughed through low-altitude turbulence, grey clouds whipping by the window at hundreds of miles an hour, just inches from her face. The pilots had given them the weather forecast as they started their descent – low cloud, rain and gusty wind.

She was no stranger to adverse weather, but she preferred to endure it on the ground, standing on her own two feet. Not hurtling through the sky and being thrown around inside this oversized tin can.

Her only consolation was that, according to her seat-mounted TV screen, they were less than five minutes out from their destination.

In five minutes she would be on the ground. It couldn't come soon enough.

The seconds seemed to tick by with agonising slowness as Drake sat at his table with bad music blaring from the cheap speakers overhead, all his attention now focused on the corridor at the far end of the arrivals lounge. At any moment the automatic doors would shudder open and the first groups of passengers would start to appear.

184

Once again his radio crackled into life. 'The plane is at the gate. They will start disembarking now,' Miranova said. 'Stand by.'

'Copy that,' Drake replied.

He looked over at Mason. His friend, his former teammate, once one of the best specialists he knew. Now a desperate man with suspect motives, a worryingly insubordinate streak and 18 months' worth of pent-up resentment to contend with. For better or worse, he was the only person within 1,000 miles that Drake could trust.

'Ready?'

The older man nodded, his eyes now clear and focused. The experienced Shepherd operative ready to go into action once more.

The only question was what would happen next.

As soon as she was out through the doorway and clear of the plane, Anya quickened her pace, eager to escape the slow, death-like procession of weary travellers trudging up the jet bridge. She had places to be, and the one place she didn't want to be was right here.

Her only belongings were stuffed inside a small canvas satchel slung over one shoulder. She had no luggage to collect, allowing her to breeze straight through baggage reclaim while her fellow travellers dawdled and waited for the conveyor belts to disgorge their suitcases.

Anya always travelled light these days, ready to leave wherever she was staying at a moment's notice, and rarely carrying anything that couldn't be easily replaced. Even the contents of her satchel could be dumped without causing any real problems. She had committed any important phone numbers, names, locations and other operational details to memory as a precaution.

She was a ghost, existing for most people only as long as she was within their line of sight, and vanishing again when they parted.

She supposed it had been that way for most of her life. She had never been inclined towards sentimentality, never desired mementos or keepsakes to mark the things she had done. It was just as well, because her world had been turned upside down so many times that she now possessed almost nothing of the life she'd been born into.

No evidence of the person she'd once been, and could have become.

Passport control was another hurdle easily overcome, the bored-looking customs officer giving her only a cursory glance before swiping her fake passport through the electronic reader. Passports were becoming more sophisticated these days and therefore harder to forge, but there were still a few people with the skill and the resources to produce reliable forgeries. And Anya knew most of them.

With her documents returned, Anya adjusted the satchel on her shoulder, tucked her passport into the front pocket of her jeans where no one could get to it without her knowing, and strode eagerly towards the arrivals lounge.

'This is it,' Drake hissed as the automatic doors shuddered open and the first crowd of passengers emerged into the arrivals lounge. Few were moving with any great speed or urgency, not that he could blame them. If he called Chechnya home, he wouldn't exactly be excited to be back.

Nonetheless, he was thankful for the relatively slow pace as his eyes darted from face to face, desperately seeking the one he needed. Anya was no stranger to disguises, and he expected her to have altered her appearance, but he was sure he would recognise her. There were some things that went far deeper than superficial looks.

'You see her?' Mason whispered, scanning the new arrivals. He too had encountered Anya during her rescue the previous year, though it had been brief to say the least. Drake had little faith in Mason's ability to spot her, disguised or not.

In any case, he wasn't going to waste time talking now. All his attention was focused on the passengers making their way out through the automatic doors, some in groups, others as couples and some travelling alone. Each one was rapidly analysed, compared with the memory of the woman he knew, and discarded.

On some level he was aware that his intense stare would catch the attention of anyone looking his way, but he couldn't help himself. This might be his one chance to find Anya before things escalated out of control. It had to work.

His radio crackled. 'We see nothing yet,' Miranova reported, her voice showing the strain for the first time. 'Anything at your end, Ryan?'

Keeping his eyes glued to the crowds, Drake reached down, felt around and pressed his transmit button. 'Nothing yet. Stand by.'

'Copy that.'

He could feel his heart hammering in his chest. His mouth was dry, his palms coated with a faint sheen of sweat. The thump of the bad music in the overhead speakers was matched by the pounding of his pulse as his silent, strained vigil continued.

An old man and woman holding hands, neither of them the right height or age for Anya. No good.

Behind them, a middle-aged woman with long greying hair, overweight and matronly. Move on.

Then he spotted her.

Partially hidden behind a group of men in expensive but unfashionably cut suits was a tall slender woman with blonde hair, dressed in a dark coat and jeans. The same sort of coat he'd seen Anya wearing in DC. She walked with the long, purposeful strides of one used to exercise and exertion, and who was in a hurry to get somewhere.

'Look sharp, mate,' he whispered, tensing up, preparing to move. 'Behind the three businessmen. Dark overcoat.'

'I see her,' Mason confirmed. 'You got positive ID?'

Drake peered closer, trying to get a proper look. One of the businessmen, taller than his two companions, was partly blocking Drake's view. Her head was turned down, either because she was absorbed in something or because she was trying to avoid being spotted on security cameras. Either way, strands of blonde hair had fallen in front of her face.

'Almost,' he hissed, eyes locked on her as she strode towards them, sidestepping the slower businessmen. 'Stand by.'

Slowly he eased his chair back from the table. He didn't want anything getting in his way when he went for her. It had to be perfect.

In his mind he imagined Mason barking into his radio that he'd spotted the target, jumping up from his seat and rushing towards some unsuspecting traveller while the rest of the undercover FSB agents scrambled to get there first. At the same moment, and with everyone's attention focused on the spectacle of armed officials tackling a man to the ground, Drake imagined himself moving in on Anya.

She wouldn't be panicking at that moment. He couldn't imagine her ever panicking. But she would have gone into survival mode, her keen mind quickly assessing the situation and the threats facing her before deciding on a course of action. Whether that course of action involved trying to slip unobtrusively away or killing anyone in her path, only time would tell.

But she would see him long before he reached her – of that much he was certain. She was always aware of her surroundings, and she knew him well enough to recognise him in a crowd. A great deal would depend on what happened in the second or two after she spotted him – whether she turned and ran, or trusted him enough to let him approach.

He could only hope she knew he wouldn't betray her to anyone.

Drake tensed the muscles in his legs, planting his feet firmly on the ground in preparation for his move as Anya moved out from behind the group of businessmen and glanced up at the overhead signs.

But it wasn't Anya, he realised as he got his first proper look at her. The woman in question was easily a decade younger, with a rounded, soft-featured face and eyes that had seen none of the hardships Anya had endured.

It wasn't her. He'd been wrong.

'Stand down,' Drake said, letting out the breath he hadn't realised he'd been holding. He was torn between relief, crushing disappointment and dismay that it had been a false alarm.

'Shit, that was close,' he heard Mason gasp.

'Ryan, we have no contact here,' Miranova's voice buzzed in his ear. 'Repeat, no sign of target.'

The traffic from the arrivals gate was thinning now as the last of the passengers wandered out, and Anya wasn't amongst them.

'I don't get it. This was the right flight,' Mason said, equally perplexed. 'Where the fuck is she, Ryan?'

Drake had no answer for him.

Chapter 24

Tbilisi, Georgia

The weather had abated a little by the time the automatic doors parted and Anya strode outside, taking her first breath of real air in what felt like days. It was still chilly, but the rain had eased off and, looking up, she even saw tantalising glimpses of blue sky through tears in the patchy clouds.

Not bad for December in Georgia.

It would have been foolish in the extreme to have flown under the same identity she'd used to rent the car that had got her out of DC. It would have been all too easy for a skilled and dedicated signals technician to use such a digital trail to track her down.

The real Olga Vorontsova whose identity she had borrowed for the car rental had indeed flown from Montreal to Moscow. Anya had no idea what the woman, chosen because she bore a passing resemblance to herself, had done after that, nor did she care. Olga had served her purpose of misdirecting Anya's pursuers and buying her some time.

Anya meanwhile had taken a different flight under a different name that had no possible connection to the sniper attack in DC, and which she had no fear of being compromised. A transatlantic flight from Montreal to Amsterdam had been followed by a relatively short hop to Georgia, a former Soviet republic lying on the south-western border of Russia.

And now, after almost twenty-four hours and several thousand miles of travelling, she was close to her rendezvous.

Spying signs for the taxi rank, she hurried onwards and selected the first vehicle she came across, not caring whether the rates were competitive. The driver, an overweight man with a thatch of wiry grey hair that reminded her of a bird's nest, certainly seemed grateful for her business as she approached.

'Where would you like to go?' he asked, speaking his native Georgian with the slight wariness of one used to dealing with clueless foreigners.

'Central Tbilisi,' Anya said, settling herself in the back seat. The cab looked surprisingly clean, but smelled of cigarette smoke and other less savoury odours that she suspected belonged to the driver rather than the vehicle. 'Freedom Square.'

'No problem.'

Chapter 25

Norilsk, Siberia

McKnight, along with Stav and the floor manager, were crowded on to a massive freight elevator with a dozen other miners as it slowly descended the main shaft of Norilsk nickel mine into the bowels of the earth. More than a few curious and sometimes leering glances had been thrown her way, but the presence of Stav had been enough to deter further interest.

Frost, much to her chagrin, had been left behind in the manager's office to trawl through his computer and printed records in search of any evidence of tampering on Umarov's part. McKnight knew she would much rather be here in the thick of the action, but her task was an equally important one. If they brought Umarov in and he wasn't inclined to talk, they needed evidence to confront him with.

As a passing nod to safety, she had been forced into over-sized protective gear, with a bulky helmet, eye goggles and a portable air-filtration unit slung over her shoulder like a rucksack.

'Every unit has an electronic tag in it,' the manager had explained. 'So we know who enters and leaves the mine. But it is dangerous down here. If something happens to you, I am not responsible.'

She'd understood him well enough. He was taking no blame if she was killed by falling rocks or crushed by a loader.

The minutes ticked by and still they kept descending. McKnight felt herself growing more uncomfortable by the moment. She'd never had much of a problem with enclosed spaces, but by now she was acutely aware of the thousands of tons of rock above her head. It was not a pleasant thought.

'How deep is this mine?' she asked, hoping her unease was lost in translation.

'One thousand three hundred metres. Some of the shafts go much deeper.'

Almost a mile below the earth's surface. Great, she thought as the elevator continued its slow, measured descent.

'You don't like underground, yes?' Stav prompted.

'You could say that.'

'It is same for me.'

She glanced at him. His face betrayed not a hint of apprehension or unease.

'Really?'

'*Da.* When I was kid, I got lost in caves near my home. Six hours I was stuck there in the dark before my father find me. He took me home and calmed me down. Then he beat the shit out of me for being stupid and careless.' He snorted in amusement. 'I did not get lost again after that.'

What a wonderful childhood that must have been, she thought.

Finally, after what seemed like hours, the huge lift bumped to a halt. The steel gates keeping them penned in were opened by a soot-stained worker on the other side, and the miners shuffled forwards to clock in and begin their shift.

Emerging from the main shaft, McKnight found herself staring at a maze of galleries, tunnels, cross-shafts and smaller access passageways that confronted her, all of them thronging with miners moving to and from the loading areas. In stark contrast to the frigid Arctic environment above ground, down here the air was warm and stifling. Harsh electric lights shone bravely through the dust and fumes.

She was grateful for the goggles and air purifier she'd been given. She couldn't imagine spending any length of time in such conditions without them.

The shift manager started speaking and pointing off into the distance.

'He says the foreman's office is that way!' Stav translated, having to yell to be heard as a massive-wheeled loading truck trundled past, its bulldozer-like bucket piled high with rocks waiting to be deposited in one of several ore chutes nearby. 'This is fucking dangerous place, man. Stay close to me, and watch where you walk!'

With little option but to obey, McKnight hurried after him down one of the main tunnels, skirting groups of workers as they went. Easily thirty feet wide and liberally illuminated by electric lamps, the shaft reminded her more of a subway tunnel than a mining area. The scale of the operation here was staggering.

Stav was beside her. A solid, menacing but strangely reassuring presence in that confusing and dangerous underground world. Coming as she did from a military background, Samantha wasn't the sort to be easily intimidated, but even she appreciated having someone to back her up. Especially a mile below the surface of a foreign country.

'Most of these guys haven't seen a woman in weeks,' Stav remarked, guessing her thoughts. 'You would be very popular here, I think.'

'Can't see myself changing careers any time soon,' she replied, not altogether comfortable with the direction his humour was going.

He laughed out loud at that. 'Don't be so sure. These crazy guys make more money than either of us. They stay a few years, make their fortune then move on. Some die, but what the fuck, right? We all do.'

She didn't quite share his fatalistic appraisal of the situation. Still, she wasn't inclined to pursue the matter, especially when the shift manager pointed further down the tunnel and started talking.

'Foreman's office is up ahead,' Stav announced.

Squinting through the dusty air, Samantha could make out the square shape of a Portakabin-like structure about 30 yards away. Several men were gathered near the entrance. One in particular, with a walkie-talkie in one hand and a flashlight in the other, was in the midst of issuing orders to the group.

The foreman pointed to him and shouted something in Russian that Stav didn't bother to translate.

'Leave this to me,' he said. 'I will scare the shit out of him, then we take him in.'

A moment later she saw him stride past her, heading straight for the group. Instinctively she picked up the pace, wanting to be close by when they lifted him.

The group had noticed Stav now and were watching him as he approached, curious but not yet wary. This was a big mine with lots of employees, and he was dressed just as they were.

'Borz Umarov?' he demanded, his tone making it clear this was no casual enquiry.

'*Da*,' the man with the walkie-talkie replied. His face was partially hidden by the respirator, but even Samantha could sense his unease.

Stav barked out another stream of Russian, she assumed to tell him he was to come with them and answer some questions. He was holding himself ready in case Umarov tried to run, but otherwise looked as if he had little to fear from the smaller and older man.

Umarov stood his ground, seemingly torn about what to do.

It happened fast. Realising his subject needed some persuasion, Stav reached inside his overalls for the automatic he'd insisted on taking with him. Umarov, however, was able to bring a far more primitive but equally effective weapon into play.

Unhooking the long metal flashlight from his tool belt, he swung it around like a shortened baseball bat and caught the FSB agent on the left temple, just below the edge of his work helmet. There was a muted thump, a crunch of broken glass as the flashlight shattered, and a groan of pain as Stav staggered sideways and collapsed.

'Shit!' McKnight cried, rushing forwards to his aid even as Umarov dropped the improvised weapon and retreated down the main tunnel.

Skidding to a halt beside the downed agent, she leaned in close. 'Stav, can you hear me? Stav!'

Through the cracked safety goggles she could see that his eyes were glassy and unfocused like a punch-drunk boxer, but they did slowly move around towards her.

'*Da*,' he managed to say, his voice thick and heavy. He might have been suffering from a concussion after the sharp blow, but he was alive.

Umarov was the priority now. Reaching into Stav's overalls, she felt around until her fingers closed on the butt of the automatic he hadn't quite been able to draw, then yanked the weapon free.

'Get him to a doctor!' she shouted to the workers who had gathered around, hoping they understood her intent if not her actual words. 'Doctor!'

Rising to her feet, she pulled back the slide on top of the weapon. A brass cartridge flew out of the ejection port, telling her a round had already been chambered, but it was better safe than sorry. The last thing she needed was to pull the trigger only to hear the ping of a firing pin striking an empty chamber.

Gripping the weapon tight in her gloved hands, she rushed down the main passage in pursuit of her target. Her air filter was struggling to keep up with her lungs as they greedily sucked in more oxygen, feeding the urgent demands of her body.

She had no idea where the passage led. Umarov would know these tunnels like the back of his hand and might well try to double back somehow, making for the elevator. McKnight's only option was to keep going and hope she could chase him down before he vanished.

Rounding a wide curve, she suddenly found herself faced with three separate tunnels, all leading in different directions. Umarov could have taken any one of them. There was no way of tracking him.

Spotting two men working on the engine of a nearby loading vehicle, she sprinted over, waving the gun to get their attention. 'Hey! You seen a guy come running down here?'

Both men stared at her with a mixture of fear, incomprehension and anger. No doubt they were less than pleased to be confronted with a woman waving a gun and jabbering in a language they didn't understand.

'Umarov!' she shouted, then pointed to the tunnels up ahead. 'Borz Umarov!'

The brighter and more cooperative of the two seemed to get what she was after, and pointed to the left tunnel while also spouting off a stream of Russian that she suspected was less than complimentary.

She ignored it. She had what she needed now.

With her flashlight beam haphazardly lighting a path ahead of her, she rushed down the left passage. This one wasn't as well illuminated as the others, with only a couple of dim bulbs still functioning. Perhaps it was an older tunnel that had since been abandoned; she imagined there were lots of passages like that in a mine of this size and complexity.

She hadn't gone far before the noise of the mining operation had faded into a dull echo, and the ambient light diminished to the point where she was forced to rely on her own flashlight to see. The ground beneath her feet was rough and uneven, and covered with loose rocks that had fallen from the roof over the years.

'There's nowhere to go, Borz,' she called out, having no idea whether it was true or not. There could be a dozen elevator shafts leading back to the surface for all she knew. 'We've sealed the mine off. You might as well give yourself up.'

Even if he spoke English she doubted he'd be inclined to believe her, but she had to give him the chance to surrender. In any case, there was no response to her offer. The tunnel remained eerily quiet compared to the roaring activity behind her.

She slowed her pace, straining to see, straining to hear anything above the thunder of her own heartbeat and the dry tinny rasp of her respirator unit.

She couldn't go any further like this. Knowing the air purifier would limit her awareness of her surroundings, she pulled it off and laid it on the ground, taking her first experimental breath. Straight away the dry dusty air attacked her nose and throat, and unable to help herself, she coughed and retched several times before regaining control.

Spitting to try to rid herself of the acrid taste, she rose up and continued onwards.

'All I want to know is who you sold those explosives to,' she promised, her eyes eagerly scanning the darkened tunnel. 'We can make a deal. We'll protect you.'

Something was lying on the ground up ahead. Creeping forwards with her weapon at the ready, she looked down at the work hat and brightly coloured overalls discarded on the tunnel floor in front of her. Umarov had removed anything that could give away his position.

'Shit,' she breathed, by now very much aware that she was only one person surrounded by darkness, armed but alone, and unaccustomed to moving through such an environment. Umarov knew every inch of this mine and how to use it to his advantage.

He knew it, just as he knew where to lead her.

She started to back up, realising the mistake she'd made by rushing in here alone, allowing excitement and eagerness to override professional caution.

The logical course of action should have been to alert the manager who had remained at the elevator and instruct him to shut down the mine, preventing anyone from entering or leaving. With Umarov thus cornered, they could search for him at their leisure.

But no sooner had she taken a step backwards than a figure leapt at her from a darkened alcove to the right. Instinctively she spun round and brought the pistol into the firing position, but the crushing impact of the 200-pound man barrelling into her midsection caused her grip on the weapon to slacken. A single gunshot echoed throughout the tunnel, the round impacting somewhere overhead, while the recoil of the shot caused the weapon to fly from her grasp.

Knocked flat by the rough tackle, she landed hard on the uneven tunnel floor with Umarov's bulk on top of her, sharp rocks tearing clothes and skin. She felt as though the life was being crushed out of her.

Instinctively she lashed out, feeling her fist connect hard with the man's ribcage. She might as well have tried pounding the tunnel walls. The impact jarred her arm and felt as though it had broken her knuckles, but it barely seemed to faze her opponent.

Though she was likely far more skilled at hand-to-hand fighting than Umarov, the great weight of him pinning her down meant she could do little real damage, and she lacked the brute strength to force him off. In effect, she was trapped, unable either to attack or to retreat.

It didn't take long for her opponent to capitalise on this.

She looked up just as his fist came crashing down against her, trying to dodge aside at the last second but with his weight preventing her from moving far enough.

The thunderous impact felt like a car crash inside her head. White light flashed before her eyes as the world began to fade out. She was in serious trouble now. Even dazed and hurt as she was, she knew this fight wasn't going to end until one of them was dead. And right now, the likely candidate was herself.

She saw Umarov's darkened form twist aside and grope blindly for a moment before picking up something. A rock, detached from the tunnel roof months or years earlier; easily the size of a brick and more than enough to stave in her skull.

Hefting the crude weapon in his gloved hands, he sat up and raised it above his head to strike.

McKnight's reaction was one born from a combination of instinct and training. In the military she had been taught to be flexible in her thinking, to adapt her strategy to changing circumstances and overcome them. She couldn't overpower Umarov in a fair fight – that much was obvious – so the only option was to make the fight unfair.

Taking rough aim, she drew her right knee up to her chest and forced her boot into his groin with all the strength she could muster. Her aim was true. Even through her heavy work boot she felt the impact as his delicate organs took the full force of the kick. The rock fell from his grasp as he doubled over, groaning in agony.

With her ears still ringing and strange blobs of light dancing across her vision, McKnight rolled over and scrambled away from him, desperately searching for the gun he'd knocked from her grip.

She could taste blood, and felt her jaw grinding as she opened her mouth to suck in a lungful of dusty air. Her clothes were torn and sticky with warm blood seeping from several deep cuts. She didn't doubt she'd regret this little tussle later, and she certainly wouldn't be doing any swimsuit modelling for a while, but adrenalin was doing a good job of suppressing the pain.

For now she had only one priority – subduing her enemy. He was down, but he wouldn't stay that way for long, and she had no desire to go toe to toe with him again. She needed the gun.

It wasn't easy. The ground was covered with small rocks, dips and depressions, any of which could be obscuring the weapon. And without her flashlight she was reduced to scrabbling around amongst the rubble, hoping to get lucky before her time ran out.

At last feeling her fingers brush against the weapon's bulky frame, she snatched it up and turned to face Umarov. It had taken her only a few seconds to find the automatic, but the delay had bought him enough time to drag himself to his feet and stagger down a side passage.

'Fuck!' She sprinted after him, determined not to let him escape now that she had him on the run. They were both injured, both hurting. But she had the edge.

The passageway seemed to be some kind of cross-tunnel that ran between the main shafts. At the far end she could see the glow of work lights, and silhouetted against them was Umarov, doubled over but still struggling forwards.

'Stop!' she yelled, levelling the weapon. With her vision still blurred from the blow to the head, she knew her chances of hitting him were far from good. 'Stop or I'll fire!'

Emerging into the main tunnel beyond, he glanced back over his shoulder as if sensing her thoughts. He might have failed to kill her, but he could still escape her. And with her limited knowledge of this mine, it would take precious minutes to work her way back to the main shaft, and even longer to make herself understood.

His distraction lasted only a second or so, but it was enough.

Suddenly a horn echoed down the tunnel, and Umarov turned, frozen like a deer in the headlights as the rock loader barrelled straight towards him. Then, in a storm of metal and a sickening crunch, he was gone, leaving only a bloody smear on the tunnel floor where he'd been.

Chapter 26

She was afraid.

For the first time in a long time, she was afraid.

With her hands cuffed behind her back, she was dragged down the bare concrete corridor, her boots rasping on the floor, tendrils of dirty hair hanging down around her face. Her combat uniform was ripped and torn and bloodied, her body bruised and cut; mute testimony to the vicious, desperate fight she had put up before her capture.

She had done what she could, holding off her enemies until she had almost run out of ammunition, and buying vital time for her team to escape. She could count three kills at least. Three more added to the tally of death against her name.

She had long since lost track of how many men she'd killed.

The two soldiers dragging her were dressed in camouflage fatigues, stained with dust and smelling of sweat and burned cordite. They were Spetsnaz – Soviet special forces, part of the unit that had ambushed her team.

The loss of their comrades would be at the forefront of their minds. Vaguely she remembered kicks and punches raining in on her earlier, delivered with vicious hatred that knew no bounds of gender. She could feel the deep ache of heavy bruising all over her body.

She smiled to herself, though it would have appeared to anyone watching as a fierce, predatory grimace. Kicks and punches like that

203

might have cowed many people, but not her. She had been through far worse in her short life, and she could take it.

She could take anything, she told herself.

Up ahead, a heavy steel door was thrown open and she was dragged inside. The room beyond was shrouded in shadow. From her limited field of view all she could make out was the same bare concrete floor as outside, and a simple wooden chair standing alone in the centre of the room.

It didn't take much imagination to work out who the chair was for, and her suspicions were confirmed when she was unceremoniously dumped on to it, her hands quickly secured to the back. One of the soldiers delivered a backhanded slap to the side of her head that jolted it sideways and left her ears ringing, though they held off further attacks.

She knew they wouldn't seriously harm her. Not yet, at least.

For the next several seconds, nothing happened. Silence descended on the room, and she waited with the two Spetsnaz operatives glaring at her. She felt her heartbeat quicken despite her efforts to still it, and a growing urge to swallow made her acutely aware of the apprehension creeping up from the pit of her stomach.

She had faced combat many times without fear, knowing she was at least in a situation she could control. She could anticipate and react to threats, make decisions, protect herself. Here that control was gone. She was helpless, and as much as she tried to ignore it, she was afraid.

She heard a dull metallic rasp from behind, followed by the faint crackle of burning paper as a cigarette was lit. Then, a few moments later, an exhalation of breath, long and slow and controlled. She smelled tobacco smoke.

'I said once that you were capable of remarkable things, Anya,' a voice remarked. Low, smooth and rich, and under normal circumstances pleasant to listen to. But not today. 'It seems I was right.'

Those words sent a shiver of fear down to her very core, because she knew who that voice belonged to, and she knew what it meant for her.

He had found her. Somehow he had tracked her down to this remote corner of the world, expending every resource at his disposal. And now he had her.

'You didn't really think you could play this little game and get away with it, did you?' he asked, his tone one of sympathy mixed with simmering anger. 'Believe me, I played it long before you, and I'll be playing it long after you're gone.'

Still she said nothing in response. She kept staring straight ahead, resisted the urge to swallow.

'I want you to do something for me, Anya. I want you to forget the world as you knew it, because you're no longer part of it. East and West, America and Russia . . . it's all gone. Here, all of that is irrelevant. Here, there is only you and me, and we have all the time in the world together. I want to know why you betrayed your country, Anya. I want to know why you betrayed me. And you will tell me.'

She remained silent while he took another drag on the cigarette, slow and thoughtful. 'Don't feel like talking?' He chuckled with amusement. 'You will. Believe me, you will.'

Tbilisi, Georgia, 22 December 2008

Anya had never been one for visiting churches. She was all too aware of the things she had done in her life, and was under no illusions about where she sat on the great spectrum of morality. She neither needed nor desired the comfort and forgiveness that churches purported to give the faithful.

Indeed, she had never really known religious faith. She had grown up in the Soviet Union, where organised religion was all but outlawed and the State had become the highest power known to the masses. Churches and those who worshipped in them were seen as anachronisms; strange and primitive relics from a vanished world. And later, in other places, she had seen for herself the shocking excesses and barbarity that people committed in the names of their beliefs.

There was little to be found in any religion that appealed to her.

However, she certainly did appreciate peace and quiet, and those were two things that the ancient building in which she now sat provided in abundance. Its thick walls protected them from the din of the busy city outside, leaving the interior bathed in cool, quiet darkness.

The only other inhabitants were a couple of old women sitting near the altar, their bent backs and deeply lined faces making them appear almost as ancient as the church around them. So near the ends of their lives, she supposed they had nothing better to do than linger in such places.

The Anchiskhati Basilica was the oldest church in Tbilisi, dating all the way back to the sixth century. Various invaders, from the Turks to the Persians, had tried to destroy it over the years, but still the ancient building stood – a quiet, dignified monument to the power of endurance.

That was another quality which Anya appreciated.

Sitting in a simple wooden pew near the ancient brickwork of the outer wall, she was oddly conscious of the sense of age and remembrance that hung over this place. How many other people had sat in this exact spot, seeking forgiveness, inspiration, guidance or just a hint that they weren't alone in the world?

She closed her eyes and bowed her head, not in prayer, but

in a simple moment of reflection. For the first time in what felt like days, she allowed her guard to drop a little, allowed her restless attention to wane and her thoughts to grow still. Just for a moment, she was at peace.

She became aware of the approaching footsteps as soon as they entered the church, heading towards her at a slow, measured pace. Exactly on time, just as she'd known he would be. Everything he did was timed and planned to perfection.

She heard him shuffle along the narrow space between pews and ease himself down next to her, the old wooden seat creaking under his not inconsiderable weight.

'Many come here in search of absolution,' he whispered. 'Are you one of them?'

Anya opened her eyes slowly as if waking from a dream, then turned to look at her contact. The man at the very centre of everything that was happening. The man whose great mind had engineered a plot to bring down one of the biggest intelligence agencies in the world.

Never had she seen a more unlikely candidate for such an undertaking.

He was the kind of man one passed a dozen times a day and never noticed. Short, overweight and balding. With small eyes nestled in fleshy folds behind a pair of old-fashioned wire-framed glasses, his face was rounded and genial looking. The kind of face to which it seemed smiles and laugher should come easily.

But they didn't. Not for him, not now.

He was no soldier, no hired killer, no black operative with years of training and experience to call upon. He'd started his journey as a simple man, a family man with little ambition beyond making a good life for himself and those he loved.

Fate, however, had taken Buran Atayev down a very different path.

'It was you who chose this meeting place,' she reminded him.

She had no idea how he'd arrived here, or what the travel arrangements for the rest of the group had been. Likewise, they had no knowledge of her movements. Everything had been set up so that no one element of the group could compromise any other.

Her objective was simply to be here at this church, at this precise hour. How exactly that happened was up to her.

'It was.' Atayev nodded towards the stained-glass window behind the altar, depicting a scene of St George slaying the dragon. 'Rather appropriate, don't you think?'

She couldn't say for sure whether Atayev saw himself as a virtuous man fighting a good fight against an evil enemy – whether that was the higher purpose he used to excuse his actions. But in any case, the task standing before them made the slaying of a dragon seem easy by comparison.

'It's good to see you again, my friend,' Atayev went on, genuinely meaning it. That was one thing Anya, with her intuitive ability to read body language and sense deception in others, had always appreciated about him. When he said things, he meant them.

'And you,' Anya said quietly.

Letting out a slow, thoughtful breath, Atayev bowed his head. To anyone watching it would appear he was deep in prayer.

'They've found the link to the explosives,' he said. 'The FSB are in Norilsk now, along with a pair of CIA agents.'

Anya raised an eyebrow. It wasn't unexpected, though she was surprised at how quickly they had made the connection between the bomb and its origin. And the mention of CIA agents immediately set off alarm bells in her head.

'What is the CIA's stake in this?' she asked, unable to keep from looking at him. Anya was used to keeping her deeper thoughts hidden, but even she couldn't hide the faint anxiety in her eyes, or the tension in her voice.

She saw a flicker of a smile on his fleshy face. He'd picked up on it too.

'One of their operatives has become involved in the investigation. A man named Drake – Ryan Drake.'

Anya felt her heart sink. She should have known Drake wouldn't be able to leave it alone after their close encounter in DC. The man was relentless, pursuing her with every resource at his disposal. She could only assume it was part of some misguided attempt to protect her, though in reality his interference might have the opposite effect.

'It seems this man Drake is more intelligent than his FSB colleagues,' Atayev went on. 'Some of his team have been dispatched to Norilsk, but he himself is in Chechnya.'

It was all she could do to keep from gritting her teeth with exasperation. Drake was unbalancing their plan, moving things forward more quickly than they should be. And if he continued, he could well destroy everything she was working for.

'Have they guessed the next target?'

'I don't believe so. Not yet, at least. But we must move quickly.' His expression remained neutral, but his eyes told a different story. 'You realise of course that if this Drake stands in our way, he becomes an enemy like any other?'

'I do.' She spoke truthfully, but she'd hesitated for a moment too long.

Atayev had seen it too. He leaned a little closer and lowered his voice. 'I've never had reason to doubt you, Anya. I know you're an honest person, and I must ask you to be honest with me now. Too much is at stake for me to take a chance on someone who could fail me at a crucial moment. What do you know of Ryan Drake?'

Anya met his searching gaze, knowing she had little choice but to give him the honesty he desired. 'We've encountered each other before,' she admitted, unwilling to go into further detail.

The man's eyes betrayed no hint of the shock and surprise she might have expected at such a revelation. He knew, or had at least guessed, the truth already. He'd simply been testing her.

'So Drake knows who you are. He could compromise you, and all of us.'

She knew she had to tread carefully now. Atayev posed no threat to her in a physical sense, but he nonetheless possessed the ability to destroy at a stroke everything she hoped to achieve.

'I don't think so,' she said, hoping it was true. 'He trusts me. If he's involved, it's because he's trying somehow to protect me.'

'I want to believe you, Anya. But you realise of course that this puts me in a very difficult position. Whether or not you trust his intentions, he remains a threat. Therefore, that makes you a liability.'

'There are risks in every operation,' she reminded him, hoping she looked and sounded more composed than she felt. 'I'm still your best chance of achieving your goal.'

He exhaled slowly. 'That may be so. But if Drake threatens our plan, I must know that you will deal with him. If not, you can go no further with us. Speak honestly now, and I'll believe you.'

Anya's face paled at the thought of killing Drake. And yet, even as her conscious mind rebelled against it, another part of her began to take hold. The soldier, the survivor who always did what was necessary to stay alive, to achieve her objective at any cost. That part of her had long ago pushed aside such notions of weakness and compassion, because they were luxuries she could ill afford.

Just as she couldn't afford them now.

Atayev was right. Too much was at stake to risk it all on one man. If Drake stood against her, she would have no choice but to act as she always had – without mercy, without fear or weakness.

'Drake won't stop us,' she promised him. 'I'll make sure of that.'

Another man might have questioned her further, might have doubted her resolve despite her protests, but Atayev knew better than that. For him, Anya's word was as good as the truth.

'Good,' he said, settling back in the pew. He reached into his pocket and carefully held up a little black chess piece shaped into the distinctive form of a knight. 'Because it's time for our next move.'

That was why they were really here. Anya had spent weeks studying and committing every detail of her part in the operation to memory, going over it again and again in her head just as she had done when she was an active operative.

As with the travel arrangements, each member of the group knew the part they had to play, but only Atayev's mind encompassed the full scope of their plan. Whatever he lacked in experience, Buran Atayev more than made up for in intelligence, tireless work and unwavering attention to detail. He was the key, the lynchpin on which success or failure turned. Without him, nothing could happen.

Everything with him was planned to perfection.

Casting one last glance at the depiction of St George and the dragon, he rose from the pew. 'Shall we take a walk?'

Chapter 27

Resembling a cross between a dilapidated bus depot and a besieged fortress, Norilsk's central police station was a big imposing office building facing out on to the city's main square. All of its ground-floor windows were protected by wrought-iron bars, though that hadn't stopped some determined vandals from having a go at them. Several had been smashed and boarded up.

The square itself was at least better maintained than most of the streets in town. Snowploughs had worked hard to clear the worst of the drifts, and the street lamps were still functioning. Cars and buses chugged along, venting diesel fumes as they ferried workers to and from the immense industrial complex in the distance.

It was here, in a small conference room on the second floor, that McKnight and Stav had been brought to lick their wounds after their ill-conceived foray underground. Neither was seriously injured, though they had little to show for their efforts besides plentiful cuts and bruising, and in Stav's case, wounded pride.

'Nice going, dude,' Frost said as she surveyed the injured FSB agent. She had been given a brief summary of events in the mine, but had yet to learn the details. 'You were supposed to be on protective detail. What the hell happened down there?'

Far from being irritated by her harsh criticism, he looked almost sheepish now. He had screwed up by underestimating their opponent, and had very nearly paid for it with his life. 'Umarov made a run for it. He was faster than I expected.'

Frost stared at him. 'You . . . don't . . . say.'

'That's enough, Keira,' McKnight interrupted, an ice pack pressed against the side of her head. She appreciated her companion sticking up for her, but pointing fingers wasn't going to get them anywhere right now. Anyway, her head was still killing her and the sound of Frost's tirade wasn't doing it any favours. 'It wasn't Stav's fault. We both under-estimated Umarov.'

She knew from what little time they'd spent together that Frost could be temperamental and difficult, and that it certainly wouldn't pay to make an enemy of her. But at the same time McKnight knew she had to keep her in line. Drake had entrusted her with the task of finding leads in Norilsk, and whatever their personal issues she wasn't going to be responsible for screwing this up.

Frost chewed her lip for a moment, seemingly on the verge of carrying on anyway, but reluctantly allowed the matter to drop. 'Fine,' she conceded unhappily. 'So the way I see it we're fresh out of leads. Any ideas?'

'Well, we won't be getting anything from Umarov,' McKnight confirmed. Being hit and then crushed by a high-powered rock loader didn't leave much to chance. His funeral would definitely be a closed-casket affair. 'Did you find anything in the warehouse records?'

She shook her head. 'Everything's handwritten. It's the worst goddamned inventory system I've ever seen. Anyone could have falsified the log.'

'Shit.' Rising from her chair and doing her best to ignore the pounding in her skull, McKnight walked over to the grimy window and surveyed the darkened world beyond. In the distance stood the towering chimneys of the smelting works, still pumping out smoke like there was no tomorrow. The glow from furnaces was reflected off the low-hanging clouds.

For a moment McKnight caught herself wondering if things had gone downhill in Norilsk since the fall of Communism, or whether it had just always been a shithole.

She had operated in former Communist countries that had suffered greatly since the collapse of the Soviet Union. Everywhere there had been remnants of the bold future that their governments had tried to build – huge communal swimming pools and leisure complexes, massive public buildings and wide boulevards built to Stalinist architectural ideals. Operating in such places was like going back through some kind of time warp to a faded, decayed 1950s vision of how the future ought to look.

She spotted an old woman hobbling along the icy, litter-strewn pavement opposite. She was a sad figure, her bent old frame wrapped in what looked like three separate jackets, all worn and patched up and ratty looking. She was clutching several plastic bags as if her life depended on it, probably on her way home after picking up some shopping.

Nodding to herself, McKnight turned back towards the two members of her makeshift team. 'I want to take a look at Umarov's home,' she decided. 'If there's anything in this shithole that might help us, it'll be there.'

Chapter 28

Grozny, Chechnya

A couple of thousand miles away, the mood was rather less focused.

'What the fuck was that?' Ivan Masalsky raged, pacing back and forth at the end of the conference table like a caged lion. The regional FSB director had summoned Drake and the others there after it had become obvious their target wasn't on the plane. 'I have half my security teams on alert, an airport on the brink of being locked down, and for what? Nothing!'

Miranova dared to offer an explanation. 'Sir, we—'

Bad move.

'Shut the fuck up!' Masalsky snapped, jabbing a finger at her. 'I don't want your excuses.'

Drake winced inwardly. Masalsky might have vented his frustration on Miranova for the time being, but his true anger was reserved for Drake himself – the outsider, the interloper, the unwelcome party crasher.

It didn't take long for Masalsky's attention to rest on him.

'And you, Mr Drake? Do you have an explanation for this?'

Drake had nothing to offer. He was just as dismayed at having failed to locate Anya, and for once he hoped it showed.

'Our intel must have been flawed,' he said, knowing how weak it sounded. 'We were wrong.'

For a second or two, Masalsky actually looked taken aback by his frank admission, as if he expected elaborate excuses

216

and attempts at passing the buck. The notion that a man could simply admit a failure was almost foreign to him.

However, his surprise didn't last long.

'You were wrong?' he repeated mockingly. 'Is this some kind of joke amongst the CIA, Mr Drake? Because right now I don't find it very funny. You have wasted our time and resources with your little wild goose chase.'

'That wasn't my intention.'

'Do I look as if I care about good intentions?' He placed his hands on his hips in what he probably thought was an intimidating posture. 'I want to know what you are going to do about it.'

'What would you like me to do?' Drake asked, knowing there was no answer he could give that would satisfy the man.

'I would like you to stop wasting my time, get the fuck out of my country and never come back.' He turned his baleful gaze on Miranova. 'Make the arrangements. I expect you to be on the first available flight out of here. If not, I will be having a talk with Mr Drake's superiors.'

Throwing a final simmering glare at Drake, he turned and strode out of the room, leaving a stunned silence in his wake. As far as dressing-downs went, this one took some beating.

'Keeps his cards close to his chest, huh?' Mason remarked sarcastically.

Miranova, however, was focused on the failure of their operation, rather than the fallout from her boss. 'I don't understand how this happened. We all saw the pictures of the target getting on that flight. How could he have vanished?'

'He must have switched flights somehow,' Drake suggested. 'Maybe during the layover in Moscow.'

'Or the guy was a decoy,' Mason suggested.

Miranova glanced at him irritably. After their run-in on the flight here, she had little time for Mason's opinions on anything. 'What?'

'He might have allowed himself to be caught on camera to draw our attention here. Meanwhile the rest of his group gets to go about their business without interference.'

'We have a lot of theories, and no facts to support them.' The FSB agent turned her attention back to Drake, eyes narrowed with suspicion. 'Unless there is something else going on that I don't know about.'

The pointed way in which she said it suggested she wasn't referring to the elusive group behind the attack in DC. Drake, however, said nothing, hoping she would be discouraged enough to let the matter drop.

No such luck.

'Is there something you want to tell me, Ryan?'

'What exactly are you getting at?' he challenged her.

'This whole operation was based on mutual trust,' she reminded him. 'I would hate to think that trust was misplaced. If there is something you are keeping from me, you should tell me now before we go any further. It would be a shame for both of us if I was to find out by myself later, if you know what I mean.'

Indeed he did. Her instincts were telling her that something wasn't right. He'd expected it sooner or later – Miranova clearly wasn't stupid – but he'd hoped the doubts would have taken longer to surface.

Now she was testing his resolve. Like a poker player raising the stakes, she was applying a little pressure to see if he would break.

Drake met her gaze without flinching. There was no question of backing down now, even if he'd been having second thoughts. Despite her assurances, he knew that to admit his deception would be akin to painting a target on his head.

Neither he nor Mason would ever make it back from Russia alive.

'You and I both want the same thing,' he promised her, speaking truthfully. 'We both want to find the people responsible for this. Believe that.'

Miranova maintained eye contact a few seconds longer before finally relenting. She had pushed as hard as she could, for now at least.

'As you say,' she said, though she sounded far from convinced. 'Either way, it does nothing to change our situation. Masalsky wants us out, and he will get his way.'

'What about your buddy Surovsky?' Mason asked. 'Call him up, get him to pull some strings.'

'Director Surovsky is not my "buddy", as you put it,' she replied. 'And he was not enthusiastic about this idea from the very beginning. An admission of failure now might turn him against us too.'

'Fuck,' Drake said under his breath.

Pushing himself away from the table, he strode over to the window to stare out across the rain-swept runways and the dreary pine forests that lay beyond the airport perimeter. He was tired and frustrated, and increasingly aware that they were losing whatever chance they'd once had of tracking down Anya.

More than once over the past twenty-four hours he'd privately questioned whether he should be looking for her at all. He'd played it over in his head again and again. Whatever reasons she might have had for launching that attack in DC, he could see nothing good coming from it. By attacking such a high-profile figure, she was exposing herself to a level of attention that no one could escape from. What the hell was she planning to do – take on the FSB and CIA single-handed? And why involve him?

His dark contemplation was interrupted when his phone started buzzing in his pocket. It was McKnight. Hope mingled with apprehension welled up inside him as he answered it.

'Sam, tell me you've got good news.'

'I could, but I'd be lying,' the woman replied, her voice almost drowned out by the rumble of an engine in the background. 'I was right about the explosives. There was a man on the inside who smuggled them out. Borz Umarov – a Chechen national working for the mining operation.'

'So why isn't that good news?'

'He tried to make a run for it when we approached him, walked straight into an ore loader.' He heard a sharp intake of breath as if she'd hurt herself. However, she quickly recovered and carried on. 'He's roadkill.'

Drake got the picture. A promising lead, perhaps their only remaining lead, had just been lost to a freak accident. He also hadn't missed her brief pause, and felt a momentary flash of concern that overrode his own problems. 'You all right?'

'Stav and I got a little roughed up. Injured pride, mostly,' she added, trying to lighten the mood. 'What about you?'

Drake hesitated, tempted to ask more about her injuries, though he didn't want it to be misconstrued as overprotectiveness.

'Our target wasn't on the plane,' he said, deliberately omitting Anya's name. 'We've got nothing to go on right now, and the FSB aren't happy.'

'Then maybe we can help,' she said. 'We're en route to Umarov's apartment now. If he was responsible for supplying the explosives, he must have had contact with the buyer prior to that. We'll turn his place over, see what Keira can dig up.'

'Understood. Keep me updated.' He hesitated a moment

before going on. 'I don't suppose I need to tell you to watch your back out there?'

'You know me,' she replied. 'So for once, trust me.'

With that, she ended the call.

Drake hadn't missed the sharp tone in her voice when she expressed that final sentiment, just as he hadn't forgotten the angry confrontation that had almost flared up between them back in DC. And as much as it galled him to admit it, he knew she had every right to be angry with him.

'What was that about?' Miranova asked.

'Don't go booking that flight just yet. My team in Norilsk might have a lead.'

The FSB agent glanced at the wall clock. 'Then I hope they find it soon.'

Drake said nothing to that. He could do nothing to influence events in Norilsk. For now, all he could do was sit and wait.

Chapter 29

Norilsk, Siberia

Sitting in the back seat of the Merc as it rumbled along the potholed, slush-covered road, McKnight was forced to conclude that Norilsk didn't look any better up close than it had from a distance. They were lost in a ghostly, frozen world of dreary five-storey apartment blocks festooned with big old-fashioned satellite dishes. Their bare concrete walls were scarred and weathered like those of ancient castles.

'Umarov's apartment is just a few blocks from here,' Stav announced after consulting his GPS. Norilsk seemed to be laid out as one big grid, its streets and buildings designed with simple utilitarianism in mind. However, most of the street signs were rendered unreadable by thick ice and wind-blown snow.

As they made their way deeper into the city, McKnight was surprised by the number of people out and about at such an early hour. Most were men, wrapped in heavy fur coats and hats, their backs hunched as they trudged through the drifting snow.

Factory workers, heading off to start another shift. In a city of constant darkness, the concept of night and day had ceased to exist, replaced instead by the relentless demands of industry.

'We are close,' Stav said as they pulled off the main road and into a parking lot crammed with cars that looked as if they were held together by the sheer willpower of their owners. Most were half-buried in grey snow.

Rolling to a stop in the centre of the parking lot as if they owned the place, their driver killed the engine, opened his door and stepped out without saying a word.

Stav, one side of his head covered by a gauze dressing, twisted around in his seat. 'We walk from here.'

'I'd guessed as much,' Frost replied acidly, clearly not thrilled at the prospect of venturing outside into sub-zero weather. According to the Merc's dashboard computer, the outside temperature was a balmy minus 20 degrees Celsius. She believed it.

Stav said nothing to that, turning away and opening his door. With little option but to follow, the two specialists exited the vehicle. The cold began to attack them straight away, numbing their fingers and making their eyes water.

Traffic rumbled past on the main drag; a mixture of heavy trucks and beaten-up saloons, all caked in mud and ice. The air was thick with engine fumes, mixing with the output from the nearby factories to form a choking smog that left a bitter taste in McKnight's mouth. The freezing temperatures prevented it from dissipating into the atmosphere, instead lingering over the city like a blanket.

The tenement buildings around them were all of the same basic design: square and uniform, with boarded-up windows and heavy doors leading to dimly lit stairwells that no doubt stank of urine and God knew what else. Surprisingly, there was almost no graffiti anywhere. Then again, in weather like this, who would want to stand around spray-painting?

After consulting with the giant, who was waiting a short distance away, Stav turned to address the two women. 'His apartment is in that building there,' he said, pointing to the nearest tower block. 'Come, I will show you.'

With that, he turned and started trudging through the snow towards it, with the giant leading the way. McKnight and Frost followed in their wake, eager to escape the cold. However, their relief at escaping the biting wind and driving snow outside was short-lived.

Even by Norilsk standards Umarov's apartment building was a dump – a cold, draughty, poorly lit edifice that would have been condemned for demolition if it had been in the US. As it was, scores of families eked out an existence here. McKnight could hear the blare of televisions, the rumble of washing machines and the occasional muffled argument from behind battered steel doors. In this strange world where night and day had ceased to exist, life went on.

The main corridor was lit by two bare bulbs, one of which was flickering as if it was on the way out. It was a dark and dingy place, with just enough illumination to navigate by.

'This is it,' Stav said, nodding to apartment number 412. The giant was already at the door, and reaching for something inside his coat.

Umarov's front door, like the others here, was heavy wood reinforced by metal sheeting to prevent anyone kicking it in.

'Don't you need a warrant or something to go in there?' Frost asked.

Stav looked at her with amusement as the giant pressed something against the door lock. It looked like a small bulky pistol linked to a high-pressure air canister. It was a bolt gun – the kind of thing used to execute cattle at slaughterhouses. When fired, the pneumatic bolt would spring forwards with enough force to shatter the animal's skull and destroy the delicate organ within.

Bracing himself, the giant held the barrel of the gun against the lock, turned away and pulled the trigger. There was a dull, heavy thump followed by the splintering of broken wood as the bolt slammed forward, obliterating the entire locking mechanism.

'This is our warrant,' Stav said, drawing his sidearm. 'We go first. You wait here.'

With that, he pushed the broken door open and advanced inside, with the giant right behind. After her experiences in the nickel mine McKnight was happy to let them spearhead this little foray into uncharted territory. In any case, neither she nor Frost was armed.

'It is clear!' she heard Stav call from within.

Waiting no longer, she pushed through the door and into a narrow, rubbish-strewn hallway. There was mess everywhere – empty beer cans, newspapers, cigarette packets, food cartons. It was just scattered all over the place as if the owner hadn't even heard of a bin. Clearly Umarov hadn't been houseproud.

The air was hot and clammy, and smelled of damp, cigarette smoke and other less savoury odours. The heating must have been running 24/7. Then again, with minus 20-degree temperatures to contend with outside, that was understandable.

To her left was the kitchen, in a similar state to the hallway. The cheap worktops were stained with coffee rings and spilled food, and covered with unwashed dishes, cutlery, spanners, screwdrivers, empty beer cans, broken electrical appliances and a host of other things.

There was nothing there that interested her, and she wasn't feeling up to investigating the bathroom so instead pushed on to the living room where Stav and the giant had congregated.

It was a cramped, messy, claustrophobic room that made her skin crawl the moment she entered, as if years of deprivation had soaked into its very fabric. Much of its limited

225

floor space was given over to a threadbare couch that sagged noticeably in the middle, a cluttered computer desk in one corner that was positively groaning under the weight of unsorted letters and documents, and a TV stand in the other. DVDs and old VHS tapes were piled up next to it, many of them pornographic.

Much like the kitchen, there was trash everywhere. Everything from discarded clothes to takeaway food boxes, empty bottles, books and magazines. McKnight could barely see the dirty lime-green carpet beneath it, which was perhaps a good thing, she reflected.

'Jesus, almost makes Drake's place look good,' Frost remarked, wrinkling her nose in distaste as she surveyed the room.

Something about the place puzzled McKnight, however. 'I don't get it. This place is a shithole. I thought you said miners earned a fortune working here?' she said, addressing her question to Stav. 'Umarov was a foreman. Shouldn't he have been rolling in money?'

'Maybe he was saving for retirement,' Frost suggested. Looking around, she spotted several calling cards on the table, all with pictures of scantily dressed and barely legal girls. Most of them had phone numbers handwritten on the back. 'Or maybe he had a taste for the ladies.'

She tossed the cards aside, unconsciously wiping her hand on her trouser leg.

Stav, however, had found something else of interest: a small metal cigar tin that had been hidden beneath the couch. Opening it up, he carefully lifted out a small plastic bag half-filled with white powder. A couple of razor blades were in the tin beside it.

'I think whores were not his only vice,' the FSB agent observed.

It didn't take a genius to see how Umarov had frittered away his considerable monthly pay cheque on drink, drugs and prostitutes. In a place like this, it wasn't as though there was a stimulating cultural scene to keep one occupied.

Still, petty drug abuse was the least of McKnight's concerns at that moment. They had come here for clues to the missing explosives. And somewhere in this mess of an apartment lay the answer.

'Keira, see what you can find on his computer,' McKnight said, nodding to the desktop PC in one corner of the room. 'Stav and I will make a start on his paperwork.'

'That piece of shit?' Frost asked, staring at the machine as if it were a museum exhibit, which it very well could have been. It was a bulky old-fashioned model, its beige casing stained black with soot around the air vents in testimony to its long years of service. 'It looks older than I am.'

'Believe me, it'll be a lot more fun than my job,' McKnight assured her as she looked over the daunting pile of letters, bills, invoices, scribbled notes and countless other documents that had been strewn around the room. Sorting through it all could take days.

Unfortunately neither they nor Drake had that long.

Chapter 30

Grozny, Chechnya

Drake's phone was ringing again. Hoping it was Frost or McKnight with an update on their investigation, he was disappointed to find instead that Franklin was calling.

'Yeah, Dan?'

'I guess there's not much point asking where you are right now, huh?' The tone of his voice made it plain he was far from pleased that Drake had gone behind his back.

'If you don't ask, I won't tell,' Drake replied.

'Then tell me this. Have you found what you were looking for?'

Drake glanced over his shoulder at Miranova. She was busy working on her laptop, perhaps compiling a report for her superiors in Moscow, and paid him no heed.

'We're working on it.'

'Then you'll want to get your ass in gear,' his friend advised. 'Cain's been snooping around. He knows you're up to something.'

Drake cursed silently. As if he didn't have enough to worry about at that moment; having Marcus Cain breathing down his neck was the last thing he needed.

'Even if you find her, I can't guarantee the kind of reception you'll get when you come home.' Halfway around the world, Franklin sighed. 'You may want to consider using your security blanket.'

Drake had guessed as much. A security blanket was a contingency fund set up by deniable operatives like himself for situations in which they were burned by their handlers and needed to disappear. For obvious reasons nobody admitted to having one, but everyone with a grain of common sense had hidden away the money and resources to start a new life. Drake was no different.

In essence, Franklin was advising him to cut all ties with the Agency and go dark for good. There would be no coming back from this one. He'd be a hunted man for the rest of his days.

'I'll keep it in mind,' he said, unwilling to go any further. Deep down he'd always known there would come a time when he'd have to part company with the Agency, but he wasn't ready to jump ship yet. To do so would vindicate Cain and give the man the perfect excuse to hunt him down.

'It's your call. I've done what I can, Ryan. The rest is up to you.'

'I know. And . . . Dan?'

'Yeah?'

'Thanks. I mean that.' There wasn't much he could say beyond that. Whatever their differences, Franklin had risked a lot to protect him.

Silence greeted him for the next few seconds. Then: 'Just get this done.'

The line went dead.

'Has something happened?' Miranova asked as he closed down the call. Apparently she hadn't been quite as absorbed in her work as he'd hoped.

'My boss giving me a hard time,' Drake said, pocketing the phone. 'He'll be the death of me one day.'

She flashed a pained smile and gestured to the computer. 'Then it seems we have something in common.'

'Surovsky?'

She nodded.

'Yeah, I got the impression he's not exactly a people person.'

'He is not,' she admitted. 'But then, I think his job demands a certain . . . detachment. Much like our own, yes?'

He used to feel the same way. His job as a Shepherd team leader had once been an easy one, at least from an emotional standpoint. He'd always maintained a professional distance between himself and the targets, thinking of them simply as an objective to be captured or safeguarded.

That way it was easier to accept when they came home in a coffin.

That had all changed with Anya. The wall, the barrier that allowed him to do what he did with a clear conscience, had vanished. Everything had changed with Anya.

'We're not machines,' he replied at length, not altogether pleased that she was pressing him on this issue again.

'But we are soldiers, trained to fight a war,' she reminded him. 'Perhaps a different kind of war, but a war all the same. Given your background, you should understand this more than most.'

Drake eyed her darkly. Her purposeful tone wasn't lost on him. 'What exactly do you know about me?'

'The FSB keeps files on most people of interest. Needless to say, you became interesting to us a couple of days ago.'

'You didn't answer my question.'

She leaned back from her computer, exhaling slowly as if weighing up what to say. 'You were born in England in 1972. You earned high academic marks at school, and won a scholarship at Cambridge where you studied structural engineering. You joined the British army afterwards, then transferred to the Special Air Service a few years later. We know little beyond this, except that you left the military in 2003 and moved to the CIA not long after. There was no official reason on your service record.'

Drake wasn't surprised by the first part of her brief summary of his life. His education and early military service were, after all, a matter of public record and accessible by anyone with a computer. The rest of it, however, had stirred up memories of a time he'd much rather forget. He couldn't help wondering if she knew more about his departure from the military than she was letting on.

'You are an interesting man, Ryan Drake. You seem to have done a lot of things in your life. But not for long.' She leaned a little closer, noticing his change in body language when she'd mentioned his change of careers. 'This makes you uncomfortable?'

'You have me at a disadvantage,' he said, trying to change the subject. 'You seem to know a lot about me. I don't know anything about you.'

'One of the benefits of having the backing of my agency,' she reminded him with a sardonic smile. 'Anyway, I think there is another reason. If I had to guess, I would say you didn't leave the military of your own free will.'

'I'm sure that's none of your business,' Drake replied tersely.

'It is if it has a bearing on our investigation—'

'It doesn't,' he cut in, his sharp look warning her not to pursue this further. 'And I didn't come here to play *This is Your Life*.'

He was finished talking with her, especially about this. He needed time to cool down, to regain his composure. He glanced towards the door, which he knew to be guarded on the other side by a pair of armed FSB agents in case he decided to go sightseeing. 'I'm going to the bathroom.'

The woman nodded, her expression making it obvious she'd scored a point. She had exposed a point of weakness that could be exploited later, if she chose.

'One of our agents will escort you.'

'Is he going to hold my dick for me as well?'

Miranova remained annoyingly unperturbed. 'Only if you can't find it by yourself.'

In the restroom nearby, Mason popped the lid on his bottle of painkillers and tipped a couple into his hand, eyeing the innocuous little pills with a mixture of distaste and resentment. He shouldn't need these, he kept thinking to himself.

A few years ago he'd been in the prime of his life; strong and physically fit, and possessing a robust vitality that kept him in excellent health. He could scarcely even remember the last time he'd had to visit a doctor.

Now he had to take these fucking pills just to get through the day. His shoulder was aching, and no amount of concentration could hide the slight tremor in his hand as the previous dose of painkillers wore off, leaving behind their inevitable legacy.

It started with trembling hands, but it didn't stop there. Headaches, sickness, fatigue, disorientation; he'd experienced it all the last time he'd tried to stop using them. That had been six months ago, after the final corrective operation on his shoulder.

He hated it, but right now he knew he needed them. He couldn't afford to let Drake or himself down on this job. He had to get through it.

Swallowing the pills, he chased them down with a gulp of water from the faucet and let out a sigh that was somewhere between relief and resignation. The pills packed quite a punch, and it didn't take long for them to kick in.

He was just straightening up when the door opened behind him. Startled, he spun around to find himself face to face with Drake.

'Ryan!' He tried for a relieved grin while at the same time moving a little to the left, putting himself between Drake and the bottle of pills that was still resting on the edge of the sink. 'Jesus, you scared the shit out of me.'

But Drake wasn't smiling. 'Caught you at a bad time, Cole?'

'A man's allowed to take a shit break, isn't he?' Turning away, he bent over the sink and turned on the tap again. At the same time he reached for the bottle, closing his hand around it before Drake could get a look. 'Any news from McKnight?'

'Nothing yet.'

Mason splashed some water on his face, trying to ignore Drake's dubious glance in the mirror. 'They'll find something. McKnight seems pretty squared away. And Keira . . . well, she's Keira, right?' He looked up and managed to summon a playful grin. 'She doesn't quit until the job's done.'

Drake folded his arms. 'You're right about that. I always could rely on Keira,' he said, putting a certain emphasis on that last word. The meaning wasn't lost on Mason.

He felt himself growing more on edge as the seconds crawled by, expecting his friend to challenge him at any moment. Had he seen the pills? Did he understand what they were?

Wiping his face and slipping the bottle unobtrusively into his coat sleeve, he straightened up and turned to face Drake again. 'Give them a chance, Ryan. They might just surprise you.'

He hoped his meaning wasn't lost on Drake either. Leaving his friend to think on that, he brushed past him and headed for the door. He was just reaching for the handle when Drake called out to him.

'Oh, and Cole?'

Turning, Mason was just in time to see Drake toss something towards him. Instinctively he raised his left hand – his good hand – to catch it. Then, remembering the bottle of pills he'd hidden up his sleeve, he turned slightly and snatched at it with his right. It was a clumsy catch, but he held on all the same.

He managed to hide the flash of pain from his shoulder at the sudden movement, and glanced down at the folded hand towel Drake had thrown his way. He knew right away why the younger man had done it. The son of a bitch was testing him.

'Remember to wash your hands,' Drake advised.

Chapter 31

Norilsk, Siberia

'Yes!' Frost cried, punching the air. 'Got you, you son of a bitch!'

McKnight looked up from the stack of documents she'd been sorting through with Stav, turning her attention to the technical specialist. Frost had plugged her own laptop into a USB port on Umarov's computer, using its sophisticated hacking and decryption software to break through whatever security protocols he'd had in place so she could trawl his hard drive for useful data.

Like a cyber hunter stalking her digital prey, she had slashed through its defences to get at its vulnerable underbelly. Now it seemed she was poised to make the kill.

'What have you found?'

'Our roadkill friend has been busy lately, mostly deleting stuff,' Frost explained. 'Unfortunately for him, deleting something doesn't get rid of it. All it does is flag that disk partition as available to overwrite, and even then a trace of the original data can stay for—'

'Just give me the short version,' McKnight interrupted. As fascinating as the technical aspects of her profession were, she was more concerned with the information Frost had uncovered than how she'd found it.

'Jeez, what a way to kill my buzz,' Frost griped. 'Anyway, I managed to reconstitute several emails between Umarov and

235

a guy called Anatoly Glazov. They started a few weeks ago. I had to run them through a translator program, so they read like a pair of fucking Martians talking to each other, but the gist of it seems to be that Glazov asked Umarov to supply him with several cases of D, which I guess refers to Danubit – the explosive.' She paused a moment to read on a little further in the emails she'd only just finished reconstituting. 'Umarov says . . . it'll be risky but he thinks he can do it.'

'Fuck the translator program,' Stav said, sensing she was having difficulty. Tossing aside the papers he'd been examining, he strode over to her computer. 'Bring up the original emails, please.'

Hesitating, Frost glanced at McKnight, who nodded her assent.

Hitting a couple of keys to revert to the original Cyrillic versions, Frost leaned back from the computer. 'Knock yourself out, big guy. Not literally, of course,' she added with a fake smile. 'You did that already.'

Giving her a look of annoyance, Stav went to work, his eyes quickly darting across the screen. Even Frost was surprised at the rate he was able to take in information.

'She is right,' he said at last. 'It seems the two men were old work colleagues. Glazov approached Umarov asking him to supply the explosives, and offering fifty thousand roubles in return.'

'So where did they go?' McKnight asked.

'According to this, Umarov was to take the explosives to an abandoned warehouse on the south side of the city, where some men would be waiting with his payment. There is nothing more beyond that.'

McKnight nodded. It wasn't perfect, but it was a whole lot more than they'd had a few minutes earlier.

'Then we need to find out who Anatoly Glazov is, and

where he lives,' she decided. 'If the two of them were old work colleagues, he should be on the mining company's personnel database.'

'This is not problem,' Stav said, reaching for his phone. 'FSB will find what we need.'

It took less than a minute for Stav to be connected to the right department within the FSB's immense organisation, and even less time for him to put forth his request for information. With the enquiry submitted, he hung up and folded his arms, whistling under his breath.

Sensing their eyes on him, he smiled. 'Chill and be patient, my friends. We wait.'

'I'm chilled enough,' Frost assured him.

Thirty seconds later, his phone pinged with an incoming message. Manipulating the comically small touch-screen phone with his massive hands, he called up the message and scrolled down to read.

'Well?' McKnight prompted, eager to know more.

Stav let out a snort of amusement as a grin slowly split his face.

'You will love this.'

Chapter 32

'We have him,' Miranova announced, reading off the information forwarded by FSB headquarters in Moscow.

McKnight had called them with the news of their breakthrough only moments earlier, quickly explaining the email chain they had found between Umarov and Glazov, and that all available information on Glazov would be sent on to them.

Miranova turned her laptop around, allowing Drake and Mason to see what she was looking at. Staring back at them was a passport photo of a ruggedly handsome, practical-looking man of middle age, the sort who seemed as though he belonged in a sawmill or a factory. The date stamp announced that the photo had been taken seven years previously.

'Anatoly Glazov, born here in Chechnya in 1948. He served in the Red Army engineer corps for nearly a decade,' she explained, rapidly summarising the information in his dossier. 'When the Cold War ended, he moved into the private sector and started working for Norilsk Nickel as an engineering contractor.'

Mason could see where she was going with this. 'The sort of guy who'd be responsible for rock blasting, that sort of thing?'

'Precisely. He retired from mining operations about three years ago due to ill health. He has been living off a company pension ever since.'

Drake was elated. As far as the evidence went, it didn't get much better than this. They were dealing with a man with possible sympathies to Chechen separatism, and who had the knowledge and experience to build improvised explosive devices.

'So he could be the guy behind this,' Mason reasoned.

'Possible, but unlikely,' Miranova countered. 'He was not flagged by our internal security directorates, and his file shows no history of political activity. Even his military record mentions no anti-government sentiment. He does not fit the profile of a terrorist leader.'

'But he *is* hard up for a few quid,' Drake chipped in.

The FSB agent frowned at the unfamiliar expression. 'Excuse me?'

'He's a Brit,' Mason apologised on Drake's behalf.

Drake gave him a disapproving look before continuing. 'He wouldn't be living here if he had the money to get out. A guy like that might be willing to build bombs for the right price, especially for a fellow Chechen.'

'That is my theory also.' He saw a faint smile; a tacit acknowledgement that they were both on the same page. 'His last known address is less than twenty miles from here.'

For Drake, the next course of action was obvious. 'Then let's pay Mr Glazov a visit.'

Chapter 33

Anatoly Glazov grasped the edge of his chipped, stained kitchen sink, his thin body convulsing in another coughing fit that felt as though it was tearing him apart from the inside. With a final racking gasp, he spat a glob of foamy mucus into the sink, trying to ignore the fact that it was pink with blood.

He turned on the tap to wash it away, then straightened up and ran a shaking hand across his mouth. The attack had left him feeling sick and weak, but it had passed now. It always passed.

Reaching for the bottle of vodka on the shelf beside him, he poured a generous glass and took a gulp, forcing the stinging liquid down his throat. It made him want to gag, but gradually the pain subsided as a languid warmth began to spread outwards from his stomach.

He was just laying the glass down when he caught a glimpse of his reflection in the grimy kitchen window. He saw his face, gaunt and haggard, his clothes hanging slack on his spare frame, his hair thinning and grey. He was barely sixty, yet he felt decades older.

Twenty years ago he'd been a strong, vibrant man in the prime of life. A little thick around the midsection perhaps, and an inch or two shorter than he might have liked, but still ruggedly handsome and with a successful army career under his belt. Now it was all gone. Chechnya had eaten away his life just as Norilsk had eaten away his health.

Still, none of that mattered now. Now he had the means to escape this war-torn hellhole. A quarter of a million roubles had just been deposited in his bank account; generous payment for a few days of easy work. The buyer, whose name he'd never learned, had promised him justice and retribution for the Chechen people, claiming his work would change the course of history and other such bullshit. In truth, Glazov had no interest in it. He had never considered himself terribly nationalistic, and was too old to start now.

He had agreed to the man's offer for the money, and in that regard he was very passionate. A quarter of a million roubles was enough to get him booked on a flight out of Chechnya, enough to get him the medical treatment he could never afford before. Enough perhaps to give a man a second chance at life.

He was just pondering the future that lay ahead when the phone in his living room started ringing. Turning his eyes away from the unpleasant reflection, he shuffled through the untidy hallway and into the cramped, cold room that smelled of damp and mould and decay. The room that served as both his main living space and, in light of his declining health, his prison.

He scooped up his phone, irritated at the distraction. 'Yes?'

'You're in danger.'

The voice that spoke to him was deep, pleasant sounding, clearly belonging to an educated man. Glazov knew exactly who it was. It was the man who had just given him a second chance at life.

Only now he seemed poised to take it away again.

'W-what did you say?'

'You're in danger,' the man repeated. 'The FSB are on to

you. They found Umarov and unless he was very careful, they're likely to make the connection to you.'

Glazov's breath caught in his throat. Umarov, his old friend from the days when the two of them had worked for Norilsk Nickel together, had smuggled out the explosives he'd needed to build the bombs. He'd assured Glazov that he would take care of any red tape, and that the matter was unlikely to receive any police follow-up.

'But . . . how?' Glazov asked. It should have been an angry demand, but instead it came out as a pathetic whimper.

'Perhaps I should ask you the same question. You assured me the bomb wouldn't compromise us.'

'And I meant it,' Glazov stammered, feeling utterly helpless. He was afraid, and there was no hiding it. His hands were starting to tremble, and he was beginning to wish he hadn't left his glass of vodka in the kitchen. 'I don't understand how this happened, but it wasn't me. I didn't let you down. You have to believe that.'

'But you *are* a liability. If the FSB capture you, they could make you talk.'

Glazov was practically shaking with fear. He knew well enough the ruthless measures the FSB took with suspected terrorists. Man or woman, old or young, sick or healthy, it made no difference to them.

He wasn't cut out for this sort of thing. Even during his army days he'd been an engineer, not a soldier. He'd never killed a man in his life, and had certainly never been hunted and shot at.

'What do I do?' he asked, pleading for help, for understanding. How could he make this man understand that he wasn't the enemy, that he hadn't betrayed him? 'Tell me what I can do.'

Agonising silence greeted him for the next few seconds.

He was a condemned man waiting for the judge to pass sentence.

'I can get you out, but we must move quickly,' his employer decided. 'Pack some warm clothes and be ready to leave. I'm sending someone to pick you up. They'll identify themselves with the password *Alexander*. Do you understand?'

Glazov swallowed, trying to force down the bile that seemed to be rising in his throat. 'Y-you promise you'll help me?'

'You're a man with skills, Anatoly,' the voice admitted. 'Skills that could be valuable to us in future. If you agree to work for us, we can protect you. Now get moving. Good luck.'

With that, the line went dead.

Laying down the phone, Glazov turned and slowly surveyed the room: the threadbare furniture, the old-fashioned TV and the peeling wallpaper. His home, his life, his prison.

It took all of three seconds for him to make his decision.

'Fuck this,' he said, hurrying into his bedroom. If he had to throw in his hand with a bunch of nationalistic zealots, so be it. At least he'd be alive.

The rest he would figure out later.

Chapter 34

Drake braced himself as the 4x4 ploughed through another deep hole in what was laughably called a road, the impact practically jolting him out of his seat. The dipped headlights illuminated a grey world of leafless woods, muddy overgrown fields and the occasional crumbling ruins of long-abandoned homesteads.

He hadn't seen a single electric light in the past ten minutes, and it didn't take much imagination to guess why. Most residents here would have cleared out during the First Chechen War, with few willing to return to a country scarred by conflict and suffering.

And yet here, in the midst of this remote war-torn landscape, Anatoly Glazov had chosen to make his home. Drake couldn't wait to pay him a visit.

Gearing up for a house assault was a ritual he'd gone through more times than he could count, and always it involved the same round of last-minute equipment and weapon checks, the same worries over trivial details, the same recitals of whatever plan they were expected to carry out.

In this case there wasn't much of a plan to follow. Their objective was simply to get to the isolated farm where Glazov had set up shop, find him and secure him for questioning. With little knowledge of what to expect once they were on site, it was impossible to formulate a more sophisticated strategy.

Still, the FSB were clearly erring on the side of caution. He, Mason and Miranova were accompanied by a pair of tactical agents in full body armour and woodland BDUs (Battle Dress Uniform).

They were certainly ready for a fight. Drake had spotted tear-gas canisters, breaching shotguns and stun grenades amongst their gear, but their weapon of choice seemed to be AKS-74s: compact and modern variants of the legendary AK-47 assault rifle. Such weapons were accurate and reliable even in severe weather, and powerful enough to punch through most body armour without difficulty.

It rather smacked of overkill to apprehend one frightened old man, but as the saying went, it was better to have a weapon and not need it than the other way around.

Drake glanced down to inspect the weapon he'd been issued with – an MP-443 Grach. A big, chunky automatic pistol, the Grach was a relatively new weapon that had only been adopted by the Russians a few years back. It felt solid and durable, but Drake had a feeling the balance was wrong for him and would hurt his accuracy. This one had been fitted with an integrated flashlight and laser sight for night operations, which further added to the weight. Still, he was confident he could hit most man-sized targets at up to 30 yards.

Holstering the weapon, he glanced at Mason, who was busy lacing up his boots. He seemed to be making a real meal of it, as if his fingers weren't listening to the commands from his brain. He could see the tension in the older man's face, as well as the faint sheen of sweat on his brow.

'You all right?' Drake asked, perplexed by his behaviour. Even if he'd been out of the game for a while, he was an experienced operative who had done this sort of thing dozens of times. Why was he acting like a rookie on his first mission?

'I'm hot as hell in this thing,' Mason replied, shifting uncomfortably inside his winter BDUs. The layered, thermally insulated uniform had bulked out his already large frame.

Drake frowned, sensing there was more to it than mere discomfort. 'Need a hand with that?' he asked, gesturing to his bootlaces.

Mason flashed him an angry look. 'The day I can't lace up my own fucking boots is the day they put me out to pasture.'

With a final hard yank he finished tying the lace, then reached up and wiped the sweat from his brow. He looked as though he'd just finished a strenuous workout.

Before Drake could question his friend further, Miranova twisted around in her seat.

'We are less than five minutes out,' she reported, having consulted the GPS unit mounted on the dash. Using a printed map to navigate in these parts would have been an exercise in futility; he doubted if most of the roads here had even been surveyed. 'When we get there, Agents Pushkin and Vasilev will handle the breach. We will go in once the building is secure. Understand?'

Drake nodded. Being the most heavily armed and armoured, it made sense for the two tactical agents to spearhead the assault. There weren't many problems that their combined firepower couldn't overcome.

'As long as we find Glazov, I don't care how it's done.'

This wasn't why he had come to Chechnya. He was here for Anya, not to get involved in the FSB's war. But there was still a chance that this Glazov, whoever he was, might lead Drake to her. He could only hope the man had something worthwhile to share with them.

He flexed his gloved hands, eager to get moving. The action itself he could handle; it was the waiting that did his head in. So much of his military career had been spent waiting – waiting to attack, waiting for support, waiting for an ambush, waiting for a release from the endless tension and paranoia of being in a hostile country.

But beneath it all, he sensed another reason for his unease. He had no cause to suspect the assault wouldn't go exactly to plan, yet something in the back of his mind wouldn't let it go.

Their adversaries had been one step ahead of them the whole time. Had they really managed to gain the upper hand now?

Chapter 35

Glazov was gasping in shallow, ragged breaths as he shuffled down the corridor, clutching a single suitcase that represented everything of value to him in this world. He had to pause every so often as another coughing fit overtook him, but somehow he found the strength to pick it up and keep moving.

Strangely, he felt little remorse at the things he was leaving behind. There was nothing here that meant much to him. He'd moved back here to his family home years ago for no other reason than because he couldn't afford to buy a place of his own. He'd even tried to sell the farm and its surrounding land to anyone who would buy it, but such a desperate scheme had been doomed to failure from the start. All of the adjoining farms had long since been abandoned, and no property developer worth his salt would buy land here.

No, he wouldn't miss this place one bit.

He paused for a moment at the entrance to his old workshop, still strewn with the tools he'd used to construct the bombs. Such a task had been easy for a man of his experience. He'd dealt with explosives throughout most of his life, both in the army and as a civilian engineer, and knew how best to employ their effects.

He hadn't asked too many questions about their intended targets, partly to guarantee the security of the buyers but mainly because he just didn't want to know. It was easier to justify if he knew nothing. In fact, it had almost been possible to forget he'd done it.

Almost.

Pushing those thoughts away, he hurried past, heading for the living room.

He was just laying down the suitcase when the front door resounded with a hard, almost violent blow. His already labouring heart went into overtime at the realisation that someone was right outside.

Was it the FSB come to arrest him, or his buyer come to rescue him?

Either way he was taking no chances. Reaching into his coat, he pulled out a Makarov pistol; a relic from his days in the Red Army. He hadn't maintained it very well over the years, but the weapon was so simple that there were few things to go wrong with it. He was confident it would still fire if he pulled the trigger, though he prayed it wouldn't come to that.

With the pistol gripped tight in sweating hands, he advanced slowly towards the front door. It was heavy and solid, built in the days when strength was the best deterrent against theft, and secured with a deadbolt on his side. Nothing short of a battering ram would break it down.

The door rattled in its frame as it took another hard blow. Whoever was out there clearly wasn't one for waiting around.

'Who's there?' he called out, trying to sound braver and more dominant than he felt. The Makarov in his hand offered less reassurance than he'd hoped. There could be a dozen armed men out there for all he knew, and one rusted pistol certainly wouldn't stop them.

Then, to his surprise, a woman's voice called out in answer: 'Alexander.'

Relief surged through him. He hadn't expected his saviour to come in the form of a woman, but he certainly wasn't about to question it at that moment. If anything, her prompt arrival here was a telling indication of how powerful and organised his new benefactor was. Shoving the Makarov in his pocket, he hurried forwards, unbarred the door and swung it open.

The woman who stood before him was tall and strikingly attractive, her short blonde hair damp from the rain, her icy blue eyes locked with his. She was dressed in woodland camouflage gear, and judging by the mud splattered on her boots and trousers, she had already hiked some distance to get here.

Without saying a word she stepped in over the threshold, and instinctively Glazov backed off a pace or two. There was something about her, some hidden aura of menace, that made him shiver from more than just the cold.

'W-who are you?' he stammered, wishing he'd kept the Makarov in his hand.

For a moment he caught a glimmer of something in her eyes; something that put him in mind of a field mouse about to be pounced on by a hawk. She hadn't come all this way to help him, he realised at last. Why would they go to all that trouble for a sick, crippled old man?

She had come to silence him before the FSB got here.

In a moment of blind panic, his hand went for the gun in his pocket.

He was far too late. He saw her draw a weapon from a holster behind her back, saw the long tapering barrel of a silencer as she swung it up towards his head in a single fluid motion.

His last sight was of her cold, remorseless blue eyes staring into his as she squeezed the trigger. There was a flash, a moment of sickening blackness, and then he saw no more.

Lowering the silenced M1911 automatic, Anya looked down at Glazov. He was lying in a heap in the hallway, his blood slowly soaking into the floorboards beneath. His face still bore an expression of blank, uncomprehending shock, his eyes wide and glassy. A single .45-calibre round to the forehead had ended his life before he'd even hit the ground.

She didn't allow herself to feel bad for him. He might have been a sick man of advancing years just trying to make some money, but to do it he'd knowingly constructed bombs designed to kill innocent people. Men like him deserved no pity.

Her thoughts were interrupted by the faint rumble of a car engine in the distance. Returning to the door, she peered out into the darkened woods that surrounded the isolated farm.

Sure enough, she could just make out twin points of light bouncing and jolting between the tree trunks. A single vehicle trying to negotiate the muddy, neglected road that wound its way up here.

It could only be the FSB, coming here to arrest Glazov. Little did they know that they were already too late.

At a guess, she would put them half a mile away, with a top speed of no more than 20 miles per hour over such rough terrain. She had a minute, perhaps two at most, before they got here.

She would have to move fast.

Emerging from the forest road that had snaked its way uphill, the 4x4 found its path barred by a 15-foot-high chain-link fence that apparently marked the boundary of Glazov's farm. A pair of big double gates straddled the road, on which a couple of signs had been crudely drawn in Cyrillic. Drake guessed they conveyed the Russian equivalent of *Trespassers can fuck offski*.

Normally such a barrier would have presented a serious obstacle, but fortunately their driver had the right idea. Dropping down a gear, he jammed his foot on the gas and held on tight as the big vehicle catapulted forwards, blasting straight through the chain-link gates as if they weren't even there. No doubt the paintwork would suffer for this, but it wasn't as if he was paying the bill.

Carrying on for perhaps another 50 yards, he hit the brakes and brought them to a halt in a spray of mud and exhaust fumes. The farmhouse lay directly ahead, brightly illuminated now in the 4x4's headlights.

It was an old-fashioned two-storey wooden structure, its shape and general appearance reminding Drake of Dorothy's house from *The Wizard of Oz*. This property, however, was in serious need of attention, with peeling paintwork, warped boards and hastily patched sections of roof that he was sure must be leaking in this weather. There were no lights that he could see.

The two tactical agents wasted no time throwing their doors open and rushing outside, converging on the house with their weapons up, crouched down low to present smaller targets. Drake, Mason and Miranova were right behind them, ready to move in as backup once they'd made entry.

Drake saw Pushkin reach for the breaching shotgun slung over his shoulder, saw him work the pump action to draw the first shell into the breech before levelling the weapon at the door.

Two seconds later, the sharp crack of the breaching gun split the air, followed by the crunch of shattered wood as the door gave way. The solid slug had done its work well, blasting a 6-inch hole in the door and destroying whatever bolt had held it closed.

Pushkin raised his foot and kicked it open while the next

agent moved forwards, assault rifle up to his shoulder. For a moment the beam from the under-barrel flashlight pierced the smoky darkness beyond.

Then suddenly the entire scene vanished in a blinding flash that seared itself on the backs of Drake's eyes, and instinctively he threw up his arm and turned away. An instant later a thunderous boom rolled around the clearing as if a bolt of lightning had struck right in their midst. Even from this distance he could feel the sudden, intense blast of heat.

With his eyes streaming, Drake turned back towards the building. A cloud of white smoke had engulfed the front entrance and much of the farmhouse, obscuring what was going on inside. But even he could see the red glow of flames spreading rapidly to encompass much of the ground floor.

'They set a trap!' Mason hissed. 'They're torching the fucking place.'

Drake said nothing. He recognised the distinctive chemical odour in the air following the detonation. It was a flashbang grenade, designed to produce an intense flash of light and sound that would blind and disorient enemies. It must have been triggered when the first agent made entry.

The unlucky man who had triggered it was lying sprawled in the mud near the main entrance, trying to rise but failing miserably. Drake knew from experience that the blast would have deafened him and disrupted his equilibrium, rendering him useless for the next couple of minutes at least.

Straight away Drake understood what their adversary was up to. If all he had wanted to accomplish was to destroy the house and its contents, he could have done that long before the FSB arrived. Instead they had waited until the team tried to breach, setting fire to the house to create a diversion and triggering the phosphorous grenade to temporarily blind them.

'He's making a run for it,' he hissed. 'Cole, go left and circle around behind. Anika, move in from the front. Go now!'

Without waiting for a reply, Drake charged towards the house with the automatic up and ready. Flames were licking from the ground-floor windows, accompanied by the tinkle of shattering glass as they began to give way. Despite the rain's onslaught, Drake could feel the heat searing his exposed skin. He guessed the ground floor had been liberally doused with petrol to help the fire spread quickly.

There was no way in through the front door. The hallway was already a mass of flames, the old floorboards probably starting to give way as the growing blaze consumed them.

He veered right, making to circle around behind the building and cover the rear. He could only hope Mason had listened to him and was approaching from the other side.

He spotted something in his peripheral vision. His gaze swept upwards, just in time to catch sight of something hurled from one of the upper windows. It landed with a heavy thump perhaps ten paces in front of him.

He knew what it was right away, and instinctively threw himself on the ground just as the grenade detonated, engulfing the area in white light. His quick thinking saved his vision, though the delay bought his adversary a few precious seconds in which to act.

With his ears ringing from the blast and splashes of light blurring his eyes, Drake picked himself up and peered through the haze of phosphorous smoke. He was just able to make out a figure in camouflage fatigues leap down from the upper floor, land and roll in the mud to absorb the impact, then leap upright again and sprint off through the darkened woods beyond.

Clearly whoever they were dealing with tonight, it wasn't Glazov. This was not the work of a frightened, frail man, but of a capable and resourceful operative. But whoever this person was, there was enough chaos left behind for him or her to be a mile or more from here by the time Miranova and the others figured out what had happened.

Scrambling to his feet, Drake keyed his radio.

'Target exiting rear building, heading for the woods. I'm in pursuit!'

'Ryan, stop,' he heard Miranova protest. 'Hold your position and wait for support.'

Drake ignored her. To delay now would give their target time to open the distance and slip away. Their only chance to prevent this was to strike now.

'Cole, where the hell are you?' he demanded.

'Ten seconds, Ryan,' Mason replied, already sounding out of breath. 'It's a fucking assault course around here – there's shit piled all around the house.'

That was ten seconds he didn't have. With his heart pounding and rain sluicing down around him, Drake charged through the muddy clearing, leapt over a bank of tangled undergrowth and pounded into the woods beyond.

His target was fast despite the darkness and the mud and the clawing brambles and bushes underfoot, darting with nimble grace through the difficult terrain and somehow managing to avoid any serious obstacles. Drake was hard-pressed just to keep up, and unfortunately not blessed with the same instinct for avoiding trouble.

Vaulting over a fallen tree trunk in an attempt to gain ground, he landed right in a patch of thorny briars left over from the previous summer. Unless he wanted to spend the next hour untangling himself, there was nothing to do but power through them, ignoring the pain as their wickedly barbed thorns tore through fabric and skin.

As Drake had learned during his days with the SAS, the key to evading pursuit in woodland is not speed, but rather

255

direction. Amateurs often assume that escaping simply involves putting as much distance between themselves and their pursuers as possible, and therefore tend to run directly away in a straight line, making them easy to track.

Experienced operatives would constantly switch direction as they retreated, using any available cover to interrupt their opponents' view before darting off left or right, constantly wrong-footing them and forcing them to second-guess their own movements.

Based on what he'd seen so far, Drake knew he was dealing with anything but an amateur tonight.

Sure enough, his target seemed to be everywhere and nowhere at once, disappearing behind tree trunks and bushes only to reappear somewhere else entirely. Once or twice Drake was convinced he'd lost his target altogether, but always he caught a fleeting glimpse that allowed him to resume his pursuit.

The one problem with constantly switching direction was that if the target failed to lose the pursuers quickly, then he or she would be slowed down by the efforts to escape. As the glow of the burning house receded into the distance Drake sensed himself gaining ground, and that knowledge spurred him on to greater efforts.

Then, just like that his opponent seemed to vanish, as if the ground had simply swallowed the person up.

With a final burst of speed, Drake sprinted to the point of disappearance, only to find himself facing down a steep, heavily forested slope. Above the roar of the burning farm and the pounding of his own heartbeat he could hear the distant rumble of a river, and through the trees he could just make out the muddy track of a road that paralleled it.

His target was already halfway down the slope, zigzagging down to the road where a car was likely waiting. To slip and fall now would risk a disabling injury and certain capture. Instead whoever he was pursuing was playing it safe.

The only way to catch this person was to do the opposite. Drake didn't stop to think it through. If he did, he'd undoubtedly realise what a bad idea this was and abandon the plan. Sometimes the only option was to act.

Holstering his automatic and checking that it was securely fastened in place, Drake backed up a pace, took a deep breath to psyche himself up and get more oxygen into his bloodstream, and threw himself over the edge.

He'd made it about 5 yards down the slope before his boots lost purchase on the muddy ground and he began to slide, his pace rapidly increasing as his own momentum carried him onwards. Unable to control his descent, he could do little except brace himself and hope for the best.

The contours of the slope were carrying him towards a gnarled spruce tree that clung precariously to a steep section of ground. A collision at this speed would undoubtedly break bones and damage internal organs. Throwing his weight to one side, he narrowly avoided slamming into the trunk, but the movement overbalanced him and, unable to prevent it, he began to roll.

There was no thought of exerting any conscious control now. All he could do was tuck his limbs in and endure the fall as his body tumbled down the slope like a rag doll, branches and sharp briars tearing at his flesh, jutting rocks slamming against him with bruising force. And all the while the world spun and lurched around him, all concept of direction now lost.

Only when he turned slightly and stabilised for a few seconds did he regain his orientation, catching a glimpse of the road directly below, along with his target leaping over a large boulder in the haste to escape.

For a few seconds at least, Drake held the advantage.

Allowing himself to slide the last few yards, he pitched over a stony outcrop and landed hard on the muddy, winding track that represented a road. He rolled once as he'd been trained to do in his SAS days, allowing the momentum of his fall to bleed away.

Breathing hard and trying to ignore the pain of the countless cuts and bruises he'd endured on the way down, he drew out his automatic just as his target leapt down on to the road about 10 yards away. A short distance beyond them stood a battered-looking 4x4.

'Freeze!' he yelled, levelling the weapon at the target's centre mass.

His order was obeyed immediately. Not many people will try to flee across open ground when they have a gun trained on their back.

'Hands where I can see them! Fucking get them up now!'

A pair of gloved hands was raised, neither of which held a weapon. There was no urgency in the movement, no hint of fear or tension in the set of the shoulders or the body posture. Instead it seemed as if having a gun pointed at his or her back was a mere inconvenience to be dealt with before moving on.

He didn't care how confident this person felt. He had the advantage.

'Turn around,' Drake ordered.

And then, just like that, it all changed.

'Are you going to shoot me, Ryan?' The voice that spoke was a woman's voice, low-pitched and faintly accented. A voice he knew all too well.

As the figure turned slowly to face him and the dim moonlight cast the facial features in sharp relief, Drake's heart began to pound even harder in his chest.

It was Anya.

Chapter 36

For the next few seconds the two of them remained frozen in position, each taking the measure of the other, neither moving a muscle as the rain continued to pour down around them.

Despite himself, despite everything he'd seen and endured over the past couple of days, Drake found himself taking in every detail of the woman standing before him. The woman he'd risked everything to protect.

Like him, she was soaked to the skin by the downpour, her blonde hair hanging limp and wet around her face. Her camouflage fatigues were splattered with mud and torn in places; evidence that even she hadn't been able to entirely avoid the sharp thorns that had shredded his uniform. She was breathing hard after the strenuous run from the farmhouse, her warm breath misting in the air around her.

But her eyes, or rather what lurked behind them, remained just as he remembered. Fierce, cold, predatory, constantly assessing every move he made and looking for weaknesses to exploit. By pointing a gun at her, he'd become a threat. And that was not a good position to be in.

'You don't give up, do you, Ryan?' she remarked with a grim smile, nodding to the slope he'd just hurled himself down. 'Even when you should.'

He rose up from his knees, lowering the weapon at the same time. 'Can't imagine where I get it from.'

Anya allowed her arms to fall by her sides. 'Why are you here?'

'Why do you think? I'm trying to stop you getting yourself killed,' he hit back, shaking with barely suppressed anger now he was at last face to face with her. 'Enough people have died already because of you. What the hell are you involved in, Anya?'

'This has nothing to do with you.'

'Like hell it doesn't. You made this my business when you contacted me in Washington. Either you wanted me to find you, or you were trying to frame me for that sniper attack. For your sake, I hope it was the first option.'

At this, he caught a fleeting look of surprise and confusion in her eyes. The same look he'd noticed during their momentary encounter on that rooftop in DC before she had vanished. But Anya, always the master of her own emotions, quickly pushed it away.

She shook her head, a loose tendril of damp hair falling across her eyes. 'Listen to me, Ryan. Listen well. I don't need your help or your protection. If you were any other man, I would have killed you already for the problems you have caused me. But if you interfere with my work again, I won't be so lenient. That's all I have to say.'

Her brief but chilling message delivered, she turned and began to walk away, heading for the 4x4.

'Stop!'

She halted, keeping her back to him. She didn't have to turn around to know she now had an automatic pointed at her back.

'I can't let you leave,' Drake said. 'Not without answers.'

'You're making a mistake,' she warned, her voice low and deceptively calm. 'Walk away before you make another.'

Drake stood his ground. He wasn't going anywhere. 'Not this time.'

There was a moment of inaction, of silence broken only by the relentless hammering of the rain around them. Then he heard a faint sigh, as if she were disappointed with how things had turned out.

It happened fast. Reaching into the combat smock she was wearing, she turned and hurled something straight at him. A green metal cylinder no larger than a can of soda, with a simple time-delay fuse fixed to one end.

Drake's instincts kicked in immediately. He started to turn aside, throwing up his arm in a vain attempt to shield himself from the imminent phosphorous detonation.

Then, just like that, he stopped. Even Anya would never be so reckless as to use a grenade like that at close quarters. The blast would just as likely injure or blind her, not to mention attract any FSB agents within 5 miles.

It was a bluff, a decoy designed to buy her time. Time to close the distance.

Recognising his mistake, he turned towards the woman who was now charging straight at him, and brought the weapon to bear on her.

His realisation had come a moment too late.

Reaching out, Anya clamped her hand around the barrel of the gun and twisted it upwards before he could get her in his sights. Her other hand shot out like a piston and delivered a hard strike just below his eye, stunning him. His grip on the weapon slackened, stars and flashes of light now blurring his vision.

Capitalising on his momentary weakness, Anya yanked the automatic out of his hand, drove a boot into the back of his left knee to buckle his legs, and finally delivered a second blow to the face that sent him sprawling in the mud.

Blinking and trying to refocus, Drake looked up at his opponent. Anya stood a few yards away, pacing around him in a slow circle, arms by her sides as if they were conducting a casual conversation instead of fighting. She had a knife sheathed in a harness at her left shoulder, though she had made no move to draw it, as if Drake wasn't worthy of such attention.

She glanced down at the weapon she had taken from him with such ease. Then, turning aside for a moment, she drew back her arm and tossed it into the swirling waters of the nearby river, swollen by the recent rain. 'Go home, Ryan,' she said in a tone of mild irritation, like a mother dealing with a stubborn child. She was breathing a little harder from her exertions, but otherwise showed no sign of fatigue. 'You're not ready for this.' Anger welled up inside him at the casual dismissal in her voice, as if he were a lackey to be summoned or discarded at her whim. As if everything he'd sacrificed to help her was for nothing. As if none of what they had been through over the past eighteen months meant anything to her.

'Forget what you're thinking and stay down,' she warned, sensing the flame of defiance growing inside him. 'You don't have what it takes to stop me.'

She meant what she said. She had no interest in fighting him; she had already accomplished what she'd set out to do tonight. If he stayed down, she would likely leave without further trouble. All he had to do was stay down.

He couldn't say for sure what it was that prompted him to get up. Perhaps it was a determination to make her explain her actions, perhaps it was because he didn't fully trust that she wouldn't attack him while he was down, or perhaps it was nothing more than wounded pride.

He'd been a boxer once upon a time. He'd fought dozens of opponents in his short career, taken plenty of hits along the way and even been knocked to the canvas a few times, but never had he failed to get up. He certainly didn't intend to start today.

Whatever the motivation, the result was the same. Rolling over and placing his hands beneath him, he forced himself up from the muddy ground, placing himself between Anya and the 4x4 further down the road. His fists were clenched, arms up and ready to defend himself.

Saying nothing, he spat bloody phlegm on the ground at her feet.

Anya shook her head. 'Suit yourself.'

Drake's mind was racing, trying to predict her next move. Anya's instincts would be telling her to finish this quickly, before the fight degenerated into a slugging match in which Drake's superior size and strength would inevitably take their toll. And before the FSB agents back at the farm found their way here.

She was going to attack.

She came at him again, moving fast to get in close before he could strike her. He had the longer reach, and she wanted to cancel out that advantage as quickly as possible.

Drawing on the skills he'd earned through hard experience in the ring years earlier, Drake saw her next punch coming and twisted aside to avoid it. Realising he'd caught her off balance and that he had mere moments to take advantage of it, he reached up, grabbed the knife still sheathed to her webbing and yanked it free of the scabbard.

Drake had less than a second to act before she realised the danger and retaliated. He had to make her back off, had to make her understand that he wasn't going to let her simply slip away.

He had to give her a sting.

Slashing downwards with the knife, he aimed for her flank. Experienced as she was with such close combat, she saw it coming and threw her weight to one side, but nonetheless the wickedly sharp blade sliced through fabric and skin.

That was it for her. She was done playing with him. Allowing her momentum to carry her, Anya twisted around to face him and lashed out with a vicious kick to the stomach. Drake grimaced in pain, feeling the bile rising to his throat. Coughing and gasping for air, he looked up just in time to see her knee rushing towards his face. He had no opportunity to block it, and could only close his eyes in preparation for the impact. White light exploded across his eyes, and his head was jerked sideways by the force of the blow. He could feel the warm slickness of blood flowing from the newly opened wound at his temple.

Before he knew it she had seized his left arm and twisted it behind his back. Her eyes flashed with anger as he began to buckle, trying to go with the movement. There would be no holding back this time, he knew.

Her other hand rose up, poised for a moment before the strike. Drake winced inwardly, knowing what was coming but powerless to prevent it. The blow landed right on the overtaxed shoulder joint. It was hard, clinical and precisely targeted for maximum effect. There was a crunch, an explosion of pain, and Drake let out an involuntary scream as his arm was dislocated from the socket. Knowing he was no longer a threat, Anya grabbed the radio microphone secured to his throat and yanked it off, taking the portable radio unit with it. This done, she released her hold and allowed him to collapse on the muddy ground.

The fight, such as it had been, was over.

Grimacing with pain, Drake rolled on to his back, his left arm limp and useless at his side. He looked up at her, half blinded by the deluge and the pain that blazed outwards from his dislocated joint.

Dropping the radio, Anya drove her boot heel into its plastic casing, crushing it into the ground and destroying the internal components. Her blue eyes held a mixture of anger and pity.

'Consider this a warning,' she said. 'There won't be another. If you stand in my way again, I'll kill you, Ryan.'

Drake could do nothing but watch as she turned and strode off down the road. A few moments later, the 4x4's engine rumbled into life and the vehicle took off in a spray of mud, leaving him alone.

Chapter 37

Afghanistan, 28 September 1988

Breathing hard, gritting her teeth against the pain, Anya could do nothing but hang there, swaying slowly back and forth like a piece of meat in a slaughterhouse. Her bound hands were looped into a steel hook fixed to the ceiling, her feet dangling a clear foot above the dirty concrete floor. She was naked, as she always was for these sessions.

'Once more, why did you turn against us?'

She couldn't see the owner of that voice. She could never see him. He was always behind her, or standing in the shadows, or speaking to her through microphones.

He had ceased to be a physical person in her mind. He was just there, an omnipotent presence that permeated the very fabric of this room, all-seeing and all-knowing; existing both around her and within her. She couldn't hide from him, couldn't escape him, couldn't fight him.

Perhaps it had all been an illusion. Perhaps he had always known what she was doing. She no longer trusted herself to make that judgement.

That was what she dreaded most about these interrogation sessions. Not the pain or the humiliation, but the doubt. No longer knowing what was real and what wasn't, whose motives she understood and whose she didn't.

He had been right. He'd played these games long before her.

She said nothing in response to his question. She never spoke, never gave anything.

She heard the faint hiss as the whip arced through the air, followed by the harsh crack as it connected with her flesh. Pain burned through her body as the coiled leather sliced through her skin. Already her back had been reduced to a raw mass of bloody welts and torn flesh – so many she could scarcely feel individual wounds. She knew she would carry the scars of this for the rest of her life, however long that might be.

She clenched her teeth so hard she felt they must surely break, managing to keep from crying out by sheer force of will. Only a strangled groan of agony escaped her lips.

They would come for her. Over and over she told herself this, willing it to be true. They would come for her. They wouldn't forget the sacrifices she had made, the great things she had done for them. They looked after their own – that was what she had been told.

They would find her and they would rescue her and take her back to a safe place. She had only to hold out until then.

'I know what you're thinking, Anya,' the voice said, sounding almost consoling, sympathetic. 'You're thinking you've been trained to resist interrogation, that you're strong and determined and different from the others. You won't break, no matter what we do to you.'

Cain will find me, she thought as she raised her chin a little. He'll take me away from this place, away from you. I'll heal and be whole and strong again. And one day I'll come back for you.

'Everyone who has ever been brought into this room has thought the same thing, and each of them eventually came to understand the truth,' he went on. 'The truth is, everyone breaks sooner or later. Everyone. It's just . . . a matter of time. And time is something we have plenty of.'

Her stubborn silence elicited only a faint sigh of disappointment. She heard footsteps as the guard behind stepped closer, but there was no whistle of an incoming whip this time.

Instead she felt him smear something on her back. A liquid, cold and almost oily. A moment later, when she caught the scent of medical alcohol, she understood what they were doing.

Her body went rigid as the first wave of pain struck like a physical blow, reverberating around her body like echoes in a cave. This time there was no holding it inside. She threw her head back as an agonised scream tore from her.

Chechnya, 22 December 2008

The old Russian army jeep bumped its way down the muddy forest track at top speed, swerving and skidding dangerously as the road twisted and turned, headlight beams piercing the darkness to illuminate the dense ranks of fir trees that crowded close. Snow and hail blowing in fitful bursts pattered off the windscreen like shotgun pellets.

Far from slowing down in response to the appalling driving conditions, Anya stamped harder on the accelerator, prompting a throaty roar from the old engine and a renewed surge of speed.

The sturdy vehicle wallowed through dips and bumps, straining the suspension, but Anya didn't care. She was gripping the wheel so hard it made her joints hurt.

Over and over she replayed her encounter with Drake, the harsh words they had exchanged, and the short but intense confrontation that had followed. She was angry with herself. She should have been able to overpower him easily, yet more than once he'd almost got the better of her.

Why couldn't he have stayed down like she'd told him to? What had he meant about her contacting him in Washington, and why was he now pursuing her so relentlessly?

Yet even as she asked that last question, she already knew the answer. It was the same reason she'd tracked him down in Afghanistan, the same reason she'd kept watch over him since they'd parted ways in Iraq the previous year.

The same reason she found her thoughts lingering on the night they had spent together amongst the endless dunes of the desert, searching and finding each other in the flickering light of a campfire.

Neither could let the other go.

And more than any fight or enemy, that frightened her.

Forcing those thoughts to the back of her mind, she reached for her cellphone and dialled Atayev's number from memory. It rang only once before he picked up.

'Were you successful?' he asked without preamble.

Her own reply was equally succinct. 'Yes.'

'And the FSB?'

'They arrived as I was leaving. I had to create a distraction.'

In truth, it had been a close-run thing – closer than she was prepared to admit to Atayev. Had she delayed any longer in setting out to neutralise Glazov, she might well have found an FSB assault team waiting for her.

That prompted a moment of silence. 'But you got clear.'

'I did.' As she'd hoped, she had managed to escape the area before the FSB could coordinate an effective search.

'And what about Drake?' he asked.

If possible, Anya gripped the wheel even harder. 'Injured, but alive.'

'You're playing a dangerous game. He could compromise you.'

'Let me worry about Drake,' she said, managing to keep her voice cold and dispassionate despite her private thoughts. 'Just be ready to act.'

'We'll be there,' he assured her. 'How long?'

Anya glanced at her watch. 'Ten minutes. I'll signal once I'm in position.'

'Understood. Good luck.'

With that, the line went dead.

Tossing the phone on to the passenger seat, Anya swung the 4x4 around a wide bend and stamped on the gas once more.

Chapter 38

Breathing hard, Drake backed up against the stout trunk of a towering pine tree, sliding down the rough bark until he was on his knees, shivering as the adrenalin rush of his pursuit faded. He was relieved to be out of the rain, but the deep penetrating cold was slowly working its way into his limbs.

His left arm hung slack by his side, lightning bursts of pain flashing outwards from the dislocated shoulder joint with every movement.

Ahead of him stretched the steep rock and tree-covered slope leading back up to the farm; a formidable enough obstacle even for an able-bodied climber, never mind an injured and half-frozen man with a dislocated arm.

Even now he could scarcely comprehend the depth of Anya's betrayal. He had risked everything to find her, to warn her, to protect her, yet she had breezed through him as if he were nothing. What had happened to her? What madness was driving her onwards?

And what was she going to do next?

He gritted his teeth, slamming his good right hand into the unyielding tree trunk as anger welled up inside him. This wasn't over yet.

But first he needed to sort himself out. The cuts, grazes and bruises from his fall down the slope weren't a problem, but he had to do something about the dislocated shoulder before he went on.

Reaching up, he felt around the injured joint, manipulating the slack humerus to work out how best to fit it back in. There was no great secret to fixing dislocations – all you had to do was get the bone at roughly the correct angle, then apply sufficient force to pop it back into the socket. Of course, it was usually a two-man job, with plenty of painkillers thrown in to sweeten the deal. This one was going to be a different affair altogether.

Dragging himself to his feet once more, he used his good arm to brace his left elbow against the tree trunk, holding it at right angles from his body and doing his best to line up the head of the bone with the joint. He took a deep breath and closed his eyes, trying to summon up the will to do what he had to.

For a moment he saw Anya standing over him as he lay injured on the ground, drenched by the rain but undaunted by his efforts to subdue her. He saw the pity and contempt in her eyes, felt her disappointment at the pathetic fight he'd put up, and instantly a flame of defiance leapt up inside him.

Don't think about it, a voice in his head warned him. Just get it done.

Opening his eyes and clenching his jaw, Drake leaned back a little, paused just a moment, then drove his elbow into the tree trunk. In a sickening moment the force of the impact travelled like a shockwave up his arm, displacing the bone back towards his body.

There was a moment of straining, tightening resistance as the head of his humerus struggled to find its way back into the glenohumeral joint, the bone seeming to flex under the pressure. Then, with a grinding pop and an explosion of pain, it finally slipped back in.

Falling to his knees on the muddy ground, Drake closed his eyes, gritted his teeth and let out a low, almost animalistic growl, fighting to keep from crying out as wave after wave of pain radiated out from the newly realigned joint.

After what seemed like a lifetime, the pain receded to a more tolerable level. He looked down at his hand, clenched and unclenched it a few times, then tested the strength of his grip. He tried moving his arm at the shoulder, and though he was left wincing in pain, he nonetheless found that the limb moved freely. It worked, and right now that was all that mattered.

Trying to get his breathing under control, he reached into his webbing for his cellphone. Anya had destroyed the tactical radio linking him with Miranova and the other agents, forcing him to improvise.

He did his best to shield the phone from the rain as he dialled with frozen fingers. The shivering was really kicking in now, further hampering his efforts.

Miranova would likely have silenced her own cell to prevent it going off during the assault, but with luck she would have kept it switched on. It rang out for a good ten seconds before a connection was finally made.

'Ryan?' she said, her voice broken and distorted by the poor signal.

Drake grimaced as he shifted position and his shoulder protested against the effort. 'Yeah.'

'Where are you? You were not answering your radio.' The anger and concern in her voice were obvious.

'I lost my radio. I'm at the . . . base of the slope near the river,' he managed to say through chattering teeth.

'Are you all right?'

That was a matter of perspective. 'Yeah.'

'What about the hostile?'

Drake glanced over to where Anya's vehicle had been parked. She was long gone by now. 'I lost them.'

His report was met with a moment of silence. 'Stay there. We will come for you.'

Drake shook his head. 'Forget it. I'm coming back up.'

With no one to extinguish the flames, the wooden farmhouse had become a raging inferno that was still burning a good half hour after the disastrous attempt to breach it. Even from 100 yards away on the edge of the clearing Drake could feel the heat of the flames, though in this case he was glad of it.

He had been exhausted, soaked through and chilled to the bone by the time he'd clawed his way back up the slope. Shivering, bleeding and gasping for breath, he had practically stumbled into Miranova and Mason, who had been attempting to follow his confused and zigzagging trail by flashlight.

'Christ, you look like you got into a fight with a fucking lawnmower,' Mason decided, surveying him properly for the first time in the crimson light of the flames. Wet, bedraggled, cut, grazed and bruised, his clothes shredded and stained with mud and blood, Drake was a sorry-looking sight indeed.

He gave Mason a sharp look. He was in no mood for playful banter after his confrontation with Anya.

'How do you feel?' Miranova asked, standing a few paces away with her arms folded. The look in her dark eyes was enough to make the others keep their distance. The tension in the air around her was almost palpable.

Drake glanced up at her. 'Like shit.'

'Good.'

He snorted with grim amusement. 'Thanks for the sympathy.'

'What do you expect?' Taking a step forwards, she jabbed

a finger at him. '*You* were the one who went charging off into the woods alone when I told you to wait!'

'Wait?' Drake repeated, rising to his feet as simmering frustration got the better of him. 'Wait for what? Wait for them to get away? Wait for you to get your arses in gear?'

'So instead you tried to track an armed opponent alone?' she challenged him, bristling with anger. 'You were lucky you didn't get yourself killed. How you have survived this long with such stupidity, I have no idea.'

'Okay, knock it off,' Mason said, leaping to Drake's defence. 'Both of you. While you're sat here bitching at each other, our assassin is getting away.'

Miranova looked at him for a long moment, though not with the casual dismissal she normally displayed. For once she actually seemed to be heeding his words.

Letting out a sigh, she turned away for a moment and pushed a lock of soaking black hair out of her face, doing her best to regain her composure.

'Then let us start with what we know,' she said at last, turning her attention back to Drake. 'Tell me what happened out there.'

Drake sniffed and rolled his shoulder, wincing in pain as he did so. 'I went after him, lost my footing on a slope and, well, guess what happened.'

Miranova frowned, unconvinced. 'So you did not see Glazov's killer?'

He shook his head. 'It was dark. He was too fast.'

Which led her to one conclusion. 'Then we have nothing.'

'We know we were right about our targets being in Chechnya,' Drake reminded her. 'And it wasn't coincidence they got here just before us. They sent someone to take out Glazov before he could talk, which means someone warned them.'

At this, she gave him a sharp look. 'You are suggesting someone tipped them off?'

'Just telling it like I see it. They seem very good at staying one step ahead of us. If you can think of a better explanation, I'm all ears.'

For this, Miranova had no answer.

'We can drive ourselves crazy playing spy games like this,' Mason interrupted. 'The question is, now that Glazov's out of the picture, what are our friends going to do next?'

'We will learn nothing more here. We will return to Grozny and report our findings. And we can get you to a hospital,' she added, surveying him with a look that might have been grudging sympathy.

Drake shook his head. 'I'm fine.'

'You don't look fine.'

He stared her hard in the eye. 'What was it you said to me in DC? We're expected to keep going until we can't. Well, I still can, so back off and let me do my job.'

'As you say.' She moved closer to Drake and lowered her voice. 'Tell me, Ryan, what happened to your sidearm?' she asked, gesturing to the empty holster at his hip. She was watching his reactions closely.

Drake shrugged, trying to appear dismissive. At the same time, however, his heartbeat felt as though it had doubled. 'Must have lost it when I fell.'

Miranova nodded thoughtfully. 'Interesting that you lost your radio *and* your weapon. It must have been quite a fall.'

She held his gaze a few seconds longer, the tension between them growing with every passing moment. She was hoping that Drake would feel compelled to speak up, to challenge her suspicions, to do something to break the silence.

Then, after what seemed like hours, Miranova finally backed off a little.

'But then, I suppose these things can happen to the best of us,' she remarked, laying a hand on his shoulder. It was meant to be a conciliatory gesture, but Drake knew why she'd done it. He managed to keep his face impassive as she squeezed a little.

'I hope this will not slow you down, Ryan,' she added, letting go.

Drake watched as she walked away to rejoin the others, though it was some time before his heart rate returned to normal.

Chapter 39

Grozny, Chechnya

Corporal Vadim Yerzov rolled his shoulders, trying to relieve the dull ache as the straps of his combat webbing bit into his flesh. Standing guard duty was an unpleasant job at the best of times, and it wasn't helped by the chill wind that gusted across the open space in front of the checkpoint, each blast carrying with it a thousand tiny pellets of dry snow that stung his exposed flesh.

The temperature had fallen with the onset of night, and the driving rain of the day had given way to icy snow flurries.

The tearing roar of jet engines in the airfield behind prompted him to turn his eyes skywards, and he watched enviously as a commercial airliner ascended into the darkened sky, soon swallowed up by the low clouds so that only the flash of its recognition lights was visible.

'Lucky bastards,' he mumbled, thinking about the passengers sitting in their comfortable seats, heating vents blasting hot air all around them as they watched Grozny recede into the distance.

He could only try to imagine how it must feel. His tour of duty in Chechnya would be over in another month or so, and then at last he would be out of this shithole for some well-deserved leave. It couldn't come soon enough. He was sick of this bleak war-torn place; sick of the cold, sick of the weather, sick of the people and the ruined buildings and the squalor and the misery.

'Wonder where they're going,' Private Georgy Banin remarked from the other side of the main gate, watching the same aircraft like a starving child surveying a banquet.

'Who the fuck cares?' Yerzov replied. 'Anywhere's better than here.'

'I hear you.' Banin shivered as another icy blast buffeted them. 'Maybe those FSB pricks should spend some time out here freezing their asses off.'

Not likely, Yerzov thought. The FSB personnel in the secure compound behind them were more than content to remain in their comfortable offices, allowing the Russian army to guard them day and night. Taking all the risks for none of the rewards.

Unsurprisingly, the men burdened with such a thankless task had started thinking up all kinds of colourful acronyms for their charges. Fucking Safe Bastards was this month's most popular.

Yerzov looked up as a vehicle, painted in standard olive-drab military colours, turned off the main drag and headed down the muddy potholed road towards them. It was a UAZ-469, one of the old-fashioned but very sturdy little 4x4s that had been in use by the Russian military since the 1970s. Their reliability was legendary, as was their willingness to cross virtually any terrain – two factors that made them ideal for a country like Chechnya.

Trucks like this came and went all the time around these parts, so neither man was particularly concerned as it approached. Nonetheless, Yerzov gripped his AK-47 a little tighter as the mud-splattered vehicle slowed to a halt beside him.

The driver was a woman he realised as he approached the

cab. And an attractive one at that he thought with an approving glance at her tanned skin and blonde hair. Clearly she hadn't been in Chechnya for long, or she would have been just as pale and pasty as Yerzov and his comrades.

She was dressed in olive-drab military fatigues like himself, though he saw no rank, name or unit insignia anywhere on her uniform. A sure sign that she was FSB. But judging by the mud splattered across it and the various rips and tears in the camouflage pattern, she'd had a far more eventful day than him.

Apparently she wasn't one of the pen-pushers he was assigned to guard. She was a field agent.

'Identification?' he said, a little more wary now. Being around FSB agents always put him on edge, as though he was being assessed or tested in some way.

'Of course,' she replied, handing over her ID documents.

His suspicions were confirmed immediately. Anya Sherkova, an operative with the FSB's counter-terrorism bureau. Retreating to the gatehouse for a few moments, he swiped her card through the magnetic reader, which promptly verified she was who she claimed to be.

He hadn't seen her before, but that was more the rule than the exception in a major intelligence hub like this. New personnel came and went so often that it sometimes felt like standing guard at the gates of the Kremlin.

Returning outside, he surveyed the jeep that now sat idling, exhausts venting steam that was quickly carried away by the chill wind. 'Just you in this vehicle?'

She nodded.

'And your business here?'

She looked him in the eye then. Her gaze was enough to send a shiver through him that had nothing to do with the cold weather. 'My business is none of yours.'

'As you say,' he conceded, not wishing to press the point. 'If you'd please shut down the engine, we'll search your vehicle and process you through.'

The woman glanced away for a moment as if struggling to hold in check her rising temper. He heard a slow exhalation of breath as she calmed herself. 'Corporal, I've been travelling for the best part of two days without sleep to get here. I didn't do it so I could have a pair of grunts rifling through my underwear. Unless you want to make an issue of this, I suggest you open the gate. Now.'

On the other side of the checkpoint, Private Banin looked expectantly at him as if waiting to see what he would do. To back down now would be a humiliation in the presence of his subordinate. Much as Yerzov was tempted to do it, he knew he'd never live it down.

The corporal raised his chin, summoning up whatever sense of authority he could before speaking again. 'I'm sorry, but I have my orders. All vehicles passing through here must be searched, regardless of rank. You're aware of the increased security after the attack in America?'

'Why do you think I'm here?' she asked with a sharp look. 'Believe me, I'm all the security you need.'

Yerzov resisted the growing urge to swallow, knowing it would be taken for what it was – a sign of weakness. 'The head of FSB operations in Chechnya is here, along with most of his senior staff. I'm afraid their safety takes priority over all other concerns.'

Sherkova wasted no more time on him. Instead she turned away, snatched up a cellphone from the passenger seat and dialled a number. It didn't take long to be answered.

'Director Masalsky? I'm sorry to disturb you, sir,' she said, her voice now smooth and polite. 'It's Sherkova. I'm afraid there's been a problem at the gate. The corporal on the checkpoint won't allow me through.' She glanced at the name tag on Yerzov's body armour. 'A Corporal Yerzov. Yes, sir, I explained why I'm here. Perhaps he might listen to you?'

She turned her attention back to Yerzov and held the phone out to him. 'The director would like to speak with you, Corporal. Now.'

Yerzov's eyes opened wide in fear. She was on the phone to Director Masalsky himself, the very man whose life he was here to safeguard. Yerzov could almost imagine the FSB regional director glaring down at the checkpoint from his office on the second floor, making a mental note of the dumb prick who was holding up one of his trusted employees.

That was more than enough to destroy the last of his wavering resolve. This was the kind of confrontation that could end careers, and he really didn't need the hassle. Not with only a month left on his tour.

'There's no need for that,' he said, handing back her ID documents. 'Everything seems to be in order here.'

The woman smiled. 'Everything's fine, Director. Sorry to have troubled you,' she said, shutting down the call.

She gave Yerzov a faint nod as the barrier was lifted, then gunned the engine and drove off into the compound beyond.

'Real ball-breaker, eh?' Private Banin remarked, giving Yerzov a sidelong grin as they watched the truck turn left and vanish behind a building.

Yerzov could feel a blush rising to his cheeks despite the cold. 'Fuck off.'

With a canvas kitbag slung over one shoulder, Anya made her way down the corridor at a steady, unhurried pace, barely pausing to acknowledge the FSB agents she passed along the way. She was a travel-weary operative fresh in from the field, in search of nothing but a hot shower and a cup of coffee.

Most of them knew better than to mess with someone like that.

The key to situations like this, as she had learned long ago, was confidence. If you looked and acted as though you belonged somewhere, then few people would have the nerve to challenge you. She had known covert operatives to bluff their way through military checkpoints without even showing identification – it just took a touch of panache and no small measure of courage.

The accommodation block in which she now found herself stood adjacent to the FSB's main office complex; the two buildings linked by a covered walkway to protect against inclement weather. The office complex was the nerve centre of their operation in Chechnya, home to planning and intelligence-gathering teams, conference rooms, secure communications suites and, of course, the senior executive officers.

The sensitive nature of its contents meant that access was restricted to those with high-level security clearance. It certainly wasn't the kind of place where front-line grunts found themselves, meaning she was going to have to alter her appearance if she expected to get inside.

Up ahead she spotted a sign for the women's restroom and made straight for it. As she'd hoped, it wasn't in use.

Fishing in her bag, she attached a *Closed for Maintenance* sign to the door, then retreated inside and used a piece of wood to wedge it shut.

Alone and with space to work, Anya dumped her equipment bag on the tiled floor and knelt down to unzip it. The first item out was a neatly pressed grey suit, blouse and shoes, all sealed within a watertight plastic bag.

Hurriedly stripping off her wet and mud-stained BDUs, Anya glanced at herself in the mirror, frowning at the gash that had been torn along her right hip during her encounter

283

with Drake. It had happened as he'd slashed at her with her own knife, the blade cleaving through the fabric and the skin beneath. She had avoided the worst of it, but the mere fact that he'd been able to hurt her had stung her pride. Perhaps that was why she had retaliated with such ferocity.

She'd barely noticed the injury at the time, having long ago learned to push past such minor discomforts, but the blood was going to be a problem now if she expected to get inside without arousing suspicion.

Fortunately she had a solution.

Using a couple of paper towels to clean off the worst of the blood, she reached into her bag and retrieved a roll of duct tape, tore off a length and pressed it against the cut. Removing it wasn't going to be fun, but that was something she could deal with later. Right now it was enough to stop the bleeding.

She donned the smart office clothes as quickly as she could manage, tucking in the blouse and pulling the jacket over her shoulders. The shoes went on next; their impractical design uncomfortable and almost unfamiliar to her after years of wearing military boots.

Next she ran a comb through her hair. It was still damp and dishevelled after her flight through the woods, but a wall-mounted hand drier took care of that. A touch of hair-spray was enough to hold it in the kind of neat, efficient style that she had seen other female FSB agents in this building wearing.

She was grateful that she was still wearing her hair short. The last thing she needed was for it to come loose and get in her eyes at a crucial moment. She'd made that mistake once before and it had almost cost her life.

The last task was the least pleasant of all. Leaning over the sink, she surveyed her reflection as she hastily applied foundation make-up and a neutral, understated lipstick. She'd always hated make-up, the pointless frivolity of its application and laborious removal, but at times like this there was no option if she wanted to blend in.

On second thoughts, she undid another button on her blouse and tightened the straps of her bra to push her breasts a little higher, revealing enough cleavage to elicit a favourable reaction from any male agent she passed. It went against her instincts to use sexuality to her advantage, but there was no denying its effectiveness in a largely male-dominated profession.

Anyway, she had paid a high enough price over the years for the simple fact of being born a woman; she saw no harm in reaping some rewards now.

Last out of the bag was something she was infinitely more comfortable with – her silenced Colt M1911 automatic. She had been using that reliable old sidearm since the very start of her career as a paramilitary operative, and in her opinion it was still one of the best handguns ever produced. It had never let her down.

She raised the automatic, checking that the magazine was firmly locked in place and the safety catch engaged. The M1911 was a single-action weapon with a manual safety, allowing it to be carried 'cocked and locked', meaning there was a round chambered and the hammer was drawn back.

Satisfied that all was well, she holstered the Colt inside her jacket, adjusting her posture a little to compensate for the extra weight of the weapon plus the bulky silencer.

She stretched, arching her back and raising her arms above her head. The joints popped as her muscles strained against them, but she felt better for doing it. Aches and pains that she hadn't noticed before were beginning to nag her, and she could guess why. Her body had taken a lot of punishment over the course of her long career, and at last the years were starting to catch up with her.

You're getting old, she thought with a wry smile as she clenched and unclenched her right hand. The hard, compact muscles in her arm bunched and contracted with the movement.

She wasn't frightened or apprehensive – she'd been doing things like this for too long to feel such emotions now – but she did feel a certain sense of anticipation. A heightened awareness, a rush of chemicals to her brain as her body readied itself once more for the primal battle of survival.

She looked at her watch again. Almost time.

Stuffing her wet, mud-stained BDUs into the canvas bag and locking it inside one of the stalls, Anya checked her appearance in the mirror one more time, remembering to pin her ID badge to the breast pocket of her jacket.

All things considered, she felt she was good enough to pass muster.

She would find out soon enough, she thought as she removed the wedge from the door and stepped out into the corridor beyond.

Chapter 40

Seated behind his expensive desk, Ivan Masalsky leaned back from his computer and stretched, rubbing the stiff muscles in his neck. Being the head of FSB operations in Chechnya was a demanding job at the best of times, and it had become even more difficult in the wake of the attack in America. Rather than sympathy, the killing of several FSB officers on a peaceful mission to a foreign country had instead stirred up potent anti-Russian sentiments amongst the Chechen population.

He should have left his office hours ago, but circumstances now found him working late into the evening trying to deal with the aftermath of the ill-conceived raid on Glazov's farm.

He was going to have some serious words with everyone involved when they returned, beginning with Miranova exceeding her authority and hopefully ending with Drake and his companion on the next flight back to Langley.

He glanced at his coffee cup. Barely half an inch of dark sludge remained in the bottom, and that was long cold. Reaching for the intercom beside it, he buzzed through to his personal secretary in the outer office: a beautiful young woman named Katarina whom he'd selected for this job by hand, as it were.

Her crisp, efficient voice answered straight away. 'Yes, sir?'

'Have some fresh coffee brought in, would you?'

No way was he taking on such a confrontation until his

brain was firing on all cylinders again. And if nothing else, it was an excuse to watch Katarina enter and leave the room. Truly the woman had the finest ass he'd ever seen. He wasn't ashamed to look at it, and he got the impression she knew full well what he was doing.

What the hell. He was old, but not that old.

'Of course, sir.'

'Thank you.'

With that pleasant prospect buoying his mood a little, he turned his attention back to the computer and the stack of orders waiting for his sign-off. He was just moving his mouse to open another email when suddenly his world turned upside down.

A bright lightning flash from outside was followed an instant later by an earth-shattering boom that blew out all the windows in his office and threw him to the floor like a rag doll.

The explosion was louder and more powerful than Anya had expected. The floor beneath her feet shook visibly, streams of dust and pieces of ceiling plaster fell down around her, and a moment or two later the lights flickered and went out.

She had tried to park her 4x4 far enough away from the office complex to avoid major structural damage when the 300 pounds of industrial explosive hidden inside detonated, but it had to be close enough to cause sufficient chaos for her plan to succeed. On reflection, perhaps another 20 yards might have been advisable.

Still, it was done now. The rest was up to her.

The thunderous detonation had been followed by a few seconds of stunned silence as the analysts, support staff, planners, intelligence experts and soldiers throughout the compound tried to process what had just happened. People are slow to react to things they don't expect, particularly when that thing happens to be a car bomb that's just destroyed a good portion of their security perimeter and blown out every window within half a mile.

Moving with swift, confident strides, she hurried down the corridor and into the stairwell leading up to the third floor, her heels clicking on the hard concrete steps. It was far from an easy climb in her uncomfortable new shoes, but it was the only way – the elevators would likely have shut down already.

Anya had made it up the second flight of steps before the first alarm started blaring.

Masalsky's ears were ringing, his head throbbing from the explosion that had just engulfed the building. He could feel the warm wetness of blood on his cheek, neck and arms where slivers of glass had peppered one side of his body, shredding clothes and skin. None of the injuries seemed to be life-threatening, and he was too dazed to feel much pain yet.

The air was thick with dust and smoke, stinging his eyes and throat. Coughing and retching, he managed to push himself up from the floor and staggered over to the window.

In the open area below, chaos reigned.

Some kind of explosive had detonated near the outer wall, obliterating a large section of it and leaving behind a smoking crater the size of a bus. Nearby vehicles had been turned over and hurled aside by the force of the blast, and God only knew how many people had been killed. A pall of smoke hung over the entire area.

And then faintly as if from a great distance, Masalsky heard the unmistakable sound of automatic weapons fire. Hardly able to comprehend, he squinted through the smoke in search of the source. And sure enough, he spotted muzzle flares lighting up the murky gloom below.

This was no random car-bomb attack, he realised in a moment of gut-wrenching panic. It was a coordinated strike, using the blast to breach the outer defences and allowing an armed strike team to storm the compound.

He had to do something. Turning away from the window, he lurched and staggered across the remains of his office, his sense of balance destroyed as surely as the perimeter wall outside.

Emerging into the smaller secretarial office beyond, he looked around for Katarina. A soft moaning directed his attention left, where the young woman was curled up in the corner, a bloodied hand pressed against one side of her face.

She certainly wouldn't be called beautiful after today, he realised with a lingering sense of revulsion. A shrapnel fragment had opened up her face from chin to ear, peeling back skin and muscle to reveal the obscene whiteness of bone beneath.

He could do nothing for her, just as she could do nothing for him. Abandoning the injured woman, he stumbled through the debris of her office and into the corridor beyond. He didn't even know where he intended to go or what he would do when he got there; only that he couldn't just sit here and wait for armed gunmen to fight their way up to him. There was no telling how many there were, or what their ultimate goal was.

He had barely managed to wrench the door open when a female agent came running towards him, emerging like a wraith out of the smoke. Unlike him, she seemed to have escaped injury. Perhaps she'd been on the other side of the building when the bomb went off.

She was saying something, but with his ears still ringing from the blast he was unable to discern the words.

'Speak up!' he growled, one hand pressed against a cut at his neck.

'Are you all right, sir?' she repeated, practically yelling right in his face.

'Of course I'm not fucking all right! What the hell is going on out there?'

'Your guess is as good as mine, sir,' she admitted. 'The radio net's down. But we have to get you to the shelter.'

Like any field station, the FSB compound in Chechnya had its own secure panic room in the very core of the building, built for senior executives to take shelter in during emergencies. With reinforced walls, armoured doors and its own air and electrical supply, it was as close to impregnable as any room could be.

'Sir, do you hear me?' she asked. 'We have to go now!'

Masalsky thought about Katarina and what would happen to her if the insurgents managed to fight their way up here. For a moment he actually considered sending the agent in to get her, but the boom of a grenade explosion outside was enough to forestall such thoughts.

Masalsky nodded grimly. 'Fine. Let's go.'

With the female agent leading the way, they hurried down the corridor, their eyes watering as smoke from various small fires began to fill the air.

Halting beside the elevator, Masalsky hit the call button.

'Forget it, sir,' she called out, physically dragging him away from it. 'The power's out. They won't be running.'

He frowned as she led him onwards, throwing open a door to the stairwell. It was lit only by the dull red glow of emergency lighting. 'What's your name?'

'Sherkova,' she replied over her shoulder. 'Anya Sherkova.'

Masalsky shook his head as he hurried to follow her down the stairs. 'I don't know you.'

'I only transferred in three days ago, sir. Makes my last posting seem quite dull.'

291

He was starting to wish he had more people like her. Despite the chaos around her, Sherkova thought and acted with clear, logical decisiveness. It was almost as if she wasn't even fazed by what had happened . . .

No sooner had this thought crossed his mind than she stopped, watching as the door at the bottom of the stairwell flew open and two agents hurried through. Both male, both in their forties, and both clutching automatics. Masalsky recognised them as agents from the base's protective services division, and felt a surge of relief at their arrival.

Anya, however, was harbouring very different thoughts.

These two men represented a serious obstacle that had to be overcome quickly if she expected to get out of here alive. Still dazed and confused by the blast, they hesitated on seeing her, their weapons drawn but not pointed. They were trying to work out whether she was a friend or foe.

'I'm taking Director Masalsky to the shelter,' she said, drawing on as much authority as she possessed. She pointed back up the way she had come. 'But there are a lot of casualties upstairs that need your help.'

The one on the left, probably the more senior of the two, shook his head. 'The director's our responsibility. We'll take it from here,' he said as he tried to shove his way past her.

It was a fatal lapse of judgement. Just as he moved by, her right arm lashed out, striking him squarely in the throat. There are few more vulnerable places in the human body; a single good strike to the throat with either a blunt object or a fist can drop even the most hardened operative like a stone.

This man was no different. Temporarily stunned and unable to breathe, he let out a sharp grunt of pain and fell to his knees, choking and gasping. The weapon fell from his grasp, clattering to the concrete floor.

She wasn't going to give him time to recover. A knee to the

face sent him sprawling at the foot of the stairs, his glazed eyes and limp body confirming that it would be several minutes at least before he recovered enough to pose any threat.

Such was the speed and ferocity of her attack, his comrade was only now starting to process what he'd just witnessed. Without breaking stride, Anya drew the M1911 from her suit jacket, took aim at the second agent and squeezed off a single round. There was a loud thud as the round discharged. Even with a silencer, the .45 made a lot of noise in the confined space of the stairwell.

The thud was followed a heartbeat later by a soft wet crunch as the round obliterated his skull, along with the fragile organ it was supposed to protect. He went down, leaving a splatter of blood on the concrete wall behind.

She allowed herself but a fleeting moment of regret for what she'd just done. He had died out of necessity, not desire. But it couldn't be helped, just as she couldn't allow emotions like that to intrude on her thoughts. If they did, she was as good as dead.

Masalsky stared at the scene before him in blank shock, as if failing to understand what had just happened. Then, a moment later, survival took over.

In panic he turned and tried to flee back up the stairs, thinking to take refuge in one of the offices up there. It was a vain hope, and quickly dashed.

He hadn't managed to stumble more than a few feet before he felt something sharp fired into his back. There was a click, and suddenly white-hot pain filled every part of his body. His legs gave way beneath him and he collapsed to the floor, convulsing as thousands of volts surged through his nervous system.

When it stopped at last, he was barely conscious, unable to move. He looked up through bleary eyes and saw Anya throw aside the taser she had used to incapacitate him; then his vision swam and he blacked out.

Anya holstered her pistol and knelt down beside the unconscious man. With Masalsky down and the two FSB agents neutralised, now came the hard part – getting him out of the compound without being killed in the process.

If everything had been prepared as expected, there would be a vehicle waiting for her downstairs. All she had to do was get Masalsky down there and into it, which was easier said than done. Carrying an unconscious man weighing upwards of 170 pounds was a daunting task even for her.

She kicked off her shoes, knowing they would do her no favours now, and took a few deep breaths to prepare herself. Doing her best to distribute his weight across her shoulders, she heaved him on to her back, took a deep breath and forced herself up from the floor. Her muscles burned with the effort but somehow she managed to pick her way between the two fallen agents and through the stairwell access.

She emerged into the ground-floor corridor in time to see an overweight man stagger past clutching a bloody wound on the side of his head. He didn't even glance at her as he passed, intent only on helping himself. That suited her just fine.

Anya knew there was a fire escape about halfway along the corridor that opened out into a small parking lot sandwiched between two wings of the office complex. Breathing hard and with a sheen of sweat coating her brow, she forced herself onwards with the heavy bulk of Masalsky pressing down on her with each step.

The door was already standing ajar when she reached it, apparently having been used already. With her strength waning she staggered through into the cold, smoke-filled world beyond.

As she'd hoped, this side of the building was largely untouched by the blast, as were the half-dozen cars in the small parking lot.

Her eyes flicked from car to car until she found the one she wanted. It was a GAZ-2330 'Tigr', the Russian military's standard multipurpose all-terrain vehicle, and one which also saw heavy use by the FSB.

Ignoring the scattered groups of injured and shell-shocked office workers who were milling around trying to decide what to do next, Anya staggered over to the Tigr and felt beneath the driver's side wheel arch. Sure enough, a key had been secured there.

In short order she had unlocked the rear door and heaved Masalsky inside, unconcerned about how rough she was being with him. He'd live. For now, at least.

Pausing only to secure his hands behind his back with a pair of plastic cable ties, she returned to the driver's cab and leapt up into the seat. With his weight no longer on her shoulders, she felt light as a feather despite the burning pain in her muscles.

The engine fired up first time, and Anya wasted no time pulling out of the parking lot, having to honk the horn to get a couple of stunned-looking men in bloodstained suits to move aside.

Rounding the main building, she headed straight for the vehicle checkpoint, not bothering to slow down as she approached. No way was she giving anyone time to start thinking and questioning the situation. She spotted the two soldiers cowering behind the concrete blocks that formed part of the guard position, saw one of them scramble to raise the barrier to make way for her.

These men were concerned only with stopping enemies getting in, not hindering the passage of FSB vehicles trying to get out. For all they knew, the armoured Tigr might have been part of a counter-attack to drive the enemy back.

She caught Yerzov's eye as she roared through the checkpoint, saw the fleeting look of recognition and dawning comprehension on his face, and then in a flash he was gone. The compound, the checkpoint, the firefight – it was all behind her now.

Allowing herself to experience a fleeting moment of elation, she reached for the cellphone in her pocket and dialled Atayev's number while fighting to keep the big vehicle steady as it rumbled through potholes and patches of mud.

'I'm clear,' she said as soon as the ringing stopped.

'Do you have him?' She could hear the anticipation, the anxiety in Atayev's voice.

She glanced in her rear-view mirror at the unconscious man bumping around in the cargo area. He was a mess, and he would undoubtedly be far from his best when he regained consciousness, but he was alive. That was their agreement.

'I do.'

There was a moment of silence, broken only by the roar of her engine and wind whistling past the windows. But Anya could have sworn she heard a faint exhalation of breath over her radio.

'Good,' Atayev said at last. 'Get yourself to the rendezvous. We'll be waiting for you.'

As the phone clicked off, Anya turned hard left on to the main drag. The road surface was a little smoother now, and she pressed down harder on the gas pedal, eager to put as much distance as possible between herself and the FSB compound.

The diversionary attack mounted by the rest of Atayev's group would have been called off by now, the gunmen retreating under cover of smoke and darkness before the FSB could organise a counter-attack and bring in air assets. As some semblance of order was restored, it wouldn't take them long to figure out their director of operations was missing.

That, however, was Atayev's problem. She had fulfilled her end of the bargain, for now at least. There would be more work for her before this was over.

Chapter 41

Once again Drake found himself in the 4x4 as it bumped and jolted its way through the darkened forests of Chechnya. They had departed the farm compound less than ten minutes ago, leaving behind a newly arrived security team to police up the site.

Forensics experts would comb through the rubble once the fire had burned down, though Drake doubted they would find anything of value. Anya, true to form, had been thorough in her efforts to wipe out any evidence that could compromise her.

His thoughts were interrupted as Miranova took an incoming phone call. The expression on her face soon made it obvious that something was seriously wrong.

Straight away Drake felt his stomach knot.

'Something up?' Mason asked, picking up on her change in demeanour.

'Be quiet!' she snapped, annoyed by the interruption. She was silent for another few seconds as she digested the remainder of the message. 'There has been another attack. Our field station in Grozny has been hit.'

'How bad is it?' Drake asked, bracing himself for the worst.

She shook her head slowly. 'We are still getting reports from the scene, but it looks like a car bomb followed by an armed assault. The explosion was powerful enough to breach the outer wall and destroy most of the office complex.'

'The kind of blast you'd expect from three hundred pounds of industrial explosive?' Mason suggested, his expression grim.

Miranova glanced at him but said nothing.

'I'm sorry, Anika,' Drake said, not knowing what else to say at that moment. She could never know how much he meant those words.

He couldn't understand it. The attack in DC had been a surgical strike intended to achieve a single goal – the capture and execution of Anton Demochev. The deaths of a few FSB agents who'd stood in the way had been a matter of necessity.

This car-bomb attack was a hammer blow in comparison, crude and unsophisticated. Surely there had to be more to it than simple mass carnage?

Drake was about to speak up when suddenly Miranova's radio headset crackled into life again. It was impossible to know what was being said, but the look in her eyes told its own story. If possible, she looked even worse when the transmission at last ended.

'What is it?' Drake asked, unable to stop himself. 'What's happened?'

She closed her eyes and slowly exhaled, marshalling her emotions before responding. 'Ivan Masalsky is missing.'

Chapter 42

It happened for the first time about two weeks after her capture. The beatings and torture sessions were achieving nothing – that much was plain to everyone involved. No matter what they said, what they threatened her with, what they did, she gave them nothing in return. But like any good tactician, her interrogator knew when to take a different approach.

Hauled from her cell in the middle of the night, she was carried down the hallway to another room; a new room she had never been in before. Straight away she felt the icy prickles of fear running down her spine. A new room meant a new kind of pain, and when she saw the single steel-framed bed pushed against one wall, she had a feeling she knew what kind they had in mind.

She had fought, of course. Rational thought had given way to animal instinct by this point. She had lashed out; kicked, punched, scratched, even tried to bite her captors. But there were four of them and only one of her, and they were all bigger, heavier, stronger. And she was already weakened by the abuse she had taken.

The blows rained in against her until her vision blurred and her resistance subsided. Vaguely, as if viewed from some other point of view, she was aware of her hands and feet being bound to the steel frame, her trousers pulled down and off, her legs being spread apart.

All of it seemed strangely removed. She could have sworn it was happening to someone else. Even as the first guard dropped his trousers, even as she felt his hands roughly groping her breasts.

Only when she felt the first gut-wrenching penetration did reality snap back into place with shocking clarity. Her mask of control, her armour slipped away, shattered by the horror and disgust of what was happening to her. In an instant she was fifteen years old again, pinned face down on the desk of the orphanage administrator, feeling his hot breath on her cheek, hearing his laboured breathing as he struggled to pull her trousers down.

Instinct took over.

She cried out in pain and anger, bucked and thrashed and twisted in an effort to break free, but it was all useless. There was no escape this time. The ropes cut into the skin of her wrists and ankles, burning, slicing, drawing blood. She tried to bite at him, but all she earned for her efforts was another hard blow that snapped her head back and left blobs of light dancing across her vision.

And all the while, the stabbing pain and thrusting and the sickening feeling of helplessness continued. Once convinced of her own invincibility, she saw now just how foolish and naive she had been. She was being violated, debased, her body abused in the worst way possible, and she could do nothing to stop it.

At last her cries subsided, her resistance ceased, and the only sounds that could be heard were those of the dull wet slapping of flesh against unwilling flesh, and the straining grunts of the guard slowly building to a climax.

Anya said nothing as the nightmare went on, managed even to keep from crying out in pain. She wouldn't give the bastard the satisfaction. Instead she tried to remove herself from that room, tried to view what was happening as a simple biological process, no different from any other.

But it was different. It was very different indeed, and no number of mind games could ever change that. She squeezed her eyes tight shut, her muscles tensing one last time as it finally ended.

'Why do you do this to yourself, Anya?' a voice asked as the guard rolled off her and pulled his trousers up again, his task complete. It was His voice; cold, clinical, without remorse or compassion. 'You're allowing this to happen, and for what? For whom? No one is coming for you. No one cares about you.'

Anya kept her eyes squeezed shut, refusing to let the voice in, refusing to acknowledge its words. They had done their worst already. What more could they do to her?

'Oh, you think it's over? You think we're done now? There are many guards in this prison, Anya,' the voice went on. 'Believe me, we have all night.'

Anya kept her eyes shut even as another set of footsteps approached.

Grozny, Chechnya, 23 December 2008

Anya kept her foot on the gas as the big military truck bumped along the muddy dirt track, its suspension groaning under the strain. Ranks of dark pine trees slid by on either side, crowding close to the road. They were so densely packed that the forest floor barely saw sunlight.

The Tigr which had served so well as her getaway vehicle had become a liability now. It wouldn't take the FSB long to figure out that she had used it to make off with one of their most senior commanders. Then they would come after her with everything they had.

She was also very much aware that her blouse and business suit were wholly impractical for the task at hand. She wasn't even wearing shoes, forcing her to use her bare feet on the pedals.

It was time to make a switch.

The road opened out up ahead, revealing an overgrown clearing with a cluster of buildings in the centre. An old homestead whose roof had long since collapsed, a couple of toolsheds made from rusted corrugated iron, and a barn that had once housed trucks and tools for tree felling. Its timbers were blackened and warped with age, its roof leaking and its doors missing, but the basic structure remained more or less sound.

Anya had no idea what had become of the original owners of this place. Considering the wars that had raged in Chechnya over the past couple of decades, she doubted any of them would be returning to reclaim their land now.

Pulling into the quiet darkness of the barn, Anya killed the engine, closed her eyes for a moment and let out a slow, calming breath. Outside, the wind had died down and the snow had given way to a steady drizzle of rain. She could hear it pattering off the roof and dripping down around the Tigr, mingling with the tick of the cooling engine.

The sound of rain had always been a calming one for her.

It wasn't very often that Anya experienced moments of true peace. She'd had little enough opportunity in her life, and in truth she wasn't given to deep contemplation. But there were rare times, particularly in the wake of a successful operation, when she allowed herself to let go. She allowed her guard to lower, allowed her restless mind to ease, and just felt the world around her.

Those were the moments that reminded her most of who she was. As a child she had been relaxed and carefree; a day-dreamer who would lie on the grassy hill near her home and just stare up at the infinite sky for what seemed like hours, marvelling at the simple, unspoiled beauty of it. The idea that it could all be taken away from her in one heart-rending day had never entered her young mind.

Life, however, had since taught her otherwise.

A low, gurgling moan from the rear compartment warned

her that Masalsky was starting to come round. Refocusing her mind on the task at hand, she threw open her door, leapt down from the cab and drew the M1911 from the holster inside her jacket. She surveyed her darkened surroundings for a moment, checking that nothing had been moved or disturbed in her absence.

There were no footprints on the muddy ground, no vehicle tracks apart from her own, no sign of any recent human activity. Good.

Satisfied, she circled around to the rear of the big truck. The floor of the barn was bare earth, damp from the recent rain and soft underfoot. She could feel it squelching between her toes as she walked.

Keeping the automatic to hand, she hauled open the door and surveyed her prize.

With his suit ripped and torn by the blast, his greying hair in disarray and his face smeared with soot, Masalsky was certainly looking far from his best. But he was alive, and regaining the use of his limbs judging by his ineffective flailing.

She'd better act fast. Clambering inside, she hooked an arm beneath him and with some effort pulled him up into a sitting position. His body might not have been cooperating fully yet, but his mind was in working order. She saw a moment or two of blank incomprehension in his eyes, followed by a slowly dawning awareness as he realised the situation he was in.

'You are Ivan Masalsky,' she began. She knew full well who he was, but she wanted to be sure he could hear and understand her.

He said nothing, just stared at her.

Raising the automatic so he had a good view of the weapon, she pressed the silencer against his forehead, her face devoid of emotion. 'Let me be clear. If you're not the man I'm looking for, you die right here. Now, are you Ivan Masalsky?'

That was enough to get through to him. He nodded, still staring at her in disbelief. There wasn't much fear in his expression. Not yet, at least. She couldn't tell if it was down to shock, training or simply a strong sense of composure.

Whatever the reason, it was a relief to her. She had no time for people who cried and whimpered and pleaded. As if any of those things would make a difference.

'Who are you?' he finally asked.

'No one.'

'What do you want with me?' Again, there was little fear in his voice. He was sizing her up, trying to decide what sort of adversary she was and how he could turn the situation around.

'I don't want anything from you.'

He cocked an eyebrow. 'You infiltrated a secure compound, you impersonated an FSB agent and you risked your life to get to me. You must have done it for a reason.'

'My job is to deliver you; nothing more.' She reached into her jacket, pulled out a small flick knife and used it to sever the cable ties around his wrists. With his arms now freed, she backed off a few steps and raised the automatic to cover him. 'Now, strip.'

His eyes opened wider. 'What?'

'Don't make me tell you twice,' she warned. 'Take your clothes off. All of them.'

It wasn't unknown for the FSB to include tracking devices on their more valuable operatives, allowing them to be located quickly and easily if they went missing. Cellphones, wallets, even his shoes could have a satellite tracker hidden inside. The only option was to remove everything.

Anya kept her weapon trained on him as he peeled off his

tattered suit jacket, then his shirt, shoes and trousers, glaring at her in resentment the whole time. His movements were slow and uncoordinated at first as the feeling gradually returned to his limbs.

It was strange, Anya thought. This man was one of the most powerful figures in the FSB, accustomed to inspiring fear and respect wherever he went. But here, with the suit and the bodyguards and the security stripped away, he was nothing more than a pasty middle-aged man with narrow shoulders, thin arms and a pot belly.

When he was finished, Anya retrieved a pair of jogging slacks and a grey sweatshirt from a bag at the rear of the Tigr's passenger compartment, then tossed them to him. He got the idea and quickly pulled them on, already shivering in the chill air.

'Now lie face down on the floor with your hands behind your back.'

He did as commanded without resistance. Keeping the automatic ready, she knelt down beside him and used another pair of cable ties to secure his wrists once more. They were strong enough that no human could break them through brute strength alone, and unlike handcuffs they had no lock that could be picked. She repeated the process with his ankles, then rolled him over on to his back so he could get a look at her.

'Listen to me carefully. We're here to change vehicles. I'm going to bring a car over and help you into a hidden compartment in the trunk. It'll be cramped and hot, but if you cooperate and don't panic then you'll reach your destination alive. If you fight me or try to escape, I will hurt you. The more you resist, the worse the pain will be. Do you understand what I've just told you?'

Again he nodded. He didn't seem like the hysterical type,

but Anya had learned from long experience that a compliant prisoner was ten times easier to handle than a frightened, desperate one. The key was to explain what was happening, what was expected of them and what would happen if they resisted. Once the rules were established, it was their call whether or not they wanted to break them.

'Good. Then stay here and don't make a sound.'

Leaving him briefly, she leapt down from the truck and strode over to another car parked in the barn, dwarfed by the intimidating bulk of the Tigr. This one was a simple blue Lada Niva 4x4 that looked about as old as she was.

Still, she knew from experience that what these unassuming cars lacked in style, they made up for in simple durability. She'd tested this one thoroughly prior to the operation and knew the engine to be crude and rough, but nonetheless reliable. They were also plentiful in this part of the world, making it easier to blend in.

Retrieving the keys from the soft earth beneath the rear wheel, she unlocked it, jumped in and fired it up. There was a throaty roar as the engine kicked in. Anya eased the vehicle forwards, then backed up so its rear was facing the open back doors of the Tigr.

Masalsky hadn't moved. He was smart enough to recognise that words were the only weapons at his disposal right now.

Anya had left a sports bag filled with civilian clothes on the Lada's passenger seat. Grabbing it, she pulled herself out of the car and immediately began to strip, unbuttoning her jacket and allowing it to fall away, followed by the blouse, then finally her trousers. The duct tape she'd used to seal the cut at her hip pulled and tugged uncomfortably, though she did her best to ignore it.

Masalsky was watching her in curious silence, but she

made no move to cover herself. Modesty was an indulgence she'd long since parted company with.

'You said you were just an errand runner,' he began, having obviously decided that now was the time to make his move. 'Which means you're doing this for profit, not desire. If profit is what you're after, I can pay double whatever your employer offered.'

Anya looked at him as she pulled a pair of jeans up over her hips. 'I was part of a terrorist attack on an FSB compound,' she reminded him. 'I killed two of your agents, not to mention those killed or injured by the blast. And you would make a deal with me?'

He shrugged, apparently unconcerned. 'We all make mistakes. Don't make another one now. We both know my people will be looking for me, and they *will* find me. The question is whether you want to be around when they do. I can help you get away, make sure there is no follow-up, no manhunt. And like I said, I can give you all the money you need. It's a good deal, my friend. You should think about it.'

Anya looked at him, torn between disgust and respect. For a man pleading for his life, he was doing a fairly credible job of making it appear as though he had the upper hand.

'If any of that were true, you wouldn't be offering to bargain with me,' she observed, sitting on the tailgate of the car while she laced up her boots. 'Anyway, what I want isn't in your power to give.'

Only Atayev could give her what she truly needed. But first, she had to give him Masalsky.

'I have a wife,' he said abruptly. He was looking a little less composed now, a little less sure of himself. She wasn't the kind of person he was used to dealing with. She couldn't be bought, couldn't be bullied or intimidated. 'And a son. He's ten years old. His name is Pavel.'

Anya knew exactly what he was trying to do. She was a woman after all; it was logical to try to appeal to some kind of maternal instinct. Unfortunately for him, he'd picked the wrong woman.

'You have no children, Ivan,' she informed him coldly. 'Unless one of your mistresses gave you a son. Sometimes even I find it hard to keep track.'

Leaving him in satisfyingly stunned silence, she stood up and pulled on the fur-lined leather jacket she'd saved until last, glad of the warmth it provided. She shoved the automatic down the back of her jeans and moved forwards to help Masalsky down from the back of the Tigr.

Thirty seconds later she had him secured in the hidden compartment beneath the floor of the trunk. As she'd warned, it was a tight fit for him. He was likely in for an uncomfortable journey, though not half as uncomfortable as the destination that awaited him.

Anya tried not to think too much about that as she eased the Lada out of the barn and down the rough muddy track to the main road, leaving behind the big Russian army truck with Masalsky's clothes piled inside.

Chapter 43

The FSB compound at the west end of Grozny airport looked like a scene from the Second World War. The entire facade of the office complex had been devastated by the bomb blast, blinds and shredded curtains fluttering in jagged remains of windows. The concrete structure was scarred and pitted by shrapnel, one support beam having given way altogether to leave the floor above sagging precariously.

Nearby stood the remains of what had once been a perimeter wall, now reduced to so much broken rubble by a blast that had left a crater nearly 30 feet across. Smashed, twisted wrecks of cars caught in the explosion lay strewn about, as if some giant fist had picked them up, crumpled them and hurled them away like toys.

Police cars and ambulances were everywhere, and Drake watched in silence as shell-shocked men and women in bloodied office clothes were led away by paramedics. A pall of smoke from countless small fires lingered over the ruined complex.

'Doesn't look good, does it?' Mason remarked, surveying the scene without emotion.

Drake said nothing. The very sight of it left him feeling sick to his stomach.

His gaze returned to ground level as Miranova hurried over to him with a portable radio in hand. Their earlier disagreement was still fresh in both their minds, but like Drake, she understood the value of staying professional in times of crisis.

'How bad is it?' Drake asked, bracing himself for the worst.

'Casualties are not as high as we expected,' she replied at length. 'The building was not heavily used at this time of night.'

That made sense. They didn't exactly keep regular office hours, but even major intelligence services couldn't run at full capacity twenty-four hours a day. The news of lower casualties was cold comfort to him at that moment, but it was something.

'If they'd hit this place a few hours earlier, it would have been a different story,' Mason observed. 'We got lucky.'

The woman shot him a hard look. 'Good people were killed today. Lucky is not how I would choose to describe this, Agent Mason.'

'What about Masalsky?' Drake asked, eager to avoid another argument. 'Any idea how they got to him?'

She nodded slowly. 'Come with me.'

Drake and Mason followed as she led them into a nearby building that had escaped the worst of the blast. With much of the former base of operations now sealed off due to bomb damage, a temporary command centre had instead been set up in the accommodation block next door.

The place was a hive of activity as they made their way down the main corridor, having to squeeze past agents moving in both directions. Many sported minor injuries, their office clothes ripped and stained with blood, though few gave any sign of discomfort.

Singling out a technician who was using a laptop as a communications terminal, Miranova laid a hand on his shoulder, leaned over and spoke quietly to him.

'Take a look,' she said as the technician called up an image file.

Drake already had a sick feeling in the pit of his stomach as he moved in closer to take a look. And when he saw the image, saw the static shot of Anya leaning out of the drab-coloured military vehicle to speak to the soldiers on the gate, the rising dread quickly gave way to shocked realisation.

There could be no evasion any longer; no more denials, no more excuses. Anya wasn't just a bit player lingering on the periphery of some larger scheme – she was in this up to her neck. She had orchestrated the attack that had laid waste to the FSB's field office.

And he had allowed it to happen. He had protected her when he could have warned them. His hands were just as bloody as hers.

'Our kidnapper,' Miranova said grimly. 'She drove right in through the main gate, using a stolen vehicle and FSB identification to bluff her way past the checkpoint. The bomb was a diversion designed to create enough confusion for her to reach Masalsky and abduct him.'

'Must have taken some balls to come in here alone and pull off an extraction like that,' Mason remarked. Drake didn't look at him, but he could feel the man's eyes on him.

'Clearly she is a trained operative,' Miranova added. 'We have circulated this image amongst our field teams. Whoever she is, we will find her if she dares show herself again.'

Drake swallowed hard, tearing his gaze away from the image. He had to draw Miranova's attention away from this. 'We still need to find Masalsky.'

'His satellite tracker stopped moving about five miles north-east of here. Our tactical teams found an abandoned military vehicle there, along with his clothes and the tracking module. Masalsky was gone.'

Drake wasn't surprised, either that he'd had a locator module on his person, or that his captors had known to look for it. 'If she's half as intelligent as she seems, she'll have changed vehicles by now.'

'What about satellite imagery?' Mason suggested.

The FSB agent shook her head. 'We checked. There were none over the area at the time of the attack.'

Almost as if she knew the perfect time to make her move, Drake thought. Anya had once been one of the Agency's best paramilitary operatives, armed with a wealth of information about both her own intelligence agency's capabilities, and those of other countries. Clearly she'd used that information to her advantage here today.

However, her formidable knowledge was now five years out of date. She'd been off the grid for a long time, and while things might not have changed much for the FSB in that time, they certainly had for the CIA.

Maybe, just maybe, he had an edge on her.

He had to put a stop to this. He might have been able to explain away the attack in DC, but Anya had crossed a line here today. One way or another, he had to stop her.

Reaching for his phone, he quickly dialled Frost's number. Based on her last report a couple of hours earlier, she and McKnight should be on a flight heading south from Norilsk by now.

It didn't take long for her to answer, or to make her thoughts known. 'Ryan, what the fuck is going on? We're getting reports of car-bomb attacks right in your neighbourhood.'

'Why do you think I'm calling?' Drake replied. 'I need you to get hold of the National Reconnaissance Office, find out if we had any assets over this area at the time of the attack. Call in any favours you have.'

'Ryan, I—'

'No arguments, just get it done!' Drake cut in. 'We have a high-value FSB leader abducted. We need to find him before he ends up like Demochev.'

Anya might have managed to escape Russia's satellites, but there was a chance one of the Agency's spy birds had caught her out. At the very least it was worth a shot.

'Fine. I'll see what I can do,' she conceded at last.

'Thanks.' Signing off, he turned his attention to Miranova, who was watching him expectantly. 'Chechnya's a global hotspot. You think we don't have our eyes on it?'

She said nothing to that, though he thought he saw a fleeting look of gratitude in her eyes. If somehow they managed to get to Masalsky in time, perhaps he might allow himself to feel a little better about this whole mess.

Perhaps.

Chapter 44

Ivan Masalsky blinked as the hood was yanked off his head, his eyes flooded with harsh electric light. Temporarily blinded, he could make out nothing but darkness beyond the intense corona.

He couldn't move. His wrists and feet were still plasti-cuffed together, and as a further restraint he'd been forced into a wooden chair, bound in place with duct tape around his legs and chest.

Unable to see for the moment, he concentrated instead on his other senses. He was in an enclosed space; that much was obvious. He could feel neither wind nor rain on his skin, though the cold creeping up through his bare feet told him the room was unheated. He'd felt himself walking on rough-poured concrete when he was led in here, confirming the place had a floor. Perhaps a warehouse or some other storage space.

But wherever he was, he wasn't alone.

'Hello, Ivan,' a male voice said. 'I've been looking forward to meeting you.'

He heard footsteps behind, and twisted around as a man walked into view. He was a short, modest-looking man, small and neat. The impression was enhanced by the dark blue work overalls he wore, which looked to be a couple of sizes too big for him.

Moving with unhurried patience, he circled around in front of Masalsky and into the light shining right at him. Masalsky couldn't quite see him now, but he knew the man had taken a seat by the creak of old wood as his weight settled on a chair, probably identical to the one he himself was strapped to.

The seconds ticked by, and Masalsky felt himself growing more uncomfortable. If this man had gone to so much trouble to capture him, why was he just sitting there? What did he want?

'Who are you?' he asked, unable to take it any longer.

'Who am I?' the man repeated, apparently amused by the question. There was another creak as he leaned forward in his chair. 'I'm no one, Ivan. Just another insignificant pawn. The man you walk past a dozen times a day without ever seeing, without ever thinking about. Who I am doesn't matter you to. What matters is why I'm here.'

'And why is that?'

'I'm here to judge you for the crimes you've committed against the Russian people, Ivan. I'm here to make sure the people know the truth.'

Masalsky's eyes were beginning to adjust to the ambient light now. Off to one side, he could see the distinctive outline of a camera tripod. That explained the harsh light shining right on him – he was to be recorded.

'What are you talking about? I . . . I've committed no crimes,' he protested.

The man reached for something on the ground at his feet. Masalsky heard the faint rasp of metal on concrete, and felt a shiver of fear run through him when he saw a set of bolt cutters gleaming in the harsh light.

'We'll see, my friend,' he promised. 'We'll see.'

In the accommodation block, Miranova and her fellow agents were hard at work trying to piece together the sequence of events during the attack, while also following up on reports from their field teams as they continued the search for Masalsky. Hastily set-up workstations, phones and cables trailed everywhere.

Next to this hive of activity, Drake felt every inch the proverbial fifth wheel. He was also increasingly aware of his growing fatigue, and the pain from the numerous injuries he'd taken during his fight with Anya. His shoulder felt as though someone had wedged a red-hot knife in it, and his back was starting to stiffen up after his tumble down that hillside.

Despite his protests, Miranova had insisted he be examined by one of the field station's medics, perhaps sensing that his injuries were more extensive than he was letting on. Thus, for the past five minutes he'd endured being prodded and poked by a gruff-looking man who hadn't even bothered introducing himself.

However, even Drake was unwilling to put up with any more as the man withdrew a syringe from his kit.

'No painkillers,' he said, shaking his head. A shot of morphine was great for unwinding after a tough day, but he wasn't prepared to take anything that could compromise his awareness or his decision-making ability.

The medic looked him up and down. 'Not painkillers – antibiotics. You are cut to shit,' he explained. 'This will stop infection.'

Before Drake could protest further, the man jammed the needle in his forearm and depressed the plunger. Drake winced as the unusually large needle was withdrawn. He felt as though he'd just been shot with horse tranquilliser.

The man spared him only a brief, disparaging look before packing up his gear and moving on. No doubt there was plenty of work for him tonight.

No sooner had he departed than Mason arrived to take his place. He might have spoken better English, but Drake would have taken a hundred needles over a conversation with him at that moment.

'I need to talk to you,' he said, his voice quiet but urgent. 'Right now.'

Drake didn't look at him. 'This isn't the time, Cole.'

He could guess exactly what his friend wanted to say, but this was neither the time nor the place to be having that conversation.

Suddenly he felt Mason's hand on his shoulder, strong fingers tightening their grip to send a renewed wave of pain flooding through him. It was a silent but very effective way of getting his attention.

'Make time, Ryan,' he advised, the tone of his voice making it plain he wasn't going to be put off. 'Or we do this right here in front of your new buddies. Your call.'

Swearing under his breath, Drake looked around for somewhere that might allow some measure of privacy. One corner of the room had yet to be taken over.

Shrugging out of Mason's grip, he retreated as far from the centre of activity as he could, then rounded on the older man. 'Make it quick.'

'Don't give me that shit, Ryan,' Mason hissed. 'This is getting out of control. You had intel that could have prevented a major terrorist strike, and you chose to sit on your fucking hands. Do you have any idea the kind of shit this puts us in?'

'It was my decision, Cole.'

'Fuck you!' Mason snapped, jabbing a finger at him. 'You really think the FSB would make that kind of distinction? We're both in this up to our necks. You had no right to make a decision like that on my behalf.'

'So what would you have done?' Drake hit back. 'Go

318

running to Miranova and tell her an Agency operative was behind this, but we chose to keep it to ourselves until now? Do you think for one second she wouldn't have thrown us both in jail?'

Mason sighed and shook his head in dismay. 'Ryan, for Christ's sake listen to yourself. People, *real people*, are getting killed over this. And for what? Anya isn't going to be saved; not by you or anyone else. She made her choice when she shot up that freeway in DC. Now she's made herself an enemy of the FSB *and* the CIA. How much longer are you going to keep protecting her? How much more are you prepared to give up for her?'

Drake clenched his fists as pent-up frustration threatened to boil over. 'I don't need a moral lecture, especially not from you, Cole. Let's not forget why you're here.'

'I know exactly why I'm here,' Mason assured him, his voice dangerously cold now. 'And it's not to become a martyr. You're going to get us all killed if you don't give this up.'

He'd heard enough. 'If you haven't got the nerve for this, then piss off back to DC. Otherwise, shut the fuck up and do your job.'

Mason took a step towards him, and instinctively Drake felt himself tense up, his body readying itself for a physical confrontation.

The bleep of Drake's cellphone was the only thing that seemed to break the spell. Scarcely aware of what he was doing, he fished it out of his pocket and glanced at the screen. It was Frost.

'What is it, Keira?' he snapped, still glaring at Mason.

'Good evening to you too,' Frost countered. 'Who took the jelly out of your doughnut?'

Drake was in no mood for her attempt at humour. 'Things aren't going well here.'

319

'Then maybe this'll make you feel better.' She paused for a moment, as if to let the tension build up. 'I think we've found your missing man.'

Anya said nothing as she listened to the screams echoing from down the corridor, instead concentrating her attention on field-stripping and reassembling her M1911. It was hardly a vital task, but it at least kept her mind occupied.

There was certainly nothing around here worthy of her attention.

Thirty years ago the hardened concrete aircraft shelter in which she now sat had contained Soviet fighter-bombers, intended to launch ground attacks against a possible US invasion from Turkey. Now it was nothing but a cavernous, draughty expanse of crumbling concrete and rusted pipework. Another decaying symbol of a forgotten time.

Her Lada 4x4, which had barely been up to the task of getting here, looked faintly ridiculous parked in such ominous surroundings. Outside the rusting steel doors a frigid wind sighed past, carrying with it stinging pellets of freezing rain.

The other four men in the derelict room seemed untroubled either by the cold or by the sounds of Masalsky's torture, celebrating their success with a crate of beer as they recounted their exploits during the attack on the FSB compound. They were still pumped up after the short but intense action, filled with adrenalin and endorphins that made them giddy and excitable.

She had often heard combat described as a drug, and in truth she had once felt much the same way. There had been a time long ago when, flushed with the enthusiasm and misplaced confidence of youth, she'd even sought out the thrill that came from living on a knife edge of survival, like a junkie endlessly searching for a more powerful hit.

It hadn't taken her long to discover just how misplaced that confidence had been.

'So I turned the corner and I came face to face with this big fat fucker,' said Goran, a wily little Serbian mercenary who had become one of the most outspoken members of the small group. 'I raised my weapon to fire. And you know what he said to me?'

Aside from alcohol and violence, the thing he loved most in the world was the sound of his own voice. He was easily as old as Anya, yet he spoke and acted like a boisterous teenager, boasting about everything from the men he'd killed to the women he'd bedded.

He took a long drag on his cigarette, as if he thought it would build the tension.

'"Wait",' he finally said. 'Can you believe that? "Wait!" As if we could sit down and talk things through.' He shook his head. 'Stupid asshole. I dropped him a second later.'

His story was accompanied by raucous laughter from Branka, a fellow Serb who looked so much like Goran that the two men could have been brothers. They might well have been for all Anya knew. She had little inclination to learn more about them. All she knew was that when they were together it was virtually impossible to shut them up.

The other two men were decidedly more reserved. Dokka, a big Chechen guerrilla fighter who had served in both wars against Russia and had the scars to prove it; and Yuri, a Ukrainian who shared some of Goran's outspoken personality, but who often found himself at odds with the two Serbs.

Having finished his tale, Goran took a long pull on his beer and then turned his attention to Anya. 'And what about you, *maco*? You must have some stories to tell.'

Anya didn't look up. *Maco* was a Serbian term of endearment that loosely translated as 'kitty cat', though in a cruder sense it could be interpreted as 'pussy'. It didn't take much imagination to guess the association in his mind.

He'd started calling her by the new nickname within an hour of meeting her and, wary of destroying her tenuous position within the group, she had tolerated it as she'd tolerated so many other things in life – with brooding silence.

'Not really,' she evaded as she started to thumb rounds back into the weapon's magazine. She never knew when she might have to use it.

'Come on, don't be so fucking dull!' he taunted. 'You were in there on your own, surrounded by FSB. And you came out alive. Tell us how it happened.'

Goran's exposed arms and hands were covered with tattoos; everything from numbers to crucifixes to pictures of naked women. He didn't need to tell anyone where he'd got them from. Anya knew that the numbers and obscure symbols formed a complex code explaining which Russian gulag he'd done time in, and even which cell block.

She glanced up at him, her blue eyes like pools of ice in the gloom. 'Things went as planned. Nothing more.'

She saw a brief flash of anger in his eyes. She was embarrassing him by refusing to play along with his game, by leaving him hanging. And she guessed Goran wasn't the kind of man who appreciated being embarrassed, least of all by a woman.

Quietly Anya pushed the magazine back into the port on her M1911, applying a little more pressure until she felt the click of the locking pins engaging. If Goran tried to make a move, she would be ready for him.

Then, as quickly as it had come, the anger vanished. He smiled and inclined his bottle to her in a mock toast.

'That's what I like about you, *maco*. You're so cold when

you do this shit.' He took another drink, then glanced at Branka and switched to Serbian, thinking she couldn't understand him. 'I guess she saves all her warmth for the bedroom. Maybe I'll find out?'

Anya felt herself tense up, even though the rational part of her mind warned her to show no emotion. She couldn't help it – she'd listened to just about enough of his crude banter over the past few weeks, and was approaching the limits of her patience.

Ten years ago she'd been in command of one of the most formidable paramilitary groups on the face of the earth, equalled by none. Now here she was in a derelict aircraft shelter on an abandoned airfield, taking abuse from a man she could kill a dozen times over with her bare hands.

Just for a moment her eyes reflected her thoughts, her anger, her pain, her years of pent-up frustration and impotent rage straining to break free, held in check by nothing more than her iron will. It was only a glimpse, a snapshot, a lightning flash in the darkness that illuminated the world as it was, but it was enough for Goran. The smile faded; the fire of his bravado seemed to flicker out.

He glanced away, unable to hold her gaze.

The screams were cut off abruptly by a single gunshot that reverberated around the cellar like the pealing of thunder, signalling the end of Masalsky's 'interrogation'.

Turning around, Anya watched as Atayev emerged from a doorway on the far side of the shelter and strode briskly towards them, removing a pair of work gloves and tossing them aside. Next he unzipped the overalls, stained crimson with Masalsky's blood, and stepped out of them to reveal civilian clothes, still clean and neat. Only the tiny splash of blood on the left lens of his glasses gave any hint of what he'd just been involved in.

'Did you get what you needed?' Anya asked, rising to her feet.

'After a fashion.' Atayev patted his jacket pocket, bulging with the square frame of the video camera. Anya had no desire to view its contents. 'He was more stubborn than Demochev. Took some persuading.'

Anya said nothing to this. She had seen men take pleasure from inflicting pain and suffering, had even been on the receiving end more than once herself, but Atayev was different.

His actions weren't an outlet for some inner perversion or the festering legacy of past abuses. They were a rebirth, a renewal. When he removed his bloodstained overalls, he was shedding another piece of his previous life, coming one step closer to his transformation into something new, something better.

He seemed to sense her disquiet. Reaching up, he removed his glasses, took a handkerchief from his pocket and carefully wiped the blood away, looking almost self-conscious now.

'It bothers you,' he observed coolly. 'What we do.'

'Torture is a poor tool for any soldier,' she said, deciding to be honest.

'But I'm not a soldier.' He replaced his glasses and ran a hand through his receding hair. 'And neither are our enemies.'

Anya nodded, reluctantly acknowledging his point. It still didn't change how she felt.

'If you want to leave, I won't hold it against you,' Atayev prompted. 'You've already done more than I would ask of anyone.'

'You know why I'm here,' she replied. 'I've come too far to turn back now.'

He smiled and laid a hand on her shoulder, and for a moment she saw a flicker of the husband and father he'd once been. 'I'd hoped you would say that.'

'There's something I must ask you,' Anya said, lowering her voice. 'When I encountered Drake tonight, he believed I'd tried to contact him before the attack in Washington. I did no such thing, which means someone else did. Someone who knew where I would be.'

Although she was trying not to sound threatening, she had to know the truth from this man, had to know she could trust him. For her, the best course of action was simply to ask.

From a young age Anya had been endowed with the ability to perceive the subtle visual cues and signals that people give off without conscious awareness. She couldn't explain it exactly, but that same skill allowed her to anticipate her opponent's movements in a fight, and even to know with a fair degree of certainty when they were lying.

If that was the case with Atayev, she would kill him and the rest of the men in the hangar without hesitation, and take her chances alone. The automatic shoved down the back of her jeans was loaded and ready to be fired. What he said in the next few seconds would decide his fate.

She didn't have to say anything more. He sensed her implied threat, and the danger he was now in. 'I had no part in that, Anya. That's the truth.'

She sensed no hint of deception in either his voice or his expression. If he was lying to her, his skills at deception rivalled the best operatives the Agency had ever produced. She was obliged to conclude that he was being honest with her.

'And can you say the same of the rest of your men?' she asked, with a momentary glance at Goran and the others.

Atayev said nothing, though his expression made it obvious that he was just as unsettled by the implication as she. One or more of their group could be compromised.

The bleep of his cellphone interrupted their brief conversation. Retrieving it from his pocket, Atayev opened the incoming text message. The look in his eyes made it clear the news wasn't good.

'Is there a problem?' Anya asked.

He pocketed the phone once more, his brow furrowed in thought.

'A change of plan,' he corrected her. 'We may have to move faster than we'd intended.'

Chapter 45

Drake braced himself as the Mi-24 attack helicopter ploughed through another gusting crosswind, jolting him in his seat and straining his already injured shoulder. Steep slopes mantled by fir trees flitted past his window at over 150 knots, their features so identical that they looked like a storm-tossed sea in the darkness.

They were contouring one of the many river valleys that ran through the area, using the steep tree-covered slopes both to hide the chopper from sight and to mask the considerable noise of its engines as they approached their target.

Mi-24s were best known by their NATO code name 'Hind', but they had also been endowed with the rather more flattering nickname of Flying Tanks by their pilots, and one look at them was enough to see why. Fifty-seven feet long and half as wide, bristling with guns and rockets, and protected by a belt of armour able to withstand 20mm cannon shells, they were massive, imposing machines of war. Acting as both heavily armed gunships and troop transports, Hinds had no equivalent anywhere in the Western arsenal.

They had given the Mujahideen a few headaches in Afghanistan back in the eighties, and remained formidable aircraft twenty years later. He had never been inside one himself until today, but he supposed there was a first time for everything.

As he'd hoped, Frost had once again come through for them. One of the Agency's newest Block IV KH-11 spy satellites had been passing over the FSB compound at the time of the attack, allowing the technical specialist to track the vehicle used to abduct Masalsky.

The trail had led her to an abandoned military airfield north of Grozny before the KH-11's orbit had carried it beyond the horizon, preventing further observation until the next pass. From what Miranova had been able to learn, the airfield had once belonged to the Russian air force, used to house MiG fighter-bombers before being decommissioned after the Cold War. The years of conflict in Chechnya had destroyed what little infrastructure remained, putting it permanently out of use.

And now here they were, roaring through the darkened skies over Chechnya in a desperate race to find Masalsky before his captors executed him.

For Drake, however, this race had a far more personal goal. He was after Anya, and nothing else. She had crossed the line today. If she wanted to play rough, then so be it. He was coming for her, and nothing and no one was going to get in his way.

As the chopper banked hard right, Drake was suddenly very conscious that one slip-up could see them plough straight into the side of a mountain. The airframe shuddered under the strain as gravity fought against its 26,000 pounds of armour, fuel and engines.

'Are you all right?' Miranova asked over the intercom, her face illuminated by the red glow of the aircraft's dim internal lighting.

'Helicopters and I don't mix,' he said tersely, memories of being shot out of the sky by a Stinger missile in Afghanistan still fresh in his mind. 'How long until we get there?'

She raised an eyebrow, but wisely decided not to pursue the matter further. 'We are close. Only a couple of minutes.'

Drake clenched his fists. A lot could happen in a couple of minutes.

'Ground teams have sealed off all nearby roads, and one of our unmanned drones has been vectored in. We have the entire area covered by thermal imaging. If anyone tries to leave, we will see them.'

He wished he shared her confidence. Anya had already proven herself more than capable of both second-guessing and outwitting them. Next to her he felt like a rank amateur, even with the formidable resources of the FSB to call upon.

'So what's the assault plan?' he asked, trying to focus on the task ahead of them.

'We will fast-rope down, secure the airfield and recover Masalsky. The helicopter will provide close air support if we need it.'

Drake hadn't missed the 'we' in her statement. Clearly she intended to go in with the assault team. 'When was the last time you did this?'

'More recently than you, I think.'

She paused for a moment, head cocked as she listened to an incoming transmission.

'Stand by,' Miranova warned as the chopper's nose flared upwards, rotors beating the air as they clawed their way out of the river valley that had carried them almost all the way to their target. 'Thirty seconds!'

The speed of the full-powered ascent caught even Drake by surprise, and he felt himself pushed down into his seat by the acceleration. He felt as if he'd left his stomach behind. Chancing a glance out the window, he could just make out the dark shapes of trees skimming by frighteningly close.

Cresting the lip of the valley, their flight path at last began to even out as the Hind swung right, coming in for its final approach to the target.

'Ten seconds!'

Pushkin, the FSB tactical agent who had been with them during the raid on Glazov's farm, rose to his feet, gripping a safety strap to steady himself as the pilots fought to keep the aircraft steady. The nose was rising again to bleed off speed and bring them in to hover over the target.

Drake glanced over at Mason, who had remained more or less silent for most of the flight. Whatever their disagreements earlier, both of them knew better than to hold a grudge while their lives might be on the line.

'Good to go?'

Mason looked at him and, contrary to his usual wisecracking style, merely nodded.

Drake could guess why he was on edge. Fast-rope descents required a lot of upper-body strength, as one's entire weight was placed on the arms. Descending a rope from a swaying helicopter in freezing weather conditions was difficult enough for a fit and healthy adult, never mind someone like Mason who was coming back from a long spell of inactivity.

'If you're not feeling up to this—'

'I'm fine, for Christ's sake!' Mason snapped, anger flaring in his eyes. 'Just worry about yourself, Ryan.'

Drake never got a chance to make a comeback. Gripping the hatch release, Pushkin unlatched it and shoved hard, pushing it backwards on its rollers.

Straight away a maelstrom of wind and freezing rain assailed them. Like the rest of the team, Drake was clad in several layers of insulated fabric, but the cold seemed to penetrate right through as if they weren't even there. The *thump, thump, thump* of the rotor blades just overhead drowned out any attempt at verbal communication. It was hand gestures only for now.

Drake watched as the FSB agent reached out and clipped his line into the pylon mounted on the side of the aircraft, then gave it a hard yank to test the clip. This was the interesting part, when the team roped down to their assault position.

They were utterly vulnerable during that time, unable to return fire or take cover if someone decided to have a pop at them. The Hind's gunner was no doubt sweeping the area with his thermal optics, looking for any sign of anti-aircraft weaponry. The aircraft too was vulnerable while they waited for the team to deploy.

With his line checked, Pushkin gripped the thick nylon rope and disappeared over the edge. The next agent followed a few seconds later, and the next, until the entire tactical team had descended in short order. Miranova, like her male comrades, paused at the hatch just long enough to get a good grip of the rope, then pushed herself off the deck and vanished into the darkness.

Now it was Drake's turn.

There was no great technicality to fast-roping. In essence it involved gripping the rope with thick padded gloves, loosening it a little and allowing gravity to do the rest. It was simple and quick, the only downside being that there was no descent harness, no backup line, no safeguards. If you slipped or lost your grip, it was game over.

Wrapping his fingers around the rope to get a good grip, and trying not to think about the sickening fall that would result if he fucked this up, Drake pushed himself off from the chopper's deck and relaxed his grip a little to start his descent.

He didn't wrap his boots around the rope, even though it would have given him extra grip and taken some of the strain off his arms. Boot polish from the leather could rub off on to the descent line, making it dangerously slick.

The downwash from the main rotors was immense, jerking the rope from side to side despite his considerable weight. He felt like a kid on a rope swing, swaying uncontrolled and clinging on for dear life. The frigid air clawed his throat, rain whipping into his eyes, while pain burned outwards from his injured shoulder.

He was going too slowly. He felt as though he was still 100 feet in the air. Easing off his grip even more, he felt the tiny nylon braids slipping through his fingers, accompanied by rapidly building heat from the resulting friction. Then, almost out of nowhere, the ground rushed up to meet him.

He braced himself as he landed hard, rolling to lessen the impact and releasing his grip on the line. It wasn't the most graceful landing ever, but at least he was down. And he'd managed to take the weight off his shoulder, much to his relief.

Drawing his automatic, he picked himself up and rushed forwards, eager to get clear of the landing zone. Not only would it keep them spread out and prevent a single burst of fire from wiping out the whole team, but it would also ensure Mason didn't land right on top of him.

No sooner had this thought crossed his mind than Mason abruptly released his grip and fell the remaining 15 feet or so, landing in an awkward sprawl mere feet away. Fortunately for him, the deep mud had at least served to cushion his fall, if not his pride.

As the Hind peeled away to begin circling the target area, Drake turned to his friend, who was struggling to extricate himself from the mud. Hurrying forwards, Drake grabbed him by the arm and applied more than enough pressure to get his attention.

'What the fuck was that?' Drake hissed. 'You trying to fly in?'

'Not now, man,' Mason growled, shoving him away. He was making a show of being angry, but nonetheless Drake could tell the descent had taken a heavy toll on him.

The other agents were already spreading out to form a perimeter, moving in pairs to cover each other and bent low to present smaller targets.

Up ahead stood the first major structure Drake had seen in the facility – an air control tower overlooking the overgrown wilderness that had once been the runway. It was obvious the building hadn't been used in a long time. All of the upper windows, which must once have offered a panoramic view of the airfield and runway, were long gone. The big radar array on top was a rusting, decrepit wreck, with one entire panel missing and broken cables hanging down the side of the tower like vines.

'Come on,' Drake hissed, pulling Mason to his feet. 'Get the fuck up.'

Gripping his automatic tight in his gloved hands, he hurried over to join Miranova at the base of the control tower, with Mason right behind him. Despite the freezing air he was already sweating through his BDUs with a combination of exertion and nervous energy.

The adrenalin was flowing hard and fast as he backed up against the rough, pitted concrete wall next to her, his heart thumping so loud that it seemed anyone nearby must hear it. Taking a deeper breath to calm himself, he craned his head around the edge of the building to survey their surroundings properly for the first time.

Two aircraft hangars stood about 50 yards away. They were big structures, about 30 feet high and twice as wide, resembling giant concrete hexagons laid on their sides, with steel sliding doors covering their mouths. They were hardened strike shelters, designed to protect high-value aircraft from all but the most powerful of bombs. He'd seen plenty of structures just like them on air bases throughout America and Western Europe.

Further away stood a large two-storey building, probably once an office and administrative area, and perhaps even an accommodation block. It looked just as neglected and dilapidated as the rest of the buildings here, with broken windows, empty doorways and ivy creeping over the crumbling walls.

Trees and bushes were beginning to take root here and there, forming small forests of new growth. Nature was gradually reclaiming the abandoned airfield.

Drake heard the rustle of fabric as Miranova sidled along the wall next to him. She was so close he could feel her warm breath on his cheek. 'It is quiet here,' she remarked, clearly suspicious of the lack of resistance.

Drake nodded. The assault team had announced their arrival as plainly as it was possible to do, yet no shots had been fired. What was Anya doing?

'Anything from our eyes in the sky?' he asked.

She shook her head. 'No movement. Nothing on thermal imaging.'

He wasn't surprised. Infrared cameras were all well and good, but even they couldn't see through solid walls. If Anya was here, she was likely hidden away in one of the buildings.

'Then we do it the old-fashioned way,' he decided. 'Building by building, room by room. Take your assault team and move in on those hangars. Cole, on me. We're going for that office building over there. Ready?'

'Say the word,' Mason assured him. House assaults and urban combat had been his speciality back in the day, and he was no doubt eager to prove he could still cut it.

'I don't—' Miranova began.

'No arguments,' he said, a harder edge in his voice now. He wasn't interested in negotiating with her over who was in charge of the assault. If he had to, he'd tear this airfield apart with his bare hands to find Anya. 'We're moving now. Cover by twos, five-yard spread. Go!'

Without waiting for her response he pushed himself off the wall and took off at a sprint, keeping low to present a smaller target. The scattered trees and bushes provided some visual cover, but they would be of no help if someone started shooting at them.

He could hear Mason's boots pounding through the mud behind him. Just as he'd instructed, the man was keeping several metres back. This way they could support each other in a firefight, but maintain enough distance that a single burst of gunfire couldn't wipe them both out.

At any moment he expected to hear the distinctive crackle of automatic fire and feel rounds whistling past to churn up the muddy ground, yet no such thing happened. Aside from the distant beating of the helicopter rotors and the patter of raindrops, the airfield remained oddly quiet.

An empty doorway lay ahead, the space beyond shrouded in shadow. Pausing a moment or two to allow Mason to catch up, Drake switched on the flashlight mounted beneath the barrel of his automatic and slipped inside.

His eyes were by now accustomed to the gloomy conditions, but the darkness inside the ruined building was absolute. The narrow beam looked like a 1,000-watt searchlight illuminating the empty, desolate corridor in which he now found himself.

The place was a mess. Years of rain and wind, freezing and thawing had gradually undermined the building's internal structure. Plaster was falling off the walls in big chunks, paint was peeling, and roofing panels had collapsed to reveal the electrical wiring and rusted pipes above. The walls were streaked with mould and damp.

The flashlight beam reflected off tiny shards of broken glass scattered across the floor. About halfway along the hall, a stairwell led to the upper level.

He inhaled, tasting the scents on the air. Despite the freezing temperature, there was a strange, unpleasant odour lingering in the corridor. Stale and rotten; the festering reek of decay. The smell turned his stomach, reminding him of another time, in Afghanistan, when he and his companions had stumbled across the decomposing corpse of a man they had been sent to rescue.

Surely that wasn't possible here? Masalsky had only been abducted a couple of hours earlier.

'Come on,' he said under his breath as he crept forwards, his boots crunching on the broken glass. 'Come on. I'm ready.'

He could hear movement behind, and felt a tap on his shoulder as Mason fell into step behind him, covering his back. Whatever their earlier differences, Drake knew he could rely on the man in situations like this.

Together they advanced down the corridor, passing by an empty room on the left. The door was missing, and a quick glance inside revealed nothing save for a couple of rusted filing cabinets piled in a heap in the centre of the room.

Two more rooms also yielded nothing of interest. It felt as if no one had walked this hallway since the day the airfield was shut down.

'Fucking ghost town, man,' Mason said quietly. 'Reminds me of that city they evacuated after Chernobyl. Dishes still in sinks, kids' toys lying where they'd been dropped . . .'

Drake was about to tell him to shut up, but a sudden crash further down the corridor abruptly halted their conversation.

Both men froze at the unmistakable sound of movement coming from deeper inside the building.

Drake's heartbeat soared, and he could feel the pulse pounding in his ears as a mixture of fear and anticipation swept through him. Someone or something was in here with them.

Glancing at Mason, he raised his weapon and pointed down the corridor. The older man nodded understanding, his body held taut and ready.

Taking a deep breath and gripping his own weapon tight, Drake crept forwards. The lingering stench that he'd noticed on entering the building was growing stronger with each step, causing bile to rise in his throat.

Whatever it was, it seemed to be coming from just up ahead. Most of the rooms stood open, their doors either removed or destroyed when the airfield was abandoned, but this one remained closed and sealed. Rusted and decayed by age, the heavy steel door was an imposing barrier standing in their path.

The footsteps had stopped and silence descended on the ruined building. The place was eerily quiet as the two men crunched their way through the debris-covered floor. Even the howl of the wind outside seemed to have died down.

Drake's heart was pounding as he approached the door. The knowledge that Mason was covering his back did little to ease the sense of dread and foreboding that seemed to have descended on him.

Halting in front of it, he raised his foot and glanced for a moment at his companion. 'Three, two, one . . .'

With a single powerful kick, he sent the heavy door flying inwards, flecks of rust grating off the neglected hinges. Drake was in straight away, his weapon and flashlight sweeping the room while Mason moved in right behind him.

The damp, mould-ridden room beyond must have been an armoury when this airfield was still operational. Ammunition racks lined the far wall, all empty and corroded. A couple of cheap tables sat in the middle of the room, their wooden veneers long since rotted away. The floor was covered with paper that had decomposed into piles of frozen pulp.

His inspection was interrupted by a sudden flurry of movement as something huge and dark bounded from a darkened corner and into the centre of the room.

Drake's heart surged with a burst of adrenalin, and instinctively his finger tightened on the trigger as he brought the weapon up to fire. But at the last moment, he stopped himself.

Of all the enemies Drake had faced in his career, never before had he encountered a wolf. This one, however, was a monster, topping the scales at 120 pounds or more. Broad, shaggy shoulders gave way to long, powerful legs and wide clawed feet splayed out for extra purchase on the decaying floor. Its thick grey-white pelt, able to resist the cold far better than their own clothing, seemed to ripple as the muscles beneath bunched and coiled.

Sleek, powerful and agile, it was perfectly adapted to the environment that it called home. Its vicious predatory eyes were fixed on the two humans who had been foolish enough to wander into its territory, lips drawn back to reveal rows of wicked-looking teeth.

That explained the source of the smell, Drake thought. It had never occurred to him that with humans gone, the indigenous wildlife would have stepped in to fill the void. This wolf had made the office block its territory, and would likely defend it to the death. There was no telling how many more were lurking in the darkened rooms and corridors.

Mason was apparently entertaining similar thoughts. 'This is not a good place to be.'

'Easy, mate,' Drake whispered. 'Let's back off, yeah? No sudden movements.'

Covering the deadly predator with his weapon, Drake took a step back, then another, slowly retreating down the corridor. The wolf watched them go, hackles raised, teeth bared, ready to strike the moment it sensed a threat.

Behind him Mason took another step, eager to get out of there. Drake heard the faint rattle as he disturbed something, then winced inwardly as a rusted section of the ammunition rack gave way, landing on the floor with a horrific metallic clang that echoed down the corridor.

The uneasy stand-off was broken. In an instant, the wolf launched itself forwards, loping towards them with powerful bounds, jaws already opening wide to tear into flesh.

The report of the gunshot in the confined space was deafening, causing Drake to flinch aside. He heard a frightened yelp, and suddenly the wolf crashed to the ground, its momentum causing it to skid and roll several feet before finally coming to rest at their feet.

Spinning around, Drake saw Mason standing beside them, wisps of smoke trailing from the barrel of his weapon.

'What the fuck were you doing?' he demanded, angry both at the needless death he'd just witnessed, and the gunshot that had just given away their position.

'Saving your life, you asshole,' Mason replied, lowering the gun. 'Or would you rather I let that thing kill you?'

Drake opened his mouth to retort, but before he could say a word his radio unit crackled into life, Miranova's urgent voice resounding in his ears.

'Ryan, come in! Report.'

Still watching Mason, Drake hit the transmit button at his throat. 'We're fine,' he said, an edge of anger still in his voice. 'Just local wildlife. There's nothing here.'

She was silent for a moment. 'Then you need to come to the hangar.'

He frowned, struck by the tone of her voice. 'What have you got?'

'We have found Masalsky,' she said simply. 'He's dead.'

Chapter 46

Anya once again found herself alone, this time picking her way northwards through quiet woodland towards the border with neighbouring Dagestan. As before, she and her unlikely comrades had separated for the journey to their next location, minimising the chances of the group being compromised.

Anya had chosen this route specifically because there were no border checkpoints here. It was little more than a winding forest trail, seldom used except by the occasional hunter or logging company. She had abandoned her car some distance back, knowing it was useless in the heavily forested terrain.

She was going to have to hike across the border on foot. It made for a long walk in poor weather, but she had endured far worse.

She didn't doubt that the FSB would be out hunting for her and the others, but the Chechen border was hundreds of miles long and largely unmarked by either natural or man-made barriers. It was impossible for them to cover every avenue.

So far she had encountered nothing since leaving the main road, and had no reason to believe her way was guarded. Still, she remained wary and unhappy, particularly with the FSB's rapid advance on the airfield. Despite Atayev's apparent calm, the group had been forced to clear out of there much faster than they'd originally intended.

Only a prompt warning had saved them from capture.

Temporarily absorbed in her dark thoughts, she allowed her normally acute awareness of her surroundings to slip. Thus it took her a moment or two to heed the increasingly urgent warnings being ferried by her subconscious mind. Only when she felt a chill of foreboding ripple through her did she realise something was wrong.

She was being watched.

Cursing her carelessness, she reached for the weapon at her back.

'Forget it, *mako*,' Goran's familiar voice warned her, coming from perhaps 20 yards away. 'I've got you covered.'

Anya closed her eyes and let out a sigh of disappointment, angry with herself for not seeing this sooner. Worse, she should have detected him following her long before this.

Perhaps he was a better soldier than she'd given him credit for. Or perhaps she had allowed herself to grow complacent.

'Are you here to kill me, Goran?' she asked without turning around.

'Depends what you do next. Take your weapon out by the barrel and drop it.'

To resist now would be foolish. Anya removed the weapon as he'd instructed, then dropped it on the ground.

'Good girl. Now raise your hands and turn around.'

Turning, she watched as he emerged from behind a tree further down the slope, advancing towards her with an AK up at his shoulder. He was a fair shot, and caught out in the open as she was, she knew he'd drop her before she could find cover.

'Back up,' he instructed.

Again she did as ordered. There was no sense antagonising him. Not yet at least.

Keeping her covered, he bent down and picked up the

342

M1911 she'd dropped, turning it over in his hand. 'A good weapon,' he remarked, pointing it playfully as if he were gunning down rows of enemies. 'Like *Dirty Harry*, huh?'

Anya said nothing. Only her eyes reflected the depth of her contempt.

He grinned, undaunted by her anger now. 'You just keep staring at me with those pretty blue eyes of yours, *mako*. Maybe I'll take one as a souvenir. Would you like that?'

She didn't dignify that with an answer. 'What do you want?'

'You, as it happens. We're going for a walk together.' He flicked the barrel of the gun towards the path. 'Come on. Move.'

Miranova was right – they had indeed found Masalsky. In this case he'd been left in one of the small storage rooms at the back of the abandoned aircraft hangar.

Much like Demochev before him, the senior FSB leader had been stripped to the waist, beaten and tortured before being executed, though in this case the *coup de grâce* had come via a single gunshot to the forehead. The other gory details were, however, almost identical.

The bolt cutters, the severed digits, the single word in Cyrillic carved into his chest. Drake didn't need to be an expert in Russian to recognise the word *guilty*.

Drake knelt down in front of the body to examine something else lying on the floor, looking absurdly out of place in such gruesome surroundings. Black and gleaming, carved with great care by hand, it was a knight from a chess set.

First a rook, then a knight. Whoever was doing this was clearly moving up through the ranks. And again they had managed to slip away before their pursuers could close the net.

'Jesus,' Mason breathed, surveying the scene with his arms folded. 'Someone really had it in for this guy.'

It wasn't Anya – that much he was certain of. There could be no doubt any longer that she was heavily involved in this, that her skills had formed the cutting edge of each attack so far, but the kind of sadistic torture on display here, the chess pieces, the cryptic messages . . . none of that was her style. She was a soldier, not a sadist.

He looked over at Miranova, realising how crushing this failure must have been for her. 'I'm sorry, Anika.'

There was no response from her. Only her eyes reflected the depth of her feelings at seeing another FSB agent dead. Another comrade she had failed to protect.

Another link in the chain.

'I must say, I was impressed,' Goran admitted as he and Anya picked their way through the darkened woods. He was careful to keep her a safe distance ahead in case she tried anything. 'The way you broke into that place and brought Masalsky to us . . . You made it look so easy. Tell me, where did you learn such things?'

Anya allowed herself a wry smile. 'I could tell you, but then I'd have to kill you.'

He chuckled at that. 'I bet you would, too.'

'The thought had crossed my mind.'

'And yet here we are – me with the gun, and you with . . . nothing. Strange how things work out, isn't it?'

In that sense, she was in total agreement. 'So after we cross the border, what then?'

'Then, I take you to some friends of mine. We will hold on to you for a while before we hand you over to the FSB,' he said. 'They've seen your face. I'd guess there's a good price on your head already. A week from now it'll be even better.'

Anya paused just for a moment, spotting something on the ground up ahead that evoked a mixture of urgency and anticipation. Her keen eyes had been sweeping the area this whole time, wary of a hidden danger that only she knew about. Before it had been nothing but a hazard to be carefully avoided, but now it represented a way out. A dangerous way out perhaps, but beggars couldn't be choosers. Satisfied that she was where she needed to be, she carried on, her brief hesitation passing unnoticed.

'What about Atayev?' she asked.

'What about him? He's a lot of things, *mako*, but he's not a rich man. But you . . . you're my retirement fund. I'll retire happy, knowing I helped bring one of Russia's worst terrorists to justice.'

Lifting her foot a little higher, Anya stepped over a small, almost invisible metal prong protruding from beneath last summer's dead leaves, then stopped and turned to face her captor.

'Listen to me, Goran. I want to make you an offer. I'll only make it once, and I want you to think about it carefully before you answer. Lower your weapon, turn around and walk away. Forget you ever saw me here today, and I'll do the same. I'll tell Atayev you were killed by the FSB, and I promise you'll never see me or hear from me again. You're not my enemy – I have no interest in killing you.'

Just for a moment she sensed his resolve wavering, his cocky self-assurance briefly undermined by the conviction in her voice. Just for a moment it seemed as if he might actually accept her proposal.

And then, in an instant, his doubt vanished and his smile returned. 'A tempting offer,' he said with a sardonic grin. 'But I'm afraid it doesn't end with me being rich. Now move.'

Letting out a vexed sigh, Anya turned around and resumed her march. She had done what she could; had offered him a chance to save himself. It wasn't her fault if he refused to take it.

'And do you think the FSB won't execute you once you hand me over?'

He laughed again. 'Trust me, this isn't the first time I've done this. I have plenty of friends who can make the exchange for—'

His sentence was interrupted by a muted thump that seemed to come from within the ground at his feet, followed by a hiss as something leapt up into the air right in front of him.

Having been waiting for just such a noise, Anya reacted instinctively, throwing herself into a shallow depression and curling into a ball just as a far louder bang echoed through the woods, almost drowning out Goran's scream of pain and shock.

With her ears ringing, Anya opened her eyes and looked around, slowly uncurling her limbs and checking that everything still worked. Much to her relief, she seemed to have avoided the blast and the deadly hail of shrapnel that had scythed through the air right above her head.

The same couldn't be said of Goran. The man was lying sprawled on the ground several yards away, jerking and gurgling while blood pumped from the countless wounds torn across his chest and stomach.

Anya picked herself up and approached cautiously, watching with curious detachment as he tried to reach for the AK with the shattered, bloody stump of his right arm, seemingly unable to understand that he no longer had a hand with which to grasp the weapon.

'Strange how things work out, isn't it, Goran?' she said,

reaching down to remove her M1911 from his belt. He wouldn't be needing it where he was going.

A smoking hole in the ground nearby testified to the device that had brought him down. A bounding landmine, probably an OZM-72 or some derivative. They were designed for taking out groups of enemy soldiers, with the first man in the group triggering the device and causing it to leap into the air before detonating amongst his comrades.

Chechnya was one of the most heavily mined countries on earth. More than half a million of the things had been laid during both wars – everything from anti-tank mines to cluster bombs, to handmade booby traps, with most lying in unmarked fields. Little effort had been made to clear them, and as a result several thousand civilians were killed or injured by such unexploded ordnance every year.

Goran was staring blankly at her now. Unable to speak, he could manage only a low, bubbling groan as frothy blood seeped out from the wounds across his chest.

Normally she would have used the pistol to end his suffering, but not today. Today all she could think of was his gleeful stories of the men he'd murdered, his derisive sneers whenever he looked at her, and his ill-conceived plan to betray her to the very people he'd taken such joy in killing.

'You should have taken my offer,' she said quietly.

Replacing the weapon down the back of her jeans, she turned away and resumed her hike towards the border.

Chapter 47

The mood at the abandoned airfield was understandably subdued after they had made their grisly discovery. A temporary field station had been set up in the hangar so that forensics teams could begin the task of combing the area for clues. Drake had little hope that they would find anything useful – Anya and her companions were too good for that.

'Another failure,' Miranova said as she watched Masalsky's remains being carried away in a black body bag. Her hollow eyes and drawn appearance were mute testimony to lack of sleep, constant pressure and the stark realisation that another man was dead. 'How many more will die before this is over?'

For that, Drake had no answer.

'We should focus on what we can do for the living,' he said, trying to salvage something from the situation, though his own outlook was scarcely better than hers. 'As hard as it is to accept, Masalsky's death might have given us exactly what we need.'

The woman looked up at him. 'And what is that?'

'A pattern. Each of these killings is a link in the chain. If we want to know where it leads, we need to find whatever it is that connects Demochev and Masalsky. We find that, and we might finally have an advantage.'

Miranova sniffed and nodded agreement, rallying her flagging energy. 'You're right.'

'Can we get access to their personnel records?'

She was silent for a moment, considering his request, then finally seemed to make a decision. 'Come with me.'

A couple of laptop computers had been set up in the centre of the hangar so that the forensics teams could upload pictures of the crime scene to FSB headquarters. Making her way over to the improvised comms station, Miranova sat down and quickly logged in using her own security clearance.

'I should be able to download their service records from here,' she explained as she called up what Drake assumed to be a database search tool. Inputting her search criteria, she waited a moment while her request was processed.

'They were senior directors,' Drake felt compelled to point out. Such files would have been far beyond the reach of field agents in the CIA. 'Wouldn't their records be confidential?'

She glanced at him. 'When Director Surovsky put me in charge of this investigation, I was given a certain amount of . . . latitude. For now at least, my security clearance allows me almost unlimited access.'

Drake said nothing to that. He only wished his own superiors were so accommodating.

As the files came through, Miranova opened them up and skim-read the reams of text now displayed. Clearly the FSB kept detailed records of their people – both men's career summaries alone would have filled several pages of printed paper. And with all of it written in Cyrillic, Drake was left with no choice but to let Miranova be his eyes.

'Both of them have been with the FSB a long time,' she said after a couple of minutes. 'Their records are . . . extensive.'

'Was either man involved in disciplinary action?' Drake asked. He doubted the *guilty* reference would be anything so obvious, but it never hurt to cover the bases.

She shook her head. 'Neither has any official reprimands

on file, or charges made against them. In fact, both seemed to have been model employees.'

'Everything we've seen so far points to Chechnya,' Drake said, leaning closer. 'Anything that ties them to this country?'

'Masalsky served a number of years in Chechnya as part of his role, obviously,' Miranova said, then called up the other man's file. 'But there is no record of Demochev being deployed here.'

Drake frowned. Chechnya wasn't the link he needed. Look for a different common factor. 'Did they ever serve together?'

'Not directly. They were never part of the same unit, or even the same division for that matter. As directors, they may have met during central planning sessions.'

No obvious links to Chechnya, and nothing to suggest they had worked together. What was he missing? What event tied these two men together?

Then, just like that, an idea came to him. A question not so much of actions, but of timing. Timing was everything. 'When did Demochev become director of counter-terrorism?'

'It was . . . late 2004.'

'And Masalsky?'

She was silent for a few moments, scrolling through the man's list of official postings. Her eyes opened a little wider when she found what she was looking for. 'The same time. Both men were promoted in November 2004; part of a shake-up of the FSB's leadership after the Beslan crisis.'

That name was enough to trigger a reaction. Drake knew the grim story from the scattered news reports he'd read. Chechen terrorists had seized control of the school at Beslan and demanded immediate Russian withdrawal from Chechnya. The Russians had refused, and after a two-day stand-off, the shooting had started.

Massacre was the perfect word to describe what happened

next. The school was all but flattened after hours of heavy fighting and artillery bombardment. Casualty estimates ran into the hundreds, mostly women and children, but the Russian government had imposed a virtual news blackout on the whole affair and little more had been heard about it.

But the revelation had given him an idea. 'Was either man involved in Beslan?'

Once more she went to work on the two men's records, rapidly scanning the information scrolling across the screen. Even Frost couldn't have done a better job.

'They weren't in the same directorate, but both men were deployed in South Ossetia at the time of the attack. Demochev served as commander of a border security task force. He was in command of most of the military checkpoints in the area around the town.'

'The rook,' Drake mused. A castle: a shield, a protector to keep enemies at bay.

Miranova eyed him curiously for a moment before going on. 'Masalsky was part of the FSB's anti-terrorism directorate in the province. He was responsible for monitoring and apprehending suspected militants.'

'The knight,' Drake added, thinking about the chess piece they had found on him. A warrior, a protector intended to strike out at the enemy before they could do harm.

The symbolism was impossible to ignore. As he'd known all along, the man behind this was sending them a message with each body he left in his wake. And now, at last, the message was becoming clear.

'They're going after the chain of command,' he said, hardly believing they hadn't seen it before. Only Masalsky's death had allowed them to find the common factor. 'Everyone involved in Beslan.'

'Everyone who should have prevented it but didn't,'

Miranova said, quickly picking up on his reasoning. 'They are being tried and found guilty.'

Drake's mind was racing now as the implications finally sank in. 'We've already accounted for military checkpoints and anti-terrorist leaders. Who was the senior FSB agent on site during the siege?'

It took her less than thirty seconds to find the answer. Opening a new personnel file, she turned her laptop around so Drake could see the file photo she had accessed.

The man staring back at him was in his mid-fifties and ruggedly handsome, with swept-back blond hair, a broad square face that was just starting to turn jowly, and penetrating blue eyes.

'Roman Kalyuyev,' she announced. 'He was the special agent in charge of the crisis, flown in direct from Moscow. He was a Spetsnaz commander during the occupation of Afghanistan, specialising in urban fighting and house assaults.'

It made sense that a man with practical experience like Kalyuyev would have been brought in to manage a crisis like Beslan. Such assaults were exactly what he was used to.

'Where is he serving now?' Drake asked, eager to learn more.

'He isn't,' Miranova said. 'He retired from FSB service in the wake of the massacre.'

'Why?'

Miranova cocked a dark brow. 'I believe the Americans have a saying for this – "carrying the can"? If I had to guess, I would say that a lot of the blame was placed on his shoulders. He was likely pressured into resigning.'

'So Demochev and Masalsky get promoted while Kalyuyev takes the fall for Beslan,' Drake mused. 'Now we've got a man who's angry, bitter, well acquainted with the FSB's protocols and probably still has contacts on the inside. A man who could give our mystery woman the secure ID card she needed to access the compound in Grozny. A man who could have found out the route your convoy planned to take through DC.'

The scattered clues and fragments of information seemed to be coalescing in his mind with every passing moment, the pieces coming together at last, forming a conclusion that was so real, so solid that he couldn't believe he'd failed to see it before.

Miranova had heard enough.

'Whether he is a suspect or a victim, Kalyuyev must be our priority,' she said, reaching for her cellphone. 'We must find him.'

Physical surveillance teams would take time to arrange, but Kalyuyev's emails and phone calls could be tapped within a matter of minutes. Soon, everything he said and did electronically would be tagged, logged and analysed by a team of experts trained to look for anything out of the ordinary.

Chapter 48

Moscow, Russia

'Good evening, sir,' the security guard said, giving Roman Kalyuyev a polite nod as he swept past. He received no acknowledgement. Kalyuyev's mind was on other matters tonight.

As usual, his BMW had been started up and driven to the front door, the engine ticking over for a few minutes to give the heaters time to warm up. It was a courtesy afforded to most of the senior executives of Novobyrsk Engineering.

It wasn't a particularly cold night in Moscow, the temperature hovering close to freezing, but Kalyuyev angrily pulled up the collar of his overcoat anyway as he stomped towards the waiting vehicle.

Slumping into the padded leather driver's seat, he let out a long sigh, reached up and loosened his tie. It had been a difficult week, and not because of anything work-related. Rather, his unease stemmed from the email he'd received several days earlier.

Deceptively innocuous, tucked in amongst the spam and the work chatter and personal correspondence was a message entitled simply *Information*.

He must have read its contents a dozen times, his mind endlessly chewing over the brief missive that had so shattered the comfortable prosperity of his new life.

Dear Mr Kalyuyev,

   I have information relating to the events of September 2004 that I believe will be of interest to you. We should talk about this. I wouldn't wish for the wrong people to learn what I know.

   Please reply to this email when you're ready to speak.

He had done no such thing of course. To reply, to acknowledge it in any way would make it real, would give its author the desired proof. So less than twenty minutes after receiving it, he had deleted the email and done his best to forget it had ever happened. It was amazing what a man was capable of forgetting if he tried hard enough.

But simply forgetting wasn't enough, because the next morning another email was waiting for him, this time with a distinctly harder edge. The sender had informed him in no uncertain terms that unless he acknowledged the email, he or she would take the evidence to the world's news media, that Kalyuyev would be ruined publicly and that he would spend the rest of his life behind bars.

Faced with such a threat, he had finally bowed to the inevitable and replied, asking what his mysterious stalker wanted in return for silence. Within an hour, he'd received a simple reply:

Half a million euros, cash. I'll contact you with more information soon.

That had been three days ago. And as yet, he had not been contacted again.

With a frustrated sigh, he reached out and switched on the CD player, pulling away from his office with Tchaikovsky's Fourth Symphony playing through the car's powerful speaker system. The soothing rhythms of the composition

– his favourite of the great composer's works – always helped relax him after a stressful day, and this evening he needed it more than most.

Pulling out on to the main drag that ran parallel to the dark waters of the River Moskva, he tapped a cigarette from the pack in his jacket pocket. He used the car's lighter to get it going, taking a long slow draw as he eased his way through the evening traffic.

By the time he'd arrived back at his spacious city-centre apartment, the combination of music and nicotine had gone some way towards alleviating the tension within him. The generous glass of vodka he poured for himself as soon as he'd discarded his coat was, he hoped, enough to finish the job.

He'd barely taken his first sip when his cellphone started ringing, the vibration causing it to do a slow dance across the granite kitchen worktop.

Kalyuyev let out a sigh of vexation. Couldn't a man have five minutes to himself?

Snatching the phone up, he took a gulp of vodka before answering. 'Yes?'

'Roman Kalyuyev?' The voice that spoke was female, soft and not unpleasant, though with a cold, clinical edge to it that warned this was no idle social call.

He set his glass down on the worktop. 'Who is this?'

'You know who.'

If he'd had any doubts about the identity of his caller, they vanished in that moment. 'How did you get this number?'

'That's not important, Mr Kalyuyev. What *is* important is that I have what you want, and I'm ready to make our trade.'

'All right,' Kalyuyev said. 'I'm listening.'

'Be at Poklonnaya Hill, by the obelisk, tomorrow morning at nine o'clock. I'll find you.'

He might have laughed if the situation had been different. One of the biggest landmarks in the city, Poklonnaya Hill wasn't easy to miss. She certainly had a flair for the dramatic, if nothing else.

She was also naive enough to assume that meeting in a public place was any guarantee of safety. Even at a busy landmark like that, Kalyuyev could kill her a dozen different ways and still get away with it. He had, after all, been a Spetsnaz commander for nearly a decade before moving into the shadowy world of the FSB. He knew all too well how easy it was to make people disappear, and if necessary he'd make it happen tomorrow.

'I'll be there,' he promised.

She hung up without acknowledging him.

Kalyuyev snatched up his glass of vodka and strode through to the bedroom, kneeling down at the foot of the bed to retrieve the cardboard box hidden beneath. Taking another gulp, he flipped the lid off to reveal the gleaming black metal of a USP .45 semi-automatic.

Yes, he'd be there tomorrow all right. And whoever this woman was, he'd make sure she told him everything she knew about Beslan.

Chapter 49

Grozny, Chechnya

With surveillance teams now hard at work following Kalyuyev's every move, Drake and the others had returned to the FSB field station in Grozny to await further reports. For Drake, it was a chance to clean himself up a little and get his head together. He could certainly use the breathing room.

Leaning over the sink, Drake cupped his hands and splashed cold water on his face. He had changed out of the combat gear he'd worn for the assault on the airfield, donning civilian clothes that were still dry and relatively clean. But none of this could change the fact that he looked like shit, he concluded as he surveyed his reflection.

His face was drawn and haggard, marked by cuts and bruises from his recent confrontation with Anya, his eyes circled by dark rings of fatigue, his hair dishevelled and sticking up at all angles. He couldn't recall the last time he'd slept properly; only that it had been a couple of days and many time zones ago.

But hurting and strung out as he was, sleep was impossible now. His mind continued to race, endlessly churning over everything that had happened in the past couple of days.

Again and again the same questions assailed him. Why was Anya doing this? What was her ultimate goal? And what was she prepared to do if he stood in her way? More important, what was he prepared to do to stop her?

What *could* he do? He had tried opposing her once already, and the results were plain to see in the mirror. He was no match for her.

But if he didn't do something, the FSB certainly would. They had seen her face now, and would leave no stone unturned in hunting her down. She was responsible for the deaths of several FSB agents, not to mention two of their senior commanders. They would show no mercy once they got their hands on her.

Clenching his fists, Drake closed his eyes and lowered his head, every muscle and fibre in his body tightening in a silent cry of frustration. Over the past few days he had lied, manipulated, sacrificed innocent lives and put people he cared about at risk, all for a woman he barely even knew. How much further would he go? How many more people would he betray for Anya?

'Stop this,' he whispered to himself. 'Get it together, Ryan.'

Looking up once more, he turned away and made for the locker where he'd stowed his rucksack. But no sooner had he pulled the locker door open than the contents tumbled out on to the floor. He recognised Mason's distinctive Berghaus kitbag straight away.

'Fuck,' he mumbled, realising he'd opened his friend's locker by mistake.

Stooping down, he snatched up the bag to stuff it back in the locker, then hesitated when he saw something lying amongst the spare clothes and cellphone chargers. A small plastic bottle filled with red pills.

He didn't want to pry into his friend's affairs, yet something about the bottle set alarm bells ringing in his head. Before he could stop himself, he reached down and snatched it up, turning it over to read the label.

The moment he realised what he was holding, his face

darkened with anger. He hadn't quite put the pieces together the last time he'd walked in on Mason popping pills, and had allowed the man's unusual behaviour to slide rather than push a confrontation.

Not this time.

Clutching the bottle tight, he turned and strode out of the locker room.

He found his friend in the ops centre, watching Miranova and the other FSB agents while he sipped a cup of coffee. Even as he raised the cup to his lips, Drake noticed his hand shaking a little.

He glanced up as Drake approached, noting the younger man's expression. 'Hey, what's up?'

'I need to talk to you,' Drake said, keeping his voice low. The things he had to say to Mason were best said in private. 'Now.'

It didn't take a genius to see this wasn't heading in a good direction. Nonetheless, Mason knew better than to start an argument in front of their Russian companions. Saying nothing, he followed Drake out of the room.

A couple of minutes later, the two of them were outside in the parking lot nestled between two wings of the office block. It was a cold and breezy night, with flurries of snow carried on the fitful breeze. Still, the one advantage of the unpleasant conditions was the measure of privacy it afforded them.

'I assume there's a reason I'm freezing my ass off out here,' Mason remarked without much humour. 'Let's hear it.'

Drake wasted no time. Reaching into his pocket, he held up the bottle of pills for Mason to see. 'What are these, Cole?'

Mason froze, clearly shocked by what he was seeing. 'Where did you get those?'

'I could ask you the same question. This is pethidine, for fuck's sake.'

Pethidine, a powerful opiate with properties similar to morphine, was often prescribed to combat chronic pain found in patients with terminal cancer or severe injuries. They were only legally available on prescription, and Mason's medical report had mentioned no such prescription. Wherever he'd got hold of them, it hadn't been from a doctor.

'When were you planning on telling me?' Drake asked, torn between anger and pity. 'Or were you just hoping I wouldn't find out?'

Mason at least had the good grace to blush. Of course he couldn't have told Drake about this. The CIA would never employ field operatives who needed to be doped up on pain meds just to get through each day.

'You don't understand—'

'No, *you* don't understand!' Drake hissed, struggling to hold his anger in check. 'You think this is a game? You almost got yourself killed fast-roping from that chopper tonight. What if we'd got into a real firefight?'

'I can still do my job,' Mason said defiantly.

'Bollocks, you can,' Drake bit back. 'I saw what happened earlier. You couldn't even lace up your boots properly on the way to Glazov's place. Now I know why.' He shook his head, angry with Mason but even angrier with himself for bringing him into this. 'Forget it, Cole. You're done.'

Mason's eyes flared with anger. 'Like hell I am. We have a deal.'

'*Had* a deal,' Drake corrected him. 'You lied to me. If I'd known how fucked-up you were, I never would have brought you along.'

Mason stared back at him, his gaze holding a mixture of indignation, disbelief and above all, desperation. 'You want to talk about fucked-up, Ryan? Okay, let's talk. How about coming into work each day stinking of drink? How about being so loaded when we went into that Russian prison last year that I could smell it coming out of your pores? How about being so jacked up that I could see your hands shaking?'

The look of shock in Drake's eyes encouraged him to press on, not that he needed much encouragement. Eighteen months of festering resentment had at last found an outlet, and he wasn't about to stop now.

'Yeah, I remember that night real well,' he went on. 'I could have reported you. I could have had you relieved of command, but I didn't. I trusted you to do your job, and guess what my reward was?' He thumped a fist against his bad shoulder. 'You got your little shot at redemption, Ryan. All I got was a world of shit.'

Drake hesitated, momentarily daunted by the strength of his friend's barely restrained fury. 'Nobody wanted that to happen to you.'

'Yeah? I didn't see you shedding any tears,' Mason raged. There was no way he was stopping now. 'You know what it's like to watch everything you spent your life working for just slipping away? And for what? For Anya? Look around you! You could have prevented all this, but instead you chose to protect *her*.' He shook his head in disgust. 'You want to talk about fucked-up, Ryan? Maybe you should look in the mirror.'

Reaching out, he snatched the bottle of pills from Drake's hand and made to leave. Only when he reached the doorway leading back inside did he pause and turn around.

'And don't worry, I doubt we'll be seeing much of each other once this is over.'

He made sure to slam the door in his wake. Drake made no move to stop him. He felt numb as the full magnitude of today's events settled on him. He could have told the FSB everything he knew about Anya, shown them exactly who they should be hunting for, but instead he had done nothing.

And people had paid for it with their lives.

So absorbed was he in these dark thoughts that he barely registered the buzzing of the phone in his pocket. Still churning over Mason's words, he reached for the phone and hit the receive-call button, not even bothering to check the caller ID.

'Yeah?'

'Ryan, where are you?' Miranova demanded. 'I've been looking for you.'

'Why? What's going on?'

'We have something on Kalyuyev. I think you should get back here now.'

Drake let out a breath. Self-recrimination would have to wait for now; he still had a job to do.

'On my way.'

He found Miranova in the makeshift operations centre, bent over her laptop with a pair of headphones covering her ears. She glanced up as he approached, her expression making it obvious they'd found something significant.

'Kalyuyev just received a call from an anonymous number,' she explained, laying aside the headphones. 'The caller was a woman.'

Unplugging the headphone jack from the computer, she hit playback on an audio file.

The first voice was a man's. Coarse and gravelly, and none too pleased to be taking the call as he mumbled what Drake assumed to be a cursory greeting.

Then he heard it. A woman's voice. Strong and confident, with an underlying intensity that he knew straight away was matched by her piercing, icy blue eyes.

Anya.

'What are they saying?' he asked.

'She is telling him that she has what he is looking for,'

Miranova explained. 'And that she is ready to make an exchange of some sort at nine o'clock tomorrow morning.'

'Where?'

'Moscow, Poklonnaya Hill.' Seeing his blank expression, she added, 'It is a war memorial.'

Drake could guess what she was thinking. It was unlikely that two different women were involved in an operation like this.

'Ryan, do you understand what I have told you? We have a lead on Masalsky's killer,' Miranova pressed, bemused by his lack of enthusiasm.

'I understand,' he replied quietly.

'We are already preparing a flight out of here. If we hurry, we can be there in time to intercept them.' She stood up from her workstation, visibly excited. 'When Kalyuyev and this woman meet tomorrow, we will be ready.'

Drake couldn't bring himself to say anything. Far from being elated at such a dramatic breakthrough, he knew the true implications.

Anya was walking right into a trap.

Part Three

Intervention

In the nationwide crackdown following the Beslan Massacre, more than 10,000 people were arrested and detained by Russian police. It was the biggest operation of its kind since the Cold War.

Chapter 50

Afghanistan, 2 November 1988

The floor of the cell was freezing; nothing but bare concrete through which the relentless cold slowly seeped into her body. There was no heating, no bed, nothing. She lay there shivering, breathing in small gasps, each movement bringing a fresh stab of pain deep inside. Her only item of clothing was a man's shirt that barely reached halfway down her thighs.

Her back was a mass of wounds, some old and slowly healing over with pink scar tissue, others still painfully raw and bloody. The clotted blood had soaked into the rough fabric of her shirt so that every movement tore the fresh scabs away and reopened the cuts.

She barely felt the pain of them any more. She had grown accustomed to it.

The last interrogation session had been hard even for her to endure. Twice she had been held down and raped, though the crude remarks and laughter that had once accompanied the experience had long since stopped. Even for her guards, it had become a grim task to be completed as quickly as possible.

If anything, it was worse to look up into their eyes as they did it to her in uncomfortable silence. She wasn't even an enemy to be humiliated or reviled now. She was just a thing; just a piece of meat.

This was her life now. No one was coming for her. She knew that, and more importantly, she had at last accepted it.

She supposed she had always known, and yet she had clung to the forlorn hope that somehow there was meaning in this, that her suffering would one day be vindicated, that one day she would be rescued.

But she wouldn't. She was alone, forgotten, abandoned. Her life meant nothing, either to her enemies or to her supposed friends.

Everything, every layer of armour she had surrounded herself with, every belief, every justification she had clung to, every source of strength and solace, had been stripped away. Her once strong and athletic body, hardened by years of training and experience, had been broken and battered into submission, barely enough to sustain her life.

She would never again be the soldier she had once been.

She squeezed her eyes shut as warm tears carved little tracks down her grimy cheeks. She had come down to it at last. The end of the line.

She was going to die here in this filthy, windowless prison cell. Cowed, beaten, broken down. This wasn't the end she had imagined for herself; the glorious last stand where she could at least meet her death with honour and courage. Where she could die as a soldier should.

Not this. Not here. Not now.

Drawing her knees up to her chest, she at last gave in to the quiet sobs that she had been holding back all day as absolute, crushing despair pressed down on her like a physical weight.

Then suddenly she gasped, stirred from her grief by the horrible grating clang of a door being thrown open further down the block. She knew with terrible certainty what that sound meant.

They were coming for her again.

She felt her weary heart beat faster. Even now her broken and exhausted body was trying to help her survive, readying itself for the ancient, primal response to danger – fight or flight.

She could do neither thing. Her hands were bound behind her back, and even if they weren't she doubted she had the strength to put up much resistance now. She was helpless, utterly vulnerable.

She could do nothing but lie there and wait for the end to come.

Moscow, 24 December 2008

Moving with the subtle grace born from long practice, Anya slowly lowered herself to the ground until she was kneeling on the cool earth. She reached out with both hands, allowing her fingers to gently brush the dew-covered grass stalks that swayed all around her, then bent down and wiped her hands across her face.

The touch of the morning dew was cool and refreshing, helping to focus her mind and sharpen her thoughts, to prepare herself for what was coming today.

She had performed this ritual many times in her life. It was one of the few things she had learned from her mother that she could still remember; some lingering vestige of the ancient beliefs that she kept alive.

In her heart she knew that she no longer understood its context or purpose, that in her ignorance she was just blindly following a half-forgotten memory long devoid of meaning, but she did it anyway. Just for a moment or two it recalled some wispy shadow of the woman who had brought her into this world.

Anya had often caught herself wondering what her mother would have thought of such a ritual being used before going into battle, whether she ever could have foreseen the future that lay ahead for her young daughter all those years ago.

She had lost count of the number of actions she had fought, the number of men she had killed, the number of times she should have died but hadn't. Almost everyone she had ever cared about, everyone she had trusted and tried to protect, was gone now. But somehow she remained in this life. Old, damaged and worn down, she defiantly stood when all the others had fallen.

And once again she was going into the fray, risking her life to fight enemies she didn't hate, serving a master she didn't love. She had killed innocent men, betrayed those who trusted her, made herself a criminal and a terrorist. But it would be worth it, she told herself. To reach her final goal, it would all be worth it.

The ritual complete, she lifted her head up, opened her eyes and took her first breath of the chill morning air. She was renewed, reborn, ready.

'Forgive me,' a soft voice said. 'I didn't want to interrupt.'

Anya glanced over her shoulder to see Atayev standing a short distance away. She had been aware of a presence nearby, had heard the soft rustle of footsteps in the grass and known someone was watching her, but she had allowed it to pass.

She had also known it would be him. This was their pre-arranged meeting spot, and at this early hour the chances of a random encounter were practically nil.

'I'm finished,' she said, rising up from the ground.

The man looked uncharacteristically subdued and pensive, as if her actions had awoken a long-buried memory in him. 'Who do you pray to?'

To a casual observer it must have seemed as if she were praying, prostrating herself before the God of Islam or some other deity. Anya had never known such faith, and certainly had no need of it now.

'I don't,' she replied flatly. 'We live or we die. Prayer won't change that.'

'Spoken like a true soldier,' he remarked, then paused for a moment as if considering his next words. 'I used to pray to Him, every night. Can you believe that? Asking God to keep my wife and child safe, to give me the strength to protect them and provide for them. I used to believe that would be enough.' She saw the flicker of a grim smile cross his face. 'When I realised how wrong I was, when I realised He didn't care about me or anyone else, it was the most . . . liberating moment of my life. It freed me, to do what I had to without fear, without conscience or remorse.'

As he spoke, a change seemed to come over him. She saw that same cold, hard, remorseless look in his eyes that she'd seen when he emerged from Masalsky's torture room. It was the same look she had seen in the eyes of many soldiers over the years – men who had witnessed such suffering and horror that it simply ceased to make an impression.

The man standing before her, small and overweight and untrained, no longer cared about living or dying. And that made him more powerful and dangerous than the men he had pitted himself against.

'When this is over and I'm dead, what do you suppose they'll say about me?' he asked. 'That I was a murderer, a terrorist . . . a sadist?'

He wasn't asking for reassurance, for justification or comfort. His was a question born from idle curiosity; a man contemplating the end of his life and how it would be weighed up in the final analysis.

'It doesn't really matter now, does it?' Anya replied. 'What people say about you won't change what you did, or why you did it. That's what is important.'

'I suppose so,' he conceded. 'Is it the same for you?'

Anya met his searching gaze without hesitation. Perhaps more than anyone she'd ever met, she felt as if she could be honest with him. He wouldn't judge her, no matter what she said. 'We each do what we have to, Buran. I can live with the choices I've made. That's all I have to say.'

She knew now why he had sought her out this morning, why he wanted to speak privately with her. He had come to say goodbye, in his own way. In all likelihood they would never see each other after today.

'The others are waiting for us,' he said, assuming a more businesslike air now. 'All except Goran. I haven't heard from him since last night.'

'You won't,' Anya promised him. 'He turned against us. I had to deal with him.'

'I see.' There was no emotion, no regret over the man's death. And no question over how it had come about. 'Do you think he has compromised us?'

She had asked herself the same question many times since last night. Unfortunately, they would only find out for sure when they put their plan into effect. 'Would it make any difference?'

Atayev shook his head. Like her, he was committed now. The only choice for either of them was to see this through.

'We should leave. We don't have much time.'

Anya nodded, rallying herself for this last effort. One more move, and her part in the game would be over. Her only hope was that Drake wouldn't cross her path again.

Chapter 51

Sheremetyevo International Airport, Moscow,
24 December 2008

Christmas Eve in Moscow's main airport was about as far removed as it was possible to be from the world of war-torn cities and abandoned airfields that Drake had found himself in for the past few days. Everywhere he looked he saw cheerful decorations, robotic Santas, Christmas trees festooned with lights, expensive retailers selling last-minute gifts for frazzled travellers, and restaurants and coffee shops packed with customers.

The atmosphere of excitement, expectation and relief was the sort that one could only find in an airport on Christmas Eve. Most of the people here were on the final leg of long journeys home to spend the holiday period with their families.

For Drake too this airport represented the last leg of a journey that had carried him from Washington to Chechnya, and finally here to the Russian capital. Unfortunately for him, there was no family gathering or roast turkey waiting at the end of it.

The flight from Chechnya to the Russian capital had lasted scarcely more than four hours – a short hop compared to the transatlantic flight from DC. For him it had felt like a lifetime, not helped by the tense, brooding silence between himself and Mason. Miranova had been quick to pick up on it, but wise enough not to press either man on the source of their disagreement.

'What's the set-up?' Drake asked as they strode through the arrivals area, doing his best to get his head back in the game.

There was no messing around with passports or immigration control here. This was the FSB's home turf, and Miranova had seen to it that they passed straight through airport security with little more than a wave of her badge. Tourists and stressed-out businessmen waiting in long lines watched them with a mixture of suspicion and envy.

'We report to FSB headquarters at Lubyanka for our final briefing, then deploy at the rendezvous site and wait for Kalyuyev,' she explained. 'Our field teams have him under surveillance. The moment he makes a move, we will know.'

'How long do we have?'

She glanced at her watch. 'Just over three hours.'

Three hours, Drake thought. He couldn't help wondering what Anya was doing at that moment, how she was preparing herself for the rendezvous. He didn't imagine she was nervous or frightened. He couldn't envisage her ever feeling such emotions.

But then, she didn't know what was waiting for her.

No sooner had they reached the main concourse than a man in a suit and heavy overcoat strode over from a nearby seating area. Straight away Drake knew two things – he was FSB, and he was here to deliver bad news.

He was a thoroughly average man, neither tall nor short, neither slender nor overweight. He looked to be in his mid-fifties, with greying brown hair of medium length, side parted, and a neatly trimmed grey beard that somehow made him look like a living propaganda picture of the Revolution. His face, craggy and gaunt, was lined and hardened in the way that comes from living life that's neither short nor easy.

He shook hands with Miranova, ignoring her two companions for now.

'Agent Miranova,' he began, his voice deep but smooth, in stark contrast to his rugged appearance. He spoke English, probably for Drake's benefit. 'My name is Alexei Kamarov, Internal Security Directorate.'

That was enough to grab the attention of both Drake and Miranova. The Internal Security Directorate was an elite sub-unit of the FSB, effectively acting as a special police force within the vast organisation. Each applicant had to be personally approved by the director himself, and they were only deployed in the most critical of situations.

'I'm here to take over operational command of this investigation.'

Miranova's face paled visibly at this. She had requested an assault team to help with the takedown, not a new agent to head up the entire operation.

'There must be some mistake, Kamarov,' she protested. 'This is my operation.'

'Not any more.' Reaching into his overcoat, he handed her a printed document. 'Orders from Director Surovsky. He's no longer confident you have the necessary . . . expertise for this. My team is taking over, effective immediately.'

Drake met Miranova's gaze, seeing the disbelief at this sudden switch in command structure. She was being sidelined, brushed aside and replaced with someone more reliable. Why this change had happened mere hours before a crucial operation, he had no idea.

'So why did we fly all this way?' Drake asked, making no effort to hide his frustration. 'What do you expect us to do now?'

Kamarov's piercing gaze switched to him. 'You must be—'

'Tired and in no mood for power plays,' Drake said before he could stop himself. 'We had a deal with Surovsky. This was a joint investigation.'

375

'And so it is. You will remain part of the investigation until this matter is concluded, Agent Drake,' Kamarov said. It might have been seen as a conciliatory gesture, but his eyes told a different story. 'But make no mistake, we're in command here. The woman from Grozny is responsible for the deaths of two of our senior commanders – she will answer for this.'

Neither Drake nor Miranova said anything.

'Will this be a problem, Agent Miranova?'

'No, of course not.' Her expression, however, told a different story.

The older man nodded, the matter apparently decided. Not that there had been much to decide, Drake thought.

'Good. Then I suggest we get moving.'

The automatic doors opened ahead of them. Emerging into a world of blue skies and crisp white snow, they found themselves confronted by a pair of big silver BMW 3-Series saloons, gleaming and immaculate in the winter sun. The vehicles were a stark contrast to the yellow Lada taxis that littered the road.

'Get in,' Kamarov said, gesturing to the lead vehicle. 'Time is short.'

More than any other city on earth, the changing social and political winds of the past few centuries had left their mark on Moscow. Medieval churches and castles sat side by side with industrial factories, wide boulevards flanked by towering buildings of Stalinist architecture, blocks of high-rise concrete flats from the sixties and seventies, and ultra-modern steel-and-glass office and hotel complexes.

And everywhere there was evidence of Russia's newfound economic resurgence.

Bentleys, Mercs, Aston Martins . . . everywhere Drake

looked there were expensive luxury cars being driven by thick-necked bodyguards, ferrying rich men and beautiful young women to the Bolshoi or wherever the well-to-do hung out in Moscow.

New skyscrapers, hotels, shopping centres and office blocks were flying up everywhere. Construction cranes, gantries and steel frames were visible from almost every street. Whoever had been smart enough to buy up property in Moscow after the Soviet Union fell apart must have been laughing all the way to the bank now.

The city's road system was designed like the spokes of a wheel, with motorways radiating outwards in all directions and a concentric series of ring roads circling the Kremlin – the spiritual and literal heart of the city. Their course south-east from the airport took them more or less right past the walls of the ancient fortress.

When they stopped for a moment at the intersection of Tverskaya and Okhotny, Drake was just able to make out the vast sweep of Red Square backed by the Kremlin's towering outer walls. The place was packed with tourists, most of them in big coach groups with guides busy spouting off about the history of the place. Others were milling around Lenin's Mausoleum, probably annoyed that they had missed the brief period each day when it opened its doors to the public.

'Impressive, isn't it?' Miranova remarked.

Drake didn't reply. Thirty years ago this would have been considered the enemy's back yard, and here he was about to walk through their front door.

After fighting its way through traffic for another fifteen minutes, the big BMW at last rumbled to a halt at Lubyanka Square, the headquarters of the Federal Security Bureau.

One thing Drake had to commend the Russians on – when

it came to government offices, they really knew how to do things with flair. A massive, rectangular, yellow-bricked building fashioned in the neo-baroque style, it dominated a vast cobbled square the size of several football pitches.

Now more than a century old, it had started life as the headquarters of an insurance company of all things. After the Revolution, the Bolsheviks had taken a liking to it and requisitioned it as the headquarters of the Cheka, the secret police back in the day. Since then it had been occupied by the NKVD, the KGB and most recently the FSB.

The name of its owners might have changed over the years, but its basic purpose hadn't. Countless political dissidents, criminals and plain unlucky civilians had disappeared into its warren of underground cells and interrogation rooms, most of them ending up dead or deported to a gulag, never to return. There was even an old joke, told with typically grim Russian humour, about Lubyanka being the tallest building in Russia because you could see Siberia from its basement.

Drake, however, soon found himself in a far more welcoming part of the building as he exited the official car and made his way in through the main entrance. The decor was lavish and sophisticated, reminding him more of a museum or art gallery than a working office complex. He was particularly impressed by the gigantic mural stretching across the tiled floor, depicting the FSB's emblem of a two-headed eagle backed by a sword and shield.

Another agent was waiting to receive them, and exchanged a few hushed words with Miranova as they hurried over to a bank of elevators at the rear of the lobby. Stony-faced security guards with automatic weapons watched them every step of the way.

Arriving at the nearest elevator, Kamarov hit the call

button, and a few seconds later the doors slid open with barely a sound.

'Nice place you've got here,' Mason remarked as they whirred their way up. Beyond the elevator's glass walls, the inner courtyard of the building stretched out beneath them.

These days it held nothing more interesting than storage warehouses and a couple of delivery trucks, but back in Stalin's day it had been the site of almost daily executions. To cover up the sound of gunshots, car engines had been run and allowed to backfire.

The female FSB agent nodded agreement. 'Lubyanka has a long history, a long memory. Like Russia herself.'

Kamarov said nothing to this, and it was hard to tell what was going on behind the craggy, impassive mask of his face.

A few minutes later all four of them, along with several other FSB field agents who would be on site during the operation, were gathered in one of the building's richly furnished meeting rooms.

In appearance, it was a strange combination of nineteenth-century grandeur and twenty-first-century high technology. Lofty ceilings and elaborately carved cornices stood in marked contrast to the sleek computers and telephone units set up on the long antique wooden table running down the centre of the room.

The view from the third-floor windows was spectacular, with what looked like the whole of Moscow stretching out before him like a model, afternoon sun glinting on glass and concrete. About a mile away, he could make out the towering spires of St Basil's Cathedral and the ancient red-brick walls of the Kremlin.

Kamarov kicked the briefing off without preamble.

'Kalyuyev's rendezvous is scheduled to happen here, on Poklonnaya Hill,' he began, indicating a map of the monument complex pinned to the whiteboard behind him. 'According to our phone intercepts, his contact has requested to meet at the base of the obelisk in the centre of the complex. We will deploy to intercept once they make contact with him.'

He paused a moment to survey the agents gathered around the table. 'Our on-site task force will be divided into two teams – Anna and Boris.'

Drake nodded understanding. The Russians used a different writing system and therefore a different phonetic alphabet from that of their Western counterparts. It took a little getting used to, but the principle was the same. In any case, Drake had heard all sorts of weird and wonderful radio call signs over the years.

'We will also have an armed tactical team on standby in the parking lot to the north. They will move in only on my orders. Is this clear?'

On the whiteboard beside the map was a printed image of Anya, lifted from the surveillance footage of the Grozny attack.

'Our primary target is this woman,' Kamarov went on. 'She is likely to be armed and should be considered extremely dangerous. Take a good look at her because you will see many faces on the hill this morning, and I don't want any false positives. She may have altered her appearances so don't rely on any one aspect to identify her. We have one chance to take her down – if we fail, we may lose her for ever.'

Despite its dramatic backdrop, Drake was beginning to understand the very practical basis for choosing Poklonnaya Hill as a meeting point. It was a popular tourist destination, with lots of people coming and going and therefore many potential targets to keep track of. And of course, any hill naturally favoured the defender if the meeting turned into a shooting match. Always the soldier, Anya had chosen her field of battle well.

None of it was likely to help her, though. Not against the forces arrayed in this room.

Kamarov turned his attention back to the map and gestured to a group of buildings to the south-west of the hill. 'Our spotter team, call sign Olga, will set up here. There is a telecommunications mast here that should provide a perfect field of fire over most of the hill.'

'Nobody said anything about snipers,' Drake interrupted, rising from his seat. 'I thought our objective was to capture the target alive?'

Kamarov was smart enough to keep his expression carefully neutral. 'And so it is, Agent Drake. But as your friends at Langley are fond of saying, I prefer to keep my bases covered. We don't know what kind of force she may bring with her. She may even have snipers of her own in the area.'

Drake glanced at the map again, seeking a counter-argument. 'That tower's got to be almost a mile from the hill,' he said, making a rough estimate based on the scale. 'You'd be lucky to hit a barn door from that range. And you said yourself there'll be civilians everywhere.'

'My men are good shots,' Kamarov assured him tersely.

I bet they are, Drake thought. Kamarov's sudden arrival at such a crucial stage in the investigation, his seemingly unlimited authority that came straight from Surovsky himself, and his fixation on taking down Anya, made it obvious he hadn't been sent here just to assume control of a failing investigation.

Kamarov was part of a kill team.

'I think Agent Drake has a point,' Miranova said, jumping into the discussion before it turned into something more serious. 'Even the best sniper in the world would struggle to make an accurate kill from that range. The risk of collateral damage would be high.'

'Then let's hope we don't have to use it,' Kamarov remarked, before turning his attention to the wider gathering. 'With so many eyes on the hill, there is no way she can approach Kalyuyev unseen. Once we have a confirmed sighting, Anna and Boris will move in to surround her and take her down. All other actions are at my discretion. Questions?'

Drake had one for him. 'Where will I be in all this?'

The senior FSB agent regarded him irritably. 'You will be here, at Lubyanka.'

'That's unacceptable.'

'It is also unacceptable that two of our most senior officers have been tortured to death,' Kamarov reminded him. 'Yet still it has happened.'

'I want to be there,' Drake persisted.

'What you want is irrelevant. This operation is FSB only. Consider yourself fortunate to even be in Moscow.'

Beneath the table, Drake clenched his fists. 'You wouldn't even know about this rendezvous if it wasn't for me.'

Kamarov's eyes flared with anger, but before he could reply, Miranova jumped in. 'Agent Drake does have a point. He has been useful to this investigation so far, and his judgement has been sound. We would do well to have him on hand.'

Kamarov held Drake's gaze a moment longer, looking as though he wanted nothing more than to introduce him to some of Lubyanka's less pleasant areas.

'Our command and control unit will be set up a short distance from the meeting point,' he said at length. 'You can remain on standby there, but no closer. Do we understand each other?'

Drake unclenched his fists. 'Perfectly.'

He spared Miranova a fleeting glance. They had eye contact only for a second or two, but it was enough to convey the gratitude he felt.

Satisfied if not pleased, Kamarov nodded. 'All right. Get ready. We leave in five minutes.'

As the brief gathering broke up, Drake turned away and walked over to the window, bowing his head as the full weight of what was about to happen settled on him.

Anya was going to die today, and the only person who could do anything about it was him. Nobody else could help him now. Nobody else could make this choice for him.

Give up Anya's life, or risk giving up his own.

There was no choice to make, and he knew it.

Swallowing, he nodded to himself as if to solidify the decision in his mind, then turned back to the room and caught Mason's eye, beckoning him over. His friend approached warily, the memory of their earlier confrontation no doubt still fresh in his mind.

'What is it?' There was no trace of his former camaraderie now.

'Over here, mate,' Drake said quietly, steering him to a corner of the room where they could speak with some semblance of privacy. 'Listen, I need you to do something for me, Cole. It's important.'

Mason cocked an eyebrow. 'This ought to be good.'

Drake sighed and looked him hard in the eye. 'I need you to get out of here.'

'Ryan, we already—'

'This isn't about what happened earlier,' Drake interrupted. 'Whatever our differences, it doesn't matter now. You were right, mate – I put you and the others at risk by going after Anya. I'm sorry for that. In fact, I'm sorry about a lot of things. But I'm not going to put anyone else at risk.'

Mason frowned, taken aback. 'So what do you want from me?'

He paused, just for a moment. An instant of hesitation. A reality check.

This was it; his last chance to back out, to give up this foolish notion before it ruined him. If he did this, there would be no going back.

An instant, and then it was gone.

'I need you to get out of here – out of the city, out of the country. Make an excuse, say you've been recalled to Langley . . . whatever. Get your arse to the US embassy. I'll direct Sam and Keira to meet you there.'

One of the other benefits of being a Shepherd team member was their ability to claim diplomatic asylum, no questions asked. Rocking up to an embassy building without a passport and demanding to be let in was hardly the height of professionalism, but if the situation called for it they could nonetheless take such an extreme measure.

Once all three of his companions were safely back on US soil, Drake could act without fear of reprisals against them. At least, that was what he told himself.

'Great. What are *you* going to do?' Mason asked.

Drake shook his head. 'Better you don't know.'

It didn't take a genius to see that he was planning something very dangerous and very stupid – sabotaging an FSB operation. Mason moved a step closer, keeping his voice low. 'Are you out of your fucking mind? They'll throw your ass in jail if you try to screw with this.'

'I have to do something.' Drake looked at his friend again, seeking acknowledgement, seeking understanding. 'They're going to kill her, Cole.'

Mason was unmoved. 'Tell me she'd do the same for you.'

Drake had seen that one coming, but it still wasn't easy to hear.

'I don't have all the answers,' he admitted. 'But I know Anya's part of something – something bigger than terrorist attacks and kidnappings and all this shit we've been chasing here. I *know* there's a reason behind what she's doing. And I think it has something to do with why she ended up in a Russian prison. Men in both countries want her dead.'

Just for a moment he felt as though he could see it all laid out before him. Years of lies and secrets, plans and hidden schemes, events and decisions all caught up together like a web, slowly reaching out to encompass everything around it, ensnaring people who fooled themselves into thinking they were safe. And in the centre of it all, alone and surrounded by enemies, was Anya.

'Anya's the only person who knows how it all fits together,' he finished. 'If I lose her . . . then *they* win. I can't let it happen, mate. I'm sorry, but it's just me now. I have to help her.'

Mason stared back at him. Silent, undecided, torn between two opposing paths.

'You know that if you go through with this, even if it works, there's no coming back from it. Ever,' he warned.

Once more Drake thought about the question he'd asked himself earlier as he stared at his reflection. *How much further are you willing to go for her?*

As far as I have to.

'I know.'

'It's your call,' Mason said at last. 'I can't stop you. But God help you if you're wrong about her.'

Drake said nothing to that. If he was wrong about Anya, then he deserved everything that was coming to him. For now at least, he still had a chance.

He looked at Mason again, his previous animosity towards

the man almost forgotten now. If he was honest with himself, he didn't blame Mason for trying to fight his way back into the Agency, for being bitter and angry over everything he had lost, even for lying about the powerful painkillers he was taking.

He couldn't blame him, because deep down he knew that the two of them weren't all that different. Neither of them had much outside of their work. Without it, without the purpose and meaning it provided, they were lost.

Giving his friend a look of gratitude, Drake reached out and shook his hand. He couldn't say what the future held for Mason, but he suspected it was a lot brighter than his own.

'Good luck, mate. I mean that.'

'Fuck that,' Mason advised. 'You need it more than me.'

Chapter 52

The morning sun rose hazy and indistinct over Moscow, its weak rays struggling through a low-lying fog that hung over much of the city as commuters began their daily drive in to work. The streets of Moscow were broad, designed to allow the easy movement of troops in the event of war, but these days they had to contend with little more than congested traffic.

Concealed in the back of a delivery truck that passed unnoticed amongst the thronging multitude, Anya sat in brooding silence, her thoughts turned inwards as she and the three men in the back closed in on their target.

The others had chosen to occupy themselves by checking their weapons were ready, magazines loaded, body armour secured and strapped tight, but Anya did no such thing. She had checked all of her gear in advance, and felt no need to do so again.

Instead she found her thoughts lingering on Drake. The man was as stubborn as he was foolish, and not one to concede defeat to anyone. Was it nothing but pride driving him on? she wondered. Did he really see her as an enemy now, or was it another reason? Was it the same reason she was so afraid to admit, even to herself?

She shook her head, forcing those thoughts away. Such doubts and fears were things she could no longer afford.

Drake couldn't stop her. No one could. Not now that she was so close to her goal.

Unbidden, the old words that had been hammered into her years earlier resurfaced once more, like the echo of a drumbeat still felt long after it had ceased.

Weakness will not be in my heart. Fear will not be in my creed. I will show no mercy. I will never hesitate. I will never surrender.

Anya clenched her fists as the van jolted over a bump in the road, drawing strength and resolve from the old words that had sustained her through some of her darkest hours. Once more she felt the anticipation and heightened awareness that always came to her at times like this, felt her heartbeat quicken and the blood rush into her muscles.

They were close now.

They would not fail.

Drake had staged operations from some odd locations over the years, but this was the first time he'd worked inside a foundry. The FSB had requisitioned the old building, lying in an industrial park perhaps half a mile from the meeting point, to use as their base of operations and on-site communications hub.

The floor was nothing but bare stone, except for the area around the old furnace where the ground had been laid with tempered bricks to resist the extreme heat. The smelting trays, metal grinders, lathes and other pieces of ancient forging equipment scattered about the room stood in marked contrast to the ultra-modern laptops, encrypted radio units and satellite uplinks that had been hastily set up.

A team of three technicians were attached to the makeshift field station, each busy manning their own terminal. One even had access to the video feeds from an unmanned drone that was circling the target area.

Drake couldn't see them, but he knew that a couple of armed guards had been stationed outside to ward off curious bystanders, and perhaps more importantly to keep him from venturing outside. Kamarov was taking no chances with him.

This was as close as he was allowed to get to the action. Here, in a dingy, unused old workshop, he was forced to sit and watch Anya meet her end.

Miranova too was in there with him, ostensibly to supervise the operation. In reality, Drake knew that Kamarov had simply brushed her aside, relegating her to an unimportant role where she couldn't interfere with his plans.

He met her gaze for a moment, seeing the tension and unhappiness in her. She knew as well as he did that she'd been shit-canned. And like him, she wasn't used to standing idly by while others put themselves at risk.

Drake could feel the vibration of his phone ringing, and a quick check of the screen confirmed his suspicion that it was McKnight. He had sent a text message on the way here advising her and Frost to part company with their FSB escorts and make their way to the US embassy where they would rendezvous with Mason.

He hadn't expected them to meekly obey, but neither was he prepared to debate the matter. For their own sakes, he needed them to listen to him.

'Yeah, Sam?' he began, retreating some distance from the comms station.

'What the hell is this message all about, Ryan?' McKnight demanded. She wasn't one for beating around the bush, he realised. Perhaps all that time spent around Frost was starting to rub off on her. 'Why do you want us at the embassy?'

He could hear music, voices and tannoy announcements in the background, and guessed she had just disembarked from her flight.

'Look, I don't have time to get into it now. I just need you to do it. Cole's there waiting for you; he'll explain everything.'

'Bullshit he will,' she retorted. 'I want to hear it from you. What exactly are you planning, Ryan?'

'There's something I have to take care of here. That's all.'

She seemed to understand, or at least guess at what he had in mind.

'Don't do it,' she said, the anger gone from her voice now. 'Not for her. She's not worth it.'

Drake closed his eyes. More than most, he regretted the way he'd treated Samantha. She had come through for him every time, had done everything he'd asked of her, yet still he'd managed to let her down.

'Sam, listen to me,' he said, speaking low and quiet now. 'I need you to do this – both of you. Whatever happens, I need to know you're safe.'

McKnight said nothing for several moments, but he heard a faint exhalation of breath. She was struggling as well, to find a way to say the things she wanted to.

'What about you?' she finally asked.

Drake had no words for her. The concern, the compassion, the sadness in her voice was almost more than he could stand. He had made a lot of sacrifices to get this far, had even betrayed people's trust, but hurting her was the hardest thing of all.

Suddenly, Miranova looked up from the computer terminal she'd been standing over. 'Kalyuyev is on the move!' she cried out. 'We just had word from the field team outside his apartment. He is in his car, heading west.'

Drake's heartbeat stepped up a gear, the doubts and fears pushed back a little now that the time had come. 'I have to go, Sam,' he said quietly. 'I'm sorry. I mean that.'

Before she could reply, he killed the call and strode over to join Miranova, putting his game face on and doing his best to put his regrets to one side.

'Do they have eyes-on?'

She nodded. 'They are in traffic behind him.'

'Anyone with him?'

Relaying Drake's question, she waited a few seconds while the reply came through. 'No. Only Kalyuyev.'

Roman Kalyuyev swore under his breath as he swung the big BMW right, weaving in and out of the slow-moving traffic. It was the early-morning rush hour in Moscow, with commuters everywhere clogging the main roads.

He was getting close now. He could already see the towering obelisk that surmounted Poklonnaya Hill rising up into the morning sky, as if to pierce the very clouds that drifted past.

He could have left his apartment earlier to guarantee a timely arrival for the meeting, but instead had chosen to delay, knowing the heavy traffic would slow him further. His mysterious contact would be expecting him to arrive early, to be eager, desperate for answers. But he would let her wait.

Soon she would start to doubt herself. Her cunning plan that had seemed so bold and brilliant would start to unravel before her eyes as she imagined all the ways it could go wrong. She would question whether he really intended to show up, or whether he had something else planned. She would see enemies in every shadow, and soon enough concern would give way to panic.

Then, when she was off balance, losing her nerve and on the verge of leaving, he would arrive. He would arrive, and he would make her wish she had never considered the idea in the first place.

Beethoven's Ninth Symphony played on the car's expensive sound system, the powerful orchestral strains perfectly matching his mood of barely restrained anger. The music was an outlet, a means of keeping his true feelings in check so he could do what he had to, so he could think calmly and logically and make sure this matter was brought to a definitive end.

The stupid, ignorant little bitch who thought she could hold him to ransom was going to feel the full force of his anger today. He hadn't fought and killed for his country, hadn't watched good men bleed and die, hadn't sacrificed his career and his honour, to have some smart-assed investigator take it all away from him.

Unconsciously he reached up and felt the solid, reassuring shape of the USP .45 automatic in the shoulder holster on his left side. When the time came, he wouldn't hesitate to use it.

More than most men, Roman Kalyuyev knew that the only true end to any problem came from the barrel of a gun.

Poklonnaya Hill had a long association with war, Kamarov reflected as he glanced around, taking in the Second World War-era tanks and self-propelled guns that sat alongside food vendors and children's play areas, their barrels empty and their engines silent.

It was here, almost at this very spot, that Napoleon Bonaparte had assembled his Grande Armée, believing such a display of force would prompt the Russians to surrender Moscow. And it was here, more than a century later, that the Red Army had dug in to fight a last desperate battle against the German blitzkrieg. Two generations of invaders who had tried and failed to conquer Russia, both remembered here in the sprawling memorial complex known as Victory Park.

And in the centre of it all, rising from the middle of a vast circular plaza, stood a black obelisk commemorating Russia's war dead. Over 140 metres from base to tip, it was one of the tallest structures in the area, and dominated the Moscow skyline. An ever-present reminder of the 12 million Russians who had died in that terrible conflict.

However, his concerns at that moment were very much in the present day. He had been informed over the radio net that Kalyuyev had left his car in the parking lot just off the main drag to the east, and was proceeding on foot along the main avenue that led to the obelisk. His path would take him beneath the shadows of fifteen enormous bronze columns that lined the way, commemorating the main fronts during the War.

Kamarov's concealed radio earpiece crackled with an incoming transmission.

'This is Anna. He is at the foot of the stairs now,' came the voice of one of the agents tailing Kalyuyev. 'On his way up.'

'Copy that,' he replied, speaking quietly into the microphone hidden inside the collar of his overcoat. 'No sign of target. Standing by.'

Even at this early hour there were people everywhere. Many were tourists, some were locals out for a morning walk, and one or two were old men who looked as though they belonged to the generation who had fought here. They weren't in uniform with their medals proudly displayed like they would have been twenty years earlier, but Kamarov sensed by the way they regarded the tanks on display that the ancient war machines evoked strong memories.

Nonetheless, keeping track of the countless new faces coming and going was no easy task, and he suspected the other field agents spread out across the hill were having similar difficulty. This meeting place had been well chosen indeed.

He would have expected nothing less from his adversary.

'Anna. He's at the top of the stairs, heading for the statue,' the agent's voice crackled in his ear. 'We won't have eyes-on much longer.'

Glacing towards the stairs as if through casual interest, Kamarov saw him at last. Tall, good-looking, broad-shouldered and dressed in a fashionable and expensive black overcoat, Kalyuyev cut a striking figure as he emerged on to the wide paved avenue that ran around the base of the statue.

He hit the transmit button in his coat pocket. 'I have him. No contacts yet. Standing by.'

The mood in the makeshift command centre was equally tense as Drake and Miranova hovered close to the three communications agents, waiting for news. The radio chatter was now being piped through a set of speakers, allowing them to listen in on events as they unfolded.

So far, nothing. Kalyuyev had arrived at the rendezvous point, a little late but otherwise unscathed, yet there was no sign of Anya or anyone else coming forward to make contact with him.

The minutes ticked by, and Drake found himself growing more and more uneasy. It wasn't in Anya's nature to be late for things. In his experience she preferred to be on station first so she could see her contact approaching. Her ability to read the subtle facial and postural cues that people unconsciously gave off also provided her with an edge in such situations.

He glanced at his watch. It was 9:16.

Had Anya sensed a trap and abandoned the meeting? Or even worse, had she laid a trap of her own for Kamarov and his kill team?

'Olga to all units, possible contact,' a voice announced. 'West side of the hill. A woman with blonde hair, moving in on Kalyuyev's position.'

Olga was their spotter team; a two-man group positioned on the roof of a telecommunications mast about a mile west of the monument. One man was armed with a high-powered camera, the other with a decidedly more dangerous Dragunov sniper rifle. At a mile distant, any shot they took would be risky to say the least, but Kamarov had insisted on their presence nonetheless.

In an instant, Drake's heartbeat doubled. Was this it? Was Anya making her move at last? And if so, how would the strike team respond?

'Boris to all units, stand by,' Kamarov ordered.

'Is it our target?' Miranova asked, an edge of tension in her voice now.

Seconds, agonisingly long, stretched out.

'Do we have confirmation?' Miranova repeated.

'Can't get a good look at her face,' the spotter admitted. 'I'm on her four o'clock.'

'Boris to Olga. Where is she now?' Kamarov asked.

'Approaching Kalyuyev. Forty metres and closing.'

'Anna. We're trying to get a better look. She's got her back to us.'

Kamarov snapped out another terse transmission. 'Do you have the shot, Olga?'

'Yes. Thirty metres.'

Something wasn't right about this, Drake knew. It had been nagging at him all morning, but with his mind consumed by what would happen during the actual takedown, he hadn't had time to consider why Anya would risk herself by making contact like this.

'Twenty metres. Kalyuyev is turning towards her.'

Anya was no fool, and she would have to assume the people hunting her weren't either. Killing Demochev might not have been enough to make her goal obvious, but Masalsky was the game changer. She must have realised they would make the connection between the two men and work out that Kalyuyev was her next logical target.

'I will lose the shot in ten seconds,' Olga said. 'What are your orders?'

'Give me that headset,' Drake said, practically snatching it off the communications officer nearest him and stabbing the transmit button. 'Hold your fire. It's not her.'

'Drake, get off the net,' Kamarov growled.

'Olga. Five seconds. Fire or hold?'

'It's *not her*. She would never expose herself like this,' Drake practically shouted into the radio. 'We both know the woman you're dealing with, Kamarov. This isn't her.'

Stunned silence greeted him.

'You know I'm right,' Drake said, ignoring Miranova's astonished look. 'She's better than this.'

'She's right on him,' Olga called out. 'Do I take the shot?'

'No,' Kamarov said at last. 'Hold your fire, Olga.'

On Poklonnaya Hill, Kamarov watched as the woman in question appeared from around the side of the massive concrete plinth supporting the obelisk. Tall, slender and with short blonde hair, she bore a passing resemblance to his target, but nothing more.

He watched as she strode right past Kalyuyev, who appeared equally surprised at her lack of interest, and embraced another man a dozen paces beyond, kissing him on the cheek and smiling affectionately.

'Boris to all units,' he said, speaking into his radio. 'It's not her. Stand down.'

If only you knew how close you came, he thought as the woman started taking snaps of her companion against the backdrop of the city.

Chapter 53

Drake's hands were shaking, his heart thumping in his chest as he laid the headset down, ignoring the incredulous looks of Miranova and the three communications specialists in the room. In some part of his mind he was aware there would be repercussions from this. He had revealed his hand to Kamarov, but in that moment he was past caring.

He had just prevented an innocent civilian from having her head blasted apart by a high-powered sniper round.

He glanced at his watch – 9:20 a.m.

'You have some explaining to do, Ryan,' Miranova warned, her dark eyes smouldering. She wouldn't have figured it all out yet, but she would know there was more to his presence here than he was letting on.

His cover was blown. He was well and truly in the shit now, and unless he wanted to spend the rest of his life in a prison like the one he'd rescued Anya from, he knew it was time to part company with his FSB comrades.

He looked at Miranova, eyeing up the side arm that he knew was holstered inside her jacket. The technicians weren't armed, and he was fairly sure he could wrest the weapon away from her. He wouldn't kill her – there was no way he was prepared to sacrifice another life for this – but perhaps he could restrain her or even use her as a hostage.

Either way, he saw little choice but to act, and act fast.

'You're right,' he admitted. 'I do.'

He had just taken a step towards her when suddenly the foundry's main door exploded inwards in a hail of wood and metal fragments, its lock disintegrated by the breaching charge fixed against it. A moment later, several small objects were hurled inside, landing with heavy thunks on the floor.

Having taken part in his share of house assaults, Drake could guess well enough what they were without having to see them.

'Get down!' he yelled, grabbing Miranova and tackling her to the ground behind the big furnace in the centre of the room as the first stun grenade exploded.

In an instant, blinding white light engulfed his vision, burning away the room and everything in it. The devastating blast that accompanied the detonation felt as though it had blown out both his eardrums, leaving him with nothing but a constant static whine, like a television that had lost its tuning.

For a second or two he could do nothing except lie there, breathing hard, water streaming from his eyes. Miranova was beside him on the ground. He still had one arm across her back, keeping her pinned down. He couldn't see or hear her yet, but he at least knew she was alive. He could feel her chest expanding and contracting with each breath.

He blinked several times, shaking his head in an effort to clear his eyes. Then at last, through blurry, sun-spotted vision, he saw her lying beside him, her face just inches from his. Her eyes were wide and staring, her mouth moving as she tried to say something to him, but the words were engulfed by a dull booming roar.

He could guess what she was saying, though. Somehow their enemies had found the safe house, and they had brought enough firepower to smash their way in, presumably taking down the two security operatives outside. He couldn't explain how or why at that moment, and he knew there was no time to ponder it.

He also knew what was coming next. Their attackers had used a trio of flashbang grenades to stun and disorient the inhabitants of the command centre, making them easy prey for the inevitable assault team that was about to move in.

Drake opened his mouth to call out to the three communications officers over by their workstations, to yell at them to send out a distress call to Kamarov and the other field teams. He was too late. A dull staccato roar echoed through the room at the same moment, and all three men jerked and twisted aside and fell, blood painting their shredded clothes where a burst of automatic gunfire had torn through them. Unprotected and unarmed, there was nothing they could do to defend themselves.

A similar fate likely awaited himself and Miranova if they didn't act fast.

Only then did Drake recognise the opportunity that now presented itself. Their attackers couldn't see them from where they stood; they might not even know they were there. Perhaps, just perhaps, that would be enough.

Miranova was apparently of like mind. Pushing his arm aside, she drew the automatic and backed up against the side of the lathe, staring right at him and holding a finger to her lips in a plea for silence. Verbal communication was impossible with their ears still ringing, and would in any case announce their presence. It was hand gestures only for now.

Easing himself up from the ground, he crept over to the edge of the furnace, a little unsteady as the flashbang had disturbed his equilibrium. Under normal circumstances he would have listened for the telltale crunch of boots on the debris-covered floor, but with his hearing gone he knew that was impossible.

Instead he took a breath and leaned out just far enough to survey the room. The air was thick with smoke, burned cordite and chemical fumes from the grenades, limiting visibility. The only good news was that it worked both ways.

He spotted three figures moving through the artificial mist, their weapons sweeping the room in search of more targets, before he ducked back behind cover. He looked at Miranova again and held up three fingers.

Tapping her chest, she pointed off to the left, moving her hand in a curving motion, then pointed to him and gestured for him to move right. Drake nodded, grasping her hastily conceived plan immediately. He would make a bolt for it, trying to draw their attention, while she went left to outflank and open fire on them. It wasn't much of a battle plan, and it meant putting himself right in the line of fire, but he couldn't think of anything better.

Trying to be as quiet as possible, he gulped in a couple of deep breaths to get more oxygen into his bloodstream. Adrenalin was flowing thick and fast now, lending new energy to his tired body. Good. He would need every ounce of strength and aggression and violence that he could summon up.

He caught sight of movement in the murk, and looked up just as a pair of figures emerged from behind the hulking shape of a machine lathe. Both were clad in dark combat gear, face masks and full body armour, and both had MP5 sub-machine guns up at their shoulders. Excellent weapons for close-quarters action like this, and able to spit out close to 800 rounds per minute.

This was it.

Bracing his heels against the floor, Drake launched himself at the nearest man, tackling him like a rugby player. His opponent was neither big nor strong, and Drake had the advantage of momentum. Staggering backwards under the sudden assault, he barrelled straight into his companion, knocking him off balance to land in a sprawl against the lathe.

It was one on one, at least for the next couple of seconds. He certainly had their attention now, and could only hope that Miranova was moving into position to open fire on them.

But none of that would matter if Drake couldn't get the weapon off his new friend. Clamping a hand around the gun's foregrip, Drake yanked it upwards, forcing his opponent's arms with it and exposing his torso.

With the weapon out of play for now, he laid into his enemy with kicks and punches, lashing out half-blind at any vulnerable spot he could find. Face, eyes, groin, stomach, throat. It didn't matter. There was no great technique to situations like this. He would do anything to hurt the fucker and put him out of action.

Still he heard no sounds of gunfire. Where was Miranova?

Drake felt his fist collide with the unyielding bones of the man's skull, and winced at the flash of pain that travelled up his arm, but carried on with his vicious assault regardless. Pain was irrelevant now; all that mattered was doing as much damage as possible.

A mistimed punch that struck his enemy's exposed throat was enough to knock the fight out of him, followed by a knee to the stomach that doubled him over. The vest he was wearing was designed to resist bullets, not blunt-force trauma attacks like this. With his grip on the weapon slackening, Drake finally managed to wrench it from his grasp.

He was taking no chances with either of these boys. He'd spray both of them on full automatic, aiming for their heads, arms or legs to nullify the body armour. He didn't care if he killed them outright, only that he removed their ability to kill him.

He was just bringing the weapon to bear when suddenly

pain exploded from the back of his head and he fell to his knees, his arms and legs no longer obeying commands from his brain. Vaguely he was aware of the gun falling from his grip before he pitched forwards, landing hard on the rough floor with stars and flashes of light filling his vision.

He could feel the warm wetness of blood on his scalp. Something had struck him at the base of the skull; most likely the butt of a gun. Whatever it was, it had been more than enough to knock him out of the fight.

He felt a boot pressed against his shoulder, rolling him over on to his back. There was a blur of movement, and then he found himself staring up at the roof. He could do nothing but watch as a dark figure in body armour loomed over him, then frowned in confusion as Anya's face swam into bleary focus.

For a moment he couldn't understand what he was seeing, couldn't reconcile this woman's face with the sudden attack on the safe house. However, his confusion vanished when she shook her head, visibly angry with him.

'I told you what would happen if you stayed, Ryan,' he heard her say over the ringing in his ears and the pounding of his own heart. Her tone carried a mixture of frustration, grief and regret.

Behind her, Drake could just make out one of the assault team wrestling with Miranova, forcing his knee between her shoulder blades while he yanked her arms behind her back. She cried out in pain as the tendons in her shoulders strained to their limit.

He saw a brief flicker of sadness in her eyes, as if she were trying to apologise for failing him. No doubt she too had fallen victim to Anya's expertise in close combat.

He tried to get up, tried to reach out to her, but Anya planted a boot firmly on his chest, preventing him from moving.

Glancing away, she gave a single curt nod, then backed off as a second man moved in. Drake felt the coarse fabric of a sack being pulled over his head, and a moment later the world went dark.

As Drake and Miranova were hauled to their feet and dragged away to the waiting vehicles outside, Anya turned her attention to the workstations that had been set up in the centre of the room. With a secure satellite uplink to the FSB's central mainframe in Moscow, each terminal represented a doorway to one of the most secure networks in the world.

And she had three of them right in front of her. The assault team had been under strict instructions to take no action that would put the computer terminals at risk. Their users were expendable, but the machines themselves were vital.

Selecting the nearest one, she reached into her pocket, withdrew a USB memory stick and inserted it into one of several ports on the laptop's side. The contents of the USB stick were designed to auto-run the moment they were plugged in, and sure enough a dialog box appeared, confirming that the program was being uploaded.

Anya stood by in silence as she waited for the upload to complete. The noise of the assault would surely attract attention, and it wouldn't take long for the FSB to arrive here in force. That was one battle she had no interest in fighting.

Finally the laptop pinged and a dialog box appeared notifying her that full system access had been granted. Reaching for the cellphone in her pocket, she selected a text message she had composed prior to the attack: the agreed code phrase to signify that the Trojan had been uploaded and that the FSB's network was now ripe for the taking.

Our table is booked. See you soon.

There was only one recipient – Atayev. Without hesitation she hit the send button, then turned her attention back to the terminal. She had fulfilled her end of the agreement, but she had one other task to complete here.

She needed one small scrap of information from the vast repository now available to her. One little piece, and all of this would be worth it.

Forcing calm into her mind, Anya inputted her search criteria and waited while the program went to work.

Chapter 54

Poklonnaya Hill, Moscow

'Boris to Gregory. Respond,' Kamarov growled into his radio. 'I repeat, respond.'

Gregory, the call sign for their base of operations at the disused foundry, had dropped off the radio net a couple of minutes earlier. They weren't transmitting, and they apparently weren't receiving either.

'Boris to all units. Anyone have comms with Gregory?'

'Nothing from Olga,' the spotter team replied.

'Anna has nothing.'

Swearing under his breath, Kamarov removed his radio earpiece and reached for the cellphone in his jacket pocket, quickly dialling Miranova's number. The seconds stretched out, with no response.

That was enough to decide him.

'All units, switch to alternate encryption now,' he ordered, quickly switching channels on his own radio before barking out further orders. 'The meeting was a diversion. Gregory may be compromised. Anna and Boris teams converge on that location. Go now!'

Pain.

Noise and jolting movement.

The smell of petrol and old leather and cigarette smoke. The feeling of rough, cold metal against his cheek. The pressure of handcuffs biting into the flesh of his wrists.

With his mind lingering on the edge of consciousness, Drake struggled to process any information beyond simple physical sensations. He opened his eyes with great effort and looked around, only to be rewarded with darkness.

Of course. A hood had been placed over him back at the foundry. He could feel the fabric clinging to his face every time he inhaled, hot and clammy and smothering.

Unable to see, he concentrated instead on his other senses, using touch and sound and smell to glean what he could about his surroundings.

He was lying on his side in the cargo compartment of some kind of commercial vehicle. That much was obvious from the movement and sounds. The floor beneath him was bare metal, corrugated for extra grip, and interspersed with small holes for latching straps to stop cargo rolling around.

They were taking him somewhere. That single revelation was enough to kindle a fire of hope within him. They could have killed him at the foundry, but instead they had opted to take him with them.

They wanted him alive, for now at least.

Another hard jolt, this one violent enough to slam his head on to the metal floor with painful force. Where was he? More importantly, where was he going?

He raised his head up to look around, and was promptly rewarded with a kick to the shoulder that drove him down against the floor again.

'Stay down,' a gruff voice warned.

Another man mumbled something under his breath in Russian, followed by an amused chuckle. So there were at least two of them in the van. He had no idea if Anya was amongst them.

He heard the faint hiss of an indrawn breath, and then a moment later a spent cigarette was flicked from somewhere behind him to land on the metal floor, still smoking. The acrid smell stung his nostrils.

With a final shuddering lurch, the van halted, the engine still ticking over.

More urgent voices talking in Russian, and suddenly he felt strong hands grip his right arm, one at his elbow and the other at his wrist. Instinctively he began to struggle, trying to break out of the hold, but a sharp blow to the back of the head was enough to put paid to that idea.

'Don't move. You've been implanted with a tracking device,' Anya hissed in his ear. So she was here after all. 'You know what I have to do. Don't move or I will sever an artery.'

A moment later Drake felt something sharp pressed into his forearm, the pressure increasing until with a tear and a warm trickle of blood, the skin parted and the blade made entry.

Strangely, it didn't hurt as much as he'd expected. He was aware of the bleeding, but the sensation was more akin to a shaving cut. Perhaps his senses were still dulled by the injuries he'd taken earlier, he thought with a pang of hope.

No such luck. The moment he felt the metal tweezers inserted into the newly opened wound, the pain hit him hard. He gritted his teeth, letting out an agonised groan as Anya pressed the tweezers in deeper, searching for the little tracking module nestled within the muscle tissue.

At least she was familiar with procedures like this. He'd seen her perform one on herself during their escape from DC last year.

That wasn't much comfort to him as a fresh lightning bolt of pain shot down his arm. He couldn't tell if she'd touched a nerve during her probing; all he knew was that he felt as if his entire arm had been submerged in boiling oil.

Unable to restrain himself, he let out a cry of pain as the tweezers closed around the module and, with a single hard yank, pulled it free.

'That's good, Ryan,' he heard Anya whisper, her voice barely registering as he lay there on the dirty floor of the van, breathing hard, blood trickling from the wound at his arm. 'Just breathe. It is done.'

Several orders were exchanged in Russian, then with a roar from the engine, the van lurched forwards once more.

'Someone hit them hard and fast,' Agent Pushkin concluded as he grimly surveyed the scene of carnage within the foundry. 'They took out the two agents outside, breached the door and came in with stun grenades and automatic weapons. The technicians here didn't stand a chance.'

Kamarov said nothing as he picked his way through the spent shell casings and bloodstains, taking in the grisly results of the attack. It was easy to see why they had lost comms so suddenly. The three technicians in charge of the radio net were lying sprawled on the floor in pools of blood. Burn marks on the ground indicated the spots where flash-bang grenades had detonated.

He almost felt a moment of respect for his adversary. Anya had left a trail for them to follow after the attack in Grozny, had lured them out here with the promise of an easy take-down so she could hit them where they were vulnerable. It was a bold and audacious move, and he had fallen for it.

'What about Drake and Miranova?' he asked, glancing up at the younger man.

Pushkin's expression darkened further. 'We swept the building. There's no sign.'

Wasting no more time here, Kamarov turned away, reached for his cellphone and dialled a number in Moscow. Director Surovsky had seen to it that any calls from his phone were given highest priority.

'Access code, please,' came the crisp greeting of an FSB signals technician a few moments later.

'This is Alexei Kamarov, access number 501129,' he began, his tone clipped and efficient. 'I need a priority track on a previous subject – Drake, Ryan.'

Disguised as an antibiotic shot to prevent infection, a tiny RFID (Radio Frequency Identification) device no larger than a grain of rice had instead been implanted in the muscle layer in Drake's arm without his knowledge. A team of technicians and analysts had been tracking Drake's every move from the moment the device was implanted, and was still doing so even now.

At that time Kamarov had seen it as a wise precaution in case Drake turned against them, but now he sensed a far more useful purpose.

'Copy that, sir. The tracking module is active. He's moving north-east, about eight miles from you. Too fast to be on foot – looks like he's in a vehicle.'

Just as he'd thought, Anya had risked exposing herself in order to snatch Drake from the FSB's custody, but she hadn't reckoned on the hidden device. They were now able to follow her movements just as easily as if she was broadcasting them herself.

Kamarov clenched his fist. Anya had been one step ahead of them so far, but no longer. Now he had the edge.

'Good. Keep us updated. We're moving to intercept now.'

Chapter 55

Drake grimaced as the burlap sack was pulled off his head, allowing harsh electric light to flood his eyes, blinding in its intensity next to the claustrophobic darkness he'd endured for the last twenty minutes or so.

He couldn't move. He was seated on a cheap, uncomfortable wooden chair, his hands cuffed firmly behind his back and secured to the chair with either a rope or a plastic cable tie. Whatever it was, it was beyond his ability to break.

His head throbbed as if his brain was steadily expanding beyond the limits of his skull; a testament to the single powerful blow that had dropped him like a sack of rice. It was hard to know how bad the injury was. Certainly he'd experienced the pain and nausea that went hand in hand with a concussion, and just looking into the light was enough to make him want to throw up. Still, at least his hearing was returning to normal. The high-pitched whine that had plagued him earlier had receded to a faint ringing.

The congealed blood and throbbing pain in his right arm reminded him of the device recently removed by Anya with such brutal efficiency. He wondered if the woman had derived a grim sense of satisfaction from that act, perhaps feeling that she had repaid the favour after enduring a similar experience last year.

One person who hadn't been there, however, was Miranova.

He would have heard or felt her in the back of the van with him, which meant either that she'd been hauled off in a second vehicle, or . . .

He closed his eyes and clenched his jaw shut, refusing to let his thoughts stray down that path. Not now. Not until he knew more.

Just focus on the things you can do something about, he told himself.

He looked around, taking in as much of his surroundings as possible. It was hard to see with the light in his eyes, but he guessed he was seated in the centre of a room about 20 feet square. The walls were bare brick, the floor rough and uneven.

The place was in serious disrepair, with mortar starting to come away from the bricks and patches of mould inching their way up the walls. The floor was covered with damp cardboard boxes, lumps of broken concrete, cigarette ends and other pieces of discarded rubbish. If there was a door, it had to be behind him because he could see no other access points.

A table had been pushed up against the wall opposite, on which was resting the powerful work light that was the room's only source of illumination. That told him pretty much everything he needed to know.

Drake had been in enough interrogation rooms to recognise the set-up here. This was a basic job; the sort of thing Agency field teams would cobble together to do an impromptu 'debriefing' of a high-value target. But like most things in life, simplicity was the key.

'Ryan Drake,' a voice said from behind. A man's voice, Russian accented, neither high- nor low-pitched. It was smooth and clear, suggesting he was neither a smoker nor a big drinker.

411

Drake heard footsteps on the concrete floor, and glanced left as his captor walked into view, revealing himself for the first time.

Drake had encountered all kinds of men in his profession, from terrorist leaders to covert operatives, informants, soldiers, insurgents, criminals of every kind, even rogue Agency personnel. He knew the sort of people who moved in such circles, and this man wasn't one of them.

Short, stoop-shouldered and overweight, he carried himself with the unprepossessing stature of one used to being ignored and overlooked. Wire-framed glasses sat on the bridge of his long nose, while his fleshy, amiable face was crowned by a receding patch of dark hair. He was dressed in a cheap, poorly fitting brown suit that somehow reminded Drake of a middle-aged taxi driver.

All in all, he was about as far from Drake's expectation of the ruthless leader of this terrorist group as it was possible to be. To think that this man had somehow bent Anya to his will was even more inconceivable. Yet here they were, Drake handcuffed to a chair and his enigmatic captor circling around in front of him.

'My name is Buran Atayev,' he said, leaning back so that his hands were braced on the edge of the table. His frame was partially blocking the work light, allowing Drake to see a little better. 'I have been looking forward to meeting you.'

'What do you want with me?' Drake asked, still struggling to believe that this was the mastermind behind the deaths of two of the FSB's top men.

He couldn't be sure, but he thought he saw a faint smile. 'To thank you, of course. You were a worthy opponent – smart enough to see the trail I left, and predictable enough to follow it here.'

Drake had already suspected as much by now, but to

have it confirmed in such an offhand manner only served to underline his own failure.

'When you realised Kalyuyev was the next target, you chose to use him as bait rather than protecting him.' He raised a finger and wagged it from side to side as if to chide Drake for his error. 'A risky strategy.'

'He's safe,' Drake reminded him.

Again that flicker of a smile. 'For now. You, however, are not.'

Drake could see the way this conversation was heading, and knew he had to do something now if he didn't want to end up like Demochev and Masalsky. He had to give the man a reason not to kill him.

'I know why you're doing this.'

That seemed to intrigue Atayev. 'Do you?'

'You said yourself that I'd made the connection between your targets. It's Beslan. Demochev, Masalsky and Kalyuyev – all three men were involved that day. They all fucked up, they all failed to stop it from happening. That's what they're guilty of, isn't it?'

At this, Atayev shook his head, letting out a chuckle of grim amusement. 'Like I said, you are smart enough to see the obvious, but the deeper meaning is lost on you. None of those men "fucked up" as you put it. They all played their parts to perfection.'

Drake frowned, failing to understand. 'What do you mean?'

Atayev settled down on the edge of the table, making himself a little more comfortable. 'Let me tell you a story, Mr Drake,' he said with the exaggerated enthusiasm of a teacher addressing a reluctant classroom. 'It begins twenty years ago, with an ambitious young KGB agent who made a name for himself during the Afghan War. He was, as you would put it,

413

a firefighter – a man sent where the need was greatest, to deal with threats that others could not. His ambition was matched only by his complete disregard for human life, and he soon became one of the most feared KGB operatives in the country. But time was against him, and after the collapse of the Soviet Union he found himself cast adrift. Just another relic of the Cold War in a world that no longer needed him.'

In a flash, Drake's earlier phone conversation with Frost leapt into his mind once more. A former KGB agent who operated in Afghanistan with brutal efficiency, who now had a vested interest in tracking down the men behind the attack in Washington. Instantly, the pieces assembled in his head like a puzzle whose solution suddenly became obvious.

'Surovsky.'

Viktor Surovsky: the golden boy in Russia's war against terrorism and organised crime, the hard-line but nonetheless brilliant leader who had brought order from chaos, who had remade the FSB into an intelligence organisation to rival the best in the world.

Another faint smile, this time one of grudging respect. 'Indeed. But such a life did not suit our ambitious friend Viktor. He began looking for other ways to advance himself, until at last his attention came to rest on Chechnya. This was a place with many enemies to be overcome, just like Afghanistan. But how was a man to make a name for himself there? It is at this time in his life that a second man enters our story. A comrade of Viktor's from the old days, a former Spetsnaz operative now working for the FSB's counter-terrorist division.'

Another piece of the puzzle fell into place.

Roman Kalyuyev.

'It was Kalyuyev who suggested that it was fear, not accomplishments, that brought men to power. Like St George and the dragon, he needed only to create a monster, and then slay it. Viktor, blinded by his own ambition, agreed immediately with this idea. Three separate targets were chosen to maximise civilian casualties – an apartment complex in Moscow, a pair of airliners, and last of all . . . a school.'

Drake could hardly believe what he was hearing. Frost's earlier summary of Surovsky's career replayed in his mind.

'Russia got hit by a bunch of terrorist attacks from Chechen separatists. They blew up an apartment complex in Moscow, downed a couple of airliners and shot up a school in Beslan.'

'The first two attacks were merely opening moves, designed to draw attention – Beslan was his masterstroke,' Atayev went on. 'Only an attack of that scale would give him the springboard he needed to launch himself into power. Using undercover agents, Viktor and Kalyuyev were able to convince Chechen militants that a major hostage crisis would be enough to bring Russia to the negotiating table. Demochev and Masalsky were bribed into cooperating. Masalsky was ordered to cease FSB surveillance of known Chechen insurgents in the weeks leading up to the attack, while Demochev made sure that the armed group was able to reach the school unchallenged.'

'Demochev served as commander of a border security task force. He was in command of most of the military checkpoints in the area around the town.'

Miranova's words from the briefing earlier seemed like a mockery of Drake's own incompetence now.

'Masalsky was part of the FSB's anti-terrorism directorate in the province. He was responsible for monitoring and apprehending suspected militants.'

Demochev and Masalsky. Two men who had been mysteriously promoted to divisional leader positions instead of punished for their failures. Only now did Drake understand why. Only now did he perceive the pattern that had been in front of him the whole time.

'When the crisis unfolded, Kalyuyev the anti-terrorist expert was flown in from Moscow to coordinate a rescue operation. But rescue was the last thing on his mind. His orders were to storm the school and make sure every one of the hostage-takers was killed – Viktor wanted no one left to speak out against him. And believe me, Kalyuyev executed his orders with great thoroughness.'

Drake was appalled. Hundreds of men, women and children had died in the attack, caught in the crossfire between the two opposing forces. Had Kalyuyev really been willing to go so far?

'And so we come at last to the endgame, where the true nature of Viktor's plan is revealed. As the dust settled and the scale of the disaster became clear, the Russian people demanded action, their anger fuelled by leaked reports of police incompetence and cover-ups. Leaked by none other than Viktor himself. The government was desperate to find a scapegoat for the disaster, and quickly settled on the FSB. The existing leadership were either forced to resign or relegated to token positions, while our friend Viktor, the firefighter from Afghanistan, found himself promoted to the position of acting director. Kalyuyev meanwhile took much of the blame for the failed rescue operation and retired, several million dollars richer, of course.'

Kalyuyev, the successful businessman living the high life in Moscow, who had left his FSB past behind with enough money to buy his way into virtually any company he chose.

'Over the next few months, Viktor worked feverishly to consolidate his hold on power. Anyone who posed a threat was methodically hunted down and eliminated. Thousands were arrested and held without trial, while State control of the media was tightened, strangling the life out of Beslan. Foreign journalists and investigators who started asking too many questions were either assassinated or intimidated into silence. Just as Kalyuyev had said, fear became Viktor's most powerful weapon. Fear of attack was what brought him to power, and fear of reprisal is what allows him to remain there unchallenged.' He turned his head slowly look at Drake, his bespectacled eyes reflecting deep wells of grief and pain and years of pent-up fury. 'And so ends our story, Mr Drake.'

Drake was quite simply stunned by everything he'd heard. He never could have imagined the depth of the conspiracy they were dealing with, or the scale of the tragedy that had been allowed to play out.

Only then did it finally occur to him that this man standing before him was no terrorist or freedom fighter, that he wasn't driven by religious or political ideology, or a thirst for power or wealth. He had a far more personal connection to this.

'If everything you've told me is true, then I'm not your enemy,' Drake implored him. 'I can help you. I can get you to America, give you protection, find a way to get your story out. You can make Surovsky answer for what he did.'

The older man folded his arms and regarded Drake with quizzical amusement. 'Why would I need your help?'

'Don't you get it? They're on to you now. You managed to kill Masalsky and Demochev because they didn't understand what you were doing, but Surovsky will be ready for you. You can't beat someone like that with bombs and guns. And even if you could get to him, killing him would only make him into a martyr. If you want to bring him down, you have to do it the right way. Get me out of here and I'll help you destroy the fucker.'

At this, his captor merely shook his head. 'You could be telling the truth. In which case you are a better man than I thought. But I already have all the help I need.'

Glancing over Drake's shoulder, he nodded to someone who had apparently been standing there, silent and unnoticed, throughout the whole conversation.

Drake heard the soft thump of boots on the concrete floor and looked around as a woman walked into view. Tall, athletically built, with short blonde hair and piercing blue eyes.

Anya.

Chapter 56

'Goddamn it, Ryan. Pick up!' McKnight seethed, pacing the small office while her cellphone rang out uselessly.

Mason watched her in uneasy silence, wishing he could say or do something that would help. Unfortunately he had little to offer except bad news.

True to his word, he had made excuses to his FSB minders and arranged an escort to the US embassy in Moscow – a big, square, seven-storey office block located in the Presnensky District less than a mile from the Kremlin. Constructed of steel and mirrored glass and concrete, its appearance more closely resembled a corporate headquarters than a diplomatic mission.

That, however, was where the similarities ended. This particular corporate headquarters was surrounded by imposing perimeter walls and watchtowers, every inch of its property monitored by security cameras and guarded night and day by armed Marines.

The Chief of Mission there had greeted his arrival with the same enthusiasm most men felt for a piece of dog shit stuck to their shoe. Still, a little negotiation on his part had granted him entry, and less than ten minutes later he had found himself reunited with Frost and McKnight, both of whom were eager for news on Drake.

Neither had been impressed by the admission that he'd

willingly left Drake to carry out his ill-conceived plan, and McKnight had wasted no time trying to raise him by phone. Thus far, however, she'd had no luck.

'Fuck,' McKnight hissed, abandoning her attempt. 'Nothing.'

'He won't answer,' Mason said gently. 'He'll know why you're calling.'

McKnight's hazel eyes flicked to him, filled with concern and anger, though the latter seemed to be winning through. 'And for good reason. Christ, the stupid son of a bitch is going to get himself killed.'

'And you let him go through with it,' Frost added with an accusing look at Mason.

He avoided her gaze. 'It was his call.'

He heard her footsteps on the carpet, and turned around just as she squared up to him, having to tilt her head back to make eye contact.

'And that'd be just fine with you, right, Cole?' she snapped, jabbing a finger into his chest. 'Why should you give a shit now that Ryan's got your crippled ass back on the books?'

Batting her hand away with such force that even she was caught off guard, he took a step towards her with his fists clenched. 'Fuck you, Keira. If you were a man, I swear to God I'd hammer you into the floor.'

After everything he'd gone through, everything he'd lost since that disastrous night last year, how dare she even think to question his loyalty?

Another person might have backed off, might have been intimidated by his rage, but not her. She stood her ground, flashing a fierce grimace that might have been called a smile.

'Don't let that stop you,' she said. 'Come on, champ. Take a shot, see where it gets you.'

'Both of you, stop this!' McKnight shouted, forcing herself

between the two. 'You're field operatives, so start acting like it.'

Mason let out a breath, calming a little.

'We all want to help Ryan. Knocking the shit out of each other isn't going to cut it.' McKnight lowered her arms, keeping her eye on Mason who she no doubt considered the bigger danger. 'Keira, go get some air.'

The young woman's eyes lit up, no doubt feeling like she was being singled out as the perpetrator. 'There's plenty of air in here.'

'That wasn't a suggestion,' McKnight said without turning around. 'Come back when you've got a clear head.'

Both McKnight and Frost were feeling the strain of having been isolated from unfolding events for so long. The frustration at being unable to directly help their teammates had taken its toll on both of them, but this wasn't the way to deal with it.

Glowering at Mason a moment longer, Frost turned away and strode out of the room, making sure to slam the door shut behind her.

'Thanks,' Mason said, relaxing a little.

'Save it,' the woman advised. 'You fucked up by letting Ryan go through with this. But pointing the finger and yelling won't undo it.'

Mason said nothing to that. He admired her pragmatism, if not her manners.

She was just raising her phone again when suddenly the door flew open and one of the embassy staff hurried in. Midforties, bespectacled and with his shirt straining to contain his overhanging beer gut, it was obvious he wasn't part of the security detail here.

He was a signals technician, responsible for monitoring and reporting on the vast amount of data and communications that the embassy was able to intercept each day. This might have been a diplomatic mission on the outside, but like any embassy in the world it was also an intelligence-gathering hub.

'We have a problem,' he began, out of breath having run here from wherever his own office was. 'NSA just intercepted a flash warning across the Russian radio net. Looks like one of their field units was hit.'

Mason felt an icy knot of fear twist his stomach. 'Where?'

'Kutuzovsky Prospekt, near Poklonnaya Hill. They're scrambling tact teams in the area.' He paused for a moment, taking a breath. 'There's talk of agents missing in action.'

McKnight let out a breath, paling visibly at the news.

'Ryan.'

Chapter 57

Anya surveyed the bruised and bloodied man handcuffed to the chair before her with cold, clinical detachment. Ryan Drake, the man who had freed her from the hell she'd been imprisoned in for four long years, who had given her back her life, who had helped her regain some vestige of humanity.

Only she had the power to liberate him now.

'As I said, I owe you my thanks,' Atayev said. 'Without you, this woman never would have found me. And without her, none of this would have been possible.'

Drake paid no heed to Atayev's words now. All his attention was focused on Anya.

'Why, Anya?' he demanded, his voice icy cold despite the fire in his eyes. 'Just answer me that. Why?'

He didn't understand. Of course he didn't understand. How could he?

'You should have taken my advice, Ryan,' she admonished him. 'I warned you what would happen if you tried to stop me. Why couldn't you have listened?'

She saw him waver just a little, saw the doubt growing within him as another piece of his faith and trust crumbled away. But still he held on, still he refused to believe it.

'Anya, this isn't you,' he implored her. 'I know you. You're better than this.'

Anya shook her head, looking at him with pity in her eyes.

'You don't know me. You never did. You only saw what you wanted to see, what you needed to see.' She spread her arms, gesturing at their surroundings. 'Tell me, what do you see now?'

It was too much for him. He had clung to the belief that there was something to this whole thing he wasn't seeing, some deeper truth that would justify her actions. Only now did he realise it didn't exist. Only now did the knowledge settle on him that he had put his faith in something that was never real.

'I protected you. I risked my life for you,' he spat, straining against the cuffs that held him securely in place. 'Keira was right all along. We should have left you to rot in prison.'

He was livid with rage, his muscles trembling with barely suppressed fury, his green eyes boring into her. But beneath it all Anya sensed something far worse – pain. The pain of betrayal.

Anya knew better than most how it felt to put faith and belief in someone, to risk her life for them only to realise it was all for nothing. And here she was visiting that same betrayal on a man who had shown her nothing but loyalty.

She couldn't carry on this conversation, couldn't see her actions reflected in him any longer. Taking a step forwards, she drew back her fist and slammed it into Drake's face, snapping his head back with the force of the impact. He opened his eyes slowly, struggling to focus as blood dripped from his mouth.

'There's something . . . you need to know,' he whispered. 'It's important.'

Anya leaned forward a little. 'Tell me.'

'You hit like a girl,' he said, forcing a bloody smile.

That was all the incentive she needed.

Moving with slow and deliberate care, Anya circled around

behind him. Bound to the chair and unable to turn, he was forced to remain there, heart pounding against the walls of his chest. She could almost feel his fear. He had no idea what she was about to do, but he sensed it was going to hurt.

His suspicion was proved horribly correct a moment later as she seized the little finger of his left hand.

'You're still a good man, Ryan,' she whispered in his ear. 'In a bad world.'

As Anya began to bend his finger backwards, he closed his eyes and braced himself, knowing what was coming. The joint held for a moment against the pressure, bone and sinew strained beyond their limits. Then suddenly there was an audible pop, and a starburst of agony exploded through Drake's brain as the joint finally gave way. He gritted his teeth, groaning in anguish but stubbornly refusing to cry out.

He wouldn't give her that satisfaction.

Anya had done what she had to do here. Standing up, she backed away and glanced at Atayev. 'We don't have much time.'

He nodded. 'I'll see you outside.'

Drake couldn't see Anya leave, but he heard the creak of a door being opened, followed by a harsh metallic clang as it slammed shut behind her. His mind was racing as his captor rose from the table and drew himself up to his full, if modest, height.

'It seems we are finished, Mr Drake. I don't imagine we will see each other after today.' He took a step towards the door, then paused as if he'd just remembered something. 'By the way, I have a gift for you.'

Reaching into his pocket, he carefully lifted out a single white chess pawn and laid it on the table. Drake had seen two pieces already, one on Demochev and the other on Masalsky, and recognised the style well enough – this one belonged to the same set.

'Think on this, my friend,' he said, placing a hand on Drake's shoulder in an almost fatherly gesture.

Then a moment later he was gone, and Drake was alone.

Chapter 58

'Satellite tracking has locked down his location!' Pushkin said, raising his voice to be heard over the roar of the engine as their black Mercedes-Benz E-Class wove in and out of slower-moving traffic, its blue light flashing. Two more such vehicles were close behind, each packed with armed agents. 'It is a heavy goods truck, moving east on the M7.'

'How far?' Kamarov asked.

'Six miles.'

'I want constant coverage of that truck. Have them launch a drone if we're going to lose the satellite. And advise all police units in the area to be on standby.'

'We're on it, sir.'

Kamarov nodded, satisfied that for now at least, they had the situation in hand. However, all the technology and resources at his disposal would mean little when the shooting started. If the woman they'd been sent here to recapture was waiting for them in that truck, some of the men accompanying him would undoubtedly die.

Twenty years ago in Afghanistan he'd had the element of surprise on his side. He'd had an entire platoon of Spetsnaz operatives at his disposal, and still he had lost three men in the vicious firefight.

And he was old now.

The pain in the joints, the slightly impaired reactions, the

427

gradual loss of strength. He hadn't felt any of it back then, but he did now. He was old, his body slowly failing him as the years wore on. And yet here he was, once again preparing to take on the most dangerous opponent he'd ever faced.

How could she be anything else?

After all, Anya had been the director's favourite; his student, his protégée. Her betrayal had cut as deep as any physical wound.

And now he wanted her back.

Drake hadn't been alone for long before the door swung open once more and another man sauntered into view, holding what looked like a bag of tools. Gratefully laying the heavy burden down on the table, he turned to regard Drake for a long moment of thoughtful silence, as if he were a workman sizing up a job.

He was a small man, lean and wiry, the veins in his exposed arms standing out hard against stringy muscle as he reached into his pocket and retrieved a pack of cigarettes. Remembering his manners, he held the pack to Drake.

'You want one, my man?' he asked, speaking in a heavy Slavic accent.

Drake shook his head.

'Don't smoke, huh?' The man smiled with amusement. 'Very wise, my friend. Bad for your health.'

Helping himself to one, he lit up and took a long, slow draw, still watching Drake as if he was a task to be undertaken.

'My name is Yuri,' he said at length. 'Pleased to meet you, man. You are Drake, yes?'

'That's right.' There was little point in lying to him.

Yuri smiled and nodded. 'You are English. That is good. I like English, I have cousin there.' His eyes lit up as an idea came to him. 'Hey, Manchester United, huh?'

'Yeah, Manchester United,' Drake agreed, not sure where this was leading.

'Ronaldo. He is fucking good player, yes?'

If you say so, Drake thought. He knew as much about football as he did about flower arranging. 'Good player. Yeah.'

Yuri leaned back and took another long draw, apparently satisfied that he'd broken the ice. 'I like you, man. We are bros now. Yes?'

'Yeah.' Somehow Drake didn't imagine they'd be Skyping each other when this was over, but he was content to keep him talking.

'Okay, bro. Here is the deal. You are going to die here in this room. This is bad, I know. But there are lots of ways to die. Some are easy,' he said, reaching behind his back and pulling an automatic from his belt. Drake couldn't see it very well in the harsh light, but its small frame suggested a Walther PPK or something similar.

Unzipping the bag, he emptied the contents on to the table before him. An array of electric drills, saws, hammers and knives clattered to its surface, many of them rusted and stained from long use.

'And some are hard.'

Satisfied that he had made his point, Yuri laid the handgun on the table and turned back towards Drake. 'I can make this really easy for you, man. One round to the head. *Bang!* And it's over. I want to do this for you, because you are my bro and I want to help you, but you have to help me too, man. If you tell me everything you know about the FSB, I promise I will make this quick and simple. You won't even feel a thing. But if you want to be a crazy guy and hold out on me, I think you'll be having a really bad day.'

As if to emphasise his point, he lifted up a cordless drill and pressed the trigger to test the batteries were still good.

Sure enough, the rusty, bloodstained drill bit turned with a high-pitched whine.

'So you think about that, man,' Yuri advised. 'You think about that really hard while I get ready.'

Flicking his cigarette away, he reached into the bag for a pair of white plastic overalls; the kind worn in car body shops for spray-painting. Only in this case, the waterproof coating was designed to resist splashes of blood.

Drake, however, had no intention of ending up as Yuri's next torture project. He was simply biding his time, waiting for his would-be torturer to get distracted long enough for him to act.

Anya had done far more than break his finger during their brief conversation earlier. Just before she snapped the digit, he had felt her press something into his other hand. Something small, ridged and metallic.

A key.

He didn't understand how or why she had done it, and now wasn't the time for seeking answers. What mattered right now was freeing himself and taking out the man who was just itching to use that cordless drill on his kneecaps.

As Yuri laid the overalls down in front of him and began to step into the legs, Drake knew his chance had come. Fumbling with the small key until it finally slipped into the lock, he gave a single quick turn. There was a moment of taut resistance before he felt and heard the faint click as the lock disengaged.

He wasn't going to waste time fucking around with the second lock. Not now. Shrugging his wrist out of the cuff, he pulled it through the loop of plastic cable tie securing it to the chair, took a single deep breath to get more oxygen in his bloodstream and launched himself at his enemy.

There was no time to consider a detailed strategy for

attack. His first, last and only concern was taking Yuri down and keeping him there.

Alerted by the sudden movement, his opponent looked up from what he was doing just as Drake barrelled into him, knocking him backwards to crash into the table, which promptly gave way under the impact. Tools, knives and other instruments clattered off the tabletop to land all around them, while the work light, the only source of illumination, fell sideways and shattered against the floor, plunging the room into darkness.

The two men, groping blindly in the near-pitch darkness, were now locked in a desperate struggle for survival.

Yuri might have been small and lean, but what he lacked in size he more than made up for in aggression and resilience. Having recovered from the shock of Drake's escape and his bruising collision with the table, he immediately went on the offensive, lashing out with fists, boots and even fingernails.

Drake laid into him with a hammer-like blow to the side of his face, gashing his cheek to the bone, yet the man barely seemed to react to it. Growling with rage, he clawed at Drake's eyes, trying to blind him. Drake dodged and weaved like the boxer he'd once been, desperate to avoid his hands while at the same time pummelling his chest and stomach with punch after punch, ignoring the stabs of pain from the broken finger. That would be the least of his worries if Yuri managed to blind him.

He was just drawing back his arm to strike again when suddenly the smaller man lunged at him, mouth open wide and teeth bared like an animal. An instant later those same teeth clamped down on Drake's neck where it met his shoulder, puncturing the skin. He let out an involuntary cry of pain as they started to tear through the muscle layer beneath. The little fucker was literally going for his jugular, and only

431

sheer luck had caused him to miss his target. But that luck wouldn't last for long.

This was one fight that needed to end now. Yuri was already doing serious damage, and Drake couldn't force him off without taking a chunk of his neck away at the same time. He needed to give the man some incentive, and he had a pretty good idea what to do.

Abandoning his fruitless attempts to pound Yuri into submission, he reached down between his legs, clamped a hand around his genitals and twisted with every ounce of strength he could summon.

There are few men who could endure an attack like that, and Yuri wasn't one of them. The grip on Drake's neck slackened, and a low primal growl of pain began in his throat as Drake's fist tightened around his most vulnerable area.

Drake wasn't about to give him a chance to recover. At last managing to free himself from the man's tenacious grip, he pulled back and butted Yuri full in the face, feeling the crunch of cartilage giving way under the impact. A sudden spurt of warmth on his forehead told him he'd broken the man's nose.

Yuri was in trouble now, and they both knew it. Clutching at his nose, he threw himself backwards and tried to kick and scramble away from Drake while snarling something in his own language.

Drake knew he had to silence the man before his cries warned the others. Unable to see much in the near-darkness, he instead groped around for the tools that had been knocked off the table during the fight. He would have loved to chance upon the automatic Yuri had brandished earlier, but the chances of finding it quickly were slim.

He felt his fingers brush the plastic casing of some kind of power tool. Either the electric drill or a circular saw that

Drake had also seen amongst Yuri's implements. Whatever it was, he ignored it. He had no time to fumble with the controls in the dark, and in any case, he needed to kill Yuri quickly, not patiently slice pieces off him.

Then at last his hand closed around a long wooden handle with a metal striker mounted at one end, and he knew he'd found what he needed. As his father had once told him, technology was all well and good, but sometimes what you really needed was a good solid hammer.

Snatching up the instrument with his good hand, he closed in on Yuri, following the curses and groans of pain, took aim and brought the hammer down on the top of his head. There was a dull wet crunch as the metal striker cleaved its way through bone and brain before finally stopping as the handle struck what remained of his skull.

The effect was as profound as a gunshot. Yuri's cries ceased instantly and he went down, collapsing face first on to the concrete. A long, low groan and a spasmodic jerking of his legs was the only sign that he'd been alive only seconds before.

It was over.

Breathing hard, Drake let go of the hammer and reached up to touch the bite mark on his neck. His hand came away slick with blood. He couldn't tell how bad the injury was, but he could still turn his head despite the growing pain as the damaged muscles started to seize up. If he'd severed an artery, he would already have been dead.

As for the rest of him, the picture was less rosy. His head still pounded from when Anya had knocked him down, and his broken finger throbbed with waves of pain that travelled up his arm like electricity, mingling with the dull ache in his damaged shoulder. His tussle with Yuri had left him with more cuts and bruises to add to the list.

Still, he could move and think, and he needed to do both now.

Reaching out, he rolled the dead man over to search him, quickly locating the petrol lighter he'd used to spark up his cigarette. A small dancing orange flame leapt up on his first attempt, allowing Drake a proper look at his immediate surroundings for the first time.

If there had been any doubt that Yuri was dead, one look was enough to confirm it. The hammer still protruded from the top of his head, the metal striker deeply embedded in his skull. A sticky pool of blood, brain matter and pieces of shattered bone gleamed in the light of the flame, while his eyes stared blankly up at the ceiling, now dull and unfocused.

A quick check of his pockets revealed a couple of spare magazines for whatever automatic he'd brandished during the torture session, a packet of cigarettes that were of no use to Drake, and a cellphone in his back pocket.

'Thanks, bro,' Drake whispered, helping himself to the phone.

Closing his eyes for a moment and searching his frantically racing mind for the right number, he punched it in and waited in anxious silence for the call to connect.

Like most major American embassies, the Moscow branch featured an extensive communications suite, allowing it to stay in secure contact with Washington and other diplomatic missions around the world. The fact that such a suite also allowed the staff there to monitor transmissions in their host nation was a natural by-product, and for this reason most embassies had a contingent of Agency personnel.

'What more do we know?' McKnight asked, barely able to contain her impatience as several technicians worked to uncover more details of the incident that seemed to have Moscow's law-enforcement units shitting bricks.

'Details are still sketchy,' one of them warned. 'It takes time to decode their transmissions.'

'Any word on survivors?' she persisted. 'Or even where the FSB are directing their field teams?'

'We're working on it.'

'Goddamn it, one of our operatives is out there!' she snapped, causing a momentary silence to fall on the room. 'While you're working on it, he could be dying.'

Mason winced, surprised to see her lose her cool so soon after quelling the argument between himself and Frost. He sympathised with her, and even shared her frustration, but shouting at these men would achieve nothing except to have them removed from the room.

'Sam, take it easy, okay?' he said, gently steering her away from the bustling communications centre. 'I know you're worried about Ryan. But you've got to let these guys do their job.'

'That's not all I'm worried about.' She looked at him, her gaze betraying doubt and uncertainty. 'What if he's not a hostage, Cole?'

'What do you mean?'

'He said he was going to protect Anya, right?' She lowered her voice. 'What if Ryan's the one responsible for this "incident"?'

Mason hesitated, not sure what to say. He found it hard to believe Drake would go that far, but neither could he definitively deny it. When it came to Anya, all bets were off.

His thoughts were interrupted when McKnight's phone started ringing. Snatching it up, she frowned at the unknown number before hitting the receive-call button.

'Who is this?'

'Sam, it's me,' a low, urgent voice said. A British voice. Drake's voice.

Her eyes lit up, and she raised her free hand to snap her

fingers several times, getting the attention of every agent in the room. 'Ryan! Jesus Christ, what's happening? Where are you?'

'The safe house was hit. I'm in some kind of basement, don't know where. You need to . . . trace this call.' There was an urgency in his voice, but it was also heavy with pain. He was hurt.

McKnight jerked a finger at the nearest technician. 'Have someone trace the call on my cell right now. And start recording the conversation. Move!'

As they went to work, she turned her attention back to the call. 'Talk to me. What's your situation?'

'I'm alive. I don't know about Miranova,' he evaded. 'Listen, I might not have much time. The man behind this is called Buran Atayev. He's convinced that Beslan was a false flag operation planned by the FSB. He's trying to punish them for what they did.'

'Is he there?' she asked, hastily scribbling down the name.

'He was, but he's already gone,' Drake admitted. 'I think he's planning to go after Surovsky. And he has Anya with him.'

McKnight closed her eyes. The edge of pain in his voice was more noticeable when he spoke her name. 'I'm sorry, Ryan.'

'You don't understand; she's the reason I'm not dead. She helped me escape. I don't know what her plan is, but she's not a hostile, Sam. You have to believe me.'

McKnight said nothing to that. She was inclined to take any such opinions of Anya with a grain of salt. 'Okay, sit tight and keep the line open. We'll find you.'

'I'd love to, but it's only a matter of time before they find out I'm loose,' Drake replied. 'Anyway, I have to go after Miranova. She's here somewhere.'

'Ryan, you can't—'

'I have to,' he interrupted. 'She trusted me. She doesn't deserve this.'

'And what about you? What do you deserve?'

'Sam, listen to me,' he implored her. 'There are . . . a lot of things I've wanted to say to you. I wish I hadn't left it so long, but . . . you were right. I should have trusted you. I'm sorry.'

McKnight said nothing. She could feel her throat tightening, could feel her eyes watering. She turned away from the other agents in the room, not wanting them to see her.

'Don't be,' she managed to say at last.

She heard a faint sigh on the other end. 'Look, whatever else happens, you have to keep the FSB out of this. They'll kill Anya the first chance they get. Miranova's not running this op any longer; they've brought in some guy called Kamarov. I don't know who he is, but I'd bet my life he's here to end Anya's.'

McKnight clenched her teeth. 'We'll do what we can.'

'Thanks, Sam. Thanks for doing this.' There was a momentary pause, both of them aching to say things they knew they couldn't. 'I have to go. I'll contact you again if I can.'

'Take care,' she said as the line went dead.

No sooner had she ended her conversation with Drake than she turned to the technician charged with tracing the call. 'Tell me you have something.'

He nodded, listening intently to his own phone while information was relayed from Langley. 'We've got him.'

Chapter 59

Using the dim light from the cellphone's screen, Drake began to search amongst the debris for the automatic lost during the fight. There hadn't been time to look for it earlier, but now at least he had a few moments to recover the weapon.

He found it beneath the table, partially covered by the tool bag that had fallen on top. Drake snatched it up and, unable to see properly, racked back the slide. He heard the distinctive ping of an ejected round hitting the floor, confirming that there had already been one in the chamber. Still, he'd rather lose one round now than have the weapon fail to fire at a critical moment.

As he'd suspected, it was indeed a Walther PPK, a German semi-automatic whose design dated back to the 1920s. James Bond might have cemented their iconic reputation, but their reliability and compact size had made them ideal concealed-carry weapons long before that. They'd been manufactured by different countries and in different calibres over the years, and he suspected the one he was holding was a cheap Romanian or Hungarian model. Still, presumably it would go boom when he pulled the trigger, and that was good enough.

A look around the fallen torture implements yielded another less sophisticated but perhaps more useful weapon. He wasn't interested in hacksaws or power drills, but the small metal-framed hatchet he found on the far side of the collapsed table might be of more use. Running his thumb along the edge of the blade confirmed it was still sharp enough to be a viable weapon. It didn't have the range of the PPK, but neither would it alert every gunman in the building when he used it.

Now armed, he allowed himself to calm down a little and take stock of his situation. First impressions weren't good. He was alone in a building whose layout was unfamiliar, inhabited by an unknown number of hostiles, all probably armed.

Direct confrontation was a bad idea. The PPK was light on stopping power and only came with an eight-round magazine, and he'd lost one already. Hardly an arsenal worthy of the task at hand, and a hatchet wouldn't do much to change that.

The most pressing question was what to do next. He had to assume Miranova was still alive, for now at least. He'd seen them handcuffing her back at the foundry, presumably for transportation like himself. They wouldn't go to that kind of trouble if they were planning to execute her straight away.

Anya was also an unknown. Clearly her presence here wasn't all that it seemed. She had given him the key that had saved his life, though apparently she was incapable of taking any overt action to aid him. He certainly couldn't count on her help if it came down to a shooting match, but neither was he willing to abandon her.

Letting out a long, slow breath, he closed his eyes and allowed his head to rest against the PPK's frame. 'Anya, what the fuck are you doing?' he whispered.

There was no answer for him, just as there hadn't been since the attack in DC. Anya's motivations and final goal remained a mystery.

He opened his eyes, pushing those thoughts aside. Anya could look after herself – that much was obvious – and he had enough problems to contend with already.

The room's only door was shut, but a sliver of light was visible beneath, providing just enough illumination to move around. Creeping across the room with the weapon at the ready, he felt around until he found the handle, and turned it, edging the door open.

Beyond lay an empty brick corridor, lit by bare bulbs strung up at intervals. He could see the cable that looped between each one, and in the distance he heard the faint rumble of an engine. He was willing to bet it was a generator, which suggested the building didn't have a mains power supply.

Where the generator was, he suspected he'd find Atayev as well. The question, however, was where he might find Miranova. The only thing he knew for sure was that he wouldn't find her by standing around.

One way or another, he had to move. It wouldn't be long before someone swung by this room to check on Yuri. As soon as they found the body they would know Drake had escaped, and they would waste no time hunting him down.

Gripping the PPK tight, he pushed the door open and advanced into the corridor beyond.

'I don't care what your credentials are,' said the weather-beaten, grey-haired man standing before McKnight. His name was Don Walters, the station chief for the US embassy in Moscow. 'You're not taking armed personnel on some goddamned joyride across Moscow. We get caught staging something like this, and we'll have a fucking international incident on our hands.'

Heads of diplomatic missions were not known for their close cooperation with Agency field teams. At best they viewed them as an annoying inconvenience to be tolerated, and at worst an outright menace. Walters, it seemed, fell into the latter category.

'We've got a man out there, for Christ's sake,' Frost said, barely able to restrain her temper. 'What do you suggest we do? Sit on our asses and let him die?'

Walters's baleful gaze rounded on her. He was a career veteran with thirty years' experience of diplomatic missions behind him, and not used to being browbeaten by someone half his age.

'I suggest you notify Russian security services and have them pick him up,' he said tersely. 'This is their city, not ours.'

McKnight shook her head. 'You don't understand. They'll kill Drake if they find him. His only chance is for us to get there first.'

Walters was unmoved by her plea. 'I'm sorry, but I can't sanction this. Not without authorisation from Washington, and it's one in the morning over there.'

McKnight had heard enough. As far as she could see, there was only one course of action still open to her. It was a gamble, and it had the potential to land them in a whole world of hurt if it didn't pay off, but in this case she could see little choice.

Fishing out her cellphone, she hurriedly dialled a private number and waited in anxious silence while it rang out. She was certain the recipient kept the phone on at all times; the only question was whether her plea would be answered.

Finally the ringing stopped and a hushed voice answered: 'Franklin.'

'It's McKnight, sir,' she began. 'We've got a problem and we need your help.'

For the next thirty seconds Franklin listened while she poured out everything that had happened in the past couple

441

of hours, her voice growing more strained with each passing moment.

'Ryan needs our help,' she finished. 'We have to get to him before it's too late.'

'Jesus,' Franklin breathed, stunned by everything he'd heard. 'You know you're asking a lot, McKnight. If you get caught—'

'We're running out of time, sir,' she interrupted, unwilling to delay further. 'If we don't do something now, he's as good as dead. Will you help us?'

This was the moment when her gamble would be decided. Franklin would be well within his rights to order their arrest by embassy security after everything they had done. All McKnight could do was hope that his friendship and loyalty to Drake were stronger than that.

The leader of Special Activities Division was silent for a long moment before finally replying: 'Put Walters on the phone.'

Chapter 60

Afghanistan, 7 November 1988

Anya looked up, struggling to focus with her one remaining good eye. The other was swollen shut from the beating she had taken. Her whole body ached, covered in cuts and bruises where her captors had punched and kicked their bound and helpless captive without mercy, slowly breaking her down over the past six weeks.

A chill wind blew across the rocky, desolate landscape, whipping dry snowflakes and locks of tangled, matted blonde hair into her face. With her body wasted away after weeks of near-starvation, the cold penetrated through to her very core, starting her shivering right away.

She ignored this, however, as she stared at the towering mountains around them, their caps mantled with snow, and the wide open plains beyond. After looking at nothing but bare concrete walls for so long, she was almost moved to tears by the stark, raw beauty of the scene.

'A good place to do this, don't you think?' a taunting voice asked.

She glanced left as Viktor Surovsky walked into view, wrapped in a heavy fur coat and hat to ward off the winter chill. Unlike her, he was still robust and healthy, his ruggedly handsome Slavic features just as striking as the day she'd first met him.

Further back, near the vehicle that had brought them out here, stood another man. Surovsky's bodyguard, his expression betraying no emotion as he stared back at her. She imagined men like him were used to seeing all kinds of things without really seeing them.

'I wanted to give this to you, Anya,' he explained. 'You put up such a brave fight, it seemed only right that you be rewarded for it.'

Anya stared back at him, saying nothing. Defiant to the end.

And this certainly was the end. She was under no illusions about why she'd been brought out here to this remote mountain pass.

'Such a shame it was all for nothing.' He sounded almost sympathetic as he said this; the victor offering comfort and consolation to the vanquished. 'How do you think I was able to find you that day, after you'd evaded me for so long?'

Anya was desperately trying not to listen, trying not to acknowledge his words, trying to ignore the twisting knot of fear that was tightening in her stomach with every passing moment.

'Your new friends betrayed you, Anya. The Americans, the ones you fought so long and hard for – they gave you up to me willingly. Because they had no more use for you.' Surovsky gestured to the mountains that surrounded them. 'This war is ending, we're leaving Afghanistan. The Americans have their little victory. And now that you've served your purpose, they want rid of you.' He took another drink and smiled. 'Lucky for me.'

His words broke through the last barriers of inner strength and self-control she had desperately clung to. Just for a moment, her eyes wavered and shone wet with tears, soon whipped away by the chill wind.

Surovsky could barely contain his triumph. After weeks of painstaking effort, it wasn't the torture that had finally broken her – it was a simple admission.

'Come on, now. You knew how this was going to end. Everyone outlives their usefulness sooner or later.'

She glared at him, wrists straining against the rope bonds. And for the first time since this whole ordeal began, she spoke. 'And what will you do when you outlive yours, Viktor?'

The look of absolute, undying hatred in her eyes was such that even he paused for a moment, daunted by its intensity. Even broken and defeated, she still had the power to unsettle him.

But not for much longer, he thought as he reached into his coat and drew out a Makarov pistol. She didn't even flinch as he took aim.

'You won't be there to find out,' he promised, then pulled the trigger.

The wide open space and gusting wind carried the sharp crack of the shot away. Anya jerked as the round slammed into her chest, then slumped backwards into a shallow ditch. A few moments of feeble writhing was all she could muster before at last her life slipped away.

Surovsky handed the weapon to his bodyguard, hardly believing how easy it had been. 'Get the car started,' he instructed.

He spared the young woman a final glance, still mystified as to why she had turned against him, why she had fought so hard to resist, for what cause she had been willing to sacrifice herself. He'd seen such potential in her, such untapped ability. They could have achieved so much together if only she'd stayed loyal to him.

He shook his head, dismissing the notion. As with so many things in life, he supposed he would never know.

He shivered as another chilly gust whipped down from the nearby mountains. He'd lingered here long enough. Turning away, he started walking back to where the jeep was waiting. Nobody would ever find her in such a remote area. Anyway, a traitor like that didn't deserve a decent burial. Better to let the scavengers pick at her remains.

The engine started up as he approached. Climbing inside, he closed the door, grateful to be warm once more. He withdrew the hip flask of vodka from his coat pocket and took a generous pull, relishing the fire it lit in his stomach.

'Let's go, Alexei. We're done here.'

In his office at FSB headquarters in Lubyanka Square, Viktor Surovsky sat at his desk, anxiously waiting for news on the operation to intercept Anya. Ground units were closing in on the truck she was trying to escape in with Drake, and air assets had been vectored in at his insistence. He wanted nothing left to chance.

Twenty years ago he had made a mistake. He had assumed Anya to be dead, had walked away and left her lying in an uncovered grave, yet somehow she had survived. Somehow she had crawled out of that hole in the ground. Broken, injured and starving, she had clung tenaciously on to life and somehow made it to safety.

The little bitch was nothing if not determined.

He had recaptured her fifteen years later at great personal expense, intending to use her as insurance to guarantee cooperation from his friends on the other side of the Atlantic. But again she had given him the slip, and ever since her escape he had been living in fear, consumed by the threat she now posed to him.

Anya alone possessed the ability to destroy everything he'd worked so hard to achieve. She had to be stopped for good.

Today he had a chance – a chance to end this, to rid himself of her once and for all. There would be no thought of imprisoning or interrogating her now. He wanted her dead, plain and simple.

He had his best man heading up the operation. Kamarov, always the loyal soldier, had never failed him in his two decades of service. Surovsky knew he wouldn't let him down now.

He reached for the glass of vodka on his desk and gulped a mouthful, tensing as his body rebelled against it. His doctor had warned him that another stomach ulcer was brewing, that he should stay away from alcohol. But he needed it today.

All of it. All the years of struggle, of fear and doubt and betrayal; it all came down to what happened in the next few minutes.

Chapter 61

With blood still oozing from the wound at his neck, Drake picked his way down a narrow corridor. Heavy steel doors ran along both sides at regular intervals, and the ceiling was low and vaulted, the brick walls showing signs of damp and decay. There were no windows, no natural light at all in fact. Two bare light bulbs hastily strung up with duct tape cast his surroundings in an eerie half-light that provided just enough illumination to move around.

What the hell was this place? It looked like a wine cellar or an underground storage space, though clearly it hadn't been in use for some time. The damp, heavy, musty air suggested he was underground and close to the water table.

Much like the room he'd just left, the place was completely dilapidated. The floor was covered with broken glass, yellowed and burned sheets of paper, chunks of masonry, and cables and steel pipes that had either fallen or been ripped down from the ceiling. Cyrillic writing had been crudely scrawled across one wall with white paint, though Drake had no idea what the slogan meant.

Some of the doors were standing open, their rusted frames protruding out into the corridor, but one or two were still latched shut. Edging closer to the nearest one, Drake reached out and tried the bolt holding it closed. It was rusted solid, and a few experimental tugs failed to dislodge it. A good hard blow with the hammer would probably be enough to free it up, though he saw little point. Clearly it hadn't been used in a long time.

The sound of voices behind drew his thoughts back to the present, and as he whirled around he saw a pair of shadows dancing across the floor at the far end of the corridor; figures moving past one of the electric lights. At least two of them coming his way.

Drake backed up into one of the empty storage rooms, clutching the PPK. Hidden behind the doorway as he was, it was unlikely he'd be spotted unless his new friends entered the room. Still, if they were headed for the torture chamber, they'd spot Yuri's body and know right away what had happened.

They were getting close now. Drake strained to hear them above the thumping of his own heart. They were speaking in Russian as he'd expected so the content of their conversation was unknown. Their voices were fast and urgent, but not necessarily alarmed. They sounded more like men gearing up for something, working against a tight schedule.

He had to act now. He couldn't afford to let them find Yuri, or to have a go at torturing Miranova. His only choice was to go at them.

He withdrew the hatchet from his jeans and tested the grip, trying to get a feel for the weight. The PPK was in his left hand. He wasn't a great shot left-handed, and the broken finger wouldn't help matters, but if things worked out the way he intended then it wouldn't matter. However, he needed the hatchet in his undamaged right hand.

What he had in mind was risky, messy and violent, but sometimes all three things were needed in his line of work.

He held his breath as the footsteps drew level with the door, closed his eyes for a moment and tried to focus his thoughts, tried to imagine the correct sequence of events playing out in his mind. Tried to imagine himself not getting killed.

The two men carried on past without breaking stride.

This was it. Gripping the hatchet, he rounded the doorway and advanced into the corridor beyond. As he'd thought, there were two of them, both dressed in civilian clothes; one in a leather jacket and jeans, the other in dark trousers and a fur-lined overcoat. Both were big men, about Drake's height, and heavier than him, judging by their bulked-out frames. Heavier usually meant stronger, which wasn't good news in his current condition.

Still, there was no time to contemplate this now. Picking the man on the right, Drake took two steps towards him and swung the hatchet in a fast, hard strike, aiming for the base of his skull. His aim was good, and the keen steel edge easily cut through the collar of his jacket, and the skin and muscle beneath, to shatter the vertebrae of his neck and sever his spinal cord.

An injury like that doesn't leave much margin for error. He jerked once as if stunned by an electric shock, then his legs buckled beneath him and he fell without a sound. If he hadn't been killed outright by such a violent blow to the head, he'd be dead from blood loss within a matter of minutes.

Drake immediately forced any thoughts of compassion or mercy from his mind as he yanked the hatchet free. It was a rotten way to kill a man, but this was not a situation in which fair play would be rewarded. He couldn't control two prisoners by himself. At least now the odds were even.

Alerted by the crunch of axe meeting skull, his companion whirled around, drawing a pistol from inside his leather jacket. Drake was half a second ahead of him, getting in close and smacking his forearm hard with the flat of the hatchet. He didn't want to sever the limb – he needed the man alive for now – but he had to take that weapon out of play before it became a threat.

There was a dull thump as the hatchet once again struck its target, and Drake's adversary let out a snarl of pain as the weapon fell from his grip. A kick to the back of his knees dropped him to the ground, and before he could recover, Drake had jammed the barrel of the PPK against the side of his head.

'Don't move,' he warned.

His new friend got the message. A pistol held against one's head was a wonderfully persuasive argument.

Backing off a pace, Drake planted a firm kick between his shoulder blades that sent him sprawling face first on the rough stone floor. He knew better than to resist as Drake pulled his arms behind his back and used the cuffs that he'd only recently escaped from to secure his wrists. Unlike himself, this man didn't have Anya around to provide a key.

With his prisoner secure, Drake crossed the hallway and retrieved the fallen weapon. Unlike the PPK, this one was a six-shooter; a Smith & Wesson .38 calibre. The sort of gun wielded by Chicago cops in the Prohibition era.

Revolvers like this were popular for home defence because they could be left loaded for long periods of time, unlike automatics whose magazine springs gradually lost their tension. A .38 revolver certainly wasn't the kind of weapon Drake wanted to go into combat with, but it was still a gun, and better in his hands than his new friend's.

Shoving the weapon down the front of his jeans, he returned to the prisoner, gripped him by the shoulders and rolled him over on to his back. As Drake had thought, he was a big man, his neck thick and bullish, his chest and shoulders bulked up by heavy weight training. His face was broad and square, his hair shaved right down to the scalp, his nose flattened as if he'd once been a boxer who favoured blocking punches with his head.

'Speak English?' he demanded.

The man in the leather jacket said nothing, apparently weighing up what to do. Still, the fact that he hadn't spoken at all gave Drake the impression that he understood.

Drake pressed the PPK against his forehead. 'Let me try that again. If you don't speak English, you're no good to me. And you end up like your mate on the floor there. Now, do you speak English?'

He saw the broad face twist in disgust. 'Yes.'

'Where's the female FSB agent?'

The big man nodded over Drake's shoulder. 'That way.'

Hope surged up inside Drake, but he knew he couldn't allow it to override caution. His new best friend might be trying to lead him into a trap.

'Here's the deal. Take me to her, and you get to stay alive. Sound good?'

He was silent for a moment. 'Yes.'

'Thought so,' Drake remarked, hauling him upright.

Miranova backed away from the door at the unmistakable sound of footsteps approaching. She had managed to loop her cuffed hands beneath her feet to get them in front of her, but otherwise she had little means of defending herself.

The steps had halted outside her door. She backed up against the wall, listening to the gritty rasp as the bolt was withdrawn from the other side, followed by the squeal of stiff hinges.

The door swung open, and she watched a squat, bulky figure stagger into the room, only to be struck from behind to fall forwards, landing face down on the concrete floor. It was then that she noticed his unnatural posture; the way his arms were pinned behind his back. Glancing down, she saw the metallic gleam of cuffs around his wrists.

'Anika!' a voice hissed.

Looking up, she let out a strangled gasp as she found herself face to face with Drake. One look at him was enough to confirm that, even though he was still very much alive, he'd been in the wars since their last encounter. His face was cut and bruised, his clothes filthy and torn, and it looked as though someone had bitten a chunk out of his neck. Blood gleamed in the wan light from the corridor.

'Ryan, what happened to you?' she breathed. 'How did you get out?'

'A little help from a friend.' Reaching into his pocket, he produced a key and set to work on her cuffs. 'The woman in the surveillance footage from Grozny. She gave me this.'

'She helped you escape?'

Drake nodded, though he avoided her gaze as he removed the cuffs and tossed them aside. Once more she thought about his words to Kamarov during the attempted ambush on Poklonnaya Hill. Both men were somehow connected to this target.

'You know her,' she said, phrasing it as the statement it was. 'How?'

'All I know is she helped me when she didn't have to. That counts for something in my book. The rest we can get into when this is over.' Pulling a revolver from his jeans, he thrust it into her hand. 'Here, a little Christmas present. I'd prefer if you didn't use it on me.'

She looked at him dubiously. 'Not much firepower.'

'It's what you do with it that counts. Come on, we have to move.'

He glanced into the cell she'd been occupying. The big man who had led him here was lying face down on the floor, though his chest was still rising and falling. He'd have quite a headache when he woke up, but he'd live.

Stepping aside, he swung the door back into place and pulled the bolt over to lock it shut. Their friend wasn't going anywhere.

'What is our situation?' Miranova asked, glancing down the corridor with the snub-nosed revolver at the ready.

'Shit, but possibly improving,' he admitted. 'The man behind this thing is called Atayev. He reckons Masalsky and the others were part of a plot to bring Viktor Surovsky into power, and he's out to punish them for it.' Reaching into his pocket, Drake held up the cellphone he'd taken from Yuri. 'My people are on their way. All we have to do is keep Atayev busy until they get here.'

'And do you have any idea how to do that?'

'Fuck, no. I'm making this up as I go along,' he admitted. 'Just stay close to me and keep your eyes open.'

'That is sound advice at any time.'

He grinned and nodded to the far end of the corridor. 'Let's go.'

They were going up. If Atayev was still here, they had to keep him busy long enough for McKnight to get here. And somehow, Drake had to find a way to stop Anya getting killed in the crossfire.

Chapter 62

'This is it!' Pushkin yelled, gesturing to a big eighteen-wheel heavy-haulage truck rumbling along the main highway just ahead of them, watery slush churned up by its passage spraying across the roadside.

'Force it over,' Kamarov ordered.

Accelerating hard, their driver brought them around in front of the massive vehicle and switched on his lights and sirens. A second car took up position on its left, while a third hovered close behind, boxing it in. The trailing car had orders to open fire on the truck's wheels if the driver attempted to ram them off the road.

However, no such thing happened. Straight away the truck driver hit his brakes and began to slow, veering right on to the loose gravel that lined the highway before coming to a complete halt.

The moment they stopped, Pushkin and a second tactical agent in the car were out and moving, their sub-machine guns trained on the truck's cab and the terrified-looking driver inside. He had already killed the vehicle's massive engine, and raised his hands to show he was unarmed.

Drawing his side arm, Kamarov hurried towards the rear of the vehicle, flanked by a pair of armed agents. Two more were converging on the big doors at the back, one of them already clambering up to secure a breaching charge to the door lock.

Giving Kamarov a nod, he leapt down and retreated a few paces, while two of his companions lingered by the doors, ready to act when the time came. Kamarov held back, bracing himself for the blast.

It came two seconds later. Sounding more like a rifle crack than an explosive boom, the small breaching charge nonetheless did its job with ruthless efficiency, blasting apart the locking mechanism as if it were cardboard.

Wasting no time, the two agents by the rear sprang into action, with one hauling open the smouldering remains of the door while the second hurled a flashbang grenade inside.

A second sharp crack echoed from within as the grenade detonated.

'Move in!' Kamarov ordered.

Once again the doors were hauled open, with a trio of sub-machine guns and flashlights now trained on the interior. It took Kamarov all of three seconds to realise they weren't going to find what they were looking for here.

'Goddamn it,' he said under his breath as he surveyed the empty cargo container.

Turning aside, he strode back towards the vehicle's cab. The driver, a squat, balding man in his sixties, had been hauled out and now sat on his knees by the side of the road, shivering in the cold breeze. His gaze flicked from the pair of sub-machine guns covering him, to the agent now approaching.

'What's your name?' Kamarov demanded.

'Oleg Ryumin.'

'And where are you taking this truck?'

'To Noginsk. I've just dropped off my load in Moscow.' His eyes, wide and pleading, stared into Kamarov's. 'What have I done wrong? I have all my documents and licences. I've broken no laws.'

This man was going to give him nothing. Whatever else he might have been, he was no terrorist.

He looked at Pushkin. 'You're certain this is the truck?'

The younger man nodded, still covering the driver with his weapon. 'Our tracking system is locked in. Drake is here.'

At a loss, Kamarov looked around him in search of answers. It wasn't until he saw the ladder fixed into the steel side of the cargo container that he began to get an inkling of what might have happened.

Holstering his weapon, he strode over to it and clambered up. The cold of the frozen steel seemed to cut right through his gloves, but nonetheless he made it up on to the roof without incident.

The top of the container was much like the sides – corrugated-steel panels built on top of internal ribs for structural strength. With no cargo to weigh it down, the whole assembly flexed a little every time another large vehicle thundered past on the main highway.

Squinting against the cold wind and the spray kicked up by passing vehicles, Kamarov glanced about him, searching for anything out of the ordinary.

It didn't take him long to find it.

Lying about halfway back from the cab was a lump of clay-like substance about the size of his fist. It was stuck to the metal surface of the container, having no doubt been thrown down from a bridge or overpass.

Hurrying over, he knelt down beside it, drew a small knife from his pocket and used it to slice the lump of material open.

And there, hidden within, was a little metal cylinder no larger than a grain of rice.

A few moments later, Kamarov leapt down from the truck and immediately headed towards the Merc a short distance away.

'Pack it up. We're leaving!' he announced, visibly brimming with anger.

Pushkin looked at him. 'What about Drake?'

The older man rounded on him. 'Drake's gone. They knew about the tracker and removed it. Now move!'

They were getting close, Drake knew as they ascended the cracked, worn set of stairs leading up from the building's basement. He could hear the distinctive rumble of the generator getting louder with each step. Miranova was following a few yards behind.

His head pounded, and he could feel blood leaking steadily from the wound at his shoulder, but he did his best to push through the pain to carry on. None of it mattered now. He had to keep going.

At last Drake reached the top of the stairs, eyes and weapon sweeping the shadowy recesses of the room beyond.

The place was a shambles. Broken office furniture had been smashed against one wall, while electrical cables had been torn down from the ceiling to hang like vines across the gloomy hallway. A big industrial heating unit, now rusted and decayed, was lying in the middle of the floor as if someone had simply dropped it in the middle of carrying it away.

However, the sound of the generator was noticeably louder now, and he could see the glow of lights coming from beyond the doorway on the other side of the room. Making his way through the debris with Miranova close behind, he crossed the derelict office, backed up beside the doorway and leaned out far enough to survey the space beyond.

Straight away he knew they had found what they were looking for.

The office faced out on to a wide-open area easily 50 feet

high and twice as wide. It looked as though it had once served as the building's main storage and delivery area. Steel girders supported the vaulted ceiling high above, beams of dusty light shining down from rooftop windows to illuminate the scene below.

A big set of steel double doors on one side provided vehicle access, while a second set off to the right apparently allowed boats to load and offload their cargo inside the warehouse itself. A long canal had been excavated down one side of the room leading from those doors, its dark oily water shimmering in the glow of work lights. Clearly this building was right on the shores of the river, designed to admit barges for loading and unloading cargo.

However, whatever goods or materials had once been stored here had long since vanished, replaced by a couple of panel vans parked near the main doors. Both were painted brown and dressed up in UPS livery. Around the vans were six or seven men, many of them armed. Drake saw AK-47 assault rifles, grenades and body armour laid out on a table near the vans – tools of the trade for the assault team who had kidnapped himself and Miranova.

And in the centre of it all was Atayev, standing over a younger man who seemed to be engrossed in the laptop he was working over. A laptop which was connected up to a satellite transmitter – Drake could see the distinctive umbrella-shaped dish pointing skywards.

'That's Atayev,' he whispered, nodding to the leader of the operation.

Miranova slithered along the wall next to him and leaned out, her keen mind quickly assessing the situation. It didn't take her long to recognise the problems they faced.

'We will not win in a firefight,' she remarked dubiously.

Drake had to admit she was right. With only two side arms

to call upon, they were hardly in a position to storm in, guns blazing. They needed backup, and fast.

He was just reaching for the cellphone in his pocket when another figure strode into view, heading straight for Atayev.

It was Anya.

Chapter 63

The warehouse was a hive of activity as Anya made her way across the wide-open space, with armed men moving back and forth, packing away gear and loading it into the pair of trucks they would use to escape Moscow. They had both been painted brown and adorned with the UPS delivery-service logo, providing an ideal cover for Atayev's men.

Only one computer was still up and running: the master terminal on which a skinny, scruffy-looking young man with spiked hair and a face full of metal piercings was working. It was he who had designed the program she'd uploaded into the FSB's computer network less than an hour ago, providing a back door through their formidable security system that he could exploit.

She had no idea where Atayev had recruited him from, but one look at him was enough to confirm that he didn't belong in her world. He was a cyber terrorist for hire, more used to wielding a keyboard than a gun. There were many like him these days, particularly in Russia where competition amongst rival companies was fierce and ruthless. Knowing a competitor's secrets could mean the difference between monopoly and bankruptcy.

'The program is working perfectly,' Atayev announced, having been standing over the hacker's shoulder. 'Tell her, Dmitry.'

The young man glanced up from the laptop, his eyes glassy as if he'd been focusing on the screen too long.

'I'm through the firewall and into their core system,' he said, speaking in a fast, jittery manner. By the looks of him, he'd overindulged in caffeine today, or most likely something far stronger. 'Five, six minutes from now I'll release a virus that'll trigger a network lockdown. Instead of protecting them, it'll seize control of their system and shut them out, turn their own security protocols against them.'

'As soon as their security is down, we'll broadcast the access protocol to every hacker and media website on the Internet,' Atayev said. 'Soon the whole world will know the FSB's secrets.'

Atayev's final blow against Surovsky and the FSB wouldn't be accomplished by force of arms, but by a far more insidious method. Rather than try to destroy them physically, he needed only to reveal the one thing they feared most of all – the truth.

But this prospect didn't please Anya as much as it did him. She could only imagine how many informants and operatives would die as a result of such a catastrophic breach in security. The repercussions of this cyber attack would make the raid in Grozny look like a minor skirmish by comparison. The entire organisation would be crippled for years to come.

'Then I'm finished here,' she decided. 'I came only to say goodbye.'

'Of course.' He offered a faint smile. 'I don't suppose you can tell me where you're going?'

'Better that you don't know,' she said honestly.

The older man nodded and held out his hand. 'Goodbye, Anya. And . . . good luck.'

Staring into his eyes, she caught herself wondering what was really going on behind them. Buran Atayev, the only one of them whose mind encompassed the entire plan, with all its interdependent elements, all its subtleties and misdirections. The only man whose intentions she could never quite read.

Releasing her grip, she turned her back on him and walked away, knowing this would be the last time they spoke. She had what she needed now, and so did he. Whether it was worth all the sacrifices, all the risks and dangers and betrayals, only time would tell.

As she walked away, Anya found her thoughts straying from Atayev and his lust for vengeance. Instead she thought of Drake, the man who had been her saviour, her protector, her redemption.

Betraying his trust had been the hardest sacrifice of all.

Anya was walking away from Atayev, her posture and body language suggesting that whatever business she had with the man, it had apparently concluded.

A moment of hope rose within him. Perhaps she was putting all this behind her. Perhaps there was still a way out of this for them both.

And then it all changed.

Staring in shocked disbelief, Drake watched as Atayev drew a pistol from his belt, calmly levelled it at Anya's back and fired a single shot.

The report of the gunshot echoed around the vast space like a thunderclap, so loud that even he started and recoiled from the doorway in horror. But still he could see the terrible scene playing out.

Anya jerked once as the round impacted, then stumbled and fell forwards, landing face down in a pool of oily water. She struggled feebly, trying to rise, trying to force her body to work even as her life blood flowed out, turning the pool crimson.

Always the soldier, she was trying to fight even now.

Approaching with slow, measured deliberation, Atayev kicked her over on to her back, raised the weapon and fired a second shot into her, finally ending her struggle.

Just like that, it was over. Anya was gone.

Drake fell to his knees as if the round had blasted its way through his own chest, tearing apart everything in its path. His breath was coming in short gasps, his eyes wide and staring, his hands trembling as shock took hold.

It wasn't possible. It was terrible, horrific; a nightmare made real.

The world around him ceased to matter in that moment, everything else fading into darkness. All he could see was Anya's lifeless body sprawled in that pool of dirty water, and the man who had killed her.

He watched as Atayev took a step back, making way for two of his men who moved forwards and picked Anya up, one taking her feet and the other her hands. Together they carried the unwieldy burden over to the canal, swung her once to build momentum and then pitched her in.

Drake heard the loud splash as her body impacted the water.

Watching without emotion as Anya's body slipped beneath the surface, Atayev replaced his pistol in the holster at the small of his back. It wasn't a fitting departure for a woman of her worth, but Anya had served her purpose. He had no further need of her, and felt no regret at seeing her go.

With the unpleasant task complete, he turned to address the others.

'We're done here,' he announced. 'Pack everything up.'

The rest of his group moved with quick efficiency, tossing the body armour and remaining grenades into the canal.

Just as with Anya, they had no further need of these instruments of war. They had all abandoned their assault gear now, instead donning civilian clothes to aid their escape.

Two of his men were dressed in brown jackets, shirts and trousers; playing the part of truck drivers. Details were important, and Atayev had always been a man who paid attention to detail.

Both men now hurried towards their respective vehicles, clambered up into the cabs and fired up the engines, while another two strode over to the main doors and unlocked them.

In a minute or two they would be out of here.

Drake had seen enough.

Shock and grief had given way to something else entirely now. Something far more dangerous and destructive. Cold, focused, absolute hatred.

Raising the PPK, he pulled back the slide far enough to check that a round was chambered, then rose to his feet. He was no longer thinking of tactics or survival, or the practicalities of their situation. All he wanted was Atayev. No matter what happened to him, no way was that fucker getting out of this building alive.

Abandoning his cover, he strode out through the door and towards the group now preparing to leave. He gave no thought to concealment or protection. He just wanted to cover as much ground as possible before the shooting started.

Beyond the trucks, the big wooden doors barring the warehouse entrance had been hauled open to reveal a stretch of open waste ground partitioned off by a chain-link fence. Drake could just make out the dark waters of the Moskva River in the distance.

'Ryan, what are you doing?' Miranova hissed. 'Ryan, come back here!'

He wasn't hearing her. He wasn't aware of anything now but the pounding of his heart, the surging blood in his veins, the desperate lust for revenge that had taken over every muscle, every bone, every fibre of his being.

He had made it about halfway across the room before one of them spotted him. A big man with tattoos covering his exposed arms, he opened his mouth to cry out a warning to his companions.

He never got the chance. Raising the PPK, Drake took aim and put two rounds through his head, blasting apart his skull with the twin impacts. The echo of the gunshots caused the rest of the group to flinch and glance around, seeking the source of the unexpected new threat.

Drake took full advantage of their hesitation, and a second man fell as he capped off the remainder of his magazine at his centre mass. At least one of the rounds found its mark, tearing through his unprotected gut. With blood painting the front of his grey sweater, he crumpled and fell, crying out in agony.

Drake could feel something stinging his eyes, blurring his vision, and angrily blinked to try to clear it. In some part of his mind he was aware that it was tears, but he tried not to acknowledge it as he focused all his attention on the desperate battle unfolding around him.

Without breaking stride, he thumbed the magazine eject button on the side of his weapon, jerking the gun downwards to aid the movement. No sooner had the spent clip fallen free of the housing than he grabbed a spare one from his pocket and slammed it home.

But his delay had bought his opponents a precious second or two to react, and even as Drake released the breach lock and allowed the PPK's slide to snap forwards, he spotted a figure moving through the shadows between two support pillars. The man emerged from his cover and into a beam of sunlight slanting down from above, and Drake saw the long, bulky frame of an AK-47 being raised.

Straight away Drake knew the man had the drop on him. He wouldn't be able to bring his side arm to bear in time, and even if he could, it was certainly no match for the raw firepower of an AK on full automatic. His brief, foolhardy attempt at heroism was about to end the only way such things could – with his death.

He felt merely a fleeting sense of disappointment that his attempt to avenge Anya's death, however misplaced, had ended so abruptly. Deep down he knew the woman would be disappointed in him.

But then, instead of the distinctive bark of AK fire, several sharp cracks resounded through the warehouse, and suddenly Drake's would-be killer staggered backwards and fell.

In disbelief, Drake glanced around to see Miranova advancing across the open space towards him, the revolver in her hand as she snapped off a couple more shots at Atayev and the several men still with him.

'Cover!' she yelled, sprinting the last few yards and gripping his arm, practically hauling him towards a brick wall that had once formed part of a smaller room within the larger space of the warehouse.

It wasn't a moment too soon. Two of Atayev's men dropped to their knees and opened up on full automatic, spraying a hail of 7.62mm slugs at them.

'Get down!' Miranova shouted, throwing herself on the ground. The wall was constructed from breeze blocks and mortar, easily 3 inches thick, but the AK rounds coming their way were more than capable of punching straight through at such range.

Drake could feel chunks of broken masonry pelting him as

a burst of fire traced its way along the wall mere feet away, blasting apart the concrete blocks that stood in its path.

Raising his head up, Drake jammed the barrel of the PPK into one of the ragged holes in the brickwork and squeezed off several rounds in the general direction of their enemies, more to keep their heads down than a serious attempt to kill them.

'Get out of here!' he shouted. 'Fall back. I'll cover you.'

'Shut up!' she yelled back, clenching her fist and punching his arm as hard as she could. 'I'm trying to stop you getting killed, you stupid bastard!'

The woman's harsh but true words were like a mental slap in the face, and Drake hesitated, seeing his ill-judged actions for what they were.

Having vented her anger for the time being, she rolled over on to her back and snapped open the revolver's cylinder to empty the spent cartridges, still smoking from recent use, then reached into her pocket to reload as more shots tore through the wall around them.

Then, abruptly, the firing ceased, replaced instead by frantic shouting, the roar of vehicle engines and the squeal of tyres on concrete.

For Drake, the reason was obvious – they were pulling out.

Rising up from behind the shattered remnants of the brick wall, he surveyed the scene in the warehouse. The first van was roaring towards the open doorway, its tyres screeching on the concrete floor as the driver gunned the engine hard. The second was also on the move, veering left to get in behind the first. Drake could do nothing but watch as Atayev and the remainder of his group escaped.

The first van shot out through the doors and into the open space beyond, turning hard left to head towards what Drake assumed was an access road away from the docks.

Then something happened that none of them had expected. Just as the van was coming out of its turn, a black BMW roared into view, skidding to a stop right in its path. A moment later, the driver and passenger threw open their doors and leapt out. A man and a woman, both armed with sub-machine guns.

Straight away Drake recognised McKnight and Mason, with Frost's diminutive frame appearing just behind them. In a storm of automatic fire, all three of them opened up on the first van, spraying the cab and windshield with enough shots to kill the driver a dozen times over.

Knowing it would be suicidal to venture outside with such firepower opposing them, the driver of the second van jammed on his brakes, bringing his vehicle screeching to a halt before reaching the doors.

Even as this was happening, the van's rear door flew open and three men jumped down, trying to make a break for it by running in different directions.

One was the young man with the spiky hair, still clutching his laptop computer. His eyes were wild with fear as he sprinted left with no apparent plan beyond getting as far from the shooting as possible.

The other two were Atayev himself and one of his group – a middle-aged man with long greasy hair tied back in a ponytail. He was clutching a Skorpion 61 – a nasty little Czechoslovakian sub-machine gun designed for concealed carrying.

He and his accomplice were making for a doorway off to the right of the main warehouse, keeping low to avoid fire from outside. Drake had no idea where it led, and he wasn't keen on finding out.

Raising the PPK, he took careful aim at ponytail man and fired.

Hitting a moving target with an unfamiliar weapon is no easy feat, but Drake had always been a good shot and his aim didn't let him down today. Ponytail man staggered sideways as the round slammed into him and fell in a crumpled heap, his greasy hair now matted with blood and brain tissue.

Reacting to the threat, Atayev spun around, levelled his weapon at Drake and opened fire. But he was no soldier, and it showed. He might have been able to hit Anya at point-blank range, but at 20 yards his lack of either training or accuracy was telling.

Still, even an amateur could score a lucky hit, and Drake was forced to duck behind one of the steel support pillars until the brief volley had ended. No way was he risking being brought down by a stray shot when he was so close to his enemy.

As soon as the firing had ceased, Drake glanced out in time to see Atayev disappear through the doorway. With his heart hammering in his chest, Drake took off in pursuit, determined to end this now.

Outside, the three Shepherd operatives were pushing forwards into the warehouse, spread out in a loose offensive line. There were only three of them, but what they lacked in numbers they made up for in skill and experience.

'Two o'clock!' Frost yelled, turning her weapon towards the cab of the second van. The driver had thrown open his door and was using it as a shield while he opened fire on them.

McKnight was in no mood for negotiating with the man, and promptly levelled her MP5 sub-machine gun at his unprotected legs. A single burst took out both knees, dropping him.

'Get him!' she cried, continuing her advance as Frost hurried over to disarm the injured man.

Nearby, Mason spotted a young man sprinting off towards the rear of the warehouse, moving with long, loping bounds that reminded him of an ungainly gazelle. Bizarrely, he seemed to be clutching a computer rather than a gun.

'Stop!' he yelled, taking off in pursuit.

However, no sooner had the young man reached the shadowy archways that ran along both sides of the room than a second figure emerged from the darkness, grabbing his skinny frame and spinning him around in front to form a human shield as he drew down on Mason.

Mason could feel the world going into slow motion as he raised his weapon and took aim. In a flash he replayed that sickening moment in the rifle range at Langley, when he'd missed his target and realised his hopes of returning to field ops had been dashed. It seemed like a lifetime ago now.

Adjusting his aim, he exhaled slowly, allowing the tension to leave his body, then squeezed off a single shot.

The would-be hostage-taker jerked once as the round slammed into his skull, then went down as only a victim of a catastrophic gunshot wound could, jerking and thrashing as the remnants of his brain misfired. His weight had pulled the skinny young man down with him.

Still covering him, Mason hurried over and kicked the dying man aside to reveal the computer hacker beneath. He was curled into a ball, weeping and moaning in pain. There was a steaming puddle beneath him that hadn't been there a few seconds earlier.

'Mason!' a familiar voice cried out.

Still keeping his weapon at the ready, Mason glanced left as Frost came running over to join him.

'You okay?' she asked, breathless after the brief firefight outside.

He nodded, surprised by the rush of adrenalin now surging through him. 'I'm good.'

He thought he saw a fleeting smile on the young woman's face, though it soon vanished as she looked around.

'Where's Ryan?'

Atayev might have had a head start, but he was a decade older than Drake and considerably out of shape. He could hear the rasp of the man's laboured breathing and the heavy thump of his footfalls even as he vaulted up the stairs in pursuit.

As he had soon discovered, the doorway that Atayev had fled through opened out into a stairwell that apparently led all the way up to the roof. But wherever the man was trying to flee to, Drake would ensure he didn't make it.

His own lungs were heaving, the muscles in his legs burning as he leapt up the stairs, taking them two at a time, but he ignored it. Pain was irrelevant to him now. Adrenalin and sheer unfettered lust for revenge drove him on with more strength than any drug.

Again and again he saw Anya stumble and fall forwards as the round slammed into her back. He saw her trying feebly to rise, defiant to the end. He saw Atayev raise his weapon and fire a second time.

He heard the squeal of a door being thrown open just above, the laboured breathing of his opponent suddenly vanishing as he fled outside. With a final burst of strength and speed, Drake ascended the last flight of steps, raised his foot and kicked the rusted steel door open.

As he'd thought, the doorway provided access to the warehouse's gently sloping roof, probably for maintaining the rows of skylights that ran down both sides of the apex. Above them, the grey clouds that had lingered over the city in the early morning had parted, revealing snatches of blue sky and thin winter sun that struggled through.

And there, not 15 yards away, was Atayev. Unable to manage more than a breathless stagger after the hard climb, he had halted altogether at the sound of the door being thrown open, perhaps realising the futility of his situation.

He was still clutching an automatic in his hand – the same gun with which he'd callously murdered Anya – but the slide had flown back to reveal an empty breech. The weapon was out of ammunition.

'Drop it.'

Hesitating a moment, Atayev looked down at the weapon and threw it aside. It skidded and slid down the roof before coming to rest in the guttering some way below.

'Turn around.' Drake wanted him to see it coming, wanted to look him in the eye when he pulled the trigger.

Slowly Atayev turned to face him, raising his hands as he did so. His face was red and sweaty after the hard climb up here, but otherwise he betrayed no emotion at seeing the weapon pointed at him.

For a long moment, neither man said a word. They simply remained like that, staring at each other across the open roof.

'Answer me one thing, Ryan Drake,' Atayev said at last. 'Did you mean what you said earlier, about wanting to help me take down Surovsky?'

Drake could feel his throat tightening. A lot of things had changed since then. 'I did.'

The older man nodded, seemingly satisfied with that. He reached up to straighten his glasses, preparing himself for what was coming.

'If you are going to do it, you should do it now. Before your friends arrive.'

Drake stared at him down the weapon's sights. At this

range he could scarcely miss. One shot was all it would take. One pull of the trigger and Anya's death would be avenged.

Atayev deserved it, he told himself. He deserved to die for what he'd done.

'Ryan,' a soft, quiet voice said. 'Ryan, lower the gun. Please.'

It was Miranova. She had followed him to the roof and now stood by his side, covering Atayev with her own weapon. Her attention, however, was focused on Drake.

'This man deserves to be punished for his crimes, but it must be done the right way,' she implored him. 'Don't become like him.'

Drake could feel tears stinging his eyes again as his finger tightened on the trigger. Images of Anya's cold-blooded murder flashed before his eyes, for ever imprinted on his mind.

Then suddenly, he remembered his actions in the warehouse below, his reckless disregard for his own life as he rushed for his enemy. He remembered the feeling of shame and disappointment, knowing that his own death would do nothing to avenge hers.

And just like that, he lowered the gun.

Atayev smiled as if in amusement as Miranova moved forwards, grabbing his arms and yanking them behind his back to restrain him.

'Remember today,' Drake advised him. 'It's the last time you'll ever see daylight.'

Atayev said nothing. But he still wore that same knowing, almost gloating smile even as he was led away.

Chapter 64

An hour later, Drake winced as a medic finished applying the field dressing to the wound at his neck. He was perched on the back of an ambulance parked outside the warehouse, with police cars and FSB vehicles all around. The entire area had been cordoned off while forensics teams pored over it.

His broken finger had been splinted, and the incision on his arm where the tracking device had been crudely removed was now stitched and dressed. He'd even been given some pills for the pain. All things considered he was in far better shape than he'd been a few hours before, physically at least.

The constant pressure, lack of sleep, and the various emotional highs and lows of the past couple of days had taken their toll on him. Over and over his mind replayed his final sight of Anya as her body was hurled callously into the canal like so much discarded rubbish. He knew it was a scene he'd be revisiting many times in the days and weeks ahead.

Even now he could scarcely believe it had happened, that her life had ended in such a pointless, empty death at the hands of a man who could barely handle a weapon. A man who had used and discarded her as so many others had done.

'You keep the wound clean. Change dressing every day,' the medic advised, finishing up her work. She slapped his hand away as he reached up to touch the wound. 'And don't scratch the stitches.'

Drake was poised to retort, then thought better of it. The medic was in her fifties, stoutly built and not about to take any shit from the likes of him. Instead he merely nodded in gratitude as she packed up her case.

No sooner had she left than a familiar voice spoke up.

'Well, aren't you a sorry-looking piece of shit?'

Drake looked up as Mason walked over to join him, with Frost and McKnight right behind. They too had had questions to answer from the FSB, starting with what exactly a CIA team were doing mounting an armed raid in Russian territory, barely 2 miles from the Kremlin. However, Miranova had been quick to deflect the attention away from them, pointing out that they had been instrumental in the capture of Russia's most wanted man.

For a moment Drake just sat there looking at the three teammates, the three *friends*, who had journeyed halfway around the world for him, who had believed in him, who had risked their lives to help him. The thanks he owed them went far beyond words.

Echoing Mason's light-hearted remark, he managed to summon up a defiant grin. 'Better than looking like shit every day.'

The older man shrugged. 'Wouldn't know.'

Despite his apparent indifference, Drake could tell he was enjoying the banter that had once flowed so easily between the two of them. And in part of his mind, he found himself missing it too.

'I would,' Frost cut in, giving Drake the harsh look of a teacher about to discipline a wayward student. Considering she was normally on the receiving end of such rebukes, Drake couldn't help wondering whether she relished the prospect. 'In the past two days I've gone from freezing my ass off in Siberia, to getting it shot off in Moscow. Next time you have one of these bright ideas, remind me to punch you in advance.'

Rising up from his makeshift seat, Drake took a step towards the young woman, staring down at her with hard, intense eyes. Then, without warning he reached out and embraced her tight, lifting her small frame right off the ground.

'Goddamn it, put me down or I really will punch you!' she warned, though he couldn't help noticing that a blush had risen to her face once he let go. 'You're just lucky you're already hurt.'

Deciding to let that one pass, Drake turned his attention to Mason. The man had joined the team under less than auspicious circumstances, and had certainly caused him to doubt the wisdom of his decision more than once, but had come through for him when it mattered most.

Just as he'd said when they were sitting in Drake's cramped office back at Langley, Cole Mason could still do his job in the field. Drake saw him through different eyes now.

'I was wrong about you, mate,' he said, unafraid to admit it. 'I want you to know that. Back at Langley . . . you were right, and I was wrong. And I'm sorry.'

Mason raised an eyebrow. 'Well, holy shit. Ryan Drake admitting he's wrong . . . Might have to buy myself a lottery ticket tonight.'

'You do that. But . . . don't go job-hunting any time soon,' Drake advised him. 'When you're ready, there's a place on my team for you.'

For a moment, the older man said and did nothing at all. Drake's words had caught him so off guard that his usual dry humour had deserted him. He wasn't even able to muster a response.

It was a conditional offer, but a genuine one. If Mason was

to be reinstated to the active duty roster, it would have to be without the painkillers, without props or aids of any kind. He would be expected to stand or fall on his own merits.

'What, and go through shit like this again?' Mason managed to flash a playful grin, but nonetheless Drake could see the emotion in his eyes. His offer meant more to the man than he'd ever know. It was a second chance – and those didn't come along very often.

His smile fading, Mason reached out and clasped Drake's hand. Drake could have sworn he saw the glint of moisture in his eyes. 'Wouldn't miss it for the world, buddy.'

'About Anya,' Frost said, looking quieter and subdued now. Her usual cocky bravado had deserted her. 'Is it true? Is she really . . . gone?'

Drake's face darkened. He hesitated, as if reluctant to admit it even to himself, but finally he nodded in grim acceptance.

To his surprise, he saw a momentary look of sadness pass over the young woman. 'I'm sorry, Ryan. I know you were . . .' She trailed off, a deep blush rising to her face.

'It was quick,' Drake said, hoping to spare her further embarrassment. 'She would have wanted it that way.'

Swallowing, Frost merely nodded.

Last of all Drake turned his attention to McKnight. Of all his companions, she was the one he wanted to speak to most, yet hers was also the conversation he would find hardest. They each had a lot of things they'd left unsaid for too long.

'Would you mind giving us a minute?' he asked, glancing at his two teammates.

Mason and Frost exchanged a look, their thoughts obvious.

'Want to grab a coffee or something?' Mason suggested with a wry smile, hoping to lighten the mood.

Frost didn't need much prompting. 'I'd settle for a beer.'

'Only if you're buying.'

'Screw you, Cole.'

The playful argument continued as the two of them walked off together, looking more at ease than they had since their reunion in DC several days earlier.

As soon as they were out of earshot Drake turned his attention back to the woman before him. For several seconds, he just stood there not knowing what to say, how to begin. He had held it together for the sake of his teammates, not wanting to burden them with his own grief and regrets, but now he felt like a dam straining to burst.

Sensing his need, McKnight made the first move; she walked forwards and put her arms around him in a firm but gentle embrace.

That was it for him. The emotion, the tension, the doubts and fears and betrayals and grief and sadness that were churning just beneath the surface of his mind at last broke through, and he closed his eyes, clinging to her as tears began to flow down his cheeks.

'It's okay,' he heard her whisper in his ear, her own voice close to breaking. 'It's okay, Ryan. I know.'

Drake could say nothing as he held her. He could do nothing for the next few seconds but let out everything he'd tried so hard to suppress. And at last he grieved for Anya; the woman who had touched his life so profoundly, but who had remained always an enigma to him.

'I'm sorry, Sam,' he said, wiping his eyes as he finally let go.

'Christ, you don't have to apologise for this,' she promised him. 'Ryan, after everything you've—'

He shook his head. 'I don't mean this. I mean . . . the things that happened before.' He looked at her frankly, his green eyes betraying the full depth of his regret. 'I'm sorry for shutting you out, Sam. For pushing you away, for not trusting you when I should have. It was a mistake, and it was my mistake.'

She said nothing in reply. She could sense that he had more to say, and was content to wait, content to let him find his own way of saying it.

'I know what you gave up to join us. I know what you left behind. You trusted me, you showed faith in me, and I let you down. I found excuses not to take you into the field because it was easier than telling you the truth. The truth is . . . I was afraid.'

'Afraid of what?'

Drake swallowed, trying to find the right way to say what he needed to. 'Afraid I'd lose you. Afraid you'd trust me with your life and I'd fail you.'

Only now did he realise how foolish he'd been. Only now did he see how his ill-judged attempts to protect her had only served to drive her away.

He sighed, letting out a breath that was still ragged from his outpouring of grief. 'I already lost one person I care about today. I can't do it again.'

For several seconds she just looked at him, her expression difficult to read. He didn't know if she was about to embrace him or slap him across the face.

Then at last her look softened a little. She sighed and took a step towards him. 'Ryan, look . . .' She swallowed, searching for the right words. 'I know what it means to do the job we do. I know there are no guarantees, and I accepted it a long time ago. I was putting my life at risk before I met you, and I'll probably do it again, because that's my life and my choice. You don't get to make it for me.'

She was speaking quietly, her voice measured and controlled, but there was a firmness in it too, a resolution to make him understand and accept how she felt.

'It's not any easier for me, you know,' she went on, looking into his eyes now. 'When you go out into the field. I know you might not come back, but I accept it because that's the decision you've made. I respect you enough to abide by that.' He felt her hand on his, warm and soft, her grip firm. 'All I want is the same from you, Ryan.'

She wouldn't back down on this, and if he was honest, he hadn't expected her to. But this was a conversation that had been coming for a long time. He'd needed to tell her how he felt, somehow make her understand what was holding him back.

She understood, she accepted it, but she wouldn't submit to it.

'All right,' he said at last, feeling as though a weight had been lifted somehow.

He saw her lips turn upwards in a smile. It was faint, tentative, but it was genuine. 'Good,' she said, the smile broadening. 'Because if you don't, I'll kick your sexist ass.'

Even Drake couldn't help but smile at that. It was just like her to make light of something like this.

'So where do we go from here?' she asked.

Drake looked over her shoulder, seeing another figure he recognised amongst the police and FSB agents hurrying back and forth. A woman, bruised and bloodied and dishevelled, her clothes ripped and torn, reminding him strangely enough of the first time he'd met her.

Miranova.

His momentary glimmer of good humour abated, the look in his eyes hardening with resolve as he thought about what she represented, the masters she served. And most of all, he thought of the man she'd taken into custody.

'I've got a few things I still need to sort out with the FSB,' he said, looking at McKnight again. 'You mind if I have a word with Miranova?'

McKnight's dark brows drew together in a frown. She had seen something in his eyes, something that left her with a sense of foreboding.

'You sure you're okay?'

He nodded, reached out and took her hand in his. 'I'll be fine. I just need to put this one to bed, Sam. I have to make sure it's done right.'

Hesitating a moment longer, she finally nodded acquiescence.

'I'll go round up Frost and Mason before they cause any more trouble,' she said, turning away. 'Just watch yourself, okay?'

Drake managed to catch Miranova's eye as he approached. She smiled a little in greeting, though the fatigue in her eyes was difficult to hide. She too had been in the wars over the past couple of days, and like him she was feeling every moment of it now.

'How are you feeling?' she asked, looking him up and down.

'Ready for Round Two,' he said, managing a weak smile. 'You?'

'I will pass on that.' She sighed and looked up at the warehouse, and the sunlight shining through broken cloud overhead. 'You saved my life, Ryan.'

Drake blinked, surprised at her sudden shift in tone.

Reaching out, she laid a hand on his and squeezed gently. 'You risked your life to get me out of there. I won't forget that. And I will make sure that you and your team have no trouble from us.'

Drake wasn't sure what to say, but somehow he didn't think he was worthy of her gratitude or her help. He had lied to her, used her, put her life at risk more than once over the past few days. If only she knew, she wouldn't be thanking him now.

Sensing she'd made him uncomfortable, she pulled her hand back. 'We recovered the computer from Atayev's technical expert,' she said, adopting a more businesslike tone. 'From what he has told us, they were planning to open up the FSB's computer systems to every hacker on the Internet. An attack like that would have crippled us for decades.'

'But it's safe now, right?'

She nodded. 'He proved very cooperative once we threatened him with life imprisonment. Everything he did has been undone.'

Drake sighed, reached into his pocket and held up the chess piece that Atayev had left with him. A pawn, its polished white surface glistening in the winter sunlight.

'Kind of makes you wonder, doesn't it?' Drake asked, staring at the piece.

'Wonder what?'

He turned his vivid green eyes on her. 'What they would have found.'

If Atayev had been right, if Beslan and the other terrorist attacks that had devastated Russia had indeed been orchestrated by the FSB, this might have been the only chance for the world to know the truth. And he had helped cover it up.

'I don't suppose we will ever know.'

'No,' Drake agreed. 'I don't suppose we will.'

Miranova decided to let that one pass. Drake had been through a lot over the past few days, and men under stress often said things they regretted later.

'We have divers in the canal looking for the woman's body,' she said instead. 'But it feeds directly into the Moskva River, and the currents are strong there. I'm afraid we may never find her.'

Drake merely nodded. He didn't think he could stand to

see Anya now anyway. Not like that. Perhaps it was better that she was lost to them.

Miranova glanced around and lowered her voice. 'I have to ask, Ryan. Who was she? Really, I mean?'

Drake looked up at her, his eyes reflecting the full depth of his loss. He knew things about her – snatches of information, camera flashes illuminating brief moments of her life – but the woman behind it all had always been a mystery to him. He had hoped one day to learn the truth, to somehow find a way through the layers of armour she had built around herself.

Not now.

'I don't know,' he said at last.

Sensing he would say no more on the subject, Miranova wisely decided to let it drop. 'For what it is worth, I'm sorry things worked out the way they did.'

'Yeah,' Drake said, slipping the pawn back into his pocket. 'Yeah, me too.'

'What will you do now?' she asked. 'Go back to Langley?'

Perhaps, though Franklin's earlier suggestion about parting company with the Agency still weighed on his mind. If he did return to Langley, there would be repercussions from this ill-judged foray into Russia. Repercussions he might never recover from.

But that was a question for another day. There was something he had to finish first.

'I want to speak to Atayev,' he said. 'Before I leave. I want to debrief him.'

Miranova looked dubious, as well she might. 'After what he did, I'm not sure that is—'

'I have to do this, Anika,' he persisted. 'I have to know the truth. You understand, don't you?'

She was silent for a long moment, clearly torn about what

to do. Her logical, pragmatic mind would be telling her it was unwise to allow an exhausted, injured and emotionally volatile man access to a suspect like Atayev. But there was no denying the debt of gratitude she owed him.

Finally she nodded.

'I will speak to my superiors,' she said, and for a moment he saw a flicker of amusement in her dark eyes. 'They may even want to speak with you. After all, you are the hero who brought Atayev down. You may find yourself a popular man in Moscow now.'

Drake raised an eyebrow. After his actions in Khatyrgan Prison last year, that would certainly make a change.

'As long as there are no photographers around.'

Rising to her feet, she laid a hand on his shoulder. 'No promises.'

Part Four

Illusion

Former FSB agent Alexander Litvinenko publicly alleged that the Russian government was complicit in the events at Beslan. Litvinenko died from acute radiation poisoning in November 2006, shortly after meeting with two Russian officials. The Russian government denied responsibility for his death.

Chapter 65

Once again Drake found himself back in Lubyanka, the seat of power for Russia's intelligence services for five generations. Once again he was standing in that same expansive conference room, staring out across the magnificent cityscape of central Moscow. It was late afternoon now, with the evening sun shining down from an almost cloudless sky, its rays glinting off the onion domes of St Basil's Cathedral.

Sunlight and unseasonable warmth, after enduring near constant wind, rain, snow and hail since that evening in DC. It felt like a lifetime ago.

'It's a funny old world,' Drake remarked as he took a sip of tea, served strong and black in the traditional Russian style.

Miranova, seated on the other side of the table, glanced up from the report she'd been engrossed in. 'What was that?'

Drake smiled a little, keeping his back to her. 'Nothing. It's not important.'

His thoughts were interrupted by the sound of the door opening.

'Ah, you're here at last,' a deep, gravelly Russian voice announced. It was a voice he recognised well enough from the brief teleconference held at the Russian embassy in DC.

Steeling himself, Drake turned to face Viktor Surovsky.

He recalled his earlier surprise at the image that had presented itself on the television screen during the conference call, in stark contrast to Surovsky's public image as a bold, determined and powerful leader. That impression was only highlighted on seeing him in the flesh.

The FSB director was a short, frail, ill-looking man, with thinning grey hair and a lined and pockmarked face prematurely aged by too much drinking, too much smoking and too many hard decisions. His suit was expensive and no doubt tailor-made, yet it seemed to hang awkwardly on his spare frame. Drake had always believed that 'the man maketh the clothes' rather than the other way around, and Surovsky was living proof of that.

Miranova was gracious enough to handle the introductions, and immediately rose to her feet. 'Ryan Drake, may I introduce FSB Director Surovsky.'

Surovsky smiled and thrust out a hand. 'Good to meet you properly, Mr Drake.'

Drake did his best to paste on a fake smile. Despite his spare frame, Surovsky's hands were still big and square, the skin roughened by years of manual work. It seemed he was no stranger to hardship, at least in his younger days.

'And you, sir,' he lied.

'It seems I have much to thank you for,' Surovsky went on, his gaze flicking left to encompass Miranova. 'Both of you. Thanks to you, one of the most dangerous terrorists in Russia's history has been brought to justice.'

Drake wasn't so sure. If Atayev was right, the most dangerous terrorist in Russia's history was standing in this very room.

'We did what we could,' Drake said, trying to be diplomatic.

'Ha!' Chortling with amusement, Surovsky slapped him across the shoulder. Drake tried not to flinch as a wave of pain rippled outwards from the injured joint. 'I love the British sense of modesty. But in this case, take credit where it is due, Mr Drake.'

Turning away, the FSB director walked over to an antique cabinet set against one wall. A decanter of what Drake assumed to be vodka had been set there.

'It may seem hard to believe now, but it is worth remembering that this all started with a peaceful mission,' Surovsky said as he removed the stopper and began to pour. 'A chance to foster greater cooperation between our two agencies.'

Having poured three generous glasses, he returned to them and handed one each to Drake and Miranova.

'It might not have come about exactly as intended, but perhaps we achieved our aim after all.' He raised his glass and looked at them both. 'To friendship.'

'To friendship,' Drake repeated, practically having to force the words out. He was grateful to down his drink so he didn't have to maintain his genial expression.

One sip was enough to tell him that Surovsky had spared no expense when it came to alcohol. Drake was a whisky drinker by preference, but even he appreciated the quality of the Russian spirit.

Laying the empty glass down, Surovsky adjusted his belt as if to signal it was time to get down to business. 'Now, Agent Miranova tells me you wanted to speak to the leader of the terrorist group?'

Drake nodded. 'That's right.'

Surovsky surveyed him for a long moment, his dark eyes shrewd and assessing. 'May I ask what you want to talk to him about?'

'I only want the truth.'

Some of the tension seemed to leave Surovsky. 'Then I think we have something in common, Agent Drake. Two of my colleagues, both good men, are dead because of him.'

If he was expecting sympathy from Drake, it was misplaced. After a moment or two even he seemed to recognise this.

'Come, then,' he said, nodding towards the door. 'You too, Agent Miranova. You have a right to be there too.'

Ten minutes later Drake was standing in an observation room, behind a bulletproof two-way mirror and a bank of computer monitors displaying security camera footage from every conceivable angle of the room opposite.

All of this technology was in place to monitor and record the interrogation room's sole occupant. Buran Atayev was seated at a metal table in the centre of the brightly lit concrete cell, his hands and feet cuffed and chained to the floor. He was dressed in an orange jumpsuit of the type worn by prisoners at Guantanamo Bay and countless other prison facilities the world over.

His face was completely serene, his eyes closed as if he were meditating. He was sitting with his back straight, his chin raised, his chained hands folded on the table in front of him.

'He has said nothing to us since he arrived here, sir; not a single word,' explained the guard manning the observation room, watching the prisoner as if he were an enigma that refused to be solved. 'He has not moved a muscle. He just sits there.'

Surovsky nodded, unfazed. 'Mr Drake here wants to speak with the prisoner.'

The guard hesitated a moment before complying. 'Yes, sir.' He looked at Drake. 'The prisoner is secured, but two armed agents will accompany you.'

Drake got the message. They weren't there to protect Drake from Atayev; they were there to protect Atayev from Drake.

Surovsky folded his arms and looked at him. 'Ready, Mr Drake?'

He took a breath and raised his chin a little. 'I am.'

*

Roman Kalyuyev pushed himself away from his desk, having decided to finish work early today. What the hell – it was Christmas Eve after all. Most of the other executives were clocking off early themselves, and after everything he'd been through in the past couple of days, he felt he'd earned it.

His mysterious blackmailer had never shown up for her rendezvous on Poklonnaya Hill. Kalyuyev had waited a full hour past the deadline before finally deciding to cut his losses and leave. Either the whole thing had been a hoax designed simply to intimidate him, or she had got cold feet and wisely decided he wasn't a man to fuck with.

In either case, it had saved him the trouble of having to kill her and dispose of the body. It had been a long time since he'd had to do anything like that, and if he was honest with himself, he was getting a little old for such nonsense.

That was part of the reason he'd retired from FSB service in the first place, taking Surovsky's generous retirement package as a farewell gift and using it to invest heavily in a small but growing engineering firm. Spying and counter-terrorism was a young man's game. If you stayed in too long, sooner or later your luck ran out.

Now perhaps he could put it behind him. Perhaps he could look forward to a better future, free from the secrets and mistakes of the past.

With those thoughts fresh in his mind he snatched his coat off the peg, closed his briefcase and left the office, remembering to lock the door behind him.

Atayev opened his eyes as the electronically locked door buzzed open and Drake entered the room, with a pair of armed agents following close behind. He was forced to squint to see, his glasses having been removed in case he tried to harm himself with them.

'Agent Drake,' he said, bowing his head a little in acknowledgement. 'You will forgive me if I don't stand to greet you.' He held up his manacled hands as if to apologise.

A chair was sitting opposite him. Saying nothing, Drake pulled it out and lowered himself into it, staring at the man on the other side of the table the whole time. Atayev met his gaze without flinching. He was waiting for Drake to make his move.

After a long moment, Drake reached into his pocket. The two agents in the room tensed a little, their hands moving slightly closer to the weapons they carried within their suit jackets.

However, they relaxed when Drake gently laid a single white chess pawn down on the metal table. The same pawn Atayev had left with him earlier in the day.

A flicker of amusement showed in Atayev's grey eyes. 'If you wish to play against me, I'm afraid you will need more than that.'

'I didn't come here to play games,' Drake said. His tone was calm and even, but his eyes reflected something else entirely.

'Then why *did* you come here?' Atayev asked. 'To gloat? To rant and scream at me?' He leaned forward a little, his tone conspiratorial. 'To kill me?'

Beneath the table, Drake's hands clenched into fists. 'Would you like that?'

Atayev tilted his head a little, pondering the question. 'Since I am at your mercy, what I would like or dislike is not important. The more relevant question, Mr Drake, is whether you are prepared to face the consequences of killing me. A trained man like you could snap my neck with his bare hands if he chose, but then the two agents stationed in this room to protect me would either kill or incapacitate you, in which case you would die or spend the rest of your life in prison.' He nodded to the pawn on the table. 'Like in chess, every decision has its risks and its rewards, and every victory requires sacrifices. A man's potential is limited only by the sacrifices he is prepared to make. Since I have nothing to lose, I am perfectly free of limitations. Can you say the same?'

'You're the one in handcuffs, facing life in prison,' Drake pointed out. 'How free do you feel now?'

Atayev glanced down at the cuffs and smiled. 'Handcuffs can be removed. Prisons can be breached. But fear and doubt are restraints you can never escape from.' He leaned back in his chair, surveying Drake for a long moment. 'So, you did not come here to kill me. And you do not seem like the kind of man to gloat. So I ask you again, why are you here, Ryan Drake?'

They had come down to it at last – the endgame. Drake had only one move to make. The only thing he had come here to do.

In his mind he imagined himself making the move; like a coiled spring suddenly unleashed. He imagined himself leaping to his feet, reaching out and gripping Atayev's head, and slamming it down on to the table, aiming for the pawn he'd positioned with such care. He imagined the polished wooden point, hardened by the long years, shattering his skull and carving its way into the delicate brain tissue within.

He imagined the brief moment of satisfaction, knowing he'd killed the man who had ended Anya's life. The grim triumph that would be his before the guards moved in.

But before he acted, he had to know the truth.

'Why?' he asked, the pain in his voice impossible to hide. 'Why did you kill her?'

Atayev said nothing for a long time. He just sat staring at his opponent across the table. The grandmaster preparing to reveal the final decisive moves of his strategy.

And then, at last, it came.

'Do you know the secret to chess, Mr Drake?' he asked, gently reaching for the pawn and lifting it up, turning it slowly in his hand. 'Illusion. Not what you do, not what you could do, not what you *will* do . . . but what you make your opponent believe. You present him with threats; threats which must be dealt with. Threats which he becomes so consumed with eliminating that your true purpose, your true goal, is kept hidden from him.'

In the observation room, Viktor Surovsky leaned forwards, his hands resting on the desk in front of him as he watched the conversation play out.

Despite everything, despite the security and the guns and the bulletproof glass and the cameras everywhere, he felt a momentary twinge of uncertainty. Eternally paranoid as men in his profession often were, he caught himself wondering if his position, so strong and unassailable only moments ago, was quite as dominant as it had seemed.

He was tempted to order Drake removed from the room so the true interrogation could begin. The only reason he had even allowed Drake in there was in the hopes he or Atayev might inadvertently reveal something that Surovsky could later use to his advantage.

However, sheer curiosity compelled him to keep watching. What harm could it do, after all? Drake and Atayev would both be dealt with once this was over. He'd prefer to spare Miranova's life, though it might be necessary to eliminate her as well before he was finished.

For now, though, he waited.

'Once you make your opponent believe that a threat is real, you need only justify that belief,' Atayev went on. 'You give up those pieces which are no longer useful, allowing his confidence to grow with each sacrifice, allowing him to come closer and closer to victory while always keeping it just beyond his grasp. And all the while you carefully position your truly important pieces; the ones which seem so harmless and insignificant throughout the whole game, just waiting for the right time to make your move.'

He reached up to scratch the tip of his nose before going on.

'And at that moment, even as your opponent reaches out to seize victory, you strike.'

As usual, Kalyuyev's car had been brought round to the main entrance in preparation for his departure, the engine ticking over smoothly, the twin exhausts billowing small clouds of steam into the chill December air.

Tossing his coat into the back seat, he gratefully entered the vehicle's warm interior with the heaters already working hard. Just for a moment, he closed his eyes and let out a faint sigh of relief. Relief mingled with weariness.

It had been a trying couple of days, but it was over now.

Opening his eyes, he reached out and hit the play button on the car's CD player. But instead of the soothing tones of Beethoven, he instead found himself assailed by the dramatic, intense immolation scene from Wagner's *Götterdämmerung*.

He frowned, confused. He certainly didn't recall putting that CD in. Perhaps one of the men charged with moving his car had decided to play a prank on him, or had taken his expensive car for a little cruise while he was working. In either case, he wasn't amused.

He was just reaching out to eject the disc when suddenly something inexplicable happened. The car's central-locking system engaged, all four doors clicking shut.

'What the fuck . . . ?' he mumbled irritably, pressing the unlock button on his key fob. There was no response. The doors remained locked.

The entire central-locking system must have failed.

Feeling a twinge of unease now, Kalyuyev tried to open the door manually, only to meet with the same result. He was trapped inside his own car. What a ridiculous end to an already difficult couple of days. Now he would have to suffer the indignity of calling for help.

Twisting around in his seat, he reached for his coat and the cellphone he'd left in the inside pocket.

That was when he saw it, gleaming and black on the rear parcel shelf. A small, intricately carved bishop from a chess set.

Suddenly a muted boom shook the car's chassis from below, startling him. What the hell could have caused that? Had the engine failed as well?

It was only when he smelled smoke that he looked down and saw wisps of it starting to filter through the vents. More of it was drifting by outside his windows, and as he glanced out the windshield, he saw flames licking from beneath the bonnet.

The car was on fire!

Panicking now, he frantically grabbed at the door handle, trying to wrench it open, but still it wouldn't budge. He tried to hammer on the window, but the toughened glass intended to deflect bullets firmly resisted his efforts.

'Help!' he yelled as the first flicker of orange flames began to appear below. The air was thick with acrid smoke now, stinging his eyes and searing his throat. 'Somebody help!'

He could see movement outside, could see the panicked faces of the men he walked past so nonchalantly every day. He heard the faint thump as they hammered on the windows, trying to break them, trying to reach him.

And all the while, the piercing strains of Wagner's *Götterdämmerung* continued to resound through the car.

Coughing, trying to draw breath from the searing, choking black smoke now filling the car, he desperately tried to clamber between the front seats, only to find himself stuck there.

The flames were growing fast now, greedily licking upwards to consume the upholstery, the carpets, and the fabric of his trousers.

Blinded by the smoke, and able to hear nothing now but the final tortured strains of Wagner's last opera, Kalyuyev let out an agonised scream as the flames surged upwards to consume him.

No sooner had Atayev finished speaking than the electronic door buzzed open, signalling a new entry to the interrogation room.

Drake glanced over, wondering if Surovsky had heard enough and ordered Drake removed from the room. To his surprise, however, it was Miranova standing in the doorway.

He hesitated a moment, wondering what she had come to tell him.

But his surprise and curiosity immediately gave way to shocked disbelief as the woman raised her side arm, levelled it at the two agents standing behind Atayev and pulled the trigger.

The first agent went down instantly, the well-aimed round blasting out the back of his head to leave a bloody smear on the white concrete behind. The second barely had time to go for his weapon before a second shot reverberated around the room and he too crumpled and fell.

There are times to think and times to act. Times when even a momentary delay could mean the difference between life and death. This moment was definitely the latter.

Hurling his chair aside, Drake sprang to his feet and rushed at the woman. He had no idea what was going on, but he certainly didn't intend to become victim number three.

He hadn't made it more than two steps before Miranova's weapon swung around to face him.

'Don't,' she hissed, staring at him down the sights, her eyes completely devoid of mercy or compassion. She was a trained killer, a professional operative like himself, and one wrong move on his part was all the justification she needed to pull the trigger.

Skidding to a halt, Drake stared at the woman in disbelief.

'The other thing you should always remember about chess, Mr Drake,' Atayev said, having sat calmly through the entire confrontation without even flinching. 'Even a king can be brought down by a humble pawn.'

Chapter 66

Washington, DC, five days earlier

'I want to go over that revised speech as soon as it's ready,' Anton Demochev said, flicking through the incoming messages on his cellphone as he talked. Outside, the rain-lashed buildings of central Washington swept past. 'We need more emphasis on the fact that this is our initiative.'

Like the vain, egocentric fool that he was, Demochev was relishing the prospect of making the announcement of a joint US–Russian counter-terrorism strategy to the country's media. No doubt he intended to take most of the credit himself, even though the deal and the bulk of the negotiations over shared intelligence would be handled by far more deserving subordinates.

None of those things concerned Miranova at that moment, however, as she'd just felt her own cellphone vibrating. Quickly reaching for it, she opened the newest message.

As expected, it was simple, direct and to the point.

Now.

Reaching down, she checked her seat belt was firmly in place, took a deep breath and braced herself for what was coming.

It happened fast. A sudden explosion of glass and blood up front announced the impact of the high-powered sniper round, killing the driver instantly.

Such was his complete disbelief at what had just happened, Demochev could muster only a single word. 'What?'

Miranova said nothing. With no one to direct it, the car slewed sideways on the busy freeway, clipping another vehicle as it went. Miranova stared out through the shattered windscreen as a concrete barrier hurtled towards them. A heartbeat later the car made contact with the solid obstacle in a sickening, crunching, jarring impact that jerked her forwards in her seat with bruising force.

And then, just like that, an unnatural stillness descended on the car, as if a storm had just passed over them. Miranova opened her eyes and looked around. Spots of light were swimming across her vision and the blood pounded in her ears, but she was alive and, as far as she could tell, unharmed.

'Jesus Christ!' Demochev gasped, staring around in wide-eyed shock. 'What the fuck happened? Andre, what's going on?'

Andre Lagonov, Demochev's personal assistant, never got a chance to respond. With a crunch of metal, the passenger door beside him was forced open. Lagonov turned just in time to see a silenced pistol thrust through the gap, and jerked violently as a single round entered his forehead.

The door beside Demochev was forced open in similar fashion, only this time a taser was levelled at the car's occupant. Demochev let out a startled cry as the weapon discharged its payload of several thousand volts, and slumped forwards to curl up in a foetal position in the footwell.

Miranova said nothing while this was happening, and made no move to intervene as the semi-conscious man was dragged from the wrecked vehicle.

She looked up into the gaunt, unsmiling face of Goran, one of Atayev's hired thugs, then glanced at the automatic he was holding. Supposedly it was loaded with low-powered, soft-lead slugs; the kind that the Kevlar vest she was wearing should easily see off. But she was under no illusions – this was going to hurt.

'Ready?' he asked.

She nodded. 'Lower right side. Don't go for the chest.'

The last thing she needed was to break a couple of ribs.

Without hesitation he took aim and fired a single shot. The impact felt like a cannonball fired straight into her gut, and she buckled forwards, coughing and gasping. She could taste bile in her throat and fought the urge to throw up.

'You all right?'

'I'm . . . fine,' she managed to say. 'Help me up.'

She stifled a groan as he hauled her out of the wrecked car and towards the waiting ambulance, having to support the injured woman while she got her breath back. Demochev was already on board and restrained, ready to be ferried to the underground parking lot where they would switch vehicles.

After that, the pain of the crash would be the least of his problems.

Miranova wasn't looking forward to it much herself. Her part in the charade would require her to be tied, hooded and forced into a hidden compartment within the van they'd be using. It was a task she didn't relish, but it was necessary if she was to gain the trust of the CIA.

And in the end, the rewards would more than make up for it. Despite the pain, she allowed herself a triumphant smile as she clambered into the ambulance, surveying the once-powerful FSB leader lying curled on the floor.

In the end this would all be worth it.

Chapter 67

Drake could summon up no words as he stared at the woman he'd trusted, whom he had thought he knew, and who was now standing with her weapon trained on him. All traces of emotion had left her.

Only now did the full magnitude of his mistake finally settle on him like a crushing weight.

Anika Miranova, who had miraculously survived the attack in DC that had killed all her colleagues; who had conveniently led them out of that storage lock-up mere seconds before it exploded; who had been instrumental in forging a joint investigation between the CIA and the FSB; whose convenient leaps of deduction had led them to Glazov, then to Kalyuyev; who had always provided just enough information to keep them in pursuit of their adversaries while never quite allowing them to gain the upper hand.

'Once you make your opponent believe that a threat is real, you need only justify that belief. You give up those pieces which are no longer useful, allowing his confidence to grow with each sacrifice, allowing him to come closer and closer to victory while always keeping it just beyond his grasp.'

Miranova, who had survived the shoot-out at the foundry, who had allowed herself to be taken prisoner so she could end up by Drake's side for the final confrontation with Atayev.

Miranova, who had just killed two of her fellow agents,

and was even now working to unlock Atayev's restraints with one hand while keeping Drake covered with the other.

'And at that moment, even as your opponent reaches out to seize victory, you strike.'

'How can you do this?' Drake spat, his eyes burning with anger and disgust. 'Killing your own people for this man?'

'They are not *my people* any more than they are yours, Drake,' Miranova hit back, showing not a hint of regret for what she had done. 'Now get down on your knees and put your hands behind your head. Do it now.'

He didn't doubt she would shoot him dead if he resisted. She was a trained killer, and had already demonstrated her ability with ruthless efficiency. With little choice but to comply, Drake placed his hands behind his head, interlocking his fingers, then lowered himself on to his knees.

With a twist of a key, Atayev's cuffs slipped loose. Rubbing his wrists, he rose up from his chair with unhurried ease and stretched, as if awakening from a deep sleep. He glanced at the pawn still in his hand, smiled in amusement, and laid it carefully back down in the centre of the table.

Frisking one of the dead agents, Miranova withdrew an automatic from his bloodied suit jacket and tossed it to Atayev, then hurried from the room.

At last Atayev's plan was rendered chillingly obvious. Drake's capture at the safe house, his escape from the torture chamber and call to Miranova for help, the computer virus attack, the assault on the warehouse and the deaths of Atayev's men, even the capture of Atayev himself had been nothing but a carefully crafted deception to make them believe Atayev was beaten, that they had won and he had lost.

All of the killings, the sacrifices, the betrayals, all of it planned and executed with absolute precision to bring

Atayev to this place, at this moment, with his most hated enemy of all.

The final piece.

The black king.

'It was all for him, wasn't it?' Drake said, hardly believing the scale of their failure to anticipate his plan. 'Surovsky.'

Atayev nodded. 'He was untouchable. There was no other way I could get to him.'

'How did you manage to turn her?'

'I didn't,' Atayev said simply. 'She joined me willingly, agreed to dedicate her career to finding the truth about Beslan. For four years she has been the perfect FSB agent, working her way up until she was in a position to give me what I needed.'

His queen. The most dangerous and vital piece at his disposal, and nobody had even recognised the threat she posed.

But her ruthless attention was turned elsewhere at that moment, giving Drake a precious few moments in which to act. He eyed the weapon in Atayev's hands, weighing up his chances of disarming the older man before Miranova returned.

He was armed with an MP-443 Grach; a modern 9mm handgun that was now ubiquitous amongst the FSB, and more than capable of making a mess of anything that wasn't protected by several layers of Kevlar. Atayev was no expert with firearms, but even he couldn't miss from this range. Drake would have two or three slugs in him before he could close the distance. No good.

'Forget it,' Atayev warned as if sensing his thoughts. 'Cooperate and you might live through this. Resist and you certainly won't.'

The decision was rendered moot a few moments later as Miranova appeared with Viktor Surovsky in front of her, his hands cuffed behind his back, his thinning grey hair in disarray and his eyes wide with fear. He grunted in pain as Miranova shoved him roughly down into the chair that Atayev himself had occupied only moments earlier.

Straight away Atayev's demeanour changed. The layers of logical, calculated self-control seemed to peel back as Drake watched him, revealing the core of absolute, unquenchable hatred within.

'Hello, Viktor,' Atayev said, practically spitting out each word. 'I've been waiting a long time to speak with you.'

Surovsky began to spout off something in Russian.

'Now, now,' Atayev chided. 'Speak English for Mr Drake here. I want him to understand every word.'

'W-who are you?' Surovsky stammered. 'How do you know me?'

'Who am I?' Atayev repeated, taking a step towards him. 'Of course, you don't know who I am. There is no reason why you should ever have heard of me. I am nothing to you.'

Atayev held out a trembling hand to Miranova, who reached into her pocket and gently handed him a small, old, creased and faded photograph. He stared at it for a long moment, his eyes holding a look of such sadness and longing that even Drake could see how much it meant to him, then slammed the photo down on the table.

'Look at it, Viktor. Look at it!' he shouted, grabbing the older man's head and forcing him to look straight at the picture.

It was an image of a young girl, perhaps ten years old. She was sitting cross-legged on the porch of some house, beaming a dimpled smile right at the camera. Even in the tarnished image, Drake could see the sparkle in her eyes, and her resemblance to Atayev.

'There is no reason you should know her either, is there?'

Atayev asked. 'Let me tell you. Her name was Natasha, twelve years old. Killed by a Russian Army bullet. She was my daughter. And she was one of four hundred other innocents who died at Beslan because of you, Viktor. Because of *you.*'

'I . . . I don't know what you're talking about,' Surovsky pleaded. 'This is madness.'

Balling up his fist, Atayev swung a right hook against the side of Surovsky's face. It was a clumsy, uncoordinated strike from a man clearly not used to using his fists, but it was delivered with such unrestrained fury that it snapped Surovsky's head sideways. The older man let out a cry of pain as blood began to flow from a cut over his eye.

'Do not lie to me!' Atayev shouted right in his face. 'You engineered the attack at Beslan, just as you did the other terrorist attacks. You sacrificed the lives of hundreds of the same people you swore to protect. You turned our country against itself. You silenced everyone who tried to get at the truth. And you did it for one reason – power.'

Surovsky was trying to shake his head, but Atayev's grip prevented it. 'No! No, that is not true.' His eyes flicked to Miranova, as if hoping to reason with her. 'I would never do such a thing! Only a monster would even think of it.'

For a moment, Drake's mind flashed back to his earlier conversation with Miranova about that very same thing.

'Be careful fighting with monsters, lest you become a monster.'

'And a monster is exactly what you created,' Atayev said, releasing his grip. 'Along with your partners in crime.'

On cue, Miranova handed him her cellphone. Selecting the video-playback option, Atayev turned the screen towards Surovsky as the first file began to play.

The image on the screen was of Demochev, stripped to the waist and bound to a chair, breathing hard and clearly in pain. His face was bruised and bloodied; testimony to the ferocious beating he had just taken.

'Once again, tell me your orders,' said an off-screen voice. Atayev's voice.

'My orders were . . . to suspend border patrols along a certain route,' he rasped. 'The route leading to the school. We were . . . to make no effort to stop the terrorist group.'

'Even though you knew where they were going,' Atayev's voice prompted.

Demochev closed his eyes and his shoulders began to shake up and down as he broke down in tears. 'Yes.'

'And who gave you these orders?'

'Please . . . he will kill me if I—'

'Who gave the order?' Atayev demanded.

Demochev's shoulders slumped in defeat. 'Viktor . . . Viktor Surovsky.'

The screen went blank then as Atayev selected a second video file and hit play. This one, unsurprisingly, featured Masalsky in a similar state of duress. If anything, he looked even worse than Demochev had.

'What were your orders?' Atayev's off-screen voice asked.

Masalsky's head was down, as if he barely had the strength to lift it. When he spoke, his voice was quiet, his speech slurred.

'To suspend all surveillance activity on known terrorists, and release any members of the group already in custody.'

'And where did the orders come from?' the voice demanded.

Masalsky raised his head up then, revealing the extent of his injuries. 'The orders . . . were given by Director Surovsky.'

Having made his point, Atayev laid the phone down on the table and turned his attention back to Surovsky. 'Do you still deny it?'

509

Surovsky was staring blankly at the phone, frozen as if in shock. Then, slowly, he turned his head around to look at Atayev.

'What you did to those men . . . they were under torture,' he protested weakly. 'Their confessions mean nothing.'

'Confessions extracted under torture have always been good enough for the FSB,' he reminded his captor. 'Admit what you did.'

'Why? So you can kill me just like you did them?'

'I have no desire to kill you,' Atayev assured him. 'But over the past few days I have become very good at hurting men while keeping them alive. I no longer have the time or the tools I would like, but I can show you a little of what I learned.'

With that, he levelled his weapon at Surovsky's leg and without hesitation, fired. There was a small explosion of blood and fabric across his left thigh as the single round tore through skin and muscle tissue, and a moment later the crack of the gunshot was drowned out by Surovsky's howls of agony.

'That was only a flesh wound,' Atayev said once his cries had subsided a little. 'The next one will not be. I will give you three seconds to speak the truth, then I will shoot out your left kneecap. Three seconds later I will take your right. You will never walk again, Viktor. After that, I leave it to your imagination. One.'

In desperation, Surovsky's eyes turned on Miranova. 'Whatever he has paid you, I will triple it. Get me out of this. You will suffer no blame for what you did. I swear it!'

The woman said nothing. She was far beyond such petty bribes now.

'Two.' Atayev's finger tightened on the trigger.

'Let me go and I can get you out of Russia,' he said, turning his attention back to Atayev. 'I-I can give you money, a new name, a new life, anything. Name it!'

'Three!' Atayev warned, turning his head away to avoid the blood splatter as he pulled the trigger.

'All right!' Surovsky cried, bucking and kicking in his chair. 'All right, damn you! I admit it! I admit it.'

Atayev's grip on the weapon relaxed just a little. 'Go on.'

Surovsky let out a defeated sigh and allowed his head to slump forwards, the harsh electric light shining off the balding dome of his head. Bloodied and broken, he was a pathetic-looking figure.

'I was responsible for Beslan,' he said at last, refusing to look up when he said it. 'And the other attacks. I allowed them to happen when I could have stopped them. All those deaths . . . they are on my hands.' Finally he managed to drag his head up to look Atayev in the eye. 'Your daughter . . . Natasha, she died because of me. Because of me.'

For several seconds, nothing was said. A silence, stunned and absolute, descended on the room. After all the protests, the deflections, the manoeuvring and the threats, to hear him finally come out and say it, to face up to what he had done at last, left them simply dumbstruck.

It was Atayev who broke the silence, letting out a strangled breath that sounded almost like a sob. The cold, focused, detached self-control he had maintained all this time was at last failing him as he reached the end of his long journey. He had found the one thing he had been looking for all these lonely, empty years, driven and consumed by his need to get to the truth.

All the planning, the contingencies, the tireless work, the doubts and dangers had led to this moment, to this confession.

And now that it was over, he could finally allow himself

to experience the grief and desolation he had kept locked away since the day of his daughter's death. Drake watched as Atayev bowed his head, closed his eyes and let out a single, choking sob, tears trickling down his cheeks. Despite everything he had done, even Drake felt a twinge of sympathy for him.

Opening his eyes, Atayev let out a long, slow breath and looked at Surovsky again. 'Thank you.'

'You think this means anything?' the old man spat, his teeth bared as blood flowed from the gunshot wound on his leg. 'You think you can prove any of this? So you have your confession – what now? Even if you could escape this building, you will be a hunted man for the rest of your life. I hope this was worth it, because you just signed your own death warrant.'

At this, Atayev actually let out a chuckle of amusement. 'Do you think I would have done any of this if I cared whether I lived or died?' he asked. 'I came here for you, Viktor. I did not come to kill you, but to destroy you.'

He nodded to one of the security cameras mounted in the corner of the room. The tiny LED indicator light on the side of the unit was glowing red – it had been recording the entire conversation. Miranova had enabled the cameras that Surovsky had ordered shut down.

Atayev smiled, relishing the look of growing horror on Surovsky's face. 'Once every news outlet with an Internet connection has access to this recording, even you will not be able to silence them. I won't kill you, Viktor, because I won't have to. The world will eat you alive.'

The single gunshot startled him out of his thoughts with painful, violent clarity. Drake stared at Atayev as a small cloud of red exploded from the front of his jumpsuit. Atayev himself looked down at it, seemingly unable to comprehend what had happened, then slowly his legs buckled and he went down.

'I'm sorry, Buran,' Miranova said quietly, a wisp of smoke still trailing from the barrel of her automatic as she circled the small table to stand over him. One look was enough to confirm her shot had fatally wounded him. Frothy blood was leaking from his mouth and chest, his breathing growing laboured, his movements lacking any sense of purpose.

Reaching out, Miranova picked up the single chess piece that Drake had laid on the table earlier, turned it over thoughtfully in her hands for a moment, then dropped it on the ground beside Ayatev and brought her shoe heel down on it. There was a muted crunch as the ancient wood splintered and snapped beneath the pressure.

She surveyed the dying man with something akin to pity as the look of uncomprehending shock and disbelief in his eyes slowly faded away.

He was gone.

Chapter 68

'What is the meaning of this?' Surovsky demanded as Miranova bent down and snatched up Atayev's weapon. The old man looked just as perplexed as Drake felt at this sudden turn of events. 'What the hell are you doing?'

Releasing the magazine from the weapon, she pulled back the slide to eject the round in the chamber, then tossed the empty gun to Drake. It landed on the floor right in front of him, though he made no move to go for it.

'Pick it up,' she ordered.

Drake did nothing. Even if he didn't understand her motivation, it was obvious enough why she wanted him to take the weapon. She wanted his prints on it.

He saw a flicker of anger in her eyes now. 'One way or another, you will pick it up. It is only a question of how much I have to hurt you.'

She allowed her aim to stray lower, to his stomach and down to his groin. He got the message. She wouldn't kill him, yet, but she would put as many bullets in him as she had to.

Glaring at her, he reached out and closed his hand around the butt of the gun, just as she'd asked.

'Now throw it over here.'

With no option but to comply, he slid the gun back across the floor towards her. The weapon skittered and scraped on the concrete, ending up near her feet. Wrapping a handkerchief around her hand to avoid smearing his prints, she picked the gun up and laid it on the table, then turned her dark gaze on the old man.

'You are in trouble, Viktor. If you want to survive this, you will pay very close attention to what I say in the next few seconds,' she advised, her tone now clinical and detached. 'Here is what you are going to do. After this is over you will publicly declare me a hero for bringing Atayev to justice and saving your life when he tried to escape, and announce my promotion to Demochev's old position as head of counter-terrorism. A year from now you will again promote me to the position of deputy director of the FSB, making it known that you intend for me to succeed you. Within six months you will announce your retirement due to ill health, and publicly endorse me as the new director. If you do this, I will make sure that your confession, and those of Masalsky and Demochev, never see the light of day. You will get to live out the rest of your life, such as it is, in peace.'

Drake felt sick to his stomach. Only now did he see Miranova's actions for what they truly were. She had no interest in Atayev's cause, in finding justice for those who had died for Surovsky's greed. She had taken part in this whole thing, had gone through all of it, just to get herself a bargaining chip for the biggest game of all.

Surovsky eyed her shrewdly, the pain of his injured leg forgotten for the moment as he applied his ruthless, calculating intellect to the deal she was proposing.

'What guarantee do I have that you will honour this agreement?' he asked.

She shrugged. 'None. But you can be sure of one thing – if you do not take my deal or you try to betray me, all of your confessions will be the top item on every news broadcast around the world. Even killing me won't stop it.'

The old man said nothing. His mind was still whirring, contemplating options, other courses of action, seeking a way out of this. A beaten player desperately trying to find his way out of checkmate.

His eyes flicked to Drake. 'And what about him?'

Miranova glanced at him, and just for a moment he saw a hint of regret in her eyes. But it was quickly pushed away, replaced by the avarice and expectation of one now close to realising a long-cherished dream.

'He was killed trying to break Atayev out of FSB custody,' she said. 'He has been working against us the whole time. He even tried to take you hostage, but I took him down first.'

'You piece of shit,' Drake snarled, disgusted by what he was hearing. Only now did he clearly perceive her role in all of this. 'It was you, wasn't it? You were the one who sent me that text message in Washington. You wanted me around when that sniper attack happened, because you knew I'd get involved.'

She shrugged, seeing no need to deny it now. 'We each had our parts to play in this, Ryan. Your role was to be here at this moment, to witness this . . . and to take the blame.'

'And all of it so you could land a fucking promotion.'

'Wake up,' she hissed, rounding on him. 'This is about more than personal ambition. Atayev thought only about revenge, of destroying Surovsky's legacy. But what then? What is the point in removing one criminal only for another to take his place? I will stop that, for ever. Don't you see? Once I am director, I can make real changes in Russia, bring real freedom to our people. Even if it has to be done by playing Viktor at his own game, that is worth fighting for, worth killing for.'

She seemed to change before his eyes then, the passion and belief behind her words somehow burning through the cold facade she had adopted. Drake saw a glimpse of the perverted idealism and warped sense of justice that had driven her to commit such a callous act of betrayal.

He almost felt sorry for her at that moment, talking about 'real change' and bringing freedom to the masses. Even if she believed them, even if she believed she could make them real, they were nothing but flimsy words used by every dictator and tyrant, every terrorist and butcher throughout history. Wishing to prevent another criminal stepping in to fill Surovsky's shoes, she was simply becoming the very thing she despised.

'And all those people at Beslan who died because of him?' Drake asked, gesturing to Surovsky. 'What about them?'

Miranova hesitated, the muscles in her throat tightening as she saw a momentary glimpse of her bold, brilliant scheme through the eyes of another. Suddenly it didn't seem quite so justifiable, quite so easy to rationalise as a necessary evil.

Saying nothing, she instead turned her attention to Surovsky. 'Time is ticking, Viktor. Soon the agents upstairs will realise something is wrong. So, what will it be?'

The old man had been outmanoeuvred and they both knew it. Miranova was offering him a way out. A humiliating, dishonourable way out perhaps, but a way out all the same. The alternative was to be tried before an international court for crimes against humanity and spend the rest of his life in rooms just like this one.

There was no choice to make.

'All right,' he conceded. 'Kill Drake. Then we'll talk.'

Miranova let out a breath. It had worked. Her plan, everything she had risked her career and her life for; it had all paid off.

'Atayev was right about one thing, Ryan,' she conceded grimly as she raised her weapon. She might have shown a brief moment of regret, but even Drake could see the avarice and burning ambition in her eyes. 'Every victory requires sacrifices.'

He tensed up, bracing himself for the first tearing impact. This would be no neat execution with a single round to the head. She would have to make it look as though he had gone down fighting. His death, when it came, would be neither fast nor painless.

Suddenly the woman stiffened and cried out in pain and shock, her finger tightening involuntarily on the trigger as she squeezed off a shot that zipped past Drake's shoulder, burying itself in the wall behind him.

Caught off guard, Miranova looked down at the source of her sudden, unexpected pain. The base of the ruined chess pawn protruded from her leg, the jagged and broken tip buried in the fleshy part of her right calf. And clutching it in a desperate grip, jamming it in deeper with every ounce of his waning strength, was Atayev.

Somehow the stubborn bastard was still conscious, still clinging on to life.

Another twist, another agonising jolt of pain as the wooden chess piece tore through muscle tissue, threatening to drop her to her knees. She had to do something. Reacting instinctively, she trained her weapon downwards, aiming for his head.

On the other side of the room, Drake had watched this bizarre spectacle unfolding, watched as the dying man used the only weapon available to him to lash out at the woman who had betrayed him. The injury was little more than a flesh wound, almost comical in comparison to the death she could deal out with the automatic in her hands.

But at that moment, it was enough.

Knowing he had to act now, Drake planted his right foot

firmly on the ground, tensed the muscles in his legs and leapt forward like a sprinter off the starting blocks.

He saw Miranova register the sudden movement, saw her eyes come up and the weapon follow them a heartbeat later. It didn't matter now. He was in a race for his very life. Propelling himself forwards, he managed to take two good strides, building speed and momentum before throwing his shoulders down and launching himself across the metal table.

Drake weighed a good 190 pounds, maybe a little less after several days without proper food or sleep, but every ounce of it was now directed at Miranova. It was simple physics – mass multiplied by velocity equalled momentum, and he had more of both on his side.

He impacted hard, tackling her around the waist like a rugby player and knocking her into the wall opposite with bruising force. He heard her grunt of pain as the side of her face collided with the wall, and tried to drive his shoulder in harder, looking to crush the air from her lungs.

All thoughts of compassion and restraint had vanished now, driven away by the desperate nature of his situation. Only one of them was coming out of this alive.

Miranova might have been surprised by his sudden attack, but she was a trained operative just like him, and she knew how to handle herself in a fight. An elbow to the side of his head caused an explosion of light more powerful than the flashbang grenade that had blinded him earlier in the day, while a knee to his stomach almost doubled him over. He tasted the harsh burn of bile in his throat.

Miranova wasn't stupid. She knew that the pistol gave her the advantage, but in a close-quarters struggle like this it was also a liability. Drake was all over her, too close to get a decent shot.

But she could still use the weapon in other ways.

He saw Miranova bring the butt of the pistol down like a club, striking the recently repaired wound at his shoulder joint. Pain more intense than even he could have anticipated rippled outwards from the point of impact, and travelled all the way down his arm to leave his fingers numb and tingling.

They were both hurting now; it was just a question of who could take more.

Through blurred vision he searched frantically for the gun, knowing he had to keep it out of play. He saw the barrel rising up towards him as she tried to put a round in his stomach. Any injury there would certainly drop him.

Then suddenly an idea came to him; a memory of something he had seen Anya do in a similar situation. Reaching out, he grasped the weapon by its slide and jammed it back hard just as Miranova pulled the trigger.

Nothing happened; not even a click. The retracted slide was now blocking the firing pin, preventing it from striking the round in the chamber.

Stalemate, at least for the next few seconds.

Looking down at her right leg, he saw the bloody wound where Atayev had struck her, and in the centre of it a faint gleam of white wood. The pawn, still embedded in her flesh as she hadn't yet had a chance to remove it.

Even as she tried to wrench the weapon free of his grip, Drake raised his foot and slammed it downwards against her leg, managing to catch the protruding object perfectly.

The effect was not unlike pulling open a zipper. There was a moment of taut resistance as skin and muscle stretched to their limits, and then with an almost audible rip the pawn slid downwards by several inches, leaving a bloody track of torn flesh in its wake.

Even she couldn't endure such an injury, and with a cry of

pain she started to go down. Her grip on the weapon slackened just enough for Drake to yank it out of her hand.

Realising what he was doing, Miranova grasped desperately at the gun just as he reversed his grip on it and turned the weapon on her. He felt the barrel press against soft flesh, felt her trying to tear his fingers away from the pistol grip, and suddenly there was a muted thump as the weapon discharged.

For a moment the two of them remained frozen together like that, each holding the other close with bloodied hands, each staring into the other's eyes as if trying to make sense of what had happened. There was no pain – it had happened too suddenly for that.

Then, slowly, Miranova's eyes grew unfocused, her grip on Drake slackened and with a weary, ragged sigh she fell. Blood stained the front of her blouse. Still gripping her, Drake lowered her to the floor and watched in silence as she took her final breaths.

She looked neither angry nor frightened as her life faded away. Her expression rather was one of confusion, as if she couldn't quite understand how her plan had unravelled.

Drake said nothing as she convulsed and finally lay still. He had no words to explain what he felt towards her. For now, he was content merely to know that it was over.

'Drake . . .'

Looking over, he saw Atayev lying a few yards away, one hand pressed against the wound at his chest, the other outstretched as if reaching for something. Only then did Drake see the crumpled and faded picture of his daughter Natasha just beyond his reach.

Leaving Miranova, Drake reached for the picture and gently pressed it into the dying man's hand, then laid his arm across his chest so that she was close to him once more. He might have held on long enough to help stop Miranova, but it was obvious the gunshot wound to his chest would prove fatal.

'Don't fight it,' Drake said quietly. Whatever else this man had done, his last act had been to save his life. 'She's waiting for you. You'll see her soon.'

Atayev swallowed and nodded. He had said before that he had no fear of death, and looking at him then, Drake was inclined to agree.

He opened his mouth to speak again, but could only manage the faintest whisper. Drake leaned in close and strained to hear.

'The pawn . . .'

Frowning, Drake glanced around and eventually spotted the small bloodstained chess piece lying near Miranova. It must have come loose during their fight, and now lay alone on the concrete floor. Broken, jagged and stained with a dead woman's blood, Drake couldn't imagine why Atayev would want such a grisly memento now, but it was clear from the pleading look in his eyes that it was important.

Snatching it up, Drake tried to hand it to him, only for the man to push it away.

'For . . . you,' he whispered, closing Drake's fingers around the pawn. 'Remember . . . what I said.' He managed to raise his head a little, driven by a final, desperate need to be understood. '*Remember.*'

His head lolled to the side, where he seemed to see something that pleased him. He smiled, a peaceful, contented smile, closed his eyes and lay still.

He was gone.

Drake glanced down at the pawn Atayev had given him. Despite the bloodstains and the damage it had taken, there were still little patches of white shining through. And as he looked a little closer, he began to understand why Atayev had wanted him to have it; the final message he had tried to impart.

'He is dead?' Surovsky asked. Still handcuffed to the chair, he had been unable to take part in Drake's desperate struggle with Miranova, or to listen to Atayev's final words.

Drake said nothing. He didn't want to look at the old man, never mind speak with him.

'Then it is over.' Surovsky let out a breath, his teeth still clenched against the pain in his leg. 'Thank God.'

Drake closed his eyes. He had no wish to earn Surovsky's gratitude.

'Get me out of here,' Surovsky implored him. 'You stopped that traitor, that insane bitch. I will make sure you're rewarded for what you did.'

Rewarded. Drake might have laughed if the situation had been different. Drake's only reward from this man was to have been a bullet courtesy of Miranova. Now he was trying to act as if none of that had ever happened.

Slipping the pawn into his pocket, Drake snatched up Miranova's gun and rose slowly from behind the table. The look in his eyes was that of a predator regarding its helpless prey. Restrained and injured as he was, Surovsky could do nothing to stop him.

Christ, it would be so easy, he thought as he glanced down at the automatic. Easy, and justified. This man deserved death a hundred times over for the things he had done, and the things he might yet do. Neither Atayev nor Miranova had been able or willing to give it to him, but Drake was of a different sort.

He had learned long ago that death was the final, definitive way to stop such men. Perhaps the only way. He had hidden that lesson and the man it had turned him into beneath the facade of his new life, his new career. But it was always there beneath the surface.

It always would be.

'You are angry,' Surovsky went on, guessing his thoughts. 'You have a right to be. But none of it was true. Don't you see? I had to say something to her or she would have killed us both.'

Still Drake said nothing. He just stood there, watching the man squirm, listening to the ever-more elaborate justifications and supplications he tried to offer up.

In desperation Surovsky nodded to the camera mounted on the wall. 'They are recording everything, Drake. Don't be a fool. Use your head, and we can both walk away from this.' He winced as he shifted position, the injured leg paining him. 'Too many people have died for this already. Don't be one of them.'

Drake thought about the pawn Atayev had pressed into his hand, the final message he had tried to give. Killing Surovsky would achieve little if his memory, his legacy, remained intact. Such things couldn't be killed with bullets.

'You're right,' Drake said, laying the gun down on the table. 'You're right, Viktor.'

A sudden clang followed by shouting in the corridor outside told him that the security agents upstairs had managed to break their way in. Backing away from the table, Drake raised his hands as the electronic door buzzed open and three armed men poured into the room, their weapons covering all angles before finally homing in on Drake.

'Get down!' one of them snarled, gesturing to the floor as if Drake's hearing might have deserted him. 'On your knees! Down now!'

Drake made no move to resist as he lowered himself to the floor. He watched as Surovsky was released from his cuffs and lifted from the chair by two agents, wincing in pain with every movement.

He happened to catch Drake's eye as the two agents carried him past. His look of supplication and grovelling rationality was gone now. Despite the pain, he looked as he had during their first video conference; a man firmly in control of the situation once more, with others around to enforce his will.

The look Drake gave him in return was enough to take some of the edge off his arrogance, and he avoided eye contact as he was helped gently from the room.

Drake was afforded no such luxury. His arms were yanked behind his back and his wrists cuffed, heedless of the injuries to his neck and shoulder. He had expected as much. As far as they were concerned, he was a hostile until proven otherwise.

He looked up as another man entered the room. An older man with a craggy, careworn face and a greying beard.

Kamarov.

He surveyed Drake for a long moment, saying nothing. His expression was difficult to read, though Drake got the impression he was trying to make his mind up about something. Perhaps whether to kill him or let him live.

There wasn't much he could do about it either way.

Finally he snapped a command to the agent who had cuffed Drake, then turned away and strode out of the room.

Chapter 69

It was the second time today that Drake had found himself restrained in a moving vehicle, with a burlap sack over his head. Somehow he doubted he'd live to have a third such experience.

After being held for an hour or so in an interrogation room at Lubyanka, he'd been cuffed, hooded and hauled out to a waiting vehicle that had quickly sped off. He had no idea where he was being taken, and after a dozen turns, starts and stops had lost all sense of direction.

All he knew was that he'd come to a halt now. This was it. This was where they were going to execute him.

He heard the door being opened and felt a rush of cold air, then a moment later strong hands seized him and pulled him outside. For the next few seconds he stood there while the wind sighed around him, waiting for the single shot that would end it.

No shot came.

The bastards were toying with him, letting him sweat, trying to make him plead.

'If you're going to kill me, fucking get on with it,' he growled, now far beyond caring. 'I'm bored of this shit.'

Then, to his surprise, he felt his wrists seized in a strong grip. There was a click, and a moment later the cuffs came away. Immediately he pulled away and tore off his hood, taking in his surroundings.

It was dark. Either he'd been held in that cell longer than he thought, or the car journey had carried him further from Lubyanka than it seemed.

However, a glance upwards at the vast obelisk rising into the night sky told him he hadn't travelled far at all. He was standing in the great open-air memorial at the summit of Poklonnaya Hill, the scene of the aborted sting operation earlier in the day, and only a couple of miles from where he'd started. Below, the bright lights of the thriving city shone like beacons in the darkness.

Life in Moscow went on as if nothing at all had happened.

'I hope you appreciate the view,' a deep voice remarked.

Spinning around, Drake found himself standing face to face with Alexei Kamarov. The older man was wrapped up in a heavy overcoat, his head covered by a black fur hat. In his gloved hand he held an automatic.

'Is this supposed to be a parting gift?' Drake asked, glancing at the weapon.

A trace of amusement showed on his craggy face. 'There are men in this country who want you dead, Mr Drake. Fortunately for you I'm not one of them.'

'Very comforting. So what are we doing here?'

Placing the automatic inside his jacket, Kamarov fished a packet of cigarettes from his pocket and calmly lit one, taking a long thoughtful draw before he went on.

'I would offer you one, but you don't smoke,' he explained, noting Drake's look.

Drake frowned. He'd said it as if it were a solid, verified fact. Kamarov had known him for less than a day.

'You gave up in your early twenties, when you started training to become a boxer,' he went on, watching Drake closely. 'I know a great deal about you, Ryan Drake, because I make it my business to know things about people. For

527

example, I know that a year ago, you were tasked by your CIA masters to break into a secure facility in Siberia and rescue an inmate known by her code name Maras.'

Drake felt a shiver run through him that had nothing to do with the cold.

How could Kamarov know all this? More importantly, how could he have known all this time and done nothing about it? By any standards, Drake should be a wanted man in Russia. His actions the previous year must have earned him several life sentences, if not a summary execution.

The older man smiled, apparently amused by his discomfort. 'You did not seriously think you could get away with something of that scale, did you? One thing you will learn is that in this world, every action has consequences. How and when those consequences make themselves known is simply a matter of time.'

Drake had a feeling he might soon be making a return to that Siberian prison under rather different circumstances. 'Is this your way of saying time's up?'

'Not quite. You are just a soldier; you follow orders. It is the men giving those orders who interest me. More importantly, I was interested in why those men would go to such trouble to rescue a traitor.'

Drake blinked, wondering if he'd heard him right. 'What do you mean?'

Kamarov took another pull on his cigarette.

'You asked what we are doing here,' he said at length. 'I brought you here to tell you a story. The kind of story that has no place within Lubyanka's walls.'

'I've heard a lot of stories today.'

'You will find this one interesting, I think,' Kamarov assured him. 'It begins in the Soviet Union in the early 1980s, with a young woman locked away in juvenile prison. Both of her parents are dead and she has no one left who cares about her. She is forgotten, abandoned, alone. And above all, she is angry. Angry at the State, angry at the system that imprisoned her, angry at the life that has failed her. Her future looks bleak indeed, until one day she is visited by a man offering her a way out.'

Kaunas Correctional Facility, Lithuania, 8 March 1983

Anya sat at the interview table with her hands in her lap, her back straight and her chin up, staring straight ahead without seeing anything. It was the same posture of respectful deference she had long ago learned to adopt for such meetings.

Inside, however, she was curious, even a little unnerved by her unexpected summons.

Her review meetings were held twice a year, in January and July, during which her conduct, progress and personal development were scrutinised in depth. For sixty minutes she would sit in a hard plastic chair before a panel of three officials, giving bland answers to bland questions, telling them exactly what they wanted to hear.

Each time she would pray that this meeting was the last, that the assessment board would be satisfied with her conduct and authorise her release. And each time her hopes were dashed, and she returned to the boring routine of prison life with growing bitterness.

But it wasn't just a desire to return to the outside world that motivated her. In a few months she would turn eighteen. She would be an adult, and therefore by law she could no longer remain here in a young offender's institution. If she hadn't secured her release by then, she would be transferred to an adult prison.

She might have carved out a niche here, but in a place like that she would be a very small fish in a very large pond. She had no desire to fight her way up from the bottom again.

She looked up as the door opened and a man walked into the room. He wasn't one of the three men who sat on her assessment panel. Indeed, she couldn't recall ever having seen him before.

She guessed he was in his mid-forties; not old yet but seasoned and experienced, with the tanned and slightly weather-beaten complexion of a man who had spent much time outdoors. His features were strong and ruggedly handsome, his dark hair swept back from a high forehead, his grey eyes clear and focused.

He wasn't a tall man; perhaps an inch or so shorter than her. But despite his modest stature, he carried himself with the understated confidence of a man used to being in control of a situation. There was no swagger or bravado about him, but rather a quiet self-assurance that she found both intriguing and strangely appealing.

He was holding a large folder under his left arm that she was quite certain contained her review notes from the past three years. She recognised the worn and creased cover.

He approached and held out his free hand, his grey eyes focused on her.

'Anya, isn't it?' he asked.

Anya was taken aback. No one had ever shaken hands with her before. She couldn't recall anyone even making such a gesture. That was something men did.

Hesitating a moment, she reached out and took his hand. His grip was warm and strong, the skin on his palms slightly roughened by physical labour.

'May I sit here?' he asked, gesturing to a chair opposite.

Again she felt caught off guard. No one had asked her permission to do anything before. Her wishes and desires were not important to them.

But this man had taken the time to ask.

'Yes,' she said after a few moments.

Smiling, he lowered himself into the chair and sat with one leg folded on top of the other, the dossier resting on his lap. He surveyed her in silence for a few moments, taking in her rigid posture, her raised chin and clasped hands.

'You can relax a little,' he said, a hint of amusement in his eyes. 'I'm not a drill sergeant. I won't shout at you.'

Anya frowned. No one had ever told her to relax either. Feeling oddly self-conscious now, she leaned back a little in her chair and watched as the new arrival opened her review folder, his eyes scanning the pages.

'I hope you don't mind, but I took the liberty of reading your file on my way here,' he explained without looking up. 'According to the review board, you're a model inmate, Anya. You're respectful to the staff here, you spend most of your day in the library and you haven't been cited for disciplinary action in the past two years.'

And yet I'm still an inmate here, she thought.

'The file also says you're more than capable of defending yourself in a fight,' he added, glancing up at her. 'Is this true?'

Anya felt a deep blush rising to her face. Fights were a way of life in a place like this, where only the strong and ruthless earned respect. Anya had been involved in more than her share over the past three years, though she was careful never to be seen as the instigator. She might not start the fights, but she always finished them.

And as much as she tried not to acknowledge it, they provided some sense of release from the frustrations and disappointments of her life here.

'That . . . I mean, I only act to defend myself,' she stammered.

Again she saw that flicker of amusement. 'It wasn't a criticism, Anya,' he promised her. 'You should never be ashamed of standing up for yourself. Never. After all, who else can you depend on?'

Anya found herself warming to this man. Armed as she was with the inherent ability to sense deception and hidden motives in others, she detected none in him. He meant what he said, and when she looked at him she saw warmth, and even respect.

531

'Can I ask a question?' she said.

He laid down the folder and looked at her. 'Of course.'

Anya swallowed, almost afraid of what the answer might be but desperate to know at the same time. 'Why are you here?'

He smiled, looking like a father who has just watched his child take her first tentative steps. 'Based on everything I've read, I think you're a remarkable young woman, Anya. And I think you could do remarkable things if you were only given the opportunity.' He leaned forwards in his chair, his grey eyes intense, his entire being focused on her. 'I want to give you that chance, if you'll let me. Will you listen to what I have to say?'

Such was the intensity and sheer magnetism of his presence that Anya felt captivated, entranced. Never had anyone looked at her like this. Never had she been made to feel that she was actually worth something.

There was no other answer to give him.

'I will.'

'He told her everything she wished to hear – that she was special, that she was capable of great things, and that her country needed a young woman with her potential. He showed her the first true kindness she had known in years, and it was not long before she started to warm to him. Once he had established her trust, he offered her a deal – early release from prison, money, a new life, whatever she wanted. All he asked for in return was her obedience, and above all her loyalty.'

'Obedience at what?' Drake asked.

'Spying, of course. She was intelligent, beautiful and resourceful enough to survive in prison. Most importantly, she had a talent for spotting liars – a valuable skill which he believed he could use.

'Of all the agents he recruited, she was his favourite,'

Kamarov went on. 'The longer he spent with her, the more he grew to trust and care for her. In time, he decided to use her for a very special project he had in mind. He wanted her to defect to the United States, to work her way into the CIA and become one of his key assets within the US intelligence community. Naturally she agreed to his plan.'

Drake was aghast. It wasn't true. It couldn't be. Anya had told him the grim story of her early years: the loss of her parents and her struggle to survive in the State care system, her arrival in America, her induction into the Agency and her close relationship with Cain. She had spoken with absolute conviction, and she had made him believe every word.

'Imagine then the pain and betrayal he felt when she severed all contact with her handlers and disappeared, only to show up again in Afghanistan as part of a paramilitary group, assassinating Russian officers and causing huge damage to the war effort. Surovsky flew into a rage and vowed to have her brought back in chains, even drafting in an entire Spetsnaz unit to hunt her down.'

Drake saw a momentary flicker in his otherwise impassive eyes, saw the shadow of an old memory being replayed. It didn't take a genius to work out what he was thinking.

'You,' he said. 'He brought you in.'

The older man nodded. 'We were handed intelligence that Anya and her group were leaving Afghanistan, and that they intended to cross the Pakistani border through a remote mountain valley. That was where we sprang our trap. But even outnumbered and surrounded, they fought like nothing I had ever seen. In the end we took only one prisoner – Anya. She had sacrificed herself, holding us off until the others could escape.' He exhaled slowly, shaking his head. 'Brave but foolish. If only she had known what was waiting for her.'

Drake knew what was coming. Anya had made vague references to something that had happened to her in Afghanistan twenty years earlier, though she had refused to elaborate. But Drake still vividly recalled the spider's web of scarring across her back when she was getting dressed. To his eyes, they had looked just like lash marks.

'Surovsky showed no mercy once he got his hands on her. He demanded to know why she had betrayed him, who had turned her, but she never gave him anything. No matter what he did. No matter what he made others do to her, she never spoke a word.' He was silent for a time, taking another draw while he stared out across the city. 'Never in my life have I seen such resolve. Never. I always asked myself why she resisted, what she was fighting so hard to protect. And . . . after a time, I began to feel ashamed. Ashamed of what we were doing to her.'

'What happened to her?' Drake asked, almost afraid of the answer.

Kamarov swallowed, then raised his chin a little. 'She escaped, and against my expectations she made it out of the country alive. I had hoped that would be enough for her, that she would leave the CIA and find a new path. I was wrong.' He sighed, looking around the room. 'And twenty years later, I was brought in to hunt her down again. History repeating itself, as they say.'

'Why are you telling me all this?'

He looked around, and Drake could see the weight of the regret he still carried with him. 'Because I am getting too old for secrets, and because I know now the man I've been serving. I saw the recording of Surovsky's interrogation.' The look of disgust in his eyes was obvious, even in the dim light. 'I can't undo the mistakes I have made, but I can stop myself making another today.'

He pointed off eastwards, towards the towering walls of the Kremlin.

'The US embassy is about half a mile in that direction,' he said. 'Even you should be able to make it that far. I suggest you get yourself out of Russia, and think very carefully before coming back.'

Drake couldn't believe it. After everything that had happened, Kamarov was letting him go. 'What about you?'

The older man took one last draw on his cigarette before flicking it away. 'I will do what I always do. Survive.'

With that, he returned to his parked car, opened the driver's door and eased himself in before firing up the engine. Lowering the window, he leaned out and regarded the younger man thoughtfully for a long moment.

'You are a brave man, Ryan Drake. Not very wise, but brave,' he decided. 'I think I understand what she saw in you.'

Drake never got a chance to reply as Kamarov swung the vehicle around and drove off, leaving him alone.

Part Five

Instigation

To date, no Russian official of any rank has been reprimanded for the handling of events at Beslan.

Chapter 70

McKnight's home was a spacious two-bedroom apartment in Aspen Hill, about 10 miles from central DC. She had moved in only a couple of months ago, yet she seemed to have made the transition as easily as she handled everything that life threw her way.

The place was well ordered, tastefully decorated and furnished to take full advantage of the floor space on offer. It was a stark contrast to Drake's cluttered, untidy home with its mismatching furniture and heating system that never quite seemed to work properly.

The TV was on, tuned to CNN, though the volume was muted so as not to intrude on their conversation. Beyond the living room's bay windows lay the distant lights of DC, partially shrouded in sombre grey clouds. It was early evening in December and getting dark fast, with flurries of sleet pattering against the window.

Neither he nor Samantha was much concerned with the weather, however.

'Any good?' Drake asked as McKnight took a sip of the Sauvignon Blanc that he'd finally got around to delivering. It might have been ten days late, but he hoped the original intent hadn't been lost.

She smiled. 'Well, as far as peace offerings go, you could do worse.'

Drake wasn't about to argue. When it came to wine, he could have been drinking a glass of paint stripper and not known the difference.

'So we're even now?'

'Not even close,' she said with a playful grin. However, it soon faded as her thoughts returned inevitably to the events of the past few days. 'On the subject of peace offerings, I assume you're still on Langley's shit list?'

Drake made a face. His return from Moscow hadn't exactly been a triumphant affair. No sooner had he stepped off the flight than he'd found himself hauled back to Langley for a lengthy debriefing, starting with 'What the fuck did you think you were doing?'

The questions had continued in that vein for some time, with Drake being as evasive as possible about Anya while doing his best to make his actions appear justified. He'd been fighting a losing battle right from the start, and yet just when it seemed as though he was staring at a summary dismissal and a prison sentence, the debriefing had come to an abrupt end.

He couldn't say for sure, but he suspected this change in attitude was due in no small part to Dan Franklin taking the heat off him.

'I think someone up there likes me,' he remarked. 'God knows who or why, though.'

She snorted in amusement at that. 'And Surovsky?'

Drake's expression darkened at the mention of his name. He had seen and heard nothing of the man since his departure from Lubyanka, and for now at least he was content for it to remain that way. Challenging him directly was a quick way to get killed.

'He's going to get away with this, isn't he?' McKnight asked, taking another sip of wine as she looked out the window. 'Everything Atayev accused him of was true, and he gets to walk away like nothing happened.'

Drake didn't respond immediately. His attention had been drawn away from her, to the TV that was still playing news coverage from CNN. It was muted to allow them to talk comfortably, but Drake had a feeling she would want to hear the latest news piece.

'Maybe not,' he said, reaching for the remote.

Frowning, McKnight glanced around. And straight away found herself confronted by unnervingly familiar images of a short, withered-looking man being escorted out of a secure building and into a waiting vehicle, with crowds of reporters pressing in on both sides. The flashes from their cameras formed an almost continuous burst of light, starkly illuminating the aged, pockmarked face of Viktor Surovsky.

Beneath the video footage, a bold, urgent news feed scrolled across the screen.

Beslan Massacre – Russian cover-up?

'We see here images of Director Surovsky being escorted from the FSB headquarters building in Moscow,' the news anchor announced, an edge of excitement in his voice at what was clearly a major story. 'Neither Mr Surovsky, the FSB nor the Russian government have issued any statements yet in response to the videos which were released over the Internet in the past hour, but sources in Moscow have suggested that an official statement will be forthcoming later today. Once again, a number of video recordings have been released via the Internet which appear to show senior FSB agents admitting their involvement in the hostage crisis which claimed the lives of nearly four hundred civilians in Beslan in 2004. These recordings are too graphic to show on television, but they—'

The voice was cut off abruptly as McKnight muted the TV and turned to Drake, her expression one of incredulity.

'You?' she gasped.

He said nothing to this, just took a sip of his wine. Not too bad after all, he thought.

'How did you know?'

In response, Drake reached into his pocket and held up a little memento of his encounter with Atayev. The little white chess pawn that the man had given him as a parting gift, the top broken off in a jagged point, which held more significance than Drake had ever imagined.

A simple twist allowed him to unscrew the base, revealing a small hollowed-out compartment within.

Taking Samantha's hand, he turned the pawn upside down and allowed a little Micro SD card to fall into her palm. The sort of memory card used in digital cameras all over the world. The sort Atayev had used to record Demochev and Masalsky's confessions.

The contents of that memory card, while not enough to conclusively prove Surovsky's guilt, had nonetheless ignited a media firestorm. Within the hour, every major news network worldwide had picked up on the story and was running it continuously as reporters and investigators clamoured for more information. No amount of threats or intimidation or political manoeuvring could stop it now.

Men like Surovsky were untouchable.

Well, almost.

It wasn't mercy or compassion that had kept him from killing Surovsky in that interrogation room, but rather the growing realisation that he didn't have to. A far worse fate awaited Viktor Surovsky.

He would have to watch as everything he'd worked for, everything he had compromised and sacrificed to achieve, collapsed around him, until he was left with nothing but the memory of the power and influence he'd once wielded. The shadow of his former glory would consume him.

'He was right,' Drake said quietly, still holding Samantha's outstretched hand. 'Even a king can be brought down by a single pawn.'

It happened almost without either of them being aware of it. Tilting her head back slightly, Samantha leaned in a little closer, her lips parted as she stared into his eyes, willing him to respond in kind. And moved by an impulse that went deeper than he'd ever consciously acknowledged, he did.

All of the things they had left unsaid were forgotten in that moment, all of the admissions that should have been made were cast aside as they at last gave in to their need for each other.

The news report continued to play on the TV, but neither of them paid heed to it now. They had seen enough.

Chapter 71

'Listen to what I'm telling you, Sasha!' Viktor Surovsky growled into the phone. His angry pacing across the luxurious study was reduced to a shuffling limp by the recently treated bullet wound in his leg. 'They have nothing on me. Their evidence is non-existent. These confessions were extracted under torture, and we both know men will say anything if you hurt them enough.'

Accompanied only by a couple of loyal bodyguards, he had retreated from Moscow and the media firestorm engulfing the FSB to the isolation and comparative safety of his luxury dacha east of the city. Very few people knew the exact location of the sprawling house, set within acres of woodland purchased under a fake identity, and he had worked hard to keep it that way. It was his safe haven, his fallback position from where he could plan his next move.

The darkened snow-covered forests and the frozen lake beyond the big windows of his study were a deceptively peaceful counterpoint to the turmoil now raging within his organisation.

'I'm sorry, Viktor, but this is out of my hands. It's out of all our hands now,' replied Aleksander "Sasha" Polunin, the head of the FSB's Internal Security Directorate. 'The Kremlin's up in arms – they're already talking about appointing a special commission to investigate the claims. You have to step down as director, at least until they can make their assessment. You can't carry on like this.'

Surovsky snatched his glass of vodka from the table and took a deep gulp, hoping it would stop his hands from trembling. It probably wasn't a good idea to be mixing alcohol with the potent painkillers he'd been taking, but that was the least of his concerns at that moment.

'Fuck the Kremlin, and fuck their special commission!' he raged, frustration and desperation surging up within him. 'I could ruin all of them. Do they know who the fuck I am? Do they know the things I've done for this country?'

'That's the problem,' Polunin replied, his voice frighteningly cold and detached. Already he was pulling away, distancing himself from Surovsky. A rat deserting a sinking ship. 'They know exactly who you are, and now they're beginning to question what exactly you've done. My advice to you is to find a good lawyer. You'll be needing one.'

Saying nothing more, he hung up.

'Fuck!' Surovsky snarled, slamming the phone down in its cradle.

It was all falling apart. His career, his legacy, his very life was unravelling around him, and he was rapidly running out of means to stop it. He was calling in every favour, trying to threaten, plead or reason with influential men in the Russian government to help him in his hour of need, but none of it was working.

He was political poison. Nobody wanted anything to do with him in the light of accusations like this. People he'd known for decades brushed his requests of help aside as if he were a beggar on the street. In Russia, one quickly learned to know the difference between a man in difficulty, and a lost cause who could easily drag others down with him. Surovsky was now firmly in the latter category.

He raised the glass to his lips again, only to find it empty.

Cursing under his breath, he threw open the door and limped down the short hallway to the dacha's expansive living room.

And there, he stopped in his tracks.

The two FSB bodyguards he had employed to accompany him out here were lying sprawled on the floor, their blood soaking into the expensive rug he'd had imported from Saudi Arabia two years previously.

And beyond them, seated comfortably in one of the room's leather recliner chairs with a silenced handgun trained on him, was a woman.

A dead woman. A ghost.

The glass fell from his grip, shattering on the polished floorboards with a musical tinkling, tiny fragments peppering his feet and ankles. He was oblivious to it. All his attention was focused on the ghost, on the icy blue eyes staring back at him, piercing in their intensity.

'Hello, Viktor,' Anya said. 'It's good to see you again.'

For several seconds, not a word was said. The old man and the woman stared at each other across the open space, each taking the measure of the other.

Surovsky needed a moment to recover from the shock of seeing her again, to assure himself that she was indeed real and not some horrific, fevered product of his imagination. But she was real. And the two dead agents lying on the floor in front of her, like trophies placed there in homage to a god of war and death, were mute testimony to the terrible skills she still commanded.

He made no attempt to flee. Even if she wasn't armed, she could easily outpace him on his injured leg. Instead he stood his ground and looked a little closer at her, comparing her to the woman he'd once known.

She looked older now, Surovsky caught himself thinking. The first time he'd met Anya, she had been a young woman of seventeen, her youthful prettiness giving a tantalising hint of the woman she would one day become. Indeed, that was part of the reason he had chosen her, knowing that beauty could be a weapon as effective as any other.

She had changed in the quarter of a century since that day; grown stronger, harder, colder. The trials and hardships of the life she'd lived had left their indelible marks on her, both inside and out. She was still strikingly attractive, no doubt still able to use that beauty to her advantage just as he'd taught her, but the soul that lurked behind those icy blue eyes was one that struck fear even into his heart.

All the more so because he had had a hand in shaping it.

'I was told you were dead,' he said quietly. Drake, McKnight, and the few of Atayev's men who had survived the assault on the warehouse in Moscow, had all sworn the same thing – that Atayev himself had shot Anya dead and pitched her body into the river. How could they all have been lying?

Moscow, 24 December 2008

'I don't suppose you can tell me where you're going?' Atayev asked, his tone one of mild curiosity.

'Better that you don't know,' Anya replied honestly.

'Perhaps so,' he conceded. It made little difference to him now anyway. He held out his hand. 'Goodbye, Anya. And . . . good luck.'

Anya gripped it and held his gaze for a long moment. This would be the last time they spoke. She hadn't been told what the final stage of Atayev's plan entailed, but she knew one thing for certain – it would end with his death.

For now, however, she had her own death to take care of.

Releasing her grip, she turned and walked away, having to force herself to take each step. Turning her back on a man with a gun was foreign to her nature, especially when she knew that gun was about to be used on her.

Ten steps and he would fire. Seven to go.

Anya wasn't often inclined to entrust her life to others. She certainly hadn't had good experiences with such things in the past. But against her better judgement, she trusted Buran Atayev.

Four steps to go.

Her left hand closed around a small electric detonator hidden inside her jacket sleeve. The detonator wire trailed up her arm and into a pair of blank squibs fixed to the back and front of her vest, each with a small plastic bag of blood secured over them.

The blood was real. It was even her own, extracted from a vein in her left arm only minutes earlier, in case forensics wished to analyse it. The only fake thing would be the manner in which it was shed.

Two steps.

Anya took a breath, tensing herself in preparation. She had been shot before while wearing Kevlar vests. It was never a pleasant experience, and she was quite certain she would have some impressive bruises when this was over, but with a little luck she would be alive to see it.

She was about to find out.

She felt the impact of the bullet before she heard the shot, slamming into her back slightly to the left of her spine. Perfect. At the same moment she triggered the detonator, watching with satisfaction as blood sprayed from her chest.

She staggered forwards and collapsed into a muddy pool of water, putting on a show of trying to get up despite her mortal injury, while Atayev closed in on her. Right on cue, he kicked her over on to her back, raised the weapon and fired a second shot into the centre of her chest.

Fired at such close range, she felt the bruising impact more than the first shot, and it was all she could do to keep from crying out in pain. Instead she forced herself to slump back into the pool of freezing water.

With her 'death' complete, she allowed her body to go limp as two of Atayev's men hoisted her up and carried her over to the canal. She didn't make a sound, even as their hands pressed against the fresh bruising beneath her vest. They weren't in on this plan, so if they suspected anything was wrong, it was all for nothing.

A single swing to build up momentum, and suddenly she was released, falling like a stone into the canal. She took a breath, bracing herself as the frigid water enveloped her like a million needles pressing into her flesh all at once.

She did her best to push aside the pain, knowing the cold wouldn't prove fatal. She had always been a strong swimmer, and was no stranger to freezing water. And despite the discomfort, her clothes would provide enough insulation to keep hypothermia at bay. At least for a while.

She had made sure to include a few lead weights in her vest so that she would sink quickly beneath the surface. The water here was, she knew, murky and dark, with visibility extending only a few feet beneath the surface.

Once she was certain she had disappeared from view, she began to kick, propelling herself beneath the surface with sure, powerful strokes towards the end of the canal where it discharged into the Moskva River. She could hold her breath underwater for a good minute or so if she was exerting herself; enough to get her away from Atayev and his men, away from the warehouse, away from Drake. And away from the FSB agents who had been tasked with hunting her down.

She knew they wouldn't stop until she was dead. The only way for her plan to succeed was to give them what they wanted.

*

Surovsky saw a hint of a smile. 'Illusion, Viktor. It's the key to any game.'

He said nothing to that. Their 'game' wasn't over yet.

'How did you find me?' Only a few people on earth knew the location of his private residence. That was precisely why he'd come here, knowing he was safe from reporters, safe from investigators, safe even from his own government.

But apparently not safe from Anya.

Anya reached into her pocket and held up a cellphone. 'All I needed was your private number.'

It was all he could do to keep from sighing in frustration. The purpose of the cyber attack on the FSB's network was all too obvious now. It hadn't been done with the intention of compromising their systems and laying waste to the agency's secrets, but instead to gather a single, vital piece of information.

With his private phone number and a little resourcefulness, Anya could track him anywhere on the face of the earth. And with Moscow no longer safe for him, she had known he would retreat somewhere he believed to be safe, with only a few loyal security personnel she could easily overcome.

It had all been a ruse, he realised now. Her cooperation with Atayev, the men she had killed, the risks she had taken; all of these things had been nothing but stepping stones on her path, each one bringing her a little closer to her goal, to the man she had been pursuing with single-minded purpose.

All of it to bring her to this room, here and now. So she could confront the man who had twice tried to destroy her.

'You did all of this to get your hands on me.'

Anya rose from the chair, her eyes still fixed on him. 'You

went to a lot of trouble to get your hands on me in Afghanistan, and again in Iraq. Both times you made a lasting impression on me. I thought it was about time I returned the favour.'

'So what now?'

She raised her weapon. 'Now we go for a walk, Viktor.'

A couple of minutes later, Anya emerged from the dacha with Surovsky in front of her, his hands firmly bound behind his back. Her car was parked some distance away, beyond the building's security perimeter. The old man had a long walk ahead of him, in sub-zero temperatures at night.

She shoved him forwards, eager to be out of here. But she'd only covered 10 yards before she halted, catching something in her peripheral vision. After years of operating in environments where a single lapse in judgement could mean the difference between life and death, her senses were attuned to any tiny shift in her surroundings. And more than that, she had learned to trust her instincts.

Someone was watching her.

She gripped her M1911 tighter, took a deep breath and whirled around, dropping down on one knee to make herself a smaller target as she levelled the weapon at her enemy.

'Don't,' Kamarov warned.

He was standing about 15 yards away, covering her with an MP-443 handgun, not flinching for an instant. His face was set and grim, muscles taut, finger tight on the trigger. He had the drop on her.

Anya froze, her weapon still pointed at the ground. She knew that one pull of the trigger was all it would take to end her plans for revenge right here. Even if Kamarov wasn't an excellent marksman, which she knew from experience he was, he could scarcely miss at such range.

So she did nothing. She waited, her mind racing. She hadn't anticipated this. She hadn't anticipated him.

They remained like that for a few seconds, neither moving a muscle. The tall pine trees at the edge of the clearing swayed and rustled, stirred by the cold night breeze.

Just for a moment, a fleeting smile crossed her face. A bitter, ironic smile. Twice now this man had been pitted against her, and twice she had lost. How appropriate that he should return now, at the end.

One last obstacle to overcome.

'Remember what I said to you once, Anya?' Surovsky remarked, a triumphant smile creasing his pockmarked old face. 'I've played this game a lot longer than you. And I'll still be playing it long after you're gone.' He looked over at Kamarov. 'Kill her, Alexei. We're done here.'

Anya tensed, readying herself to act. Her first target would be Surovsky. Even if Kamarov killed her for it, no way would she allow that man to live.

To her surprise, however, the FSB agent did nothing. He just stood there covering her, his finger on the trigger but no more.

'I gave you an order,' Surovsky said, a harder edge in his voice now. 'Kill her.'

Kamarov ignored him. His eyes, staring down the weapon's sights, were locked with Anya's.

'We're both getting a little old for this, don't you think?' he said sadly.

Twenty years ago they had both been soldiers, both strong and fit and in the prime of their lives. Now, looking at Kamarov, she saw the toll that two decades had taken on him. His face, lit by the pale light of the crescent moon overhead, was deeply lined and creased, his cheeks hollow, his hair turning grey.

He was right, they were both getting old.

'Give this up,' he implored her. 'Drop your gun.'

'And go back to prison?' Anya raised her chin, defiant to the end. 'Not this time.'

For a moment she saw a flicker of the man he'd once been. The man who had rescued her from that prison cell in Afghanistan, who had shown mercy and compassion in a place where such things had been almost forgotten.

The man who had saved her life.

Afghanistan, 7 November 1988

With her weary heart hammering in her chest and her raw, bloody wrists straining against her bonds, Anya tried to ready herself for what was coming, tried to marshal whatever feeble reserves of strength and endurance she could still call upon to meet the next onslaught.

She could no longer resist, could no longer fight back or defend herself. Her only weapon was stoic, abiding silence.

She closed her eyes for a moment as the key turned in the lock and the rusted cell door swung open, silently reciting the words that had been her only source of strength.

I will endure when all others fail. I will stand when all others retreat. Weakness will not be in my heart. Fear will not be in my creed. I will never surrender.

She opened her eyes, expecting big coarse hands to seize her and haul her roughly to her feet, dragging her off for another session.

Then she froze, utterly perplexed by what she was seeing.

The man standing in the doorway wasn't one of the guards she'd come to know all too well during her time here. He wasn't leering at her as an object to satiate his desire, wasn't glaring at her with contempt or, even worse, showing no recognition at all, as if she were merely an unpleasant task to be completed as quickly as possible.

She recognised this man. Dredged from the depths of her memory, she recalled the day they had captured her, the desperate holding action she'd fought while the rest of her team withdrew. She remembered the grim satisfaction she'd felt as her ammunition at last ran out and her enemies closed in around her.

And most of all she remembered the man who had taken her down. There had been no triumph in his victory, no lust for vengeance or desire to inflict pain and humiliation on his defeated opponent. He had been a soldier like herself, each set against the other by the decisions of their masters.

That same man was standing before her now, saying nothing, just staring at her.

Why was he here? Had he come here to kill her? she wondered with mingled hope and apprehension. The prospect of dying no longer held much fear for her, but as she had learned from bitter experience over the past couple of months, there were worse things to be experienced than death.

His gaze travelled slowly across her body, taking in the filthy clothes, the bruised and cut flesh, the tangled, matted hair, the desperation in her eyes.

'My God, what have they done to you?' he whispered, his voice sounding as though it was about to break. He approached, and instinctively she tried to back away, her eyes wide with fear.

'It's all right,' he said, kneeling beside her. 'I'm not here to hurt you. I've seen too much of it already.'

Anya frowned, not understanding what was happening. What she was seeing and hearing didn't conform to the grim pattern that her life had assumed.

And just like that, she felt something she hadn't felt in a long time. Something that had almost burned out completely, but which had suddenly rekindled into a raging inferno. Hope. Wild and unfettered hope.

She did something she hadn't done since the day of her capture. She spoke.

'What do you want?'

He sighed, and in a heartbeat her hope evaporated. 'They're going to execute you today.'

Anya let out a breath, as if she'd just been punched in the chest. Of course she should have seen it coming. Sooner or later she'd known they would tire of their game, that they would eliminate her and move on to something more worthy of their time, but to hear the news delivered in such blunt, businesslike fashion was hard even for her to take.

'They're going to drive you out to the middle of nowhere and shoot you,' he went on, much to her dismay. 'And if you want to survive, you're going to let them do it.'

Reaching into his pocket, he pressed something into her hand. Something small and metallic. A key.

'Listen carefully. This key will unlock your cuffs,' he said, speaking low and fast. 'I've made sure his gun is loaded with blanks. Let him shoot you, let him drive away, then unlock yourself. Head due north, through a valley between two mountains. You'll find a small village a couple of miles away. Ask for a man named Vesh. He'll help you get across the border to Pakistan.'

Such was her complete shock at everything she'd heard, she was having trouble taking it all in. Her eyes were blank and staring, longing to believe him but frightened to let herself feel trust for anyone.

Sensing this, he reached out and cupped her jaw, forcing her to look right at him. 'Tell me you understand, child,' he hissed. 'I have no time to repeat it. Tell me you'll at least try.'

If she'd harboured doubts before, the intense, desperate look in his eyes was enough to silence them. 'I will,' she promised. Never had she meant anything more in her life.

That was enough for him. Letting go of her, he stood up and made to leave.

'Why are you helping me?' she asked, still unable to comprehend his actions.

He paused, just a moment, and looked at her. Looked at her but didn't see her. She realised then that he was looking at himself, his thoughts turned inwards.

'I'm a soldier, just like you. And you deserve life more than the men I serve.'

Saying nothing more, he retreated from the cell, slamming the heavy door shut behind him and plunging Anya into darkness once more.

And alone in the dark, she at last gave in and allowed the tears to come.

'We're both soldiers,' she said, echoing his words from twenty years earlier. 'We both fight and kill. Just remember who you're doing it for.'

For a moment Kamarov's eyes flicked to Surovsky, replaying the accusations and conspiracies swirling around him, the seemingly endless toll of death and fear and suffering that was his true legacy.

'Alexei, what the fuck are you doing?' Surovsky snapped. 'Why are you listening to her? This woman is a terrorist, a traitor, a murderer. She killed your fellow agents and she'll kill you if you give her a chance. Shoot her! Shoot her now!'

She saw Kamarov's finger tighten on the trigger, saw his body tense up in preparation for the kick of the weapon. Anya held her breath, bracing herself for the impact of the first round.

It never came.

She watched as the gun was lowered and his posture relaxed.

'If she is a terrorist, a traitor and a murderer, then she's in good company tonight, Viktor,' he remarked, his look one of absolute contempt.

'You'll die for this, you piece of shit,' Surovsky spat. 'It's over for you.'

'All of us deserve death for what we've done, and what we've allowed others to do. This won't erase my mistakes, but perhaps I'll sleep a little easier now.' With nothing more to say to his former boss, he turned his eyes on Anya once more. 'Answer me one question. Will you come after me when this is over?'

Anya shook her head. 'You saved my life once already. I'd say that makes us even.'

Kamarov sighed and nodded, satisfied with that. Her word meant more to him than Surovsky's ever had.

'Then I hope we won't meet again,' he said.

'We won't,' she promised, watching as he holstered his gun, turned away from her and walked off towards his car. He was a man approaching the end of his career now, prematurely aged by years of care and regret, yet he appeared lighter somehow, as if he'd discarded a heavy burden that had long been weighing him down.

She looked at Surovsky again. She had a burden of her own to discard tonight.

Chapter 72

Pakistan, 28 December 1988

Light. Bright light everywhere.

She blinked, opened her eyes a crack, then squeezed them shut again. The light burned her eyes.

Her next attempt was a little less painful, and as she opened them a little further, she began to make sense of her surroundings.

She was in a hospital. She knew that much from the stinging smell of antiseptic and the faint beep of a heart monitor that was coming from somewhere to her left, slow and regular.

'Anya,' a voice gasped. A voice she knew well.

She opened her eyes again, forcing them open despite the pain. She watched as a face swam into bleary focus in front of her. A youthful, handsome face now darkened by worry, as if he had aged many years in just a few months.

Marcus Cain.

'Shh. It's all right, Anya. It's all right,' he said, his voice soft and soothing. 'Just relax. You're safe now.'

'Marcus,' she managed to rasp. Her throat felt like sandpaper.

'Yes. It's Marcus. I'm here now. I won't leave you.'

'Where . . . ?' she began. Her head hurt; it was difficult to speak.

'You're in a hospital in Peshawar. Don't worry, you're safe,' he promised her. 'I don't know how you made it out of there, but you're safe now. It's over.'

Like the pieces of a jigsaw puzzle tumbling on to the floor, a disorganised mess of images and memories began to flash through her mind. She remembered the months of torture and interrogation she had endured, remembered her stubborn, almost childish refusal to give in. She saw her execution at the hands of Surovsky, saw her escape and the desperate, freezing journey on foot through the mountainous border region with Pakistan.

'I didn't give you up,' she said, her voice little more than a whisper. 'No matter what they did, I didn't betray you.'

She reached out to take his hand, though even this simple act required a great effort. Only then did she notice how thin her arms were; veins and stringy muscle standing out hard against her pale skin. Her body, once fit and strong and in the prime of life, had withered and deteriorated after months of abuse and starvation.

Cain's face seemed to crumple before her eyes at her feeble effort to reach out to him, though he made no effort to return the gesture. He bowed his head, and she saw tears falling into the bedcovers.

'Just concentrate on getting better,' he said, unable to look her in the eye. 'We'll do everything we can. I'll make sure you get the best treatment available.'

Anya frowned, confused. It was an effort just to focus on him. Her head was pounding, and she felt a rising tide of nausea threatening to overwhelm her. 'What do you mean, treatment?'

'I don't pretend to know what happened to you in there, but the doctors found evidence of . . . assault.' He swallowed and looked down, unwilling to meet her gaze. 'There are . . . complications that we need to deal with.'

It was too much. Leaning over the side of the bed, Anya curled into a ball and was violently sick across the tiled floor. Cain was there with a basin, several seconds too late. The sad, grief-stricken look in his eyes was more obvious than ever.

He couldn't even bear to look at her, as if her very appearance disgusted him. Only then did she begin to suspect the truth. Her survival had not been anticipated. She was expected to have died a heroic death for her adopted country, not to have survived and returned . . . tainted.

She was an embarrassment, to him and to the Agency. She was a blight, a sore, a gangrene. A dirty, uncomfortable little secret to be hidden away and forgotten about.

'Christ, Anya, I'm so sorry,' he said, his voice breaking.

Sorry. She was sorry too, about a lot of things. But sorry wasn't going to make things right; not this time. Sorry wasn't going to undo what had happened to her.

Nothing would.

Johns Hopkins Hospital, Maryland, 27 February 1989

Anya sat with her back ramrod straight, her hands in her lap as she listened to the doctor read out her medical report. He was an older man, probably in his early fifties, balding and overweight, his fleshy chin bobbing every time he spoke.

Cain had made good on his promise. She had indeed received the best medical care the government could provide, all the latest drugs and treatments to combat the damage done by torture and rape. He had done everything in his power to help her, but she knew it wouldn't assuage his guilt.

In the three months since her escape, she had recovered a good deal of her robust health and fitness. She had put on weight, the colour had returned to her skin and she had even resumed her once intense physical training. Outwardly she appeared to be in good health, but as she had learned many times in life, appearances could be deceptive.

'Unfortunately our tests indicate significant damage to both the ovaries and fallopian tubes,' the doctor went on. He glanced up from his report and offered her a sympathetic look, as if that would make everything all right. 'Function of both organs has been significantly impaired, and is unlikely to improve beyond its current level.'

Anya swallowed and looked down at her hands. 'Is there . . . anything that can be done?'

He shook his head. 'The reproductive system is, I'm afraid, particularly vulnerable in cases like this.' He sighed and closed his folder. 'I wish I could give you better news, but we have to be realistic here. It's highly unlikely you'll be able to conceive naturally, much less carry a baby to term.'

Anya said nothing. She didn't know what to say, didn't know what to feel. She just felt empty, all thoughts and emotions purged from her.

Rising stiffly from her chair, she nodded to the doctor. She couldn't remember his name. She didn't care.

'Thank you for your help.'

He regarded her over the rim of his glasses. 'Are you all right? We have . . . people you can talk to.'

She shook her head. 'I'm fine. Thank you.'

Leaving his office, she walked to the restroom at the end of the hallway and locked the door behind her. She stood by the sink, just looking at herself in the mirror.

She reached up to move a lock of hair out of her face, noticing with a kind of mild disinterest that her hand was shaking.

There were tears in her eyes. She noticed that too.

Yaroslavl Oblast, Russia, 29 December 2008

Bringing the jeep to a halt, Anya killed the engine, opened her door and stepped out. The cold night air hit her straight away, seeming to steal the breath from her lungs as a northerly wind sighed across the flat snow-covered steppes. She looked up, catching glimpses of the crescent moon through gaps in the ragged clouds.

All things considered it was a desolate, remote patch of wilderness, easily 10 miles from the nearest town. Anya had chosen it especially for what she'd planned.

Returning to the rear of the vehicle, she unlocked the trunk and swung the lid upwards. Surovsky lay within, bound and gagged, his knees drawn up to his chest. He looked up at her, his eyes glimmering with a mixture of fear and malice.

Saying nothing, Anya grabbed him by his arms and hauled him out, struggling a little with his weight. He wasn't big or heavy – his body was withered and diminished by age – but his awkward shape made him difficult to move.

He groaned in pain as he landed on the hard frozen ground, his injured leg absorbing the impact. Reaching into her pocket, Anya produced a flick knife whose blade she had sharpened to a razor's edge, and used it to slice through the ropes binding his wrists and ankles. Taking a step back, she folded the knife away and reached for the M1911 inside her jacket.

'Get up, Viktor,' she said, her voice low and commanding. 'Get up.'

Slowly stretching out his stiff, aching limbs, Surovsky planted his feet on the snow-covered ground and with some effort managed to rise.

Anya gestured northwards. 'Now walk.'

With a resigned sigh, Surovsky turned and started to walk slowly away from the vehicle, stumbling through depressions and clumps of snow-covered grass that would bloom with life again in a few months. Anya followed a few paces behind, keeping her weapon trained on him.

'I'm impressed,' he said. 'I told you once that you were capable of great things, and you proved me right today. You exceeded all my expectations. You were always my favourite, Anya.'

She said nothing. She was immune to such feeble attempts at flattery.

'I never had children of my own,' he went on, keeping his

back to her. 'In our line of work . . . there was little room for family. But when I met you, I felt as if I'd found a daughter. I cared for you like you were my own flesh and blood. Did you ever feel that way about me?'

Still Anya said nothing, just as she had taught herself to do all those years ago in that interrogation room in Afghanistan. But a part of her, a very small part that she hadn't consciously acknowledged for a long time, that she had buried beneath layers of hate and anger, knew the answer to his question.

'I know you lost your parents when you were still a child. I know you had no family to call your own. That you were alone, scared, angry, and lost.'

He stopped walking then, turned to face her. Somehow he had changed, had cast aside the bitterness and avaricious lust for power that had consumed him all these years. Despite the quarter of a century that separated them, he looked now like the kindly, patient man who had walked into that assessment room and spoken to her with such disarming respect.

And despite herself, despite all the pain and loss he had inflicted on her, despite everything, a tiny part of Anya's mind responded to it.

'I tried to give some of that back to you. I tried to be what you needed me to be, and I thought in some way you understood that.' He swallowed and looked away. 'That was why it hurt so much when I caught you in Afghanistan. To see you working for the Americans, knowing you'd turned your back on your country, on me . . . It was more than I could bear. I'm . . . I'm sorry, Anya. About everything.'

He was good. She had to give it to him. Of all the men she had known in her life, Viktor Surovsky was the only one who could lie convincingly to her. Perhaps because he had spent so much of his life telling lies, even he no longer recognised the distinction between reality and the warped, perverted

563

version of events he concocted to suit his own needs, to justify his own desires.

But Anya did. She knew a truth that she had never revealed to him.

'I never told you why I turned, did I?'

He frowned, caught off guard by the question. 'No, you didn't.'

No, she didn't. Not when he tortured her, when he ordered her beaten, starved, humiliated, raped. Not even then had she told him why.

She took a breath. And just like that, she let go of it; let go of that tiny part of her mind that still felt something for this man, that still held on to the hope that he was a guide, a light in the darkness of her life.

'My parents never died in a car accident,' she said, all trace of emotion purged from her. 'They were executed for "crimes against the State", because they dared to believe their country would one day be free. They were executed by *you*, Viktor. That was why you found me all those years later. It wasn't just random chance – you knew who I was, and you knew where I came from because *you* made it happen. You took me under your wing for . . . what? To assuage a guilty conscience? Or just to tie up another loose end?'

Surovsky stared at her, dumbfounded. He had no answers for her, no rehearsed lies or contingencies to fall back on. She didn't care – she didn't want to listen to whatever perverted justifications he might dream up.

'You took everything from me, everything and everyone I ever cared about. You destroyed my life, killed the person I once was, and the person I could have been. You even tried to kill me. But you failed, Viktor. You couldn't kill me.'

Surovsky's mask of fatherly kindness had vanished, thrown aside now that he knew it could serve no purpose.

There could be no coming back from this. He glared at her like the enemy she was, his face hard and grim in the moonlight, his grey eyes smouldering.

'So what now, Anya?' he asked. 'You brought me all the way out here to take your revenge. Well, here I am.' He raised his hands. 'An unarmed old man – quite an opponent for someone like you. Take your shot. Kill me and get it over with. I'm not afraid to die.'

Anya let out a breath, watching as it misted in the frigid air around her.

'You still don't understand, do you? I'm not going to kill you,' she said truthfully. 'That's your choice now.'

Raising the M1911, she levelled it at his right knee and pulled the trigger. There was a flash, a loud crack that echoed across the vast empty steppes, and Surovsky's leg buckled beneath him. He went down, screaming in pain and clutching the shattered remains of his knee joint.

'You bitch!' he cried, flecks of saliva flying from his mouth. His eyes were wild with fear, pain and impotent fury. 'You fucking bitch.'

Anya said nothing, instead cocking her head to listen as another sound drifted across the night air. A high-pitched, almost otherworldly howl, soon joined by others. A wolf pack, alerted by the sudden noise and the smell of blood on the air.

She smiled. She had chosen this spot carefully indeed, making sure it was well within the territory of a large pack. She had always found such predators fascinating, and had spent much time throughout her life observing their behaviour.

'They sound hungry,' she remarked. 'Did you know that wolves can smell blood from nearly four kilometres away? I'd say you have five, maybe six minutes before they track you down. I wouldn't want to be here when they arrive. But like I said, I came here to give you a choice.'

Reaching into her jacket, Anya withdrew a second pistol, a Makarov PPM, and tossed it on to the ground in front of him.

'There's one round in the chamber, Viktor. The rest is up to you.'

Teeth bared in hatred, the old man snatched up the weapon, levelled it at her and, without hesitation, pulled the trigger. His effort, however, was rewarded with nothing but a harmless click as the firing pin struck a dud round.

Anya sighed as if in disappointment. 'Like I said, I gave you a choice. If you really had tried to take your own life, I would have given you a live round to finish the job.' She looked at him a moment longer, no emotion in her eyes, not even disgust. She felt nothing for him now. 'Goodbye, Viktor.'

With that, she turned and started back towards the jeep.

'Anya, wait!' he yelled after her, trying to crawl in pursuit. 'You can't leave me out here! You can't do this!'

She no longer heard him. She kept her back straight, her chin up as she walked away, every step carrying her further from him. In the distance, but closer than before, she heard wolf song. A pack of hunters closing in on their prey.

'Anya! You bitch!' he screamed in desperation. 'Anya!'

Clambering up into the driver's seat, Anya calmly started the engine, eased off the clutch and swung the vehicle in a wide arc before driving away. She didn't look back.

Chapter 73

'I'll have one more,' Drake said, pushing his empty whisky glass across the bar, oblivious to the music and revelry going on all around him. With about twenty minutes left of 2008, the world was busy celebrating the start of a new year.

In DC in particular the excitement was palpable. They had a new president and a new administration to look forward to next year. Barack Obama, the first Democrat in nine years and the first black president in history, would be taking office in just a few weeks.

Drake, however, was in less of a celebratory mood as he reflected on the events of the past couple of weeks. Anya was gone, his own position within the Agency was more tenuous than ever, and Surovsky had mysteriously vanished after the fallout from the Beslan scandal, apparently never to answer for his crimes. He might have been stripped of his power and authority, and pursued by several international tribunals, but he'd still get to live out the remainder of his life as a free man. Everything they had risked their lives for had come to nothing.

As for Drake himself, he could at least feel good that he'd finally made peace with Samantha. More than that, in fact. She was a far better person than he deserved in his life, yet somehow in the midst of all this chaos and danger they had found each other. He couldn't say where things were heading for the two of them, but right now that was all right with him. That was a question for the year ahead.

She had invited him to see in the New Year with her, and as much as he wanted to, he'd known he would be poor company tonight. For him, tonight was about remembering what had been rather than celebrating what was, and what might be.

In truth, he found it hard to see the way ahead now. He would carry on living as he had for the past eighteen months – with a sword balanced over his head, waiting for that day, that inevitable moment when his luck finally ran out.

The barman eyed him dubiously for a moment. Drake had already knocked back three whiskies in the past ten minutes and showed no signs of slowing down, but what the hell, they were busy and it was New Year's Eve. He wasn't going to waste time cautioning him to take it easy.

Drake was just handing over the money for drink number four when he felt someone bump into him from behind. He heard a giggling laugh and a slurred apology before his new friend shoved her way past.

Almost without thinking Drake reached into his back pocket, checking his wallet hadn't been lifted. After everything that had happened over the past week or two, being pickpocketed would truly be a perfect way to cap it off.

His wallet was still there. And so was something else: a small folded slip of paper that hadn't been there when he left his house. Frowning, he lifted it out and unfolded it.

Scrawled across it in bold, flowing handwriting was a simple message.

Jefferson Memorial, north side. 10 minutes.

Drake could feel his heart beating faster the moment he took in the message, and immediately whirled around, his eyes searching the crowded bar for the woman who had bumped into him. The place was heaving with men and women of all ages. None of them stood out.

Turning back to the bar, he caught the barman's eye and beckoned him over.

'Hey, you see a woman bump into me a few seconds ago?'

'It's New Year's Eve, buddy. People come and go. You want something else?' he asked impatiently, eyeing the dozen or so other customers vying for his attention.

Drake looked down at his drink, then at the note. He thought he recognised the handwriting from a similar incident in Kabul several months previously, yet his logical mind cautioned him that it couldn't be who he thought it was. It just couldn't.

Yet unaccountably, he found himself smiling.

'No. Nothing at all,' he said. 'Thanks, mate.'

Abandoning the drink and the bar, he pushed his way through the crowds of revellers, ignoring the occasional irritated stare, and hurried outside.

The rendezvous was about half a mile away, on the other side of the Potomac. An easy five-minute run on any normal day, but not tonight. And he had a feeling his friend wouldn't stick around if he was late.

Located on the south shore of the Tidal Basin and well away from the iconic monuments of the National Mall, the Jefferson Memorial building is one of the lesser-known landmarks of the nation's capital. A neoclassical dome set on circular marble steps and supported by stone columns, it is nonetheless an impressive structure dedicated to the third president of the United States.

Drake had run past it many times during his morning exercise, though usually under more favourable circumstances.

He arrived there nine minutes after leaving the bar, tired and breathless after the short run through the busy streets of DC.

In stark contrast to the crowds thronging the streets near the Capitol Building and Lincoln Memorial, there weren't more than a couple of dozen people in the area, some within the open building but most walking through the stands of Japanese cherry trees that had been planted all around it.

Coming to a halt at the base of the steps on the north side of the building, he paused near the dark, shimmering waters of the Tidal Basin. The view of central DC was impressive to say the least, but he wasn't here to sightsee.

He looked at the people nearby, his eyes flitting from face to face, desperately seeking the one he wanted. Most of them were couples, hoping to see in the New Year in a romantic setting. None of them looked familiar.

The seconds ticked by and still no obvious candidates presented themselves.

He began to feel a sickening moment of doubt, wondering if this was nothing but an elaborate prank made credible only by his imagination and desperate desire to believe it. Was he really that foolish?

And then, just like that, his doubts vanished.

'I was starting to wonder if you would make it,' a woman's voice admonished him. 'You're out of shape, Ryan.'

Drake closed his eyes for a moment, letting out a breath, trying to calm himself. He could feel his hands shaking, could hear the pounding of the pulse in his ears.

It was her. Somehow, it was her.

Opening his eyes, he turned around, finding himself face to face with Anya. She was dressed in a long overcoat, her eyes shining in the glow of the floodlights illuminating the monument behind. Focused on him.

Drake took a step towards her. Small, almost tentative, as if she were a mirage that might vanish suddenly before his eyes.

Saying nothing, he reached out and gently ran a hand down her cheek, as if to assure himself she was real and solid. Her skin was warm and soft to his touch, and unlike before she made no move to stop him. He saw her eyes close, felt the warmth of her breath on the palm of his hand.

It was too much for him. Taking another step forwards, he threw his arms around her and pulled her into a tight, almost painful embrace, burying his face in her neck. He could feel the strong, steady rhythm of her pulse, could smell the scent of her hair, could hear her intake of breath. Her arms were around him, every ounce of her strength pulling him close as if to make him part of her.

Almost without him knowing it, he felt the sting of hot tears in his eyes.

'I thought I'd lost you,' he said, his voice nothing but a ragged whisper.

'I know. I'm sorry, Ryan. I'm sorry.' There was a tremble, a tension in her voice that he'd never heard before. She was holding on, but only through great effort. 'But I had to do it. There was no other way to get to him.'

'Surovsky?'

He felt rather than saw her nod. 'He won't trouble you again.'

Surovsky hadn't disappeared. Anya had made him disappear. She had gone through all of this, had risked her life, had made herself a wanted terrorist, all to confront the man who had tried to kill her.

Regaining some sense of composure, he pulled away so he could look at her properly. For perhaps the first time since he'd met her, he saw real remorse in her eyes.

'Was it true, what Kamarov told me about you?' he asked. 'That you were sent to America by . . . him?'

He saw her eyes open wider in surprise for a moment, though it soon gave way to resigned acceptance. She swallowed and nodded, admitting it at last. 'I was young, angry, frustrated. Surovsky offered me a way out. He promised me a new life, a life with purpose, and I took it. It wasn't until later that I realised the kind of man I had sold my soul to.'

'Why didn't you trust me?' The look in his eyes reflected the depth of his emotion, the fear and doubt and anger he had felt since all this started. All of it needless. 'Why didn't you tell me?'

Anya met his gaze and replied as only she could: honestly and without reservation. 'I have trusted people before, and it has not ended well for me. And . . . I didn't want you to know the truth about me. This was something I wanted . . . something I *needed* to do alone.'

He understood. In some part of his mind, he understood the suffering Surovsky had inflicted on her, the damage he had done that could never be repaired. The man's legacy was a festering wound in Anya's soul, and only she could heal it.

Drake sighed and released his hold on her. Despite all the years of danger and conflict she had seen, despite the countless times she had risked her life, there still remained that small part of her that doubted herself, that was afraid to show itself for fear of being destroyed.

'So what now? Surovsky's dead. Everyone thinks *you're* dead.' As far as he could see, there was only one conclusion to draw. 'It's over.'

'No,' she said, her gaze hardening. 'There is still one man left. The man at the centre of it all. And he will answer for the things he did.'

Drake felt his heart sink. That man was Marcus Cain,

once Anya's mentor, her confidant, her guide and her closest friend. Now he was one of the most powerful and influential men in the Agency, and likely to become the next director before too long.

This had all started with Cain last year. He was the one who had first enlisted Drake to bring Anya home. He was the one who had turned Anya's former protégé against her, who had sacrificed innocent lives to cover up his own mistakes. He was the one who now held a sword over Drake's head, and was just waiting for a chance to bring it down.

It had started with Cain, and it would end with him. Anya would make sure of it. She wouldn't stop, wouldn't relent, wouldn't give up until she had completed her final mission.

'It seems he is our common enemy,' she went on. 'He would kill you just as readily as he would kill me. But together, we might—'

'No,' Drake interrupted her, his tone hard and uncompromising. 'Not like this.'

Anya frowned, taken aback by his flat refusal. 'What do you mean?'

'We can't keep doing this, Anya. *I* can't keep doing this – you holding all the cards and me kept in the dark. You almost got me and my team killed twice over. I can't and won't let that happen again. If you want my help, if you want to work with me, then we do it as equals. No more secrets, no more lies. If you can't give me that, walk away now.'

He'd had to say it. Even if it meant parting ways with Anya right here, right now. Even if he never saw her again, he had to make her understand what was at stake. Risking his own life was one thing, but the lives of his team, of his friends, was something Drake would never compromise on.

The woman said nothing for several seconds. She looked genuinely surprised by his ultimatum, but as he held her gaze that surprise gradually gave way, replaced instead by dawning acceptance and respect.

And at last he saw a flicker of a smile.

'All right,' she conceded. 'I'll be in touch.'

A sudden flash of red light caught Drake's attention, and he turned right to look out over the Tidal Basin. The annual fireworks display had started, hundreds of rockets, mortars and barrages exploding over the capital in a blaze of colour and thunderous explosions.

A new year had just dawned. Drake couldn't help wondering what it held for all of them. And yet, for the first time since his return from Russia, he now looked towards it with a sense of hope.

They would find a way, he knew. They would find a way through this. If he and Anya worked together as they should have done all along, nothing could stop them.

'Happy New Year, Anya,' he said quietly, tearing his eyes off the spectacular display to look at the woman by his side.

But she wasn't there. She had already left, just as silent and unnoticed as she had arrived. Drake smiled in amusement; old habits died hard, it seemed.

But he would see her again; that much he knew.

And when the time came, he would be ready.

Epilogue

Marcus Cain sat alone in the living room of his spacious private residence with a glass of Highland Park whisky by his side, watching the distant fireworks display without enthusiasm. His thoughts were turned inwards as he reflected on the events of the past few days.

Drake had played his part surprisingly well, he thought. The man remained a danger to him, but a danger that he could control and manipulate. His concern for Anya, his loyalty to his friends, his willingness to risk everything for what he considered right – those were qualities that were easy to play against. Cain had long since learned how to turn men's strengths against them.

That was why he had allowed Drake to carry out his ill-conceived plan to go chasing halfway around the world in search of Anya. That was why he'd seen to it that Drake wasn't officially prosecuted for violating Agency protocols, and why the man was still free to move around instead of being locked in a 6x8 cell. That was the reason he'd made no serious attempt to recapture Anya since her escape from Iraq the previous year.

Because of Drake's actions, Viktor Surovsky was now dead. And so was Richard Carpenter, Cain's former associate who had become the shadowy head of a private military company waging a dirty war in Afghanistan. Both men had been thorns in his side for far too long, both had the ability to undo everything he'd worked for, and both had to be eliminated.

Anya, always the perfect soldier, had done her duty without fail.

Cain was under no illusions about her supposed 'death'. He'd played that game long enough to sense a deception, and had guessed her plan the moment he'd read the reports from that warehouse in Moscow. She had faked it, allowing her to get close to Surovsky so she could kill him.

Clever. Rather obvious, but clever all the same.

And now that their work was almost done, it was time to dispose of Drake and Anya.

He heard the bleep of his phone, and reached over for it.

'Yeah?' he said, his voice betraying a hint of weariness now. It was late, and this was his third whisky.

'It's me,' a female voice said. 'You were right about Drake. He was the one who exposed Surovsky. He had the videos hidden inside the chess piece.'

'I see.' It was always satisfying to have a suspicion confirmed. 'And he doesn't suspect you?'

'He trusts me,' she confirmed – not without a hint of regret, he noted. He would be mindful of that when using her in future. 'I made sure of it.'

'Good. Then we'll keep an eye on him. If I'm right, she'll make her move soon.'

'And when she does?'

'Then we'll be ready.' Cain reached for his whisky and took a sip, relishing the rich, peaty flavour. 'And when this is over, I'll make sure you're rewarded.'

She said nothing to that; another indication that she was far from pleased to be part of this. 'I have to go now.'

'I understand.' He was about to lay the phone down when

a thought occurred. 'Oh, and one more thing. Happy New Year, Samantha.'

She hung up without further comment.

Sighing, Cain took another sip of his whisky. He couldn't help thinking of the game of chess which Atayev had been so preoccupied with. Both Cain and Anya had made their opening moves, had committed and sacrificed pieces to gain position, each constantly trying to discern the thoughts of the other.

And now at last they were approaching the decisive moment – the endgame. Each was a skilled player in his or her own way, but there could be only one winner. And Cain had been playing this game for a very long time.

He would await Anya's next move. And when it came, he would be ready.

Redemption

Will Jordan

Everyone has secrets. But some can get you killed.

Ryan Drake is a man who finds people who don't want to be found.

Once a soldier in the British Army, he now works for the CIA, leading an elite investigation team that tracks down missing agents. But his latest mission – to free a prisoner codenamed Maras and bring her back onto US soil within forty-eight hours – is more dangerous than anything his team has attempted before.

Despite the risks, the team successfully completes their mission, but for Drake the real danger has only just begun. Faced with a terrible threat, he is forced to go on the run with Maras – a veteran agent scarred by years of brutal imprisonment.

Hunted by his former comrades and those willing to do anything to protect a deadly secret, Drake is left with no choice but to trust a dangerous woman he barely knows. For he has only one chance to save those he loves and time is running out...

arrow books

Sacrifice

Will Jordan

A missing man. A brutal conflict. A ruthless enemy. That's just the beginning.

Afghanistan, 2008. A Black Hawk helicopter carrying a senior CIA operative is shot down by a surface-to-air missile, its lone passenger taken hostage by a fanatical new insurgent group.

Knowing this man holds information vital to the ongoing conflict, the CIA bring in Ryan Drake and his elite Shepherd team to find and rescue their lost operative.

But nothing is what it seems, and within hours of arriving in the war-torn country, Drake and his team find themselves caught in a deadly conflict between a brutal terrorist warlord and the ruthless leader of a private military company.

And lurking in the shadows is a woman from Drake's past determined to settle old scores...

arrow books

dead
good

*For all of you who find
a crime story irresistible.*

Discover the very best crime and thriller books on our dedicated website – hand-picked by our editorial team so you have tailored recommendations to help you choose what to read next.

We'll introduce you to our favourite authors and the brightest new talent. Read exclusive interviews and specially commissioned features on everything from the best classic crime to our top ten TV detectives, join live webchats and speak to authors directly.

Plus our monthly book competition offers you the chance to win the latest crime fiction, and there are DVD box sets and digital devices to be won too.

Sign up for our newsletter at
www.deadgoodbooks.co.uk/signup

Join the conversation on: